“I'm really ha ... ry me, Chelsea.”

Slowly she reached out to take the box. “What are we doing, Gage?”

He looked into her eyes. “Being expedient, I guess.”

“You need me, I need you.”

He nodded. “I hope you need me. I sure as hell need you.”

“Because of Cat.”

Not replying, he leaned to slip the ring on her finger where it sparkled and shone, catching the hot Texas sunlight spilling in from the window. Three round ovals glittered at her, more beautiful than anything she'd ever owned.

“Cat says there are three diamonds, one for each of us, all on the same band forever,” Gage said.

“She's so sweet,” Chelsea whispered, touched.

“Are you marrying me because of my child?” Gage asked.

“Yes,” Chelsea said, and he laughed.

“Good. For a while there, I thought you might be marrying me for me,” Gage teased.

“Cowboy, you think too much of yourself.”

Dear Reader,

The thing about writing a series is that sometimes it's hard to let a particular place or family go. And so it is with the Callahan Cowboys, six brothers who lured me in with their sense of adventure and die-hard commitment to stay single. I thought it would be fun to see what happened to Irish Chelsea Myers, who had once upon a time been engaged to the eldest Callahan brother, Jonas. Now Chelsea is house-sitting at Dark Diablo, where she can write her mysteries in peace. However, a cowboy shows up on her porch one day with his teenage daughter, a child he has just discovered is his. Peace and quiet is not to be the rule of the land, as Chelsea is about to find out! Not to mention that the cowboy is kind of stubborn, incredibly hot and definitely determined to be the best father he can be. A pretty irresistible combination for a woman who always secretly wanted a man who's larger than life, even if she thought she was content to live her adventures on the pages of her own books.

I so hope you enjoy *The Renegade Cowboy Returns.* I fell in love with the town of Tempest, and the wonderfully patchwork-quilted family that the little farmhouse in Dark Diablo, New Mexico, shelters from life's storms. It's my greatest wish that you, too, will enjoy this "bonus" book—along with one other—as just-can't-say-goodbye stories to the Callahan Cowboys series!

Happy summer and the best of beach reading to you!

Tina

www.tinaleonard.com

www.facebook.com/tinaleonardbooks

www.twitter.com/tina_leonard

The Renegade Cowboy Returns

TINA LEONARD

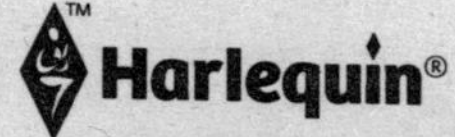

TORONTO NEW YORK LONDON
AMSTERDAM PARIS SYDNEY HAMBURG
STOCKHOLM ATHENS TOKYO MILAN MADRID
PRAGUE WARSAW BUDAPEST AUCKLAND

ISBN-13: 978-0-373-75415-1

This edition published by arrangement with Harlequin Books S.A.

For questions and comments about the quality of this book please contact us at Customer_eCare@Harlequin.ca

www.Harlequin.com

Printed in U.S.A.

CONTENTS

ABOUT THE AUTHOR

Tina Leonard is a bestselling author of more than forty projects, including a popular thirteen-book miniseries for Harlequin American Romance. Her books have made the Waldenbooks, Ingram and Nielsen BookScan bestseller lists. Tina feels she has been blessed with a fertile imagination and quick typing skills, excellent editors and a family who loves her career. Born on a military base, she lived in many states before eventually marrying the boy who did her crayon printing for her in the first grade. Tina believes happy endings are a wonderful part of a good life. You can visit her at www.tinaleonard.com.

Books by Tina Leonard

HARLEQUIN AMERICAN ROMANCE

977—FRISCO JOE'S FIANCÉE †
981—LAREDO'S SASSY SWEETHEART †
986—RANGER'S WILD WOMAN †
989—TEX TIMES TEN †
1018—FANNIN'S FLAME †
1037—NAVARRO OR NOT †
1045—CATCHING CALHOUN †
1053—ARCHER'S ANGELS †
1069—BELONGING TO BANDERA †
1083—CROCKETT'S SEDUCTION †
1107—LAST'S TEMPTATION †
1113—MASON'S MARRIAGE †
1129—MY BABY, MY BRIDE *
1137—THE CHRISTMAS TWINS *
1153—HER SECRET SONS *
1213—TEXAS LULLABY
1241—THE TEXAS RANGER'S TWINS
1246—THE SECRET AGENT'S SURPRISES **
1250—THE TRIPLETS' RODEO MAN **
1263—THE TEXAS TWINS
1282—THE COWBOY FROM CHRISTMAS PAST
1354—THE COWBOY'S TRIPLETS ‡
1362—THE COWBOY'S BONUS BABY ‡
1370—THE BULL RIDER'S TWINS ‡
1378—HOLIDAY IN A STETSON
"A Rancho Diablo Christmas"
1385—HIS VALENTINE TRIPLETS ‡
1393—COWBOY SAM'S QUADRUPLETS ‡
1401—A CALLAHAN WEDDING ‡

†Cowboys by the Dozen
*The Tulips Saloon
**The Morgan Men
‡Callahan Cowboys

The Renegade Cowboy Returns

Many thanks to Roberta Brown of the Roberta Brown Agency, who has been such a wonderful guide for the past year and a half—I can't thank you enough. I wish I knew all the names of the wonderful, magical people at Harlequin who shape the final product that becomes a Tina Leonard book, but they are numerous and work in the unspecified and sometimes unthanked shadows—heartfelt appreciation for your unstinting care. Kathleen Scheibling gently keeps me focused, and Laura Barth is kind enough to always have a cheery word. Much love to my family, who are simply my rock, and also to the awesome readers who have my sincere thanks for supporting my work with such amazing generosity and enthusiasm. I am quite blessed.

I would also like to thank someone who will never read this dedication, as he cannot, since he is a dog. Bailey, my angel, as I write this note on the eve of Christmas Eve, I would like to say thank you for all the wonderful times you kindly lay in the room with me as I wrote, and then gave me a gentle nudge to go out and take a walk with you. You raised my children and me and even my husband with joyous kindness. The past six years have been such a blessing, and I will always be grateful to the Golden Retriever rescue society for granting us your golden goodness. I know you won't be here when this book is published, and so, in your honor, I'd like to tell everyone that the best friend they could ever have is an angel from the rescue of their choice. Alternatively, a wonderful gift that keeps on giving is a donation to a rescue society. I love you, and we miss you terribly already.

Chapter One

"What's past is prologue"
–*The Tempest* by William Shakespeare

The secret to Gage Phillips's happy existence was ridiculously simple: stay far away from women, specifically those who had marriage on their mind.

He put his duffel on the porch of the New Mexico farmhouse and looked around. The rebuilding project he'd taken on for Jonas Callahan was perfectly suited for a man who gloried in solitude. Gage knew his formula for a drama-free, productive lifestyle seemed oversimplified to some people, especially ladies who wanted to show him how much better life could be in a permanent relationship with a good woman. Yet he was thirty-five and a die-hard, footloose cowboy—testament to remaining single being the best choice a man could ever make on this earth, besides finding the right career and spending hard-earned cash on a dependable truck.

He hadn't always been die-hard and footloose. Fourteen years ago he'd been at the altar, and fourteen years ago he'd learned a valuable lesson: marriage was *not* for him.

His friends were fond of saying he was just too much of a renegade to be tied down. Gage figured they might have a point. Fatherhood had been a late-breaking bulletin for him. About a year ago he'd been delivered the news. What man was so busy traveling the country that he didn't know he had a daughter?

Leslie, convinced by her parents not to tell him about his child so they wouldn't have to share custody, made a midlife decision to invite him to Laredo to come clean. He was pretty certain Leslie had told him only because she was at her wits' end with Cat—and because her teenager apparently was fond of making her mother's new boyfriend miserable.

The situation was messy.

So it was time for a little escape. This desolate, dirt-as-far-as-the-eyes-could-see forgotten hideaway was also perfect for getting away from his other problem—the family. If anybody needed quiet and a place to plot his exit strategy from The Family, Inc., it was he.

"Excuse me," a female said, and Gage jumped about a foot. "If you're selling something, I'm not buying, cowboy. And there's a No Trespassing sign posted on the drive, which I'm sure you noticed. And ignored."

He'd whipped around at her first words and found himself staring at a woman of medium height, with a slender build and untamable red hair, eyeing him like a protective mother hen prepared to flap him off the porch. Maybe she was the housekeeper, getting the place cleaned up for his arrival. He couldn't place her accent—perhaps Irish or Scottish. Either way, she seemed intent on him not getting past the front door. He plastered on a convincing smile to let her know he was harmless. "I'm not selling anything, ma'am. I'm moving in."

She blinked big, glass-green eyes. "You have the wrong address."

"This is Dark Diablo Ranch." It was impossible to have the wrong address; there were no other houses around for miles. "Owned by Jonas Callahan of Rancho Diablo, right?"

She nodded. "It is. But Jonas never mentioned anything about anyone living here."

He could see she wasn't the kind of woman who could be swayed with easy charm. Probably didn't trust strangers, which was a good thing. By the way her hand moved impatiently to rest on her slim hip, it was obvious she didn't trust him, even with his pointed mention of Jonas's name. A woman who had nice long legs like hers usually caught his eye. He loved tiny freckles, too. She had a light dusting on her pale legs and arms exposed by her green tank top. Even across her delicate nose… But she also had a healthy dose of ire clouding her brow.

Nope. This was not a lady one enjoyed for a night or two in the name of good sex.

"Sorry," he said. "I've definitely got the right address, then. Looks like we're going to be housemates."

"I don't think so." She remained stubborn, not giving an inch. "There's a run-down barn out back, and a small bunkhouse, which, though antiquated and not exactly a five-star hotel, will suit you. I'm going inside to call Jonas and tell him there's been some kind of mix-up."

"That's a good idea," Gage said. "Ask Jonas why he didn't warn me about Lucy Ricardo being my bunk mate." Gage shook his head, deliberately trying the lady's patience. "He knows I'm not a fan of redheads. There's two things in life that should be left well alone, and they both happen to be the same shade." He grinned, a rascal in denim, determined to needle her. "That'd be a stick of dynamite and a redhead, ma'am, if I need to spell it out for you."

"Really." She gave him a last annoyed look and went into the house, letting the screen door slam behind her. Gage sat on the porch, whistling to himself, leaning back on his elbows as he stared up at the jewel-blue New Mexico sky. He could hear her complaining to Jonas, and grinned as bits of dialogue confirmed to him that Jonas was verifying his story.

She wasn't happy about it, either.

"You might have told me," she said, her tone begrudging as she came back out, "that you're here to do work for Jonas."

"You didn't seem interested in my curriculum vitae," Gage said. "Better to let Jonas tell you. Funny thing, he didn't mention you to me." He gazed at her again, thinking how attractive she was, even for a redhead. "My name's Gage Phillips." He stuck out a hand, which she pointedly didn't accept. Shrugging, he shoved it in his jeans pocket.

"I don't need to know your name," she said. "You'll

be staying in the bunkhouse, as my mother and I live here."

Mother? He was going to read Jonas the riot act the next time he saw him. The ornery son of a gun had said nothing about a saucy female and no doubt equally prickly ma infesting his solitude. "My understanding is that the barn and the bunkhouse are fairly uninhabitable," Gage said. "That's part of the reason I'm here."

She pressed her lips together, catching his attention. He thought she'd be really pretty if she ever smiled—not that she seemed interested in doing much of that around him. Very tantalizing, though. He gazed at her, wondering why Jonas would have left out telling him about this very luscious detail when he'd hired him. Jonas had specifically told him he'd be staying at the farmhouse. He'd never mentioned females.

"Wait a minute," Gage said. "Where are you from?"

"Dublin, Ireland," she said, her tone stiffer than an ironing board.

"You're Jonas's ex-fiancée," Gage said, a light dawning. "I had an invitation to Sabrina and Jonas's wedding, though I couldn't make it over from Hell's Colony in time. But I heard about you."

She looked at him, not pleased. "Jonas and I are good friends, and nothing more."

He laughed. "Cupcake, I get the whole setup now. Those damn Callahans. They want everyone to share their misery."

"What are you talking about?"

Gage couldn't wipe the smirk off his face. It was

all so obvious. "You're not a United States citizen, are you?"

"No. What does that have to do with anything?"

He shrugged. "You. Me. One house. It's a setup."

"I don't think so," she said, her voice subarctic. "There is no setup."

"Sure." He leaned forward on his knee. "How long are you planning to stay here?"

"Here? As long as I can."

"And how long would that be?"

She sniffed. "I'm in the process of getting a green card."

"So you want to stay a while?"

"Being in New Mexico has had a wonderful effect on my mother's health. We're hoping to remain here permanently, if possible. Mum and I have been traveling, and we're getting to the end of my legal time here. Filing the paperwork has been a very slow process. But I don't see what that has to do with you, or—" Her expression suddenly changed from ire to horror. "You think Jonas sent you out here so I could snare you into marrying me! Because I'm his ex-fiancée? You think I just need another man to make all my problems go away, and Jonas sent you as some kind of consolation prize."

He smiled. "Don't look so shocked, cupcake."

She shook her head. "You're dumb. I'm going inside, and I hope our paths cross very rarely."

"Hang on a second."

He didn't think she'd stop, but to his surprise, she

turned to look at him with all the misgiving she'd probably have when eyeing a coyote. "What?"

"What's your name? I can't just call you Irish."

"My name is Chelsea Myers, but I prefer you don't call me anything. Look." She gave him a mulish glare. "I don't believe Jonas would try to get us together—"

"You don't know the Callahans all that well, then. They're notorious for their practical jokes."

"The two of us getting together would indeed be a joke. Jonas promised me I would have nothing but peace and quiet here for my writing. Peace and quiet is what I need, or I can't work. Does that make sense to you?" She gave Gage a look that quite clearly said he was probably incapable of understanding much of anything. "So if you like brawling, loud music or wild nights with the ladies, you'll need to go into town for all that."

"Sure thing, sweetie." He picked up his duffel and strode past her into the house.

"What are you doing?"

"If we're going by Jonas's rules, then I'm staying in here. He said nothing about a redhead with an attitude disturbing me on my own personal time-out. He said nothing about sleeping in a ramshackle bunkhouse or a caving-in barn. He said there was a quaint, newly furnished though spartan farmhouse I could live in while I create his horse program and rebuild this joint. And if you don't mind, Miss Myers," he said, his tone deliberately soft to let her know he did mind very much, "I abhor the sound of a TV, especially the soap operas you ladies love, and most particularly reality TV. When

I come home at night, I want no bickering, no bossing and no busybodying interrupting my routine. Got that?" He glanced around, seeing the redheaded storm about to erupt, and spoke to forestall it. "Now, where's Ma Myers? I'd like to introduce myself."

"She won't be here until tomorrow. She's in Diablo helping Fiona Callahan pickle vegetables for the Fourth of July family celebration. Never mind about my mother," Chelsea said. "We can't both stay in this house."

"There's a barn and a bunkhouse," he reminded her.

Her lips pressed flat again. "Mum and I will take the upstairs, you will take the downstairs."

He glanced around, liking the look of the place. Jonas hadn't been far off when he'd said it was almost new inside. He'd begun renovating the house first, then hired Gage to whip the rest of the ranch into shape. "Fine," he said. "I leave early, come in late."

"I couldn't care less what you do."

"I just don't want to catch you wandering around in your nightie, sweetheart."

"I promise not to wander around in my nightie," Chelsea said, her voice oh-so-sweet, "if you don't mind leaving your boots on the porch. The hardwood floors are new."

She had him there. His own mother would have already read him the riot act—he and his brothers and sister had learned to leave their boots outside or in the mudroom from the time they were old enough to wear them. He'd be better off dealing with a scorpion in his boot than his mother catching him wearing them in the house. "Deal. Pleasure doing business with you, Miss."

"Whatever," Chelsea said, and went up the stairs.

He watched her climb, his mouth curving a bit at the sight of female hips swaying ever so enticingly. She was a mouthy little thing, but he didn't mind mouthy so much. Mouthy could be tamed.

"One more thing I need to mention," he called up the stairs.

"What now?"

"My daughter is arriving tomorrow, so she'll be staying here with me."

Chelsea appeared at the top of the stairs. "Daughter?"

Gage nodded. "Yeah. Cat and her mom have been having a bit of mom-daughter drama. Cat's thirteen, so she and Leslie, my ex-wife, want a small break from each other."

Chelsea's eyebrows rose. "Small break? Like a couple of days?"

He shrugged. "Like the rest of summer vacation. Jonas said this was probably the perfect place for Cat and me to get to know each other better."

"I see."

Gage saw that Chelsea did in fact "see" and wasn't pleased. "I don't imagine a teenager will be much of a bother."

Chelsea disappeared from view. He went into the kitchen to check out the grub in the fridge—he'd need to make a grocery run before Cat arrived.

He hadn't been quite candid about his daughter. According to Leslie, she was a handful and they were always squabbling. Gage had offered to bring Cat out here for the summer to give mom and daughter a respite from each other, but he'd thought it'd be just the two of them.

Now it would be the four of them, one big, not-too-happy group.

CHELSEA WAS *NOT* HAPPY with Jonas Callahan, or the cowboy downstairs. Jonas was a fink for not telling her of his plans—he'd said Dark Diablo would be the perfect place to write and for her mother's health, saying nothing about a man and his teenage daughter living with them. This Gage Phillips—a handsome man with *scoundrel* written all over him, from his easy grin to his dark brown eyes that twinkled with mischief—clearly had issues. "Marriage, indeed," Chelsea muttered. "I'm not that desperate to be legal in this country. I'll stick with the slow-as-a-turtle process, thanks, Jonas."

She was going to kill the eldest Callahan like a character in her mystery novels.

Of course, she didn't have to stay here. She could tell Jonas the deal was off. Her laptop was portable; she could write anywhere, couldn't she? But truthfully, her mother would be comfortable here. They'd spent several months traveling, seeing the sights on a once-in-a-lifetime journey together. Dark Diablo was an ideal setting for her mother to rest for a while.

"I'm not leaving. Jonas wouldn't try to fix me up," she said to the open laptop where her protagonist, Bronwyn Sang, hung helplessly from a steep cliffside that the ruthless murderer had pushed her over. Bronwyn would have to dangle a little while longer, unfortunately. In the meantime, Chelsea was determined to keep so much distance between herself and Gage that he'd never even see her.

She was too ticked to write now. A nice, cold swim in the creek Jonas was so proud of was the answer. Hearing a truck door slam before an engine started and left the property—safe, for the moment!—Chelsea tossed on her emerald-green polka-dotted bikini, grabbed a towel and flip-flops and headed out. Exercise was what every writer needed to clear her head, and if Bronwyn was ever going to be rescued so she could live to fight another day, Chelsea had to get her boiling-hot emotions refocused.

In other words, she had to forget about the fact that Gage Phillips, in spite of all the "No" signs flashing all over him, was so devil-may-care, so bad-boy, that of course her hormones had noticed—she'd have to be dead not to. He was the call of the wild she'd always dreamed of, a Texas man, big and strong, and Chelsea recognized her downfall when she saw it.

If Jonas hadn't lobbed temptation into her lap on purpose, then he was the king of coincidence. Gage was right: the Callahans were pranksters, and they loved matchmaking.

But sexy, dark-eyed, dark-haired Gage from Hell's Colony, Texas, was in no danger from her.

GAGE STARED AT the bikini-clad redhead as she floated on a plastic raft in the shallow end of the creek. *Great. Just great.*

She was one hot lady. Too hot to be his housemate.

He sat down on a boulder and took off his hat, mopping his face with his red bandanna. Okay, he had three options for the temptation that lay before him.

One. He could cannonball into the water and tump her off the raft, thereby setting up total frigid conditions in the house they were sharing for the foreseeable future.

It was so tempting. In fact, it was the most tempting of the options on his short list. If she'd been any other woman, the wolf in him would have definitely been on the prowl.

There would be no freewheeling cannonballs with Miss Irish.

Two. He could clear his throat, call out that he was here so she wouldn't think he was spying on her—which he was, at this point; all that almond-colored, slightly freckled skin could not be looked away from. Not to mention she had darling breasts and—

No. She'd think the worst of him, that he'd followed her or something. He hadn't, but she would never believe it. He'd pulled his truck around to check out the barn and bunkhouse to begin making a repair list, and had found the creek Jonas had told him about. Jonas loved this part of the vast property the best, probably because bodies of water were scarce in most of New Mexico. But also, this one was special, private, and not full of rocks and stones and rough edges like the rapids where the kayakers loved to test their mettle. This was a quiet haven, and Gage could see why Jonas sought peace here.

Gage dared not call out to Chelsea. She had been distinctly displeased to see him.

The third option was all he had: turn around and walk away, pretending he'd never seen her in her green polka-dotted bikini. The vision of her languidly lying on that yellow raft was burned into his memory; he guessed it would probably haunt him for a long time.

Too bad. He turned to walk off unnoticed, glad he was able to do so.

Something cold and wet smacked him in the back, and he stumbled, surprised. A child-size football bounced onto the nearby dock Jonas had constructed.

Gage turned back, realizing that Chelsea, among her many other attributes, had perfect aim.

"You can at least have good manners and say hello," she said.

He fished for words, wondering why he was so tongue-tied. "You seemed to be resting."

"And you seem to be a Peeping Tom." She rolled off the raft, wrapping her arms around it so she could float and look at him. "I thought you were going into town."

"I am." He resented the intimation that he'd been spying on her. He was, but he wasn't. It was splitting hairs, and she was looking to split them. "I was making an initial run-through of the buildings to see where it might be best to start. I saw the creek. You're not the only one who likes to swim. And I didn't say hello because, quite frankly, I just saw you at the house, where you told me not to speak to you." He shrugged. "Make up your mind."

She gave him a long look. "Nothing's changed. I just don't like you watching me."

"Believe me, I wasn't planning on it." He turned, hoping she didn't have any more child-size missiles to peg him with. Jonas *would* have to stick him with the world's most unfriendly female.

He was going to tell Jonas that, too, the first chance he had. Gage had every intention of letting his employer know that for perhaps the first time, the Callahan matchmaking magic had fizzled out big-time.

CHELSEA QUIT HIDING in the water and got back on her raft when she knew that Gage was truly gone. Exhaling, she went back to gazing at the sky.

He was annoyed with her now, and she was annoyed with him.

Neither of them wanted to share a house.

She closed her eyes, not as relaxed as she had been. It was going to be hard to plot a mystery when the Texas cowboy kept crowding red herrings and twists out of her mind. He was tall and big and strong, incredibly handsome, and if his back hadn't made such a nice wide target, she wasn't certain she would have been able to hit him with the small football.

He'd seemed pretty surprised, but not as surprised as she'd been.

Maybe it hadn't been very nice to do it. They had to live in the same house together, so perhaps it was best not to let her Irish temper and red hair get the better of her, as her mother was fond of reminding her.

She rolled off the raft and swam to the dock, grabbing her towel as she stood in the shallows. "Hey!" she called after Gage. "Hang on a sec."

He walked back, his eyebrows raised. Taking a deep breath, Chelsea wrapped the towel around herself and stepped onto the bank. "Listen, I don't want to get off on the wrong foot here. I think it just caught me off guard that we'd be living—"

He'd been watching her as she spoke, listening, but her words stopped abruptly when he pulled a gun from his jacket, firing at the dirt to her left. Chelsea shrieked and jumped back, pinwheeling into the water, towel and all. Coughing, she rose to the surface.

He was staring down at something on the ground, then moved dark eyes to her. She pushed her hair out of her face.

"You…you crazy—" Chelsea took a deep breath. "You're not living with me! I don't care what Jonas says. I was here first." She tread water, angrier than she'd ever been in her life. "I'm not living with a man who carries a gun on him as casually as a piece of chewing gum!"

Gage looked perplexed. "Why would you want to live with a man who didn't carry a gun?"

She stared at him. "I don't know. I don't care! You're crazy, and you're not living with me. It doesn't matter if you pitch a tent, but you're not staying in the house." She didn't allow herself to think about his poor daughter, who had a maniac for a father. "Get out of my sight."

She wanted to send a few more choice words after him, but he retreated so obligingly that she held her tongue. Jonas was going to get an earful! In fact, she was mad enough to drive out to Rancho Diablo and tick him off in person.

She swam to the bank, not bothering with pulling herself up on the dock. Her towel was soaked. She started wringing it out, muttering under her breath—and realized a three-foot-long snake was lying at her feet with its head shot off. The scream that erupted from her could have been heard in the next state as she leaped back into the water.

Chelsea was shaking badly, and was pretty certain she was sweating despite being in the creek up to her neck. She hated snakes! And that wild-eyed cowboy had shot the nasty creature and left her, no doubt snickering about how freaked out she'd be when she saw it.

No cowboy came to check on her.

She grabbed the float, which had become wedged in the shallows, and sat on it, looking around for more snakes. The stupid thing had probably been slithering to the creek for a drink, or to nest in the rocks.

Shivers crawled up her skin.

"Are you out there, cowboy?" she called timidly.

"Yes," Gage answered, "but I'm not walking into your sight, Irish. Just want to make certain you're not one of those hysterical females who can't stand the sight of a little creepy-crawly."

Little! He was having a laugh at her expense. Still, she owed him for shooting the snake. She probably would have stepped right on it. "I might be just a wee bit afraid of snakes," she admitted.

"Nobody likes snakes. You did real well."

She sniffed, surprised that he was offering her some empathy. "I take back what I said about you being a gun-toting freak, or whatever I called you." She took a deep breath, still feeling goose bumps tighten her skin.

"No worries," he said. "I'm heading off now to do my errands in town. You going to be all right?"

She wasn't. She glanced around, wondering if the snake had any friends that might be nesting in the wet towel she'd dropped. "You know we don't like snakes in Ireland," she said. "Saint Patrick ran them off for us."

There was a moment of silence before Gage walked toward the creek. He fished her towel from the water and held out his hand. "I'm no saint."

She looked at him, not accepting the hand he extended. "I know that."

He shrugged. "Come on, Red. I'll walk you back to the house."

She didn't need a second invitation. Taking his hand—he felt strong and substantial, thank God, because she needed something strong right now—she let him drag her from the creek. He kept his eyes steadily averted from her, and she was out of the water and away from her snake nemesis in a blink. While Gage pinned her raft between two scraggly trees so it wouldn't blow away, she hurriedly wrapped herself in her towel, unable to stop shivering. She couldn't shake her fear that another snake might be nearby. Still, Gage didn't look her way. Didn't every man want a glimpse of a woman in a bikini?

He didn't seem to. His posture was stiff, fixed in a

deliberate stance of avoidance. Chelsea remembered that she'd told him to stay out of her sight, and he was clearly trying to obey her not-very-nice demand.

She swallowed, letting go some of her pride. "I'm sorry. I've been kind of a witch to you."

He finally glanced at her. "It doesn't seem so bad with that sweet accent you've got."

Was that a compliment? "Really?"

"No." Gage laughed and started walking. "Getting blessed out by a woman is no fun in any language or accent."

She scampered after him, not thrilled to be left behind with a dead snake. "Maybe we could start over."

"No need."

Okay. She wasn't going to beg him to accept her apology. They walked in silence back to the farmhouse. He went to his truck, and Chelsea went in the house, pulling off the dripping beach towel.

And that's when she realized she'd gotten out of the creek without her bikini top.

She shrieked, this time with rage and embarrassment. The sound of male laughter came through the open screen door before Gage's truck started up and drove away.

And he called the *Callahans* pranksters!

Chapter Two

When Gage ran into Jonas Callahan in Tempest's town square, he was ready to let all his annoyance fall on his employer's head. "Jonas, you ornery son of a gun," he began, stopping when Jonas held up a hand.

"You can thank me later," Jonas said. "I can't chit-chat now. I need to go over last-minute plans with an architect. I think I'm going to knock the farmhouse down and start over. It's just much too small."

Gage's jaw tightened. "Knock it down? It's the only livable place at Dark Diablo."

"True," Jonas agreed. "I wouldn't do it until after the summer is over. Cat will have gone back to school by then, is how I figure it. Chelsea will have finished her Great Novel, and you can park your boots in the bunkhouse."

The bunkhouse was, as Chelsea had noted, pretty old and not really inhabitable, even for someone who was as used to roughing it as he was. "This is almost the end of June, Jonas. What if I can't get the bunk-house and the barn renovated that fast?"

Jonas glanced at him. "My brothers and I can come over and crew for you if you need us."

"I'll know soon enough, I guess." Gage wasn't certain how to take this change of plans. "Why did I think the job was for about six months?"

"It is," Jonas said, surprised, "unless you finish sooner or get sick of it. Do you have a problem with sleeping in a bunkhouse?"

Gage shook his head, not bothering to point out that the roof had holes in it the size of owls. He could get those patched up in the next month. He could get a lot done—if he didn't have Cat to entertain. Secretly, he wasn't certain what to do with a daughter he didn't know that well. He'd met her only once, and he'd been nervous as hell.

The only good thing about having Chelsea and her mom on the property was that maybe they'd provide a buffer.

"Frankly, I'm scared shi—"

"Well, don't worry," Jonas said, his tone jovial as he pushed his hat down a little more comfortably on his head. "So, what'd you think of Chelsea?"

What did he think of Chelsea? Now, that was a loaded question. Gage sent his friend a suspicious glance, keeping his face unreadable. She was beautiful, for one. She had a helluva rack on her, and seeing her bare and not reacting had taken all of his self-control. Taut nipples, sweet breasts—he broke into a sweat that had nothing to do with the hot New Mexico sun. "Last I saw her, she was pretty upset about a little friend that was visiting. I'm hoping she'll calm down before I get back."

Jonas looked up from staring at his phone, his attention finally caught. "What kind of friend?"

"A snake friend. Just a small one, maybe a foot long. Nothing to get excited about. Be seeing you, Jonas." Gage nodded and went down the sidewalk toward the lumber store, not feeling any more need to socialize. Reading Jonas the riot act about sticking him with a red-haired, sexy female wasn't going to do anything but give his friend fodder for tales around the dinner table. He knew the Callahans too well.

I can take it, Gage thought. He just wasn't certain he could take Chelsea and Cat and Ma all under one roof, when he didn't know any of them at all.

"JONAS!" CHELSEA EXCLAIMED when her one-time fiancé banged on the front door. "Get in here so I can bawl you out like you've never been bawled out before!"

He came in, looking a bit wary, wearing a smile to placate her. She was not placated.

"Why didn't you tell me there was going to be someone else living here?" she began hotly.

"Everything happened quickly," Jonas said. "Both of you are making way too big a deal of this. Pretend like this farmhouse is a bed-and-breakfast. Would you care who the other boarders were?"

"No," Chelsea said, clenching her teeth, "at least not until one of them shot a gun near my feet, I wouldn't."

"Gun?" Jonas perked up. "Gage wouldn't fire a gun near you, Chelsea."

"Well, he did." She wasn't about to share the whole bikini topless incident.

"Had to have had a good reason."

Jonas's eyes began to twinkle, and she knew from experience that he was vastly amused and couldn't wait to hear the whole story, which would be retold later to his brothers and their wives with great gusto.

"Were you being mean to him, Chelsea?" Jonas asked, his tone rich with teasing.

"No, Jonas, I wasn't." He was referring to her Irish temper, knowing full well she wasn't really mean to anybody.

But she did have a temper.

Which she didn't intend to rein in now.

"Did this have anything to do with a critter you didn't want around?"

"I am quite certain, Jonas, that Gage has told you everything, if you know about the *critter*. I'm sure he couldn't wait to have a good laugh at my expense."

"Now, now," Jonas said, his voice comforting. "Gage didn't tell me anything except that some animal had been around, and you hadn't been happy about it."

"It was a *snake*," she said.

"Snakes are no fun," Jonas agreed, trying to get on her good side. "What kind was it?"

"I don't know, and I don't care," she snapped.

"It's important to know, Chelsea. If it was poisonous, I need to look for a nest and—"

"A nest!" Her blood ran cold.

He looked at her, his gaze curious. "You're really afraid of snakes, aren't you?"

"Everyone who is normal has a fear of snakes," Chelsea stated, "unless that's their line of work. And I'm not a snake charmer. Yes, Jonas, you know darn well that I'm as unenthusiastic about snakes as your five sisters-in-law and your wife would be."

"True," he conceded. "Snakes are not welcome around Rancho Diablo."

"Well, then." She crossed her arms. "Maybe you'd like to go take a look at it and catalog it. The stupid thing is down by the creek."

"All right." He ambled off, letting the screen door slam. Chelsea shook her head, thinking that men could be so dense at times. She went back to dusting, arranging the kitchen so she could start cooking tomorrow.

Cleaning made her start thinking about her heroine, who was still in danger and dangling cliffside.

This writer's block is terrible. I don't know how to get the story to flow again. I need peace and quiet and—

"Aw," Jonas said, coming back inside with half a snake dangling from his hand. "It was just a—"

Chelsea screamed, a good old-fashioned gut scream that probably moved nearby mountains.

"What?" he said. "This is just a harmless—"

"Get it out of the house!"

"All right, all right." He exited his own house in a hurry, recognizing that he and his trophy weren't welcome. Chelsea grabbed a glass of water, drinking to calm herself.

"I'm sure that snake was more scared of you than you were of it," he called from the porch.

"Shut *up,* Jonas," she said, and then she heard Gage and him giggling outside the screen door like a couple hyenas. Like children. Chelsea drew a deep breath, marched to the front door, slammed it shut and locked it.

Boys might be boys—but not at her expense.

"NOW YOU'VE DONE IT," Gage told Jonas. "I could have told you that gag wasn't going to play well. Although it *was* funny. That Irish is a screamer for certain."

His friend couldn't contain his grin. "I'm going to take it home and bring it out at the dinner table."

"Sabrina will probably let you have it upside the bean with a dinner plate," Gage warned.

"This is true." Jonas stuck his prize in a sack and went off. "Good luck, by the way."

"Good luck with what?" he asked, knowing the sentiment had been loaded.

"Getting back in the house. Ever again." Whistling, Jonas got in his truck and drove away, his conscience completely unbothered by how he'd destroyed Gage's plans to get on Chelsea's good side.

She wasn't going to let him in tonight, he'd be willing to bet. "Nuts," Gage said, thinking about the pretty breasts he'd tried so hard not to look at. Maybe it was better if he slept in the old run-down bunkhouse. Deciding there was always his truck to bed down in if he couldn't stomach the conditions, he went off, cursing Jonas under his breath.

FROM HER UPSTAIRS bedroom window, Chelsea watched Gage slink off, a veritable snake in nicely fitting blue jeans that hugged his butt and yet sagged just enough to be comfortable. She should have known that any friend of the Callahans was bound to be a bad boy.

"I know how to handle men with a wild streak," she said, setting down to her laptop. Bronwyn was in trouble, but Chelsea didn't know how to help her. It all had to do with Bronwyn's conflict, and Chelsea had yet to figure out exactly what that was. She had the feeling Bronwyn hadn't yet been totally honest with her about her real emotions, the real thing that drove her to be a detective—

"Chelsea!"

She glanced out the bedroom window. Gage was below, waving something at her.

It looked like a white flag.

Truce?

She opened her window. "I'm busy. What do you want?"

He lowered the flag. "To ask you out to dinner."

"Why?"

The question shot out of her more rudely than she'd intended. Once burned, twice shy…

"Just a friendly meal between two people who are sharing space."

"We're not," she said very sweetly. "You're out there and I'm cozy in here. But thanks." She started to close the window.

"Chelsea, wait!"

She edged it up a little and looked out. "What's the matter? Can't you just grill a snake for your supper?"

He grinned at her, the devil in denim. “I could, but I’d rather share a meal with you.”

She shook her head. “Uh-uh. You’re trouble, Texas.”

“Yeah. But you know that up front, so it’ll be easier for you. Anyway, we should try out a restaurant in Tempest. I’ll buy, since you’re mad at me. It’s the least I can do.”

“Then obviously you’ll be buying me dinner every night.”

Gage laughed, a full deep laugh that had the hair standing up on her arms. The man was too sexy for his own good—and she suspected he’d been told that a time or two by man-hunting ladies.

“You need to see the town,” he said. “Getting out will help you with your writing.”

Chelsea wrinkled her nose. He had a point—it wouldn’t hurt her to go do some exploring of her new town. Jonas had said Tempest was charming.

Anyway, she had a dangling heroine, and truthfully, she’d do anything to get rid of her stubborn case of writer’s block. “All right,” she said, not gracefully, either. This man had probably looked at her naked breasts, no doubt told Jonas she’d gotten out of the creek without her top. They’d probably had a great, knee-slapping guffaw over it. “I’m ordering steak, though. You pay for your sins around here, buster.”

“Come on down, Rapunzel. We’ll see if we can find you a steak in Tempest.”

Chelsea shut the window, closing the drapes so he couldn’t watch her change. It had been a long time since she’d had a real date, although this certainly couldn't be called a date—more like a short truce. She and Jonas had never dated—their relationship had started out as an agreement between two people who each needed something.

I wanted out of Ireland. I wanted a climate that suited my mother's health better. I wanted life beyond what I knew.

If I have to put up with a snake now and again, it's going to be worth it—even if he has brown eyes and a body to die for.

Chapter Three

"So," Gage said, as they seated themselves in a booth at Cactus Max's. "This looks like a great place for a red herring, don't you think?"

Chelsea glanced at him with some disdain in her big eyes. Gage grinned, loving yanking her chain.

"Are you trying to be funny?" she asked.

"Not really. Am I?"

"I'm pretty sure you're not." She snapped open her menu with some annoyance, and he grinned again. In the corner of the bar-and-grill-style restaurant, three pool tables were in use, the occasional clicking of balls audible over the easy conversation of the diners. About fifty people milled around, enjoying nachos and beer and other cuisine, or watching big-screen TVs that hung from all four corners, the sound muted. In the background, soothing and mellow jazz music played. Gage found himself relaxing, until he saw Chelsea's gaze fixed on him.

"What?"

She shook her head. "There's a twenty-ounce steak on the menu."

"If you can eat it, be my guest."

"I'll go with the Southwestern steak wraps." She closed her menu.

"And some wine?"

"Tea," she said, eyeing him again. "Thanks."

He laughed. "You're not letting your guard down around me, are you?"

"I can't," she said. "You got really close to me with a bullet. And do you have a permit for that gun you carry?"

They were interrupted by a dark-haired woman named Blanche cheerfully placing a lighted candle on their table. The flame gave the booth a romantic atmosphere that Gage knew would not help Chelsea relax. Not around him, anyway.

Talk about trust issues. He had a wall to climb with this redhead.

"New to town?" the waitress asked.

"We are," Gage said. "We're staying at Dark Diablo."

"Oh," Blanche said. "I know you. You're the ones Jonas said didn't like each other very much."

Chelsea's gaze shot to his, then bounced away. Gage laughed. "We're working on it, Blanche."

She smiled at him. "Well, you sure are a good-looking fellow. I like my men rugged. I can't imagine a lady wouldn't just go to jelly at the knees for you, honey."

He figured Blanche was somewhere around sixty years old, and with her infectious smile and dark brown eyes, she'd probably been able to catch whatever kind of man she wanted. "Thanks. I like my ladies round and sweet like you."

She grinned. "And what about you?" she asked Chelsea, politely trying to include her in the banter.

"I like my wraps rare and my tea cold, please," she said, and Blanche giggled.

"She's no fun," the waitress told Gage.

"She's fun sometimes," he responded, teasing both of them. "So, who's the babe in every corner of this joint?" He gestured to the four large paintings of a busty blonde in different costumes, looking like Marilyn Monroe come to life, only younger and somehow more innocent.

"That," Blanche said with the gusto of a born storyteller, "is Tempest Thornbury."

"Is that a stage name?" Chelsea asked.

"Well," she said, "when you're born Zola Cupertino, you have to consider alternatives, right?" She jammed her pencil into her abundantly tall and sprayed mass of shining dark hair. "Anyway, Tempest is our big star around these parts. She decided to name herself after our town, and the Thornbury, heck, I don't know how she came up with that. But she went off and made herself famous on Broadway, and then went overseas to live in a villa in Tuscany." Blanche shook her head. "They say she's a recluse now, which is a shame, because she's all of about twenty-eight. Can sing like a bird and dance like nothing you ever saw before."

"Why did she become a recluse?" Chelsea asked, and Gage could tell she was fascinated by the story in spite of herself.

"No one knows, exactly. Something about a love story gone wrong, and ghosts in the old family home in Tempest. Not sure how it all fits together. We've talked about it many a time in Tempest, but the truth is, when she left here, she changed so much from when she was little Zola that we don't really know what to think. Her life is very different from ours. You can still see her family home from the country road, you know, but none of us go out there much because of the ghosts." She smiled at Gage. "So are you having steak wraps, too, or did you just want to sit there and stare at the lady all night?"

Gage snapped his gaze away from Chelsea, realizing he *had* been staring. "I'll have the Aztec salad and a margarita, please."

Both women stared at him.

"Not hungry, Gage? Planning on eating the snake later?" Chelsea asked.

"Snake!" Blanche exclaimed. "Don't talk about snakes. I can't stand 'em!"

Chelsea smiled at Gage, enjoying her jest at his expense.

"I might eat the snake," Gage said, handing the menus to Blanche, "but I'm a vegetarian."

"Oh," she said, clearly rattled. "Well, I'll put your order in. If you two need anything, just give a shout."

Gage smiled at Chelsea. "Don't be mad. It really was harmless."

"Then why did you shoot it? Just to watch me hop around?"

He smiled again. "No. From where I was standing,

I didn't know what kind of snake it was. I'd rather be safe than sorry."

She looked at him with suspicion. "Why are you so certain it was harmless?"

"Because it was just a—"

"I hope you're not still talking about snakes," Blanche said, plopping their drinks on the table. "I'm telling you, I hate nothing as much as I hate them!"

"It's all right," Chelsea said, "the only snake around here right now is him."

"That's not fair," Gage said, as Blanche went off in a cloud of disapproval. "I was trying to save you."

"From a harmless snake?"

"What if it had been a rattler? Would you rather I'd just called out, 'there's a snake next to you so be careful'?"

Chelsea's face reflected a mixture of emotions. "Let's talk about something else."

"All right." He raised his margarita to her and said, "To us being good housemates."

"I think not." She didn't raise her tea glass.

Nodding, Gage glanced around at the life-size posters of Tempest Thornbury. Now that he looked at them more closely he could see that they were actually oil paintings done in careful detail, probably from photos of some of Tempest's Broadway gigs. "She's beautiful, huh?"

"Yes. But it's kind of a sad story, don't you think?"

He shrugged. "Everybody's got one, right?"

"Do you?"

"Yeah. But nothing I share with anyone but friends."

She gave him a wry glance. "Okay."

"So what's yours?"

Chelsea shrugged. "It's not very interesting."

"Yeah?" Gage watched her sip her tea with pleasure. She made everything look graceful. Even leaping into the creek she'd been graceful. He could watch her for hours, and if she lost her top again, then he could watch her for days, he was pretty sure.

"I've taken care of my mother for years. That's about it."

"What about Dad?"

She shrugged again. "Died young. Don't remember him." She glanced at Tempest's paintings. "It wouldn't be so bad to leave your roots and go do something exotic and fabulous, would it?"

"Takes a special breed of person, I'd guess. I'm much more of a homebody than that."

Chelsea laughed out loud. Reaching into her purse, she pulled out her phone. "I made notes about you, Texas, when I called back to Diablo to find out about you—after the snake incident. According to Sabrina, you're Jess St. John's cousin, who is married to Johnny Donovan at Rancho Diablo. You rodeoed most of your life, happiest on the circuit. You've never had much of a love life because the road is your life. Apparently, you mentioned once that you're never in one place for more than two or three nights, so there was never any point in calling a lady back." Chelsea slid her phone back into her purse. "I'd say you didn't lack for adventure. In fact, somebody like her," she said, indicating Tempest, "is probably exactly right for you."

He shook his head. "You'd be surprised, but life catches up with people."

Blanche placed their artfully plated food in front of them, and Gage got hungrier just looking at it. "This looks great."

"You won't find better in Tempest," Blanche bragged, "although all the restaurants here are pretty good, I'll say that. If you're a foodie, you'll find you don't want to stray far from town."

She went off again, pleased with her story.

"I like Blanche," Chelsea said. "She's happy."

Gage dug into his salad with gusto. "And proud of what she does."

"So what caught up with you?" Chelsea asked as she bit into her steak and moaned. "I could cut this steak with a spoon, it's that tender."

"I'm sure if you placed a call back to the ol' homestead, you know I wasn't exactly aware that I had a daughter."

Chelsea's eyes grew round. "All I asked was whether you were safe to live with. I didn't inquire as to your love life."

Gage grinned. "Not curious at all?"

She didn't say anything.

"We'll work on our relationship," he promised.

"I want to drive by and see the Tempest place," she said suddenly, catching Gage off guard.

"Ah, the mystery writer's curiosity at work. Feeling the blockage move?"

She wrinkled her nose. "My creativity isn't blocked."

"Jonas says it is. Jonas says you haven't been able to write in three months. He said—"

"Jonas doesn't know everything." Chelsea ate more of her steak wrap, carefully not looking at him.

Obviously, she no more wanted to talk about her problem than he wanted to discuss his. "I'm game for a late-night run to a ghost-infested family home."

Chelsea's gaze met his. "Good."

"Guess ghosts don't bother you like varmints do?"

"I'll be fine, thanks."

He polished off his margarita, thinking that for such a hot night, he was in danger of getting frostbite from his companion.

Maybe she'd warm up to him if they could scare up a ghost or two.

"IT'S KIND OF A SAD little place for such a lively person," Chelsea observed, peering at Tempest's house as Gage stopped his truck in front of the small, two-story white wood structure. Long neglected, the paint flaked and the front porch sagged. Even in the falling darkness, she could see that the roof hadn't been repaired in years.

If visiting a haunt like this didn't stir her creativity, maybe nothing would. A shudder ran through her. She'd loved ghost stories as a kid—she'd grown up on them, courtesy of her mother. "I probably learned storytelling at my mother's knee," she told Gage. "This house has secrets."

"Just looks like a deserted old house to me." He got

out of the truck and went up to the porch. "Nothing exciting about a building that needs to be torn down."

She looked in a dirty window. "You have no romance in your soul."

"You're probably right." He joined her in spying. "Looks like no one's home, Chelsea, if you're just dying to take a peek inside." He pushed the front door open, and pointed to several firecrackers that had been lit and left on the porch, probably by pranksters around Halloween. "Watch where you step."

She followed him in. "Pee-ew. Doesn't smell like a place a star grew up in."

"She was Zola here, remember. Cupertino or something."

Chelsea looked around at the moldy, sagging furniture. Everything was in a state of decay and disrepair, and she felt sorry that the house had been abandoned. "It looks like she just left everything behind."

"Nothing here was what she wanted." Gage kicked something under the sofa.

"What was that?" Chelsea demanded.

"Nothing."

"It was," she insisted. "You have to be honest with me."

"A small mouse," Gage said. "A little on the decayed side."

"I'm okay with mice," Chelsea said, walking past him into the kitchen.

"I don't know what you think you're going to find in here, unless it's your next cliffhanger," Gage said, batting some cobwebs away from his face. "These spiders are bigger than in Texas. And you know there's probably scorpions in this place—"

"You know what your problem is," Chelsea said, looking back at him. "You don't know how to relax."

"This is relaxing?" Gage moved a fallen tile away from where she was about to step. "If we want to see rotten, we could do it at Dark Diablo."

But this was where Tempest had grown up, and from here she'd gone away to seek her fortune. Chelsea could feel the ghosts of disharmony and discontentment shrouding the small house. "Whatever made her leave, it was ugly enough for her to hide herself away once she made her bundle."

"We don't know that she made a bundle."

"She made enough to live in a villa in Tuscany. Blanche said Tempest is still in demand."

"Yeah," Gage said, "Blanche was blowing smoke up your skirt. She was giving you the Tempest tale, to make their little town seem a bit more exciting. I bet no one named Tempest ever even lived here."

"Then who's that?" Chelsea asked, her scalp tightening just a little.

Gage picked up the picture that lay on the kitchen counter, long forgotten. It was of a small girl with threadbare clothes and spindly arms. He turned the photo over. "Zola, five years old."

"See? Blanche was telling the truth."

He set the photo back down in the dust. "Can we go now? I've spent quite enough time with Zola Tempest, thanks."

Chelsea followed him out. "Guess there's no need to lock the door."

Gage shook his head as he got into the truck. "Well, hope that helped."

"Helped what?" She speared him with a look of distaste as he pulled from the drive.

"You know." He pointed to his head. "With the… storytelling wheels."

"Oh, for heaven's sake," Chelsea said, irritated. "Listen, the thing about writer's block—which I don't have—is that it's the Unspeakable Thing That Must Not Be Mentioned."

"Your own ghost," Gage said.

She sighed. "If you must."

He laughed. "And ghost-hunting helps?"

"I do like mysteries and hauntings," she said stiffly.

"So an exorcism would be like a superboost to your creativity. Or a séance!" He ignored her gasp of outrage. "We could do one, Chelsea. We could get the Callahans out here, and we could sit around and burn candles and wait for Tempest to come screaming out of a closet or something."

"You are so odd." Chelsea turned her head, not about to give him the pleasure of knowing that he was getting to her. His needling annoyed her, and he knew it, and he was the kind of man who loved to devil a woman to death, until she finally gave up and gave him what he wanted.

Sex, in most cases. She'd be willing to bet her best pair of heels.

"It's not going to work," she told him.

"What isn't?"

"This pathetic attempt to scare me so badly that I'll just jump into your arms like a silly, spineless heroine."

"I'll have you know that there are lots of silly, spineless heroines who liked my arms just fine."

"Well, you can keep your stories," Chelsea said. "Enough with shooting the poor harmless snake and trying to spook me with talk of séances. You're not fooling me."

"Good to know," Gage said, amused, and Chelsea told herself right then and there that if Gage Phillips ever tried to kiss her, she was going to give him the fattest lip of his life. *Pow!* Right on his too-attractive, laughing, storytelling kisser.

In fact, she hoped he did try to kiss her.

She really did.

Chapter Four

About four the next afternoon, when Chelsea was making tea and desperately wondering why her heroine wasn't cooperating, she heard the sounds of Gage's own issue, loud and clear.

"I don't want to be here," a girl said.

"You didn't want to be in Laredo, either, sweetheart. So here you are," Gage replied.

Chelsea dried her hands on a dish towel, telling herself she wasn't eavesdropping shamelessly.

"I didn't want to come," the voice said—obviously that of Cat, the surprise daughter.

Chelsea couldn't imagine what it must be like to discover one had a teenage daughter. Gage hadn't said a whole lot about his ex-wife—and Chelsea hadn't wanted to pry. But from the words being spoken outside, he and his daughter had a lot to work out.

"You may not have wanted to come," he said, "but I wanted you here. So take your bag inside, please."

Bravo, Dad, Chelsea thought.

"There's a nice lady inside who you'll like, so let's go meet her," Gage added.

"Lady? I thought you said we were going to be alone. That's what you told Mom—that it was just going to be me and you," Cat complained, her voice getting high.

"That's what I said," Gage said, "because it's what I thought at the time. The owner of the house made other plans, and that's beyond my control. Please take your bag inside."

"You told Mom there'd be no girlfriends," Cat insisted. "You said this was an appropriate place for me to be."

Chelsea heard Gage sigh. "Trust me when I tell you that this lady and I are not romantically attached. I just met her yesterday. Either you take your bag inside right now and quit acting like a child, or I'm going to let you sleep on the porch, Cat."

Chelsea froze, waiting for them to come in.

When they did, she realized just how full Gage's hands were with his new daughter—and why Cat's mother needed a break. Cat had long black hair to her waist on one side, her head shaved on the other. She had a nose piercing, an ear cuff and what looked like a bar through her other upper ear. She had two lip rings, which gave her sort of a snakelike look.

But that wasn't the worst part. The worst was the stare Cat leveled at her, as if she hated her on sight.

"Hi," Chelsea said, recognizing she would have to tread carefully. "I'm Chelsea Myers, the upstairs roommate."

"You're not going to boss me," Cat said to her.

Chelsea blinked. "You're right. I'm not."

"Cat," Gage said. "You and I don't really know each other, but let me tell you something you should know. I don't tolerate disrespect."

Cat glared at her father. "You didn't tell Mom the truth. She always said you were the least honest man she ever met. I guess I know who I can believe."

Gage sighed. Chelsea saw no reason to explain what Gage had already told to his daughter, so she said, "I made cookies. Does anybody want some cookies and maybe some tea? I'm sure you're hungry after—"

"'Does anybody want some cookies?'" Cat mimicked. "Betty Crocker to the rescue." She set her black duffel on the floor. "Quit staring at me," she told Chelsea.

Chelsea was about to reply, wanting to head off the explosion she could tell was about to blow from Gage, when the screen door opened and her mother blew in.

"Hello!" Moira Myers exclaimed. "Goodness, the wind is picking up out there!"

Cat stared at Chelsea's mother, shocked, it seemed, by someone else's appearance taking center stage. Moira was dressed in hot pink from head to toe, from her sparkly tennis shoes to her calf-length skirt, to the short-sleeved sweater with a pink poodle on it. She even had on hot pink lipstick. Her white hair stood out in cotton candy tufts from her head, liberated from the plastic scarf she usually wore on windy days. In her hand she carried a cage with two lovebirds in it.

"What are you?" Cat asked.

"Cat!" Gage finally exploded.

"Mum, come in," Chelsea said, going forward to hug her. "You look lovely."

"She looks—" Cat began, swallowing her words on a yelp. Gage seemed to finally have had enough of his daughter's sassy mouth.

"Fiona Callahan helped me pick this out. Do you really like it, Chelsea?" Her mother smiled beatifically. "I love shopping with Fiona. She's so much fun! She made me feel ten years younger."

"Mum, this is Gage Phillips," Chelsea said, "and this is his daughter, Cat."

"Hello," Moira said, shaking each of their hands. Cat actually offered hers, either because her father had gotten it through her head that he was about to make her life miserable, or because surprise at Mrs. Myers's appearance had rendered her temporarily unable to carp. "It's so nice to meet you! And how pretty you are, dear," she told Cat in her lilting Irish accent. "Would you be so kind as to step outside and get my suitcase off the porch, please? You look like such a nice, bonny lass indeed."

To Chelsea's surprise—and Gage's too—Cat went to retrieve the bag. "There, now," Moira said when she returned a second later, "let me see. I know I'm forgetting something. I'm always forgetting something, aren't I, Chelsea, love? Oh, I know," she went on, not waiting for Chelsea to answer. Chelsea would have said she'd never known her mother to forget anything, but Moira didn't seem to need any response. "This is for you, dear," she told Cat, handing her the cage with the two beautiful lovebirds inside.

"Really?" Cat took the cage, astonished. "I mean, I don't like birds. I hate birds. I bet they'll give me allergies." She stared at them, seemingly fascinated. "They're ugly. And it's stupid to have things in a cage." She looked at her father. "Can I keep them?"

Gage looked at his daughter with some exasperation. "If Mrs. Myers has given you a gift, Cat, then I think you should say thank-you. And then you should ask Miss Myers where the best place to keep them would be."

Cat glanced worriedly at the two women. "Um, thank you," she said to Moira, as if she wasn't certain how to express gratitude.

"Let's find your bedroom upstairs. That will be a lovely place to keep them, I'm sure," Chelsea said, starting up the stairs. Cat followed, not protesting any longer, carefully carrying the birds so they wouldn't be jostled.

Thanks, Mum, Chelsea thought. *Once again, I have a feeling you saved the day.*

"This is my room?" Cat asked.

"Yes," Chelsea said. "I think your birds would be comfortable right here near the window. Not too close to feel the sunshine, though."

Cat gently set the cage on the shelf near the window. "Your mom is weird."

Chelsea smiled. "My mother is eclectic. I like that about her."

Cat looked at her. "You like your mother?"

"Of course. Why wouldn't I?"

"I don't know." The teen shrugged, watching Chelsea warily as she sat down on one of the twin beds. "You're not supposed to like your mother."

Chelsea smiled. "I love my mother. She's my best friend."

"Wow," Cat said, "you're a bigger loser than I thought."

Chelsea smiled again. "I'm going back downstairs. If you're hungry, join us. I need to get my mother settled in."

"I don't want to join you," Cat said, following her down the stairs. "I'm only coming because my dad says I have to."

"That's fine," Chelsea said. She was pleased to see Gage and her mother seated in the front room, chatting comfortably. He seemed genuinely interested in her, and Chelsea told herself that anyone wearing that much hot pink had to make people smile. "Mum, can I get you some tea?"

"You can, daughter." Mrs. Myers excused herself and followed Chelsea into the kitchen. "Quite the fun situation you've got going here."

"I suppose so. It's really just going to be me and you, though. There's a lovely creek, and the town is so pretty—"

"I think you're going to have your hands full." Moira took the teacup Chelsea handed her, drinking appreciatively. "Ah, no one knows how to make a proper tea except you, daughter."

"You taught me everything I know, Mum."

Cat came into the kitchen, obviously hungry but not wanting to seem as if she was. She glanced at Mrs.

Myers's cup. "If that doesn't have eye of newt in it, could I have some?"

Chelsea laughed. "You never know around here, Cat. You'll have to go on faith."

Cat took the cup she handed her, slurping it down quickly.

"Oh, she's hungry," Moira said. "Chelsea, where are your manners, love? Bring out the frog-toes cookies and give some to Cat."

"Gross!" the girl exclaimed.

Chelsea shook her head. "Mum," she gently remonstrated, handing Cat a plate with three cookies on it. "There's more, but you don't want to ruin—"

"My mom said this was going to be a backwater and that I'd probably have to eat some gross stuff, but I'm not eating frog toes," Cat said. "And you can't make me."

"These are homemade chocolate chip cookies, and you don't have to eat them if you don't want to." Chelsea smiled at her.

"You're both weird," Cat said, snatching the plate. "Why'd you say there were frog toes in the cookies?" she asked Moira.

"You mentioned eye of newt," Moira said, her tone pleasant. "Which of course brings to mind Shakespeare's *Macbeth*. You know it, I'm sure. 'Eye of newt, and toe of frog, wool of bat, and tongue of dog...'"

"My mom is not going to be happy that I'm living with a bunch of weirdos," Cat said, taking out a tongue piercing and laying it on the side of the china plate.

"Mmm, these are pretty good." She seemed pleased by the cookies, eagerly polishing them off.

Gage hadn't come into the kitchen. Chelsea figured he'd probably run for the hills, or maybe to the library for a *How To Be a Father on the Fly* parenting book. "Will you take this plate to your dad, Cat?"

Cat looked at her. "I don't—"

"Sure, and that's a good girl, now," Moira said. "What a lovely lass you are, Cat."

Cat took the plate and left the kitchen, looking bemused, if not surprised, at the praise.

"Now I see how you got me through my difficult teen years," Chelsea said. "Have I ever apologized for being a handful?"

"Chelsea, love," Moira said, sipping her tea, "if anything, you've always been an angel. I owe you apologies for saddling you to a life that wasn't like the other girls'. You could have done a lot more, if you hadn't had me—"

"Mum!" Chelsea exclaimed. "Don't say it!"

"Oh, well. It doesn't matter anyway, does it?" Moira asked, taking a bite of a cookie. "I rather thought the eye of newt question was clever from the lass, didn't you? She's older than her years."

Chelsea shook her head. "I don't know what to think. I guess we'll see what happens." She thought about Gage, wondering about last night. After their visit to Tempest's house, he'd brought her home and said good-night—and promptly bunked on the sofa.

It had rained all night, a vicious storm that cut the power—and Chelsea hadn't been able to sleep. She'd huddled in her bed, staring out at the rain washing the windows in sheets, wondering why she was thinking about Gage when she should have been thinking about her plot.

"He's a handsome man, Chelsea. D'ya fancy him?"

"No." She shook her head. "Mum, we're from opposite ends of the earth, trust me."

"Ah, well. So it goes." Moira grinned. "Fiona said she was pretty certain the two of you might take a shine to each other. I guess she'd be wrong this time, eh?"

"Definitely," Chelsea said. "Don't let the Callahan myth blind you to the fact that Gage isn't the kind of man I need in my life."

"What *do* you need? Do you know?"

Chelsea thought about Gage walking her through an old, falling-down house, making sure she didn't step on firecrackers and dead mice. She thought about him shooting a snake that wanted to take a swim with her. "I need someone boring," she said. "I want stable and boring."

Moira laughed. "Then that handsome rascal wouldn't be the man for you."

"That's right," Chelsea said. "When I meet stable and boring, I'll know."

JUST GAZING AT HIS DAUGHTER gave Gage a little bit of the willies. What had Leslie been thinking, letting Cat look like this? Do this to herself?

Chelsea and her mother hadn't seemed too disturbed by Cat's appearance. Maybe it was a girl thing. He was definitely out of his league with girl things, so he let his worry over this girl—his daughter—and her wild appearance go for the moment.

He didn't know what to say to her. What had come so easily for Chelsea and Moira didn't come easily for him. The two of them sat on the front porch swing, miserably not speaking.

"Guess you were surprised about me," Cat said.

Gage nodded. "It's a good surprise, though."

Cat shook her head. "No, it's not. Mom says you're just an itin…itin—"

"Itinerant," Gage supplied, thinking that sounded like something Leslie would say.

"Itinerant cowboy," Cat said with a nod, "and that you've never had two nickels to rub together because you can't keep a job. She said when you were together, you made mashed potatoes with water in them instead of milk because you were so poor."

He scratched the back of his neck, thinking that Leslie hadn't managed to spare him. But maybe he didn't deserve any sparing. "That's all true, pretty much, though I do have two nickels."

Cat didn't seem impressed. "How long am I staying here?"

He shrugged. "I guess until school starts. You like your school, right?"

"I don't know. The kids are weird."

Gage sighed, thinking his daughter wasn't doing a whole lot to fit in. In that, she was like him. "You want to know about this side of the family?"

"No," Cat stated. "I'm not going to see you again

after August. I'll never meet your family. So I don't care."

It was true she wouldn't meet the family. Gage generally stayed as far away from them as he could, leaving his sister and two brothers to run Phillips, Inc., in Hell's Colony. He wasn't cut out for politics, or family debates. "Well, it'll make good storytelling, since we're both bored."

"I could go back in and talk to the Weirdos," Cat offered. "Except I think I heard them talking about whipping up some dinner. The old lady mentioned something about dog legs and bat wool." She shivered.

Gage laughed. "Sounds delicious."

"I think you should throw them out."

"That *old* lady, Mrs. Myers, gave you a pair of pretty birds. Cut her a break."

Cat sighed. "I guess that was kinda cool. Anyway, I guess you want to bore me to death with your family skeletons. Mom says you've got such a closetful of 'em that Dracula would be impressed."

Jeez, Leslie. "Okay, there's your uncle Shaman."

"Weird name."

Gage decided *weird* was one of his daughter's favorite words. "Shaman's two years younger than me. He's in the military, been in since college. In high school, the girls were crazy for him because he was definitely anti-authority, anti-establishment. In other words, he was a hell-raiser—although, strangely, he graduated valedictorian." Gage laughed, still proud of his brother. "He's probably my favorite sibling, but I haven't seen him in years."

"Because you're on the road all the time, shifting from place to place." Cat nodded, obviously repeating her mother's side of the story.

"Then there's Kendall. She's two years younger than Shaman, and four years younger than me. Kendall is twins with Xavier. He goes by Xav."

"They're the ones who run the family business. Mom says they've got more money than King Midas, and that you got kicked out of the business because you were too bone-idle to help run it." Cat looked at her father. "Why are you so lazy?"

"Because," Gage said, ruffling his daughter's hair—the side of her head that had hair, "I'm an itinerant cowboy, and that's what we do. Let's go check on Mrs. and Miss Myers. They might need help."

Cat padded after him into the kitchen, her black-checked tennis shoes not making a sound.

"We're going into town to get some ice cream," he said. "Anybody want to join us? What is that?" he asked, staring at the two-tier confection on the kitchen counter that Mrs. Myers was frosting.

"This is dessert for people who eat their dinner and put away their dishes," Moira said. "It's coconut cake. My own mother's recipe."

"It smells wonderful." Gage's mouth began watering.

"It is." Chelsea took the spreading knife from her mother and handed it to Cat. "You finish the frosting, Cat."

The teen looked at the cake uncertainly. "I can't. I don't know how. It's just a stupid cake, anyway." She tried to hand the spreader back to Moira, who shook her head.

"There's nothing that can't be fixed, love," the woman said. "Go on, nice and easy. And when you're finished, please sprinkle these coconut bits on top."

Moira turned away to do something at the sink. Chelsea peered into the fridge, monitoring the contents, not paying any attention to Cat. Cat looked at her father, a question in her big brown eyes. He nodded, and she took a deep breath, reaching out to place some frosting on the cake.

"It tore," she said. "I can't do this! It's a stupid—"

Moira took her hand, gently showing her how to spread the frosting in a smooth, gliding motion that didn't disturb the cake. Then she turned back to the sink, and after a moment, Cat tried again.

The frosting went on like it was supposed to, and Cat applied herself more diligently to the task, silent for the moment. Gage's breath released from his chest, though he hadn't realized he'd been holding it.

"Gage," Chelsea said, "we're going to need some things from the grocery, now that there are four of us. I'll make a list, if you'd like to do the shopping."

"I can do that," he agreed, glad to be given an assignment. "I'll pay for the groceries, if you're going to be kind enough to fix meals."

"We're going to have pot roast and…" She glanced at Gage. "I forgot you're a vegetarian. You'll have to pick up the veggies and things you like to eat."

Cat stared at her father. "You're a vegetarian? That's *weird*."

Gage shook his head, having heard *weird* one too many times today. “I’ll take care of the groceries, Chelsea. Thank you both for cooking for us. Come with me, Cat. You and I will start clearing out the barn.”

“I don’t want to—” she said, putting down the spreader and following her father.

“I know,” Gage said. “It’s weird. But everybody works if they’re lucky enough to have a job, and we do. So you can help me clear the barn. I need to sketch a new structure, and then decide if this is the right location for a barn, according to Jonas’s new plans, and then we’ll talk to a few architects, let them draw up some things for the big man. How does that sound?”

“Terrible. Boring.” Cat followed her father out, almost at his heels.

Moira smiled at Chelsea. “Nothing a little cake and sweet tea won’t cure.”

Chelsea nodded. She hoped so, anyway. “I’m going to make a list for Gage, and then go write for a little while. Will you be all right?”

“I’m happy as a lark,” Moira replied. “I’m going to play with this new phone Fiona talked me into. She’s been texting me for the past hour, but I haven’t had time to look.” Moira beamed. “I want to see what my old next-door neighbor is up to now.”

“Probably something weird, to use Cat’s word.”

Moira laughed and Chelsea went upstairs to ponder her heroine’s dilemma. Life for Bronwyn Sang wasn’t getting any better. Bronwyn had been dangling off the edge of the cliff for three months. Chelsea’s book was due to her editor in one month.

She'd written only ten chapters.

"I'm in deep water here," she told Bronwyn. "I'm starting to think your problem is that you're passive. If you had an ounce of kick-ass in you, you wouldn't be dangling. *He'd* be dangling."

She sighed, and decided to write the grocery list first. That was something she could handle, a small little list that—

Chelsea stopped fiddling with her pen, her attention caught by Gage and Cat outside her window.

He was showing her how to aim his gun at a large can he'd placed on an old moldy hay bale near the ramshackle barn. "Argh," Chelsea said. "It isn't any of my business. You're my business," she told Bronwyn, turning back to her book, which was going nowhere fast. "If you were anything like Tempest, you wouldn't just be hanging around—"

Tempest. Now there was a woman who had decided she wasn't going to be a doormat to anyone, probably including evil villains. The photo of Zola as a child and the adult renderings of Tempest had been vastly different. Only the eyes had looked the same, eyes that had seen a lot in life.

Tempest, Chelsea wrote, tapping on the screen just under where Bronwyn dangled, awaiting certain death from the killer in book three of the Sang P.I. mysteries, *is a woman who knows what she wants. She walked away from her small town and she never looked back, making herself into one of the most sought-after women in the world. She is beautiful and independent, and men throw themselves at her feet. But she is in charge of her own destiny, so she doesn't need a man to save her.*

I wish I could meet Tempest.

The crack of a gun outside made Chelsea jump. She peered out at Gage and Cat. Cat was receiving a high five from her father, and the can had been pretty much obliterated.

"Really!" Chelsea muttered. There had to be another way to bond with one's long-lost daughter. Grinding her teeth, she put on her headphones and went back to Detective Sang.

"GREAT JOB." GAGE retrieved the can and set it back up on the bale. "Looks like you've got sharp eyesight and good hand-to-eye coordination. You'd probably like archery, too."

"I don't know," Cat said, looking like Eeyore. He felt sorry for his daughter with her half-shaved head. She'd be such a pretty girl without the angst written all over her. A bit of anger boiled up inside him at his ex-wife. It had been simmering ever since he'd found out Leslie had kept Cat a secret. Anger, he knew, did nothing, didn't help anything. He preferred to blot those emotions, any emotion, really. Seesawing emotions blinded one to what needed to be done in life.

But his daughter shouldn't look so despondent, even if she was a newly minted teen. "Hey, what do you say we go for a horse ride?"

"I don't know how to ride a horse."

"You live in Laredo. There are plenty of horses."

"I know, but Mom's afraid of them. So I never

learned to ride." Cat shrugged thin shoulders. "They're just stinky animals, anyway."

He remembered Leslie saying something like that. "Okay, you don't have to ride."

Cat looked around at the vast, empty acreage. "So I'm stuck here for the rest of the summer? With no friends? Surely there's somebody besides the two oddballs in there." She flipped her hand toward the house, and Gage sighed.

"First, we don't know that they're oddballs. Anyway, the truth about meeting people is that usually it's best to give folks a chance. If you talk to them twenty times and you still don't like them, then that's just the way it is. But sometimes you get a wrong first impression. It's easy to do."

"Yeah." Cat didn't sound as if she thought she'd like Moira and Chelsea on closer inspection. "So, where's your family you were talking about? Mom says you're the loner, and that none of them really like you."

Gage put his gun away and ran a hand over his daughter's long side of hair. "Here's the deal. I know you love your mom. And that's a good thing. But let me suggest that Leslie hasn't seen me in a great many years, so she doesn't know me. And I think you're old enough to make your own decisions about things." He shrugged. "I'm not saying whatever your mom said about me and my family isn't true, I'm just saying it may not all be true. And you owe it to yourself to make your own mind up."

Cat took that in for a minute. "Okay."

"Good." Gage thought his daughter probably wasn't

a bad kid, probably just confused and somehow out of place. The mouth likely got her into trouble, and the air of I-don't-give-a-damn, when she clearly very much did.

I remember that stage. It sucked.

"So, anyway, I guess I'll never meet my aunt and uncles," Cat said morosely.

Gage let out a breath and went to sit on the bale of hay. "Never is a long time."

"Yeah." She shrugged, and sat on the ground cross-legged. "Mom called your sister."

Gage's jaw clenched. "Did she?"

"Yeah. She told her about me. Mom said she was hoping maybe what's-her-name would know where you were this summer." Cat looked at him. "Mom said your sister didn't know, but gave her your cell phone number and then said some rude things about her."

Gage winced. "Don't worry about that. It has nothing to do with you, Cat. Kendall's mouth runs away with her at times."

"I was hoping for a normal family," Cat said, her tone wistful.

"We all do, sweetie. 'Normal family' is pretty much a fairy tale."

"Brittany Collins goes to my school, and she has a normal family," Cat insisted.

"That's good," Gage said, thinking that his daughter was very young, very confused. It was only to be expected that she might look around her and see girls whose lives she'd like to emulate. "We better get going to buy those groceries. And you wanted ice cream."

"That sounds boring," Cat said, and Gage laughed.

"Boring's not so bad."

"Maybe not," Cat said doubtfully. "Maybe you should ask the Weirdos again if they want to go with us."

Gage glanced at his daughter. "You wouldn't mind?"

She shrugged. "We'll look like a freak show, but no one knows me here, I guess. And the old lady was nice to bring me some birds. I really like them. Mom won't let me have pets—she says they're dirty. She'd flip out over birds, I bet." Cat sounded cheered by that. "And that lady you stare at all the time—what's her name?"

"Chelsea," Gage said, "and I do not stare at her."

"Yeah. You do. Kind of like my mom stares at Larry." Cat shuddered. "Larry is such a loser. I don't know why she stares at him. He looks like a frog." She glanced at her father. "You don't look like a frog."

"Thanks." Gage smiled. "You want to go inside and invite the ladies?"

"Do I have to?"

"Your idea."

"Ugh." Cat walked into the house to the kitchen, where she knew she'd at least find the old lady who loved pink clothes. "Hey, Dad's taking me for ice cream. He said it would be nice if you and your daughter came along to keep us company. He says we don't know what to say to each other, and that it's pretty awkward."

Moira glanced up from her cookbook and smiled at Cat. "What a bonny idea. As a matter of fact, I was thinking you and I should make a trip to the library one afternoon."

"What for?" Cat asked suspiciously.

"As we were discussing *Macbeth,*" the old lady began, and Cat shut that down in a hurry.

"*You* were discussing *Macbeth.* I just didn't want you giving me any fried newt eyes."

Moira smiled and tied on her rain cap.

"What's that for? It's not raining."

"You're right. It's not," Moira said, tying the pink polka-dotted plastic securely on her head. "Could you be a love and run upstairs and get my daughter, please? Knock first, and only go in if she says you may. She might be writing."

"Something awful, I'm sure," Cat said, her tone depressed and certain that whatever Chelsea was writing, it had to be worse than a third-grader's school paper. She banged on the door.

Chelsea opened it, smiling when she saw Cat. Cat sniffed to let her know she didn't like her. "Dad says you and your mother have to come eat ice cream with us. He says he needs you because we don't like each other very much. Your mom's putting on her hair thing, and she looks kind of weird, but she's going to take me to the library someday, so that'll be a real drag."

Chelsea nodded. "Ice cream sounds wonderful."

Cat looked past Chelsea into her room. "You're probably not a very good writer."

"Um—"

"I bet nobody would ever buy your books." Cat

looked up at her. "Anyway, you should be a schoolteacher or something."

"Why?" Chelsea asked, following her down the stairs.

"You look like one," Cat said, making it sound as if it wasn't good to look like a teacher.

"Thank you," Chelsea said. "My mother was a schoolteacher. I always admired her." A schoolteacher! No one probably ever told Tempest she looked like that.

Chelsea wondered if Gage thought she looked like a schoolteacher. She patted her hair, which had a tendency to get wild and unruly when she was writing, from constantly shoving a hand through her bangs when she was deep in thought.

"I'll sit in front," Cat said, "next to my father."

"Perfect. This is a nice truck, Gage," Chelsea said.

"I just bought it." He turned to smile at her, and Chelsea noticed her stomach give a little flip. He had such nice white teeth in his big smile, and his dark eyes seemed so full of life that it was hard not to smile back.

She saw Cat glowering at her, and wiped the answering smile off her own face. "I saw you shooting, Cat. Was it fun?"

"No," Cat said.

"Do you shoot, Chelsea?" Gage asked.

"Not unless I have to."

"I do," Moira said. "I can bag a quail at fifty paces."

"She can," Chelsea said. "Many a time we ate something Mum brought home."

"Eye of newt," Cat said.

"Maybe," Chelsea said. "In my home, we ate what

was on our plates, said thank-you, excused ourselves and cleared the table. No questions asked."

Cat turned to look at Moira. "Are you going to make me do all that?"

Moira nodded. "Of course, lamb. Otherwise, I don't cook."

"Jeez," Cat said. "This is worse than prison."

"Cat," Gage said, his tone warning.

Chelsea looked out the window, amazed by the lack of cars on the road into town. "Tempest is like an old postcard that never changed."

"I like that," Gage said. "I like that it seems preserved in time."

"I do, too." Chelsea jumped when Gage's gaze caught her eyes in the mirror above the dash.

"It looks boring," Cat said, her nose pressed to the window as she looked out at the farmland they passed. Cows and horses and an occasional llama dotted the dry landscape. "I'd be embarrassed for my friends to know I was stuck out in the middle of the desert. I'll probably get stung by a scorpion."

"That reminds me—by chance did your mom send you with a pair of boots?" Gage asked, glancing at her black-and-white-checked tennis shoes.

Cat shrugged. "I've never had boots. I don't need any, because I'm not going to be an itin…itin—"

"Itinerant," Gage supplied.

"Cowgirl," she finished, convinced she had life all figured out.

Chelsea's gaze once again caught Gage's in the mirror. He appeared a little chagrined by his daughter's attitude. Chelsea told herself that his and Cat's problems had nothing to do with her. In fact, she should be at home writing, giving Bronwyn a chance to figure her way out of her mess.

It was so much more exciting to wonder about Tempest, and how she might handle the pitfall Bronwyn had landed in.

I'm not good at pitfalls. I don't like guns. I don't like scary stuff. How did I ever wind up writing mysteries?

Maybe I write mysteries because I love puzzles. And I crave adventure—just like Cat.

She looked at Gage, thinking he was pretty much the call of the wild in real life—but she wasn't adventurous Tempest. Except for her and her mother's excursion to America, adventure came to her only on the safe pages of her novels. She would never have the courage to walk away from her life and be someone she wasn't. "Gage," Chelsea said suddenly, telling herself it was folly to get involved, "do you know when the nearest rodeo is?"

"Santa Fe. This weekend." He looked at her. "The four of us could go, if you'd want to see one. Moira, have you been to a rodeo?"

"Not a one, and I'd love to," Moira said. She shot her daughter a glance of approval, then looked at Cat.

"I've attended one, and I'd really like to go again," Chelsea said. *And give Cat a chance to see boot-wearing cowgirls and cowboys outside her hometown, doing their jobs.*

"Great. We'll go," Gage said.

"Sounds boring," Cat said.

Chelsea smiled. "We'll see."

AFTER A QUICK GROCERY RUN, they ran into Blanche the waitress at Shinny's Ice Cream Shoppe. Introductions were made, and when Moira went off to look at the photographs on the walls, and Cat and her dad were engaged in some getting-to-know-you chitchat, Chelsea wandered over to the gregarious waitress. "What flavor?"

Blanche smiled. "Peppermint. My favorite. You?"

"I think peach." Chelsea liked Blanche. In fact, she liked much of what she'd seen around the town of Tempest so far. Which brought up the name that had been stoking her curiosity, even making her wonder if she'd plotted her heroine wrong in her current book. "So tell me more about Tempest."

"You're not asking about the town, are you?" Blanche gave her a smile that reached her big eyes behind red-and-blue-swirled glasses frames.

"I want to hear about that, too. But I have to admit you caught my interest with the tale about Tempest."

"C'mon." Blanche waved her over to a black-and-white photograph on the wall. "This is Zola when she was just a wee thing."

Chelsea blinked. "She seems so thin."

"Yeah. Well, it wasn't for lack of eating, I don't think. Her mom used to send her down every day to this very ice cream shop. My husband, Shinny, over there—" she pointed to a friendly-looking, balding man who was sweeping up "—he owns this shop. He gives ice cream out to the kids, especially the ones he knows got folks who can't afford it. Zola was on his list of kids who always got a double scoop, or a milkshake if he could talk her into it. Chocolate," Blanche said with a smile, "in case you were going to ask. Shinny's special."

Chelsea moved to a photo of Tempest's most famous citizen standing in a field, looking at the camera with wide eyes. Her bare feet looked dirty and her overalls not much better. "Did she have a high school sweetheart?"

"No." Blanche pointed to a football team photo with a pretty brunette standing in a shiny uniform beside the team. "Maggie Sweet was the girl the guys went for. Not a skinny, brown-headed sparrow like Zola. Funny thing is, when she grew up and left this town behind to become Tempest, men pursued her like mad. She went through men like candy, and I don't think she was serious about a one of them. She had one serious guy, some minor royal from Scotland, I think. Anyway, she found out he had a lady on the side, and left him just like she'd left this town." Blanche smiled, remembering. "We were all afraid she'd be heartbroken, but Tempest said it was his loss."

"How do you know all this?" Chelsea had to know more. "I thought she went away and never looked back."

"She used to call back here from time to time. It's just been the last year or two we haven't heard a peep from her. About to send a delegation over to check on her." Blanche didn't look convinced that that would have much impact. "We still love her here. She'll always be Zola to us."

She'd always be that dirty little girl in the threadbare clothes, Chelsea thought. No wonder she wanted to make herself into Tempest. Chelsea could understand wanting to get away from her old life. It would be fun to be a heroine in a book for a day. *Not my heroine. She's been dangling so long she's afraid she'll never get off that cliffside.*

"Ready to go?" Gage asked Chelsea, smiling a greeting at Blanche. "I've got to get Cat home. She says she's tired after her big day of traveling. If you want me to come back later and pick you up—"

"I'm good. Thanks." Chelsea smiled at the woman in turn as she got up from the swivel seat she'd settled on while they'd been chatting. "I enjoyed the town history lesson, Blanche. Thank you."

Blanche waved a hand, reached out to pat a grumpy-looking Cat. "You come back anytime, sugar. Free ice cream for pretty little girls." She smiled at her. "You look so much like your daddy."

Gage appeared pleased. "Thanks, Blanche. I take that as a real fine compliment."

Cat glanced up at him, surprised. "You do?"

He nodded. "Sure I do."

Cat didn't seem to know what to think about that. She remained silent, following him as he went to escort Moira to the truck. Chelsea went out behind them, watching Gage interact with his daughter, thinking that for a man who'd just found out he was a dad, he was handling it very well.

"THANKS," GAGE SAID as he walked the women to the front door. Moira and Cat went on inside to check on the birds, which Cat had named Mo and Curly—he guessed Larry hadn't been her favorite of the Three Stooges—so Gage grabbed the chance to tell Chelsea exactly how he felt.

Damn grateful.

"For what?" She looked at him, surprised.

He shrugged, not certain how to express what he wanted to say. "Helping Cat make the transition. And me."

Afternoon light glowed softly on her features as she studied him. Gage waited nervously, as if he was on a first date, not certain why he felt so skittish around Chelsea. Her eyes were so kind and radiated understanding. She wasn't the type of woman who made men nervous, he was pretty certain.

Which meant…he must dig her.

A little.

The stray thought made Gage even more nervous. Since his relationship with Cat's mother, Leslie, he'd stayed busy, making no time for dating. A night or two with a lady sufficed.

He shouldn't feel differently about this russet-haired Irishwoman. For many reasons—not the least of which would be not wanting to play right into Jonas's hands.

A man had his pride. Gage looked away from the redhead with the big eyes.

"I didn't do anything for either of you," Chelsea said. "I like Cat. She reminds me of myself at that age."

He couldn't imagine any resemblance, in any way, between the two of them. But he smiled. "Thanks."

"No thanks necessary."

There was no reason to keep Chelsea outside longer than he had, either. The shame of it was he really wanted to talk to her more. His heart drummed inside him, and he wished he had his typical easy talk at his disposal. But he didn't.

And then he did the unthinkable, brushing his lips from the side of her mouth to her cheek, as "just friends" as he could manage.

God, she was soft.

"See you around," he said, not hanging in to find out what price he might have to pay for stealing a brotherly peck. He didn't know what had possessed him. He'd let his mouth do the speaking his voice couldn't. "I'm leaving, Cat! Are you coming?"

"I'll catch up in a sec!" she yelled back from upstairs. He heard the screen door close as Chelsea went inside.

Good thing, too. Or he'd be tempted to go back for another helping of "just friends."

Now that he knew how soft she was, he was going to have to put the brakes on temptation. *Hard.*

Chapter Five

Chelsea went inside to help her mother with dinner, completely stunned that Gage had kissed her. Sure, it was a non-kiss, really, as kisses went—but yesterday they hadn't even been on shaking-hands terms.

Of course, it hadn't been anything more than Gage expressing his gratitude. New-overwhelmed-dad gratitude.

He appreciated her and her mom being nice to his daughter. That was all the brief peck had meant.

It had "just friends" written on it. Quick and fast and…like it hadn't meant anything except *thanks*.

She was amazed to see Moira and Cat busy chopping vegetables. "What can I do to help, Mum?"

"Nothing at the moment. The cake is made, dinner is almost finished. We're just finishing up a big salad for Gage. And a sweet potato casserole."

Cat glanced up at her. "We get a baked chicken. Dad gets portobello mushroom skewers."

"You go write, dear," her mother said.

"You should," Cat agreed. Chelsea wondered if that was her subtle way of trying to keep Moira to herself.

"I read what was on your laptop—by accident. I went into your room to find you, but you weren't there."

Chelsea raised a brow. "And you just happened to make yourself at home on my laptop?"

"I didn't touch anything. You left the screen up." Cat shrugged. "Anyway, it's going to get read if it ever gets published."

"It is getting published, and I don't allow anyone to read my work until I say it's all right to." This was something they were going to have to straighten out pronto. Cat would have to understand that her room was off-limits.

"Anyway," the teen said, "I just thought you should know that Tempest is a real flesh-and-blood person. I can actually see her." Cat took a bite of carrot, considering her thoughts. "Bronwyn, not so much. She seems kind of wishy-washy. Cardboard."

Chelsea and Moira stared at Cat. Chelsea wasn't certain what to think about the critique—although she had a funny feeling it was dead-on. "Please don't read my work anymore, Cat, unless I give you permission."

She nodded. "I won't. Miss Moira says she's going to take me to the library and get me some books by great authors. Great texts, is what she calls them. Suitable for my advanced level." She beamed, pretty proud of that praise.

Chelsea shook her head, recognizing the teacher at work. She sank onto a bar stool and looked at Gage's daughter. "Permission aside, that was a pretty confident critique."

"I know." Cat nodded. "My teacher says I should consider journalism. Maybe even poli-sci."

The front door opened, interrupting the conversation.

"Cat!" Gage called from the front door.

"Yes, Dad?"

"I thought you were going to catch up with me?"

"I am." She put down the carrot she'd been chopping. "I'm sorry, Miss Moira. I have to go help my dad."

"You go, love," she replied, amused.

"Will you finish helping her?" Cat asked Chelsea. "There's a lot left to do." She went out of the kitchen, and the front door closed a moment later.

"Goodness." Moira laughed. "She's a bit of an old soul, isn't she?"

"Yes." Chelsea took over the chopping. "I'm not too happy with her critique, either."

"Oh, don't be angry with the lamb," her mother said. "You know our rules may be different from what she has at home. I don't sense that she gets a lot of supervision. Now that you've explained the boundaries, I'm sure she'll respect them."

Gage would insist on his daughter respecting boundaries. That much she could tell about Gage—he tried to keep distance where it needed to be.

Except when he'd kissed her.

And she hadn't even smacked him, as she'd promised herself she would if he ever stepped over her lines.

Like Cat, he'd crossed her limit so nicely. In such an ordinary way. It had barely been a kiss—and yet it had felt strangely as if there'd been deeper meaning behind it.

Boundaries.

Like father, like daughter.

"Boundaries are good," she told her mom. "We'll work on them."

DINNER WAS SET ON THE PATIO, and Gage and Cat gathered around, looking hungry, and in Cat's case, tired and a tiny bit red in the face from exertion and late-afternoon sun. They washed up and then sank down gratefully to join Moira and Chelsea.

"This is great," Gage said. "I can't remember the last time I had a home-cooked meal."

Cat looked at her dad. "That's probably because you're itin—"

"I know," he said, ruefully interrupting. "But going from job to job is how I make money, kitten."

"Mom does say you're always right on time with the child support." Cat grinned at her father. "It's the one nice thing she says about you."

"What did you two do all afternoon?" Chelsea asked, wanting to put Gage at ease.

"We went and talked to a man about knocking down the barn. Dad wants an estimate for that," Cat said importantly. "Although I think his boss will be angry if he does it." She looked at her father, not certain if knocking over buildings was really in his job description.

"And look who's going to join us for dinner," Moira said. "Just in time to say grace for us."

Chelsea looked up, surprised to see Jonas Callahan

pulling in with a horse trailer. "I'll set another place." She went to grab a plate and silverware, coming back out in time to see Jonas slap Gage on the back.

"Didn't I tell you you'd like it here?" Jonas asked, glancing around at the wonderful spread on the table. "That smells good. I love roast chicken and portobello mushrooms." He leaned over to kiss Moira on the cheek, tipped his hat to Chelsea, and said, "Who's this beautiful girl?" to Cat, who blushed, to Chelsea's delight.

"My daughter, Cat," Gage supplied. "Sit down, Jonas."

"I will." He sat down easily, filling his glass from the tea pitcher. "Hi, Cat. You like it here?"

"Not really," she said with her characteristic tact. "But will you please say grace for us? Miss Moira says you will, and we're starved. Dad's been working hard today."

Jonas laughed. "Good for him. And I'm happy to say grace, thank you for the honor."

They bowed their heads, and Jonas said grace, and then everybody began filling their plates with Moira's good cooking. Chelsea was amazed by how well Cat seemed to fit in, with just a smidgen of guidance and structure. She caught Gage watching her study his daughter, and busied herself with the chicken and vegetables. *I'm getting too involved. It's none of my business. I'm here to write, and get my heroine out of her tangle, and take care of my mother.*

Not get love-struck over a footloose cowboy.

"Fiona says to tell you hi, Miss Moira," Jonas said.

"When's she coming out to see me?" Moira asked.

"Actually, I'm to remind you all of the Fourth of July picnic at the ranch. You'll be there, won't you?" Jonas looked at Chelsea and then Gage.

"I will be," she said.

"We can all drive out together," Gage offered.

"Splendid." Jonas grinned. "You know, Aunt Fiona said you would all get along like peas in a pod, and she's never wrong about these things."

Chelsea's gaze caught Gage's by accident, and she felt herself blush—just like Cat.

Jonas grinned at her, looking like a man who was enjoying his charmed life a bit too much. Chelsea frowned at him, letting him know she didn't appreciate his statement, and he laughed.

She was going to stab him with a fork, she vowed, if he thought about trying any of the Callahan matchmaking games on *her*.

"How's the writing, Chelsea?" Jonas asked, trying to get on her good side, probably having noticed the steam coming out of her ears on his behalf.

"Fine," she said, her tone sweet for the sake of table manners, but with a definite edge of *don't bother*.

"She's still stuck," Cat said, "but Miss Moira says if we shut her up in her room for a few days, sometimes that works. And sometimes a change of scenery helps, too."

Jonas snapped his fingers. "Speaking of that, I need the two of you to run an errand for me."

Chelsea felt her eyes narrow. "The two of who?"

"You and Gage, my two trusted house sitters." Jonas

waved a fork expansively. “I need you to go sweet-talk two peacocks out of our neighbor to the north, a Ms. Ellen Smithers.”

“Peacocks?” Chelsea said. “Why peacocks and why us?”

“I want two peacocks out at Rancho Diablo, and maybe here, once we get things settled. Ms. Smithers doesn’t like us. Or at least she didn’t like the man who used to own this house. I’ve talked to her on two occasions, even took Sabrina with me. Both times the answer was an enthusiastic no.” He grinned. “She’s a stubborn thing. But Ms. Ellen doesn’t know that I’m not above using a decoy to get what I want.”

“And you want peacocks?” Gage asked.

“Always have.” Jonas nodded. “The kids’ll love ’em. Cat, be prepared that when you come to Rancho Diablo, there’s a lot of babies, and a lot of toddlers running around.”

“Great. *Sesame Street*-a-palooza,” Cat said ungraciously.

“Nope. We don’t watch much TV at the ranch. Too busy.” He winked at her. “You’ll see. You’re just about the right age to be a great babysitter.”

Cat shuddered. “My friends are never going to believe the summer I’m having.”

“That’s right,” Jonas said, his tone jovial. “We’ll take lots of pictures for you to show your friends.”

Gage shot his daughter a warning look. Cat lowered her head. “Thank you.”

“Can you leave tomorrow?” Jonas asked. “I can

stay over tonight in Tempest. I'd love to take the peacocks back with me."

"Tomorrow? Jonas, I was going to discuss the plans for the barn and bunkhouse with you tomorrow, and—"

"Always time for that. Running out of time to get peacocks on the ranch for the Fourth. I want this year to be special. Can I count on you, Chelsea?"

She didn't want to sound reluctant like Cat, but she was. Not meeting Gage's gaze, she said, "I have no knowledge of peacocks, or buying peacocks, Jonas."

"That's my girl," he exclaimed, as if she'd said "Absolutely, I'd love to."

Moira had been silently watching the interchange with a smile on her face. "Now that that's all settled," she said, "who wants cake?"

Chapter Six

"I've known you two days, and Jonas has got us chasing peacocks." Gage shook his head as he steered the truck onto the highway bound for Colorado. *"Peacocks."*

Beside him, Chelsea looked out the window. "I'm surprised Cat wanted to stay with Mum."

"What teenage girl wouldn't rather go on a wild peacock chase?" Gage was somewhat annoyed with his boss, but to be honest, there were some perks to being on the road.

Namely, his shotgun rider wasn't too hard on the eyes.

"The upside is that we won't be gone long. It's a long day at the most." He was trying to comfort Chelsea, probably not doing too good of a job. Her deadline was heavy on her mind. He understood deadlines. The fact that Jonas didn't seem as pressed about getting started on the plans for the ranch as Gage was put him on edge. He'd allotted six months for this job, hoping to wrap it up in four, depending on how fast he could secure building permits. This was no long-term job for him—Jonas knew that.

"What if this Ms. Ellen Smithers doesn't want to sell us peacocks?"

"Not our problem. We'll give it our best shot." Gage shrugged. "Personally, I couldn't care less about Jonas's damn birds." Thinking about birds made him think about his daughter preferring to hang back with Moira and Curly and Mo. He hoped Cat didn't call her mother and mention that he'd left her behind with a woman she'd just met. Leslie would probably have a fit.

"Still, Jonas seems to have his heart set on them. I can't believe Ms. Smithers is so ornery with him about peacocks. A paying customer is a paying customer." Chelsea sighed. "Sometimes I feel like we all just jump around to Jonas's tune."

"Sure. He's our boss. We signed on to his madcap adventures." Gage frowned. "Normally I wouldn't mind. If he'd sent me looking for horses, which is under my job description, I'd be fine. But the surprise element is what moves the Callahans."

"Yes."

In his peripheral vision he could see Chelsea's hands fidgeting. She still wasn't all that comfortable around him. He didn't guess she had any reason to be. They barely knew each other.

"Listen, we'll make this quick," Gage said. "We'll get you back to your computer, and me back to my kid, and we'll all have some more of your mom's delicious cake."

Chelsea nodded. "That sounds good."

Gage hoped he was right.

MS. SMITHERS WAS A TALL, large-boned woman who looked more like a woman who could tame lions than a peacock breeder. Chelsea could see why Jonas was a bit intimidated by her, not that he would ever say he was. For one thing, Ms. Smithers was almost Jonas's height—and Gage's. Both were tall men. Not only was Ms. Ellen Smithers tall, she was heavyset. She looked like a stern, no-nonsense person, and Chelsea found herself shrinking back slightly when the woman glared at her.

"You're here about my peafowl?" Ellen asked.

"Yes. We are," Chelsea said, noting that Gage seemed happy for her to lead. "We're interested in purchasing a pair."

She received a frown in return. "I mostly sell to zoos and other breeders. Not interested in selling to individuals usually."

Chelsea offered her a smile. "We're hoping you might make an exception."

"The problem is," Ms. Smithers said, "I don't know if the birds get taken care of by people who don't understand them. They're beautiful animals. They have special needs. What do you know about peacocks?"

Chelsea gulped. Gage shrugged. "That they're good watchdogs."

"True." Ellen nodded. "What else?"

"That we pay cash for them." Gage pulled out his wallet. "And that peafowl can be noisy during breeding season. I'll be building an appropriate pen with sprinklers and lots of shade."

"Hot where you are, is it?" Ms. Smithers stared at

him warily, one eye on his wallet. "Peafowl need lots of space, too. You got lots of space?"

"I'm from Hell's Colony," Gage said easily. Chelsea noticed he sidestepped saying that the birds would possibly be living on the despised ranch Jonas had purchased.

"And you?" the curious Ms. Smithers asked Chelsea. "You don't sound like you're from Texas."

"I'm from Dublin." Chelsea could tell by the look on her face that she wanted more information. "I'm in the States with my mum. She has some breathing issues, and the warmer, drier climate here is helpful." Chelsea hoped that was enough to satisfy Ms. Smithers.

"Well, now." Ellen nodded. "Come inside and have a bite while I ponder whether I have a pair of peafowl I want to sell."

"We don't—" Gage began, and Chelsea shot him a look.

"We'd appreciate that," she said quickly, and he gave her a slight squeeze on the arm that she took to be appreciation as he followed the ladies inside. "Play along," she whispered as Ellen led them into a small, bright kitchen that looked hardly big enough to contain her bulk. "Be nice."

"I'm always Mr. Nice."

Chelsea ignored that and sat at the table. Gage took the seat across from her.

"Looks like a storm is blowing in," Ellen said. "These early summer storms are strong this year. We've had a couple of tornadoes."

Chelsea took the glass of water she was offered.

Gage did, too, watching her for cues. "I've never seen a tornado," she said.

"Just hope you never do." The breeder peered out one of the windows, worrying. "Yep, here comes the rain."

Slashes of droplets suddenly hit the glass panes, loud in the small kitchen.

"Guess I should have had you move your truck into the barn," Ellen told Gage. "That's hail."

Chelsea looked at him sympathetically. "It was too shiny-new, anyway."

He didn't look amused. "So, about the peacocks—"

"I don't have any right now," Ellen said. "I've got some old ones you wouldn't want, and I've got some that are nesting, but—"

Chelsea thought Gage's head was going to pop off his shoulders.

"You didn't say you didn't have any available when I called you," he said.

"We're so eager to see some," Chelsea interjected, shooting a warning glance at him.

"You can see them. Of course, not now with this storm. The nesters are cozy in their pens right now. I don't let my peafowl roam during nesting, you know."

Chelsea had wondered why there were no peacocks roaming about when they'd driven into the red-fenced farm, heralded by a sign that read Smithers' Peacock Farm and Honeymoon Cabin.

The lights went out suddenly, plunging the kitchen into darkness.

"Well, that's that," Ellen said cheerfully.

"What's what?" Gage demanded.

"That's the end of the juice." She sounded so happy about the electricity going out. "Could be hours before it comes back on."

"All right." Gage rose, his patience at an end. He handed her a business card. "Why don't you call me when you have a pair of peacocks you'd like us to look at buying."

"I will." She nodded. "You folks be careful pulling onto the main road. This rain'll be making mud of the end of the drive. Can be tricky." She smiled at Chelsea and lit some candles. "Of course, if you want to wait out the storm, you're welcome to stay in my guesthouse. It's two hundred dollars a night, and I don't mind saying it's kind of a honeymooner's getaway. I've got about fifteen peacocks, and maybe in the night I'll remember which of them is just right for sale. I do hate to part with any, but of course they're prettiest now. They'll lose their trains at the end of breeding season. I might find a pair if I have time to go over my records."

Chelsea froze. She didn't want to be in a honeymooner's getaway with Gage. "We're not in need of—"

"We'll take it." He tossed cash on the table to cover the cost of the room, and then an extra hundred to encourage her memory. "Maybe that'll help you come up with a just-right pair for us, and cover your trouble for keeping us, Ms. Smithers."

Her eyes glowed in the candlelight as she gazed at the money. "You'll find food in the fridge. Best in the area. Everything in the Peacock Cabin is available for guests. Lots of towels, which you'll need, because I don't have a spare umbrella to offer you. You'll need this flashlight to see your way over to the cabin. Once there, you'll find candles and a torch on the entry table. As remote as we are, power outages are not unusual. Of course, you may not need the candles." She smiled broadly, winking. "Please make yourself at home, and don't hesitate to let me know if you need anything."

Gage leaned close to Chelsea as they got up to follow Ms. Smithers down a long hall. "Just a pair of birds with eyes on their tails."

"Shh," Chelsea said, trying not to giggle. She was nervous at the thought of staying in a "peacock cabin" with Gage. But it wasn't bad nerves. More like shivers of destiny and creativity finally awakening—the thrill of the unknown and adventure. And when he put his hand on her back to help her outside to the cabin Ms. Smithers pointed at, Chelsea accepted his assistance along the mud-washed, cobbled sidewalk. He clasped her hand as they ran to the cabin surrounded by trees, rain hitting them as they went.

They stepped inside, and Chelsea gasped. "Wow. This *is* the Peacock Cabin."

Gage whistled, closing the door behind them. "Little less rustic than I'm used to."

"Me, too." Chelsea took off her shoes, leaving them on the Saltillo tile floor near the door as she lit the candles on the entry table Ellen had mentioned. When candlelight threw flickering light around the room, she could see their digs for the night. The centerpiece, she noticed with some dismay, was a round honeymooners' bed covered with an emerald-green satin spread, and positioned beneath a heavy crystal chandelier. She stepped closer with a candle, seeing peacock-feathered pillows piled abundantly at the top of the bed, the colors glistening almost erotically in the candlelight. A mirrored wall backed the bed, emphasizing the florid color scheme. Chelsea lit candles on the bedside tables, noting that every wall had a painting, which seemed to be delicate nudes in a Garden of Eden–type setting, each of which included—what else?—peacocks.

"Holy smokes," Gage said. "I think the bed is motorized."

"Why?" She stepped closer to see what he was looking at.

"I guess so it can turn." He stared underneath the bed with a flashlight, checking out the contraption. "I wondered why it was set so high. When the juice, as Ellen called it, comes back on, we'll check it out."

"She certainly wants this cottage to contain everything a honeymooner needs," Chelsea said, checking out a glass-topped table with a gold-rimmed tray. "I was going to help myself to some fruit juice, but I see these are juices of a different kind."

Gage grinned as he glanced at the tray of varying fruit-flavored body oils. "Who would have thought Ms. Ellen had such a sensual side?"

"Not me." Chelsea shuddered. "Let's not think about that. Let's plan on how you're going to get those peacocks away from her. I'm pretty certain she hijacked you for the honeymooner's cabin and has no intention of letting you have any peafowl. How'd you know they were called peafowl, anyway?"

"First," Gage said, handing Chelsea a towel so she could dry off, "she didn't hijack me. She held up Jonas for the money, and he said I had his full permission to do whatever I had to do, including bribery, to encourage her to let loose some birds." He leaned down and pulled off his boots, setting them by the door next to her leather flats. "Second, once I realized Jonas was determined to get his hands on some peacocks, I did a quick study of how the creatures live."

Gaze shrugged, looking dangerous in the near darkness, his teeth gleaming whitely as he sank onto the bed. Chelsea's nervousness picked up, warning her that this situation was fraught with danger, mainly from her own attraction to the cowboy. *And I am attracted to him, I always knew I was. I just didn't want to admit it to myself.*

"You forget I'm in charge of building Jonas's grand plan for Dark Diablo. Peacocks will need pens on the ranch."

"And that means another project on your list."

"Exactly. I wanted a time estimate. Since I'd hoped this job would be a four-to-six-month project, having to stop and direct construction of pens will add on time. It's not like a doghouse or something else uncomplicated. Pens'll have to be spacious to accommodate the five-foot tails when splayed. Peacock trains can be six feet in length when not open." He sighed. "Jonas has always been a grand dreamer."

"Or schemer."

"Yeah. Anyway, that's when I picked up some peafowl lingo. I was hoping to impress Ms. Smithers, knowing she'd given Jonas a bit of a rough road."

Chelsea sank into a chair across from the bed, not wanting to get too close to temptation. "I had the strangest feeling she was giving us the runaround."

"Not as much as we're giving her." Gage bounced once on the mattress. "I wonder if Jonas got the grand tour of this joint. I'll bet he did, the old dog. This smacks of a Callahan setup."

Chelsea froze. "What do you mean?"

Rain slashed the windows, and a burst of lightning lit the room. She could see Gage's face clearly as he ruefully shook his head with a smile. "You find Ellen's fridge and those goodies she promised us. I'm going to check on Cat and your mom, if I've got cell service."

"Sure." Anything not to sit and look at him lounging on the bed. "She did say she stocked this cabin with the best there is to offer."

"Hope she lives up to her boasting. I'm starved."

He handed over the flashlight, and Chelsea went to find the fridge in the kitchenette, hearing Gage in the other room talking to his daughter.

"That's good," he said. "You take care of Miss Moira."

Chelsea smiled and got out some champagne that was chilling, and some chocolate-dipped strawberries, both dark and white chocolate. Further inspection showed a large salad and a loaf of bread, set side by side in beautiful bowls. Gage the vegetarian would eat both of those, Chelsea thought, considering the block of cheese attractively laid out on a marble cheeseboard. Almost as if it was waiting for someone. Chelsea narrowed her eyes, thinking. Ms. Smithers had had no notice that they'd be staying here tonight. Yet this food was all fresh, waiting. She pointed the flashlight at the chilled fruit, noticing that there were even bowls of fresh guacamole and dip, which looked tasty to her growling stomach. The ride up to Colorado had been longer than Jonas had claimed—his "short" ride to get the peacocks not as short as a drive into Rancho Diablo. Guacamole didn't keep overnight, usually, unless one treated it with lemon and air-proof plastic wrap, and the delicate strawberries…

Chelsea walked out with the tray of fruit and the bottle of champagne just as Gage hung up the phone.

"All's well at the homestead," he said. "Moira and Chelsea are going to the library, now that they've finished their baking to take to Rancho Diablo for the Fourth of July gathering. They said they hoped we're having fun. Jonas hung around for a while, and they all went for a dip in the creek. He's been quite the host, apparently."

"I'm sure," Chelsea said, extending the tray. Gage took a dark-chocolate strawberry and smiled.

"Champagne? That's fancy," he said. "I don't drink much champagne."

"We might as well drink it," Chelsea said, "because we've been had, cowboy."

Chapter Seven

Gage put the strawberry back on the tray and looked at Chelsea. "Had?"

"Tricked. Bamboozled."

"I know what the word means. I want to know what *you* mean."

Setting the tray near the body oils on the long, slender table by the bed, Chelsea sighed. "You were right. This is a Callahan setup."

He took the champagne from her, popping it open. The cork made barely a protest as it left the bottle. "If it is, I'm going to add on to my employer's tab. What makes you think so?"

"There's no meat in the fridge. Plenty of salads and fruit and tasty treats, but no meat. I'd say the guacamole was the ultimate giveaway."

"Guacamole is really only good fresh," Gage said. "I get why you're a mystery writer."

"It doesn't take a detective to figure this one out. Smithers knew she'd be feeding a guest who didn't eat meat. She prepared a great menu of what you *could* eat."

Gage filled two flutes with champagne. "Why?"

"Because all the Callahans are born matchmakers. It runs in their blood. And like you said, they want everyone to share their misery."

Gage looked at her. "It could be a coincidence. She could have had a customer who canceled. Besides which, Jonas is barking up the wrong tree, doll. The last thing I can handle right now is any kind of relationship. I'm not a relationship kind of guy, anyway. But the fact is, even if I were, my drama quotient's too high to add a love angle right now. Probably ever."

"Tell me about it." Chelsea nodded. "I'm going to kill him."

Gage tipped his glass against hers, the crystal clinking in the candlelit darkness. "I'll help you. Here's to killing Jonas."

They sipped, studying each other over their glasses. Gage set his down on the table. "I'm more of a beer guy."

"I'll join you in a beer. Ellen does stock the libations well, I noticed."

Gage followed her into the kitchenette, holding the flashlight so she could peruse the fridge. "You know, it could be a coincidence. Ellen might be the mischief maker here, looking to pad her monthly income. She strikes me as being a touch mercenary."

"Don't forget the fresh guac," Chelsea said, "and the lack of even one chilled shrimp. What honeymooner do you know who doesn't want a healthy helping of protein?"

"Not necessary." He reached around her for the cheese. "Not all men need meat for boundless energy."

"Why don't you eat meat, anyway?" she asked, joining him at the small table with her own small ransacking of the fridge arranged on a plate.

"None of my family does." Shrugging, he dug into the spreads and guacamole. "Never did. Dad had some disease, and my mom, considering herself a holistic type, believed that everyone could heal themselves with proper diet. As one tenet of Eastern medicine says, the four white deaths are white salt, white sugar, white flour and white fat. Mom added meat to the list. She had her own garden, even made her own pasta. It's not as limiting as you think."

"Did it help your dad?" Chelsea asked curiously, munching on the wheat cracker and cheese he offered.

"Dad's disease wasn't actually diet, it was financial. He loved money better than anything on the planet. And nothing can save a man from the lust for gold. Mom just didn't want to accept that he loved money better than all of us put together."

Chelsea looked at him. "So you're going to be a really good father to Cat."

"Yes, I am. As much as Leslie will let me. I suspect she's got her own agenda. If I have to sue for custodial rights, I will. I'd prefer to work it out with her. This summer will be a trial run on how well Leslie and I can do joint parenting."

Chelsea touched his hand. "Cat loves you."

"She might one day. Right now she's trying to figure out who I am." Gage shrugged, his typical blow-off of life's events that meant too much. "That's my only mission right now, besides my job."

"Are you going to take Cat to see your family? She mentioned she'd like to meet them."

"No." Gage dipped guac on a chip and gave it to Chelsea. "This is better than I would have believed Ellen the Amazon could fix. In fact, I find her a study in contrasts."

Chelsea smiled at him, warming him. "Ellen is a sturdy lass, my mum would say. Anyway, I think Cat has plans to hound you about her aunt and uncles."

"She can hound all she likes. I have very little to say to Xav and Kendall. I'd talk to Shaman if he was around, but my guess is he lets the military be his guide. Shaman's a helluva free spirit, believes in Native American spiritualism, tosses in a little Catholic mysticism for balance, and says screw the family tree. I agree with him on all that." Greg saw Chelsea's eyebrows raise, and decided to elaborate. "Xav and Kendall inherited our father's love of the almighty dollar, along with his penchant for making it. I stay clear."

"Should that affect Cat, though?"

"Now, Miss Marple," Gage said, not wanting to talk about his family anymore, "that's enough digging for skeletons for one day. Even a mystery writer has to put away her pen and enjoy the moonlight."

"Ugh, don't mention mystery writing. I'm behind."

"I hear. Cat says both of us have issues."

Chelsea laughed. "I guess so."

Lightning flashed through the windows, and thunder boomed over the cottage. "Well, if this was a Callahan setup, it could have been worse."

"I guess so."

Gage smiled. "You have a problem with the company?"

"Not exactly." She looked at him. "In fact, not at all."

"Good. I wouldn't want you to avoid me like you do, say, snakes."

Chelsea thumped his finger lightly. "Bad boy. You scared me out of my socks on purpose."

"I believe, doll, I scared you out of your swimsuit."

He saw a reluctant smile flash across her face. "So you did look," she said.

"Hell, yeah," he said. "I'm a red-blooded man. There's not a living guy on this planet who wouldn't have at least grabbed a fast peek at that set you've got." He raised his beer. "Believe me, the memory is as burned into my mind as that nude in there with the artfully placed peacock feathers. But in my defense," Gage continued, "once I realized you'd had a swimsuit malfunction, I heroically did not look again. And I'm hoping for points for that, minus one or two if I tell the truth and admit I would have gone for another bug-eyed ogle if you'd lost your bottoms, as well. Polka dots are great, but I have a thing for freckles. I think I deserve hero points."

Chelsea slipped her hand into his, the same hand that she'd thumped a moment ago. "I'm wondering if maybe you'd like more than points."

He swallowed, his throat suddenly tight. "More?"

"Yeah. Something to go along with the memory."

She would regret this later. It was the champagne and the lightning and the erotic wall art working her over. Gage made a last-ditch attempt to throw them both on a pyre of sanity. "My memory's pretty good," he said. "Beautiful breasts tend to stay with me."

She slid into his lap and put his hand on one of the breasts he'd thought about a hundred times. Maybe a thousand.

"Then again, touch is better than memory, as they say," he said, carrying Chelsea to the peacock bed.

"Who says?" she asked, curling into his neck and placing small kisses there. His body hit horny overload.

He could not be this lucky.

"*I* say," Gage said, and laid her on the mattress.

Chelsea thought she was going to die of the sexual attraction swamping her. A wild roller coaster of emotions threatened to overtake her senses—she knew that—but the fact was, once Gage kissed her on the lips, parting her mouth with his tongue, she was lost. And she was happy to be lost.

He was a man who wouldn't stay in her life, wouldn't want an entanglement. He was perfect.

"Are you sure?" he asked, running his hand under her blouse to her bra clasp.

"Positive," she said, undoing his belt buckle.

"Changing your mind is allowed. Just say the word."

He sounded worried, so she sneaked her hands around his muscled back and down into his jeans, kneading the skin, slowly moving to the front. He took off her bra, and she shimmied her jeans off, letting him make the final move with her string bikini underwear. Gage hesitated, his gaze on her in the flickering candlelight. And then, before she realized what he was going to do, he'd reached over and turned off the flashlight, blew out the candles and kissed his way down her stomach to her navel.

Gently, slowly, he removed her panties, kissing her there as thoroughly as he'd kissed her lips. She cried out, never imagining such pleasure existed, and when it seemed she couldn't take anymore and grabbed his shoulders for the pleasure of it all, he rose and slowly sank inside her.

It hurt, God it hurt, and she swallowed the cry she nearly uttered.

"Are you okay?" Gage asked.

"Yes," Chelsea whispered. But he knew anyway, because she was lying completely, rigidly still under him. So he rolled over and pulled her on top of him, holding her, and as the storm flashed light and fury through the windows, Chelsea knew she'd been right to wait for the only man of her impossible dreams.

"HOW ARE YOU DOING?" Gage asked, leaning over to kiss her lips about an hour later, after they'd dozed a little. Chelsea had stunned him. He'd never expected her to be a virgin. She was too pretty to have never had a boyfriend. Then he remembered that she'd mentioned she'd spent years taking care of her mother, and everything made sense.

"I'm fine," Chelsea said. She nuzzled his neck. "I think I could be better, though."

"Tell me how, doll."

His voice sounded rough in the darkness, though he'd tried to keep the moment light. The last thing he wanted was for the electricity to come back on and her to be embarrassed by their lovemaking.

"Like this," Chelsea said, moving on top of him.

His breath caught, and his body was instantly awake, roaring like a tiger. She was hot and tight and wet, and the crazy best part was that she wanted him.

Not half as much as he wanted Red right now. If she was game, he'd aim to please.

He grabbed another condom from his wallet on the nightstand.

"Come here, beautiful," he said, kissing her, turning her onto her back and moving inside her. He hesitated, waiting for her to clench up again with pain, but when she didn't, he began long, slow strokes to get her to the place he was already. At long last, he could tease her nipples, kiss them to his heart's content. "Ever since I saw these, I wanted them," he told her, his voice husky and tight like it hadn't been since he was a teenager.

Chelsea moaned in response, reaching for what she didn't know was out there, on the edge of pleasure. "Relax," he whispered, "I've got you." And moving inside her more swiftly, he listened for the sounds he needed to hear, letting him know he was pleasing her. When she suddenly went over the edge, crying out his name, Gage was startled. Burying his face in her neck, he said, "Chelsea, Chelsea," over and over again like a drowning man, and when he felt her wetness washing over him, he let go, sinking into her accepting body, knowing somehow that everything he'd ever thought and ever wanted in life had just changed, miraculously, and completely beyond his control.

Chapter Eight

As Ellen had predicted, the "juice" had not come back on by daybreak. Gage was gone when Chelsea finally stirred. She grabbed a quick, satisfying shower, grateful that the small cottage had gas heat. She wished she'd been awake when Gage had gotten up—but waking up with him would have been awkward, too.

He'd probably thought to spare her.

Thing was, she didn't regret last night. And if he was worried about her not understanding his feeling about no relationships in his life, he needn't be. She pulled on her jeans and shoes, fluffed her hair to dry it a bit, and told herself she'd never had a long-term relationship, and now wasn't the time for her to start. She couldn't even be sure she'd get her green card. Her mother needed her, and she had a deadline looming.

Clearly, this was not the time for romance.

Not to mention she was pretty certain Gage had a daughter who wouldn't accept a woman in her father's life easily. Chelsea couldn't blame her.

She went to find Gage, not surprised to see him outside with Ellen, looking over some tall, wide pens.

"I just can't part with any of my birds right now," the breeder said. "Good morning, Chelsea."

Gage gave her a slow, sexy smile that flipped her heart, then went back to his conversation. "I believe, Ms. Ellen, you might have known that you couldn't part with any last night."

Chelsea's jaw dropped. They had gotten taken for a night of room rental—and had taken full advantage of the moment to be alone. She blushed, knowing Jonas was going to be plenty annoyed when they returned without the colorful, beautiful peacocks he envisioned for Rancho Diablo.

"I said I'd *think* about it," Ellen said, her tone defensive. "The problem is that it's breeding season, as you might have heard last night."

They had heard the loud calls of the peacocks searching for partners. Chelsea found herself blushing again, remembering that Gage had said he was glad he didn't have to make those kinds of noises to get his lady into bed. And then he'd made slow, sweet love to her, feeding her a strawberry and making good use of the strawberry oil on the gilt tray, murmuring that she was his own delicious—

"What do you think, Chelsea?" Gage asked.

Her gaze snapped to his. "I think Miss Ellen has a point about waiting until after breeding season. We don't have a pen yet, and it would give us time to build one. We could come back at the end of the summer, say, September, and get a pair of peacocks then."

Nodding, Gage glanced at Ellen. "Works for me."

"Well," she said, pretending to think over the proposition, "I *would* feel better if you had your pens built. And once the ladies are done nesting, it wouldn't be harmful to transport them so far. Where'd you say you're from?"

"Hell's Colony," Gage stated.

"That's what I thought you said." She gave him a sharp eying. "I knew a man from New Mexico who wanted peacocks. I didn't like him. Didn't trust him with my birds."

Gage smiled reassuringly. "Glad you like us, then."

Ellen hesitated. "There aren't that many people in the market for peafowl. So I have to be careful."

Chelsea saw that the woman had her radar up for trouble. Nothing good could come of her asking more questions. "We'd like to make a fifty percent deposit, Ms. Smithers, and then pay the other half when we receive our pair. Would that suit you?"

Gage pulled out his wallet, retrieving green bills that caught Ellen's gaze.

"I think it might," she said.

"Good," Chelsea said. "Now we'll take a tour of your birds, and get your help picking out a likely pair we could take home in September. I'd like to snap some pictures so I'll have something to look forward to."

"All right," Ellen said, her voice uncertain. Snatching the money from Gage, she turned toward the pens. "Hope you two slept comfortably last night. Sorry about the electricity. Crazy storm we had."

"We slept fine," Chelsea said, not about to look at Gage. "Thank you for your hospitality."

"Anytime," Ellen said.

Chelsea didn't even glance at Gage as they walked toward the pens over the muddy ground. There wouldn't be a "next" time, which filled a part of Chelsea with regret.

THE RIDE BACK to DARK DIABLO was quiet. Gage had tried to talk to Chelsea about last night—and she'd shut him down pretty coolly, saying every woman wanted adventure at some point, and that the Great Peacock Chase had certainly been an adventure.

She seemed inclined to let their amazing—at least he'd thought it was amazing—night go unmentioned.

He guessed he should feel relieved she wasn't one of those needy females who wanted to discuss everything to death.

He didn't feel relieved. In fact, he wanted to tell her how special she was. Wanted to tell Chelsea that he'd enjoyed every moment of their evening together.

So he murmured something instead about how clever it had been to pin Ms. Smithers down with a fifty percent deposit—he had no idea how Jonas would feel about that, but that was his problem—and that he admired how Chelsea had handled a difficult negotiation.

She'd nodded, got in the truck, her face paler than normal, and said little else—until they were nearly back to Dark Diablo.

"Gage," she said, "you work for Jonas, and I work for Jonas keeping his farmhouse up and in order, and any other little things he decides he wants, like peacock buying. I've always heard it's bad to mix business and pleasure, and I'd have to agree with that."

Gage nodded. "That is many times true."

"I feel comfortable with our relationship." She looked at him. "I like Cat, and I want us to be friends."

"Sounds good to me." He pulled into Dark Diablo and parked, prepared to discuss the matter more, but Chelsea grabbed her purse and hopped out.

"Damn," he muttered, watching her head to the farmhouse. "Maybe I wasn't as good as I thought I was."

Cat came running out, then slowed down, trying not to seem excited to see them. Moira followed, and then Jonas walked out on the porch, looking for his infernal birds, no doubt.

"Look what Mr. Jonas bought me," Cat said, showing off a new pair of sturdy brown ropers.

"And me, as well," Moira said, pointing to a red-and-brown pair.

"Wow," Gage said. "I thought you didn't want boots, Cat."

"Mr. Jonas says it's safer to wear them," she said importantly. "He says there's sometimes snakes out here. Not so close to the farmhouse, but out where I might be working with you." She beamed at her father.

"Those are great," Chelsea said. "I'm going to have to get some, too."

Jonas nodded. "Yeah. You should."

"Thanks, Jonas," Gage said. "Appreciate you taking Cat for boots."

"Took it out of your pay, so thank me later," Jonas said.

"You don't pay me that much," Gage pointed out.

He grinned. "I know. It'll take you a while to work these boots off then."

"Why don't you pay my dad?" Cat asked. "He works hard for you."

Gage stroked his daughter's hair. "We have a different kind of deal, Cat."

"Ah." She looked at him with eyes that said *Mom was right.*

"Your daddy thinks he might want to buy a piece of this place," Jonas said easily. "Land is how he wants to be paid. He'll work a long time for me, but if he's in a settling mood, there's plenty of land to go around."

Chelsea's gaze flashed to Gage. Cat stared up at her father. He shrugged. "I wouldn't necessarily call it a settling mood."

He didn't want to talk about his plans, and Chelsea looked away, admiring Moira's boots, and then Cat's. "Okay, girls, I feel odd woman out. We're going boot shopping for me later this week."

"It's fun," Cat said, dropping the *weird* she used to describe everything. "The man who owns the store will give you popcorn and let you ride his mechanical bull."

Gage wanted badly to tell Chelsea that he'd take her into town to pick out boots, but bit the inside of his lip so he wouldn't. What the hell was the matter with him?

"We'll go shopping tomorrow," Moira said. "It will be fun. Cat and I made a trip to the library, but there's another book she wants that the library is holding for us."

"Where are my birds?" Jonas asked, unable to wait

any longer to start in on him, Gage figured, considering the fact that the truck was clearly empty of fowl.

"Ms. Smithers is everything you said, Jonas. A bit ornery, a bit of a con woman." He glanced at Chelsea.

"You don't have any peacocks?" Cat asked, seeming to notice for the first time that her father had failed in his mission. She glanced at Jonas as if to say *Oh, boy. Dad's gonna be in trouble now.*

"She claims she'll sell them to us in late summer, early fall, after nesting season. They apparently won't be as pretty," Chelsea said, "because they'll be molting. You'll just have to wait for your precious yard ornaments, Jonas. However, I did take pictures of some birds that you might get, if she doesn't renege on us, which is very possible. I'll send the pics to your phone," Chelsea added, heading into the house.

Jonas stared after her. "What got into her?"

Gage put his arm around Cat, giving her a squeeze. "It turned out to be a longer trip than we thought it would be, Jonas. I think she's worried about her deadline."

"Oh. Yeah." He thought about it for a moment. "Well, I guess you did the best you could."

Gage dug out his wallet, handing Jonas the leftover money.

"Where's the rest of it?" he asked.

"We left a deposit for a pair of birds, then you picked up the tab for the overnight stay."

Jonas smiled. "Did you sleep in the Peacock Cabin?"

Gage looked at his employer. "Chelsea did. I slept in the truck."

Jonas blinked. Gage could have sworn his friend's face fell just a bit before he schooled it to its normal expression of wily.

"Too bad," Jonas said. "You missed a great contraption. The bed rotates under a chandelier thing—"

"I get seasick easily," Gage said, and walked to his truck. "Anyway, there was no electricity."

He turned back around to stare at Jonas. "How do you know about the Peacock Cabin, anyway? Did you stay in it?"

He shook his head. "No. But Ms. Smithers tells all about it on her website. Just wondered if you'd gotten to enjoy all the bells and whistles on my dime."

"Guess not. Come on, Cat, honey. Good night, Moira."

Gage went off with his daughter, hoping Jonas had bought his tiny fib. There was no point at all in giving the matchmaking Callahans any encouragement.

They were barking up the wrong tree, anyway. He drove past the No Trespassing sign Chelsea had pointed out to him when he'd first come to the ranch, and thought she'd pretty much taken that commandment to heart.

CHELSEA WAS HAVING a burst of creativity. Words and scenes and dialogue washed over her faster than she could type. Sitting in her cozy room overlooking the side of the ranch, she wrote like a woman finally unbottled.

Bronwyn Sang was coming to life, leaving behind the cardboard shell Cat had mentioned.

Chelsea wrote until dinner, when her mother sent Cat up the stairs to ask if she was going to eat.

"Your mom made Irish stew. Don't know what that is," Cat said. "We chopped up what she called praties and stuff."

"Sounds lovely. You'll like it." She stretched, then followed Cat downstairs.

"We're going to picnic outside," Moira said. "I had Jonas set up a table before he left, and these torches. The sunsets are gorgeous here, and we shouldn't miss them." She lit the tall torches lining the drive. "I love New Mexico. I really do."

"Your mom doesn't want to go back to Ireland," Cat whispered to Chelsea.

Chelsea nodded. She knew her mom's breathing problems were so much better here. In fact, her mother seemed healthier in general. But if the green card didn't come through… Just then, Gage walked up to the table, offering her a small smile that Chelsea returned.

Then she looked away. Jonas *had* tried to set them up. She knew exactly why he'd done it. It was true that matchmaking was second nature to the Callahans, but beyond that, he knew how much healthier Moira was here. He'd met Moira in Ireland when he'd gone there to find his aunt Fiona and uncle Burke, and had remarked to Chelsea on more than one occasion since how great it was to see Moira feeling so well.

She'd gone from a brown wren to a woman who wore pink and a smile.

I'd do anything to keep that smile on her face—anything but try to hook that cowboy. Nice try, Jonas.

"Is Jonas still here?" Chelsea asked.

"He went back to Rancho Diablo." Moira smiled. "He said he'd return soon to make sure Gage was working hard on his barn."

"I could get a lot more done if my boss didn't send me off on tangents," Gage said.

"Mum, what can I help you with?" Chelsea asked quickly.

"Nothing. Everyone go inside and fill your plates. We have a lot of good food to eat."

"Are you sure you're not working too hard?" Chelsea asked her mother softly as she followed her in.

"I feel better than I have in ten years. Don't worry about me." Moira helped Cat ladle stew onto her plate. "Gage, you'll find salads and vegetables for your liking, and sugared strawberries for dessert."

Chelsea felt her face flame. She didn't dare look at Gage, knowing he was remembering the strawberries they'd eaten together.

It had been so astonishingly perfect being in his arms. Even her writer's imagination couldn't have prepared her for the wonder of making love with him.

She would never allow it to happen again.

"Looks wonderful, Moira," Gage said, giving her mother a hug.

Chelsea went cold inside. It felt almost too cozy, too family, being together like this, and she was reluctant for those feelings to come to her. They were an illusion.

She and the others went outside with their plates and

seated themselves, admiring the setting sun, which was fabulous, as predicted. Moira said grace for them and they picked up forks, ready to dig in. A black Range Rover with dark windows pulled up the drive, honking loudly.

"Whoa," Cat said, "that's weird."

Gage put down his fork and got to his feet with a long sigh.

"Who is it?" Chelsea asked.

A tiny blonde with outrageously long and beautiful straight hair jumped out of the vehicle, stalking over to them on high red heels. She wore a black, expensively cut skirt and jacket.

"Hi, Gage," she said. "You didn't return my calls, so I came to find you."

She smiled at Moira, nodded at Chelsea, then settled curious china-blue eyes on Cat. "So *this* is my only niece! Hi, Cat."

"Who are you?" the teen demanded, in her typical no-nonsense way.

"This is Kendall," Gage said, "my corporate-minded sister."

Chapter Nine

"Why are you here, Kendall?" Gage asked, after introducing his sister to everyone. He saw Kendall checking Chelsea out and knew her ever-present radar was already in high gear. Kendall hadn't liked Leslie, had called her a fortune hunter. But that was Kendall—protector of the family fortunes.

No freeloaders, no opportunists allowed. As far as Kendall was concerned, Leslie had merely been after a man with money.

Chelsea went and got an extra folding chair for his sister, and Moira filled a plate with food for her. Kendall settled in without complaint, almost happily.

But Gage knew she had come for a reason.

"I told you. I'm here to meet my niece. You, my dear, are our family's only extended relation." Kendall smiled at Cat. "The rest of us haven't gotten married yet. Only Gage was marriage-minded."

Gage flashed his sister an annoyed glance. "Did Xav send you?"

"No." Kendall thanked Moira and tasted the salads with something of a frozen expression on her face. "Cat isn't vegetarian?" she asked, watching her niece wolf down the Irish stew.

"Leslie wasn't," he reminded his sister. "It's a choice, Kendall, not a holy grail."

"Healthier," Kendall commented. "Never mind that right now. Gage, you need to bring Cat to the house. She should meet Xav."

"Why?" Gage asked. "Couldn't your twin drop in unannounced with you?"

"Not tonight, unfortunately. He's in Paris, overseeing a possible business merger. But let's not talk about boring things. I want to hear all about my darling niece."

Cat gave her aunt a curious look. Chelsea shifted, forking up some salad, appearing uncomfortable. Despite her pink outfit, Moira seemed less than her usual sparkly self. Gage resented his sister's intrusion into their peaceful dinner.

Hell, it couldn't have gotten more awkward between him and Chelsea even if his sister hadn't appeared. He leaned back, keeping his eye on his daughter. If things got too wacky with Kendall, he'd just excuse himself and head into town with Cat.

Although abandoning Chelsea and Moira to the uneven branches of his family tree didn't seem quite fair. He settled in for the long haul, until Kendall got her fill of playing Aunt Sunshine.

"We need you back in Hell's Colony, Gage," she said. She smiled at her niece. "Bring Cat, of course."

Cat looked at her father, uncharacteristically silent.

"You'll like our home, Cat," Kendall declared.

"It's not my home," Gage said, annoyed.

"Of course it is your home," Kendall said. "The four of us own it. Don't be difficult, Gage."

"You have a home, Dad?" Cat asked. "I thought you were an itin—"

"Cat," he said, "don't listen to everything your aunt Kendall says."

"You know," Chelsea said, "I need to do some writing. This was delicious, Mum, and Kendall, it was so nice to meet you. I'm sorry to eat and run, but as Gage can tell you, I'm terribly behind in my work."

"See you later," Cat said.

Gage nodded, his gaze following Chelsea. "Good night."

"I'll join my daughter," Moira said. "Kendall, if you're staying the night, you may have my room, certainly. It's nice and big, and you'd be comfortable."

Kendall smiled at Moira, then swept her gaze over the small farmhouse. "I'm actually staying at a little hotel in Santa Fe. I didn't know if I'd find Gage, or the conditions he'd be living in. But thank you."

"You're welcome. Good night."

Moira and Chelsea left, taking their dishes with them.

"You really have to come home, Gage," Kendall said, once the coast was clear.

"Because?"

Kendall leaned back, her gaze moving to Cat. "For one thing, there are papers you're going to have to sign concerning the Paris merger. Second, it's important for

Cat to know where her father is from, don't you think? And she needs to meet her uncle Xav."

"You could have brought the papers," Gage pointed out. "Courier them."

"We have to be together. All of us."

"Shaman?"

"We're planning the signatory for his next leave. Which happens to be over the Fourth of July weekend."

Gage shook his head. "Listen, Kendall, I'd rather you just buy me out. I have no interest in The Family, Inc."

"It's Gil Phillips, Inc. And you do have interest. No one's going to buy you out, Gage. You're part of the family whether you like it or not."

"It's all right, Dad," Cat said. "Can't we just fly out there so you can sign the papers, and come back?"

"We're invited to the Rancho Diablo picnic that weekend," Gage said, "and I want you to go to it." How could he explain to Cat that she was his family, and he intended to do everything he could for her? There was no reason to expose her to The Family, Inc. She belonged at a fun picnic with people who had good hearts and would really care about her.

"Really, Gage," Kendall said. "A picnic is hardly important. Shaman's leave is far more pressing, as is this buyout."

"I thought you said it was a merger."

"All right," Kendall said. "It's a buyout."

"The smoke begins to clear," Gage said. "It's never quite as simple as you make things sound, Kendall. Who are we screwing this time?"

"No one. It's an honest buyout of a distressed company."

He shook his head. "And you need me to sign off on the deal. That's the real urgency of getting me home." Leaning back in his chair, he shook his head. "Cat and I are going to a family picnic."

"Gage, Cat would have just as much fun in Hell's Colony as some county picnic. And I could take her to a real salon," Kendall said, glancing at her niece's piercings with some concern. "Would you like to get your hair done, Cat?"

"No," she said. "Thank you. I think I'll go to the picnic. There'll probably be scorpions and snakes, but I got new boots yesterday so it'll be okay."

Kendall shuddered. "Too rustic for me."

"I need to check on my birds," Cat said. "Good night, Aunt Kendall." She gave her father a kiss on the cheek and carried her plate inside.

"Awkward little girl," Kendall observed. "I remember that stage. Leslie said she and her daughter were having some issues. Gage, I think it would be best if you brought her home, let me spend some time with her."

Gage got up. "Kendall, it's not going to happen. I'm never bringing Cat back to that mausoleum you call home. Forget about it. If you need me to sign papers, I'll fly out to do it."

"I'm going to butt in here, and I know you'll tell me to mind my own business as you always do, but from looking at your daughter, I'd say she's not the world's happiest kid. Leslie was never the most stable person, as you know." Kendall gazed at him. "I think you should sue for custody. The courts would look favorably on you since Leslie withheld knowledge of your child from you for so many years."

Gage sighed. "Kendall, every situation in life doesn't require a litigious call to arms. I'm pretty sure it would upset the hell out of Cat to have her father haul her mother into court." He shook his head. "Cat and I are just finding our way right now."

Kendall's gaze flicked toward the house. "What's the deal with the Irish lady?"

He frowned. "What do you mean?"

His sister shrugged delicately. "Just wondering. She seemed to look at you a lot. I noticed you couldn't keep your eyes off her. I just wondered if there's anything going on there." She looked at her brother. "I want you to be happy, Gage. You haven't been in a long time."

He sure as hell hadn't noticed Chelsea looking at him like he was some kind of hot god—although he could conceive that he'd probably been staring at her like a hungry lion. He glanced at his kid sister, remembering that once upon a time they'd been close. Before The Family, Inc., had taken over their lives, like a spreading, sucking growth. "There's nothing going on. But I've just gotten back from Colorado, and I'm beat. Let me walk you to your car."

"You'll think about bringing Cat with you?" Kendall asked as they walked together to her Range Rover.

"No," Gage said. "Good night, sis."

"Reconsider. She's family. She deserves to know." She kissed his cheek, got in her car and drove off.

Gage turned around, seeing the light on in Chelsea's window. He thought he saw her shadow as she sat there, no doubt typing at her desk.

No. There was nothing going on between them.

But he wished there was—and cursed himself for complicating his life when he'd known he had a thousand reasons not to do it.

Thing was, Chelsea was pretty irresistible. He'd known that the moment he'd met her. The peek at her topless breasts had been the tipping point. There'd been no way he could have passed up knowing how those breasts tasted, how her lips tasted, how she would feel underneath him.

Right now, he was pretty much damned. Because it was obvious from everything about her that Chelsea wasn't going to let him near her again—ever.

"WHY DO YOU THINK DAD doesn't like Aunt Kendall?" Cat asked, as Chelsea helped her feed her birds. Cat wore pink pajama bottoms and a white T-shirt, looking very much like a little girl as she prepared Curly and Mo for the night.

"I don't know," Chelsea said. "You'd have to ask your father."

"She seems nice. Fun."

Chelsea watched the teen go into her bathroom to wash her hands, then get into bed. She pulled the sheet over Cat and sat on the mattress next to her. "So you'll take me shopping for boots?"

Cat smiled. "Maybe your mom'll come with us. I

like her. I have a grandmother, but she's not like your mom. My grandmother is more…careful."

Chelsea brushed Cat's one side of long hair away from her face. "I know she must love you very much."

"I don't know." Cat looked toward the window, where the moon hung crescent-shaped in the dark sky. "She never says she does. Her and my mom don't get along all that well. Grandma has a lot of money and she thinks my mom is wasting her opportunities."

Chelsea tried to smile. "Families have different dynamics."

"What does that mean?" Cat asked.

"It means that people act certain ways because of different experiences they've had. They don't always say what they mean, or do what they wish they'd do. I know your family loves you a lot." Chelsea patted her arm. "You're a special girl, Cat."

Cat looked at her. "I think I'd like for Aunt Kendall to take me to a hair salon like she offered."

"If she can't, you could go with me and Mum," Chelsea said, "if your father said you could."

Cat thought for a minute. "I'm thinking about taking some of my piercings out."

"Are you?"

She shrugged. "Maybe."

Chelsea nodded and rose. "Good night, Cat."

"'Night. I hope you get some writing done. Sometimes I can hear you tapping on your keyboard at night and it puts me to sleep."

Chelsea smiled. "I'll try, for that reason alone."

But when she went into her room, she stared at her

laptop, not sure where she was going. The flood of words had dried up. Glancing out the window into the darkness, she saw lights on in the ramshackle barn. Gage was probably working. She knew his sister had left some time ago, but he hadn't come back to the house. He hadn't seemed happy with his sister showing up unexpectedly.

It felt as if he had gone inside himself, into an unreachable place.

Chelsea shivered and looked down at her notes. Tempest had just walked away from everything, both painful and joyous, in her life. Chelsea wondered if she could do that, and decided she couldn't. *Although we did leave Ireland, Mum and me, to find a better place.*

And we don't want to go back.

She wrote a note to herself to call and check up on the paperwork she needed to become a legal resident. It had been a few months since she'd applied, and she hadn't heard anything.

If she wasn't granted a green card by August, she'd have to leave the country. She wouldn't even be able to go back to Colorado with Gage to twist Ms. Smithers's arm about the peacocks. As much as Cat loved her new lovebirds, she'd probably get real excited over peacocks. Chelsea thought about the girl, wishing she'd had better answers for her. Yet it wasn't her place, and that was hard, too. She'd never wanted children, or at least hadn't thought a lot about having them. But Cat, and her father, somehow managed to worm themselves inside her heart with their hard-edged-but-vulnerable personalities. It was as if they wore their hearts on their sleeves, yet were fiercely afraid of giving them away.

I completely understand that.

She wasn't in a place to give hers away, either.

"GAGE!"

He cursed and looked down from the barn roof, seeing that Kendall had returned. Hadn't disappeared yesterday as he'd hoped she might. The sun was high and hot in the New Mexico afternoon, and pulling off roof shingles was no fun task. Had to be done, though, at least in this really worn section. It was sagging, and rain would come in. Once they brought horses out to the ranch, the barn would need to be secure. He was of the mind that the whole barn needed to come down so he could start over with a technologically advanced structure, but Jonas had assigned him the Peacock Chase and then dashed off before Gage could corner him with the plans he'd developed.

People had to quit interrupting his job.

"What?" he barked down at his sister.

She waved at him to come down off the roof. He complied, but wasn't pleased.

"Chelsea said I'd find you out here, but I didn't expect to see you on a roof risking your neck," Kendall complained. "Can't you hire people to do that for you?"

He looked at his shiny sister in her tall heels and a dynamite sky-blue suit. "There's plenty of work to go around if you want to get up there with me."

"Very funny." She shot him an annoyed look and followed him inside, where a large standing fan blew around the dusty barn air. She waved a hand at the dust motes, which did little to clear them. "Gage, we have to talk about Cat."

"Why?" He wiped off some sweat with a bandanna and waited for his sister to start in about beauty treatments or clothes or something.

"Because she's our only heir," Cat said.

Gage blinked. "What do you mean?"

"You might not be interested in Gil Phillips, Inc., but you're still part of the business," Kendall said. "Therefore, even if you didn't want your share, it would go to Kendall. And as she's a minor, Leslie would then be her financial guardian." Kendall stopped for a moment to let that sink in. "I'm sure you'd agree with me that Leslie wouldn't be the most suitable guardian for Cat's trust."

No. She wouldn't be. Gage frowned.

"It's millions," Kendall reminded him. "Many millions. You need to do some serious thinking and get the paperwork moving. As much as you want to ignore that you're part of Gil Phillips, Inc., you're one-fourth of it. And Cat would one day inherit the whole thing, unless Shaman and Xav and I married and had families, which none of us seem inclined to do. You were the only one who put your heart before everything else."

It was a shock to consider this, as he'd never considered it before. He'd been focusing on the fundamental fact that he had a daughter, not that she'd be heiress to millions. If Leslie knew, things would get complicated fast. She'd always harped on the fact that his family appeared to have money, money that he seemed more than happy to live without, because he was.

Leslie had resented the hell out of that. Hence her telling Cat how itinerant and lazy he was.

Vast wealth could corrupt, in the wrong hands. Cat was delicate, fragile, unsure of her place in the world.

"Damn, Kendall," he said.

"Everybody hates the voice of reason," she said cheerfully.

"Mum wants to know if you guys want lunch." Chelsea walked into the barn, fresh and sunny in a tight pair of faded jeans, leather clogs and a white, fluttery top. Gage got hot just looking at her. He wished Kendall would disappear so he could get close enough to Chelsea to maybe catch a whiff of her fragrance, perhaps try to melt her wall of reserve.

A guy could dream.

Neither was likely to happen, either Kendall disappearing or Chelsea letting him sneak her out of that gauzy top. He wondered what color her bra was, then glanced away when he realized she was blushing.

Okay, he was pretty much telegraphing that he wanted to rip her clothes off right in this barn and take her until the sun went down.

"Mum and I saw your car, Kendall. Mum says she's planning to try her hand at an eggplant parmigiana tonight, and that you should stay for dinner, if you can." She gave Gage a glance that barely touched him. "It looks like you both could use a glass of tea."

Gage got up, brushed off his jeans. "Come on, Kendall. You might as well get inside where it's cooler so you can harangue me some more."

Chelsea walked ahead, obviously trying not to intrude on their brother-sister time. He gazed at her butt, following the bounce-bounce of her side-to-side curves with pleasure.

With animal focus.

"Goodness, bro," Kendall said, "does she know about this thing you've got for her?"

"No," Gage said. "And it's going to stay that way."

"Sure it is," Kendall said, "because every time she gets near you, you tear off her clothes with your eyes. I thought women were like ships in the night for you, going by in the dark with no visible name."

"Kendall," Gage said, "it's not like that."

"Sure it's not," she said, going to greet Ms. Myers with a smile.

Gage's gaze went straight to his daughter to make certain she was all right—she was grinning and was wearing her new boots—and then his gaze ricocheted to Chelsea, who was lining up sandwiches on plates. He felt himself smile with pleasure at the sight of her and get hard, all at once.

Okay, it *was* just like that.

But he had it under control.

Chapter Ten

"So who is this Tempest chick, anyway?" Cat asked, following Chelsea into her room. Chelsea didn't want to be downstairs with Gage and Kendall. Her mum had laid out some goodies and disappeared for a walk, and Chelsea figured now was as good a time as any to try to get her heroine off the cliff.

She turned to look at Cat. "Have you been reading my work again?"

The teen shrugged. "There's nothing to read. So no, I haven't."

Chelsea sank onto the bed and looked at her. "You and I have to discuss boundaries."

"Yeah, I know." Cat sighed and sat on the window ledge. The breeze stirred the tree outside ever so slightly. It was another hot day in New Mexico, but Chelsea had the window open. "I hear that all the time."

"You do?" Chelsea was curious about the girl's approach to making herself at home in people's lives.

"Sure. Boundaries are something I generally don't have a problem with, except when I get bored. I guess

I just want to know if you're ever going to write anything. It's been days," she complained.

Chelsea shook her head. "You haven't been here that long. I have written a little."

"At this rate, you'll make your deadline, like, never."

Chelsea winced. "Thanks for reminding me. So anyway, other people's stuff is off-limits. Okay?"

Cat sighed. "Okay. I guess the book your mom got me from the library is more interesting, anyway. I just wonder about Tempest, you know? She's more current. Although *Little Women* is pretty interesting," Cat said, brightening. "I'm a modern-day Jo."

"Maybe so." Chelsea smiled. "Maybe you should write Tempest's story."

Cat stared at her. "Me? Write?"

"Sure. Why not?" She could see the bright young girl taking up writing, with her imagination and quick mind. It could give her an outlet she needed.

"Maybe." Cat sounded doubtful. "The old lady says next I'm going to read some Shakespeare. She's got a huge list I've got to read this summer, which is booor-ing. But I hate to let her down because she gave me the birds." Cat didn't look too worried about her reading list. "I probably don't have time to write stories. Sounds like school. This isn't Dark Diablo Summer School for Young Girls, you know." Cat glared, but it was one of her softer glares.

"No. It's not." Chelsea smiled. "I'm going to get you a spiral notebook so you can write about your experiences this summer. Like a journal. That way, you can practice."

"Maybe." Cat sniffed. "Do you like my dad?"

Chelsea stiffened, caught off guard. "He's nice."

"Sometimes." Cat looked at her scraggly nails. Chelsea thought she might have been biting them. "Yeah, he's nice. I just don't want you to think so."

"What do you mean?"

Cat's eyes went round with focus. "I don't like Larry. Not one bit. I want my mom and my dad to get back together, so we can be a real family."

"Oh. I see." Chelsea wasn't exactly surprised by Cat's dream. Any girl might feel the same way. She sighed. "You need to talk to your dad about that, sweetie."

"But you won't like him?" Cat's face was earnest.

"No. I won't like him," Chelsea said softly. Of course she liked Gage, but she got what Cat was asking: *please leave the field open for my dad and mom.*

And Chelsea had to do just that.

"I guess I'll go find your mom," Cat said, wandering from the room. "Make sure she didn't get lost. Old people do that sometimes, you know."

Chelsea shook her head—Moira wouldn't get "lost"—but was glad Cat felt she needed to look out for her. It spoke to the teen's depth of heart, and that reassured Chelsea. Cat was in a difficult spot, and Chelsea completely understood that the girl would feel possessive of her new father, the prince of her dreams coming to rescue her from a fate—and stepfather—she didn't want.

Chelsea sighed and sat at her computer, finally coming to a major decision.

She was going to start the book over from the beginning. And she wasn't coming out of this room until she'd finished her rough draft.

No more temptations—of any kind.

AFTER KENDALL LEFT, finally heading back to Hell's Colony, Gage breathed a sigh of relief. He had a lot to think about, not the least of which was everything his sister had talked about.

"Hey," Cat said, walking into the barn.

"Hey." Gage grinned at his child. She'd taken out a piercing or two, unless he was miscounting. Maybe being here for the summer was a good thing—for him and for her.

"Why didn't Aunt Kendall stay for dinner?"

"Because Aunt Kendall is a busy lady."

Cat sniffed. "She's pretty."

"Yes." Gage shrugged. "So are you."

"Yeah, but not like that." Cat's eyes went round.

Gage laughed. "It costs a lot of money to look like Aunt Kendall, honey. I'm not sure you'd want to sit in a chair for as long as it takes to achieve that."

"She said she'd take me."

He smiled and waved at Cat to follow him as he carried some old horse blankets out to the trash. They were so worn that they were useless. The trash pile was growing. "She'd be happy to take you to the salon."

"Do you think Chelsea is pretty?" his daughter asked.

Gage looked at her. "Sure. Why not?"

Cat stared at him. "You don't like her, do you?"

He sank onto an old metal chair. "Of course I like her. She's a nice lady."

"She's nice," Cat allowed, "but not for a step-mother."

"Oh," he said. "You're not in the market for a step-mother."

Cat shook her head.

He sighed. "Honey, that's the last thing you have to worry about."

"Good. Because," she said, scuffing the toe of her boot in the dirt on the barn floor, "I want you and Mom to get back together."

"I'm sorry, Cat," Gage said quietly. "That's not something either your mom or I would want."

She shrugged. "We'd be a family."

"But not a happy one."

"I hate Larry!" Tears spilled from Cat's eyes suddenly, surprising Gage. "I've done everything I can to run him off, make him not like Mom, but he still comes around. I'm not supposed to knock on the bedroom door when he's there." Cat sniffled, rubbing tears off her face with the palm of her hand.

"Hey," Chelsea said, hesitating when she walked in and saw Cat was crying. "I'm so sorry to interrupt. I was going into town to get a printer and some paper, and I thought I'd take Cat with me," she said, backing away with a stricken look.

"It's all right," Gage said.

"Talk about not respecting boundaries," Cat said, sniffling some more. Gage handed her his bandanna and waved for Chelsea to stay.

"I'm going to leave you two alone," Chelsea insisted. "I won't be leaving for town for five or ten minutes. Cat, honey, if you want to get some ice cream, just...just let me know."

She disappeared and Gage tucked his daughter into a hug. "Listen, you don't have to like Larry. But if your mom likes him, it may be something you have to deal with. For now. He's not mean to you, is he?"

"No," Cat said. "He's just ugly and dumb, and I don't want him to be my father."

"Okay." Gage held her close. "Listen, you're probably too old to need another dad, okay? You've got me, and that's the way it is." He resolved to make certain that Leslie understood he intended to play a vital role in Cat's life—and if he had to utilize Kendall's scorched-earth policy when dealing with Leslie, then he would.

Cat was not going to get caught in the cross fire. Leslie's drama would just have to take a backseat to their daughter's needs.

"I never thought about being too old to need a stepdad," Cat said, cheering up. "I figured it was just something I'd get stuck with."

"I'm not saying don't be nice to Larry." Gage swallowed, and tugged his daughter's hair lightly. "Sometimes we have to be nice to people we don't like. But summers you can be with me, if you want, and in five years, you'll be at college, anyway. That's the practical way to look at things. Practical is good."

"All right." Cat snuggled into her father's chest. "I think we better go. The old lady needs me a lot. She says I make her smile. And Chelsea just wants to get me ice cream so she can snoop around town and ignore her deadline. I better let her."

Gage laughed. "Think I'll tag along, too."

"Really?" Cat perked up. "You have to work. Or Jonas might fire you. And then you'll be out of a job again, and Mom says—"

"Never mind," Gage said, shaking his head. "I can afford an ice cream cone. Come on, Cat."

She tagged happily after him. They met Chelsea outside the barn, where she was sort of fluttering with a small packet of tissues.

"I wasn't crying," Cat said, ignoring the tissues.

"I know," Chelsea told her. "Your father was sweating." She handed them to Gage, and Cat snatched one from the packet, blowing her nose.

"I'll drive," he offered. "Where's Moira?"

"Engaged in trying her hand at a vegetable lasagna." Chelsea got into the truck, after Cat climbed in the middle. "She wants us to pick her up some mushrooms and squash. Cat, she wants you to swing by the library and pick up *Macbeth*."

"Great," Cat said, but she wasn't crying anymore.

Kendall was right. Gage was going to have to make some drastic changes in the way he'd always viewed his life. It was no longer just him. And somehow he was pretty glad about that.

"The thing about Jo in *Little Women,*" Cat said, "is that she always made up her own mind."

"It's true," Chelsea said. "She was independent."

"Like Tempest."

"I guess." Chelsea sounded amused by the comparison. "I always wanted to be Amy."

"Why?" Cat asked. "She wasn't as independent."

"But she got Laurie," Chelsea said, and Gage smiled, thinking that was pretty funny for the spirited Irishwoman.

"Hello?" his daughter said. "Spoiler? I'm only halfway through the book."

"Sorry." Chelsea looked at her with a smile. "Thought you were moving on to *Macbeth*."

"Yeah, well. I like the March family."

"I did, too."

Gage was pretty lost with the whole conversation, though he got the basics. He also understood his daughter's wistful longing, and why she fantasized about him and Leslie getting back together.

"We're kind of a family," Cat said suddenly, shocking him. "An awkward family, but sort of one. At least for the summer."

Chelsea moved her head quickly, fixing her gaze out the window. Probably embarrassed. He was, too—but not completely.

Cat had only spoken aloud what had crossed his mind, too.

But it was just a fantasy—and as he'd told Cat, it was best to be practical.

"SO THE THING ABOUT Tempest," Blanche said as she brought them root beer floats in Cactus Max's, "is that the town itself is quiet. Friendly. We don't have much excitement around here. Tempest the woman was all about excitement. So we asked her if we could use her image for the tourist trade, spice us up a bit." Blanche grinned, her dark hair and eyes gleaming. "You know what sells. That's why you keep asking about her. She stokes folks' curiosity. I think that's why she keeps to herself, to keep the mystery alive."

Gage appreciated Blanche censoring herself from saying *sex sells,* for Cat's sake. It was true that people were drawn to fun, sexy things.

He certainly was drawn to Chelsea.

"But here, we're quiet." Blanche gave them each some paper napkins and shrugged. "We like quiet. The only disturbance we used to have was out at your place."

Gage glanced up from watching Chelsea. "Disturbance?"

"Yeah. The old man didn't like anybody. Wanted to keep his ghosts to himself. Kept out of sight, except when he needed something in town. Heard Jonas Callahan had to sweet-talk him for three years to buy him out." Smiling, Blanche gave Cat a couple of peppermints. "The old man kept railing about the young cuss who'd been bugging him to sell. None of us were too sympathetic. The way he'd acquired all that land was making folks around him so miserable they eventually gave up. When the economy turned down, they had no reason to hang on. And he just kept buying them out. Said he hated having anybody around him, looking at him, spying on him."

The waitress laughed. "Funny thing was, when he was a young, randy fellow, he was madly in love with Tempest's mother. In fact, I always suspected Zola Cupertino was his love child. But," Blanche said, "they never got together at the altar, so I guess not. She hooked up with her ex, and that was bad for Zola. One day the old drifter died, and no one ever knew how that happened, really. Zola's mom fell to drink. Zola became Tempest, and she went away for good. Hasn't been here in maybe ten years." Blanche shrugged. "Then the old man at your place died in that damn barn. And life changed for everybody."

"How did he die?" Chelsea asked.

Blanche glanced at Cat, who was listening, her eyes round with fascination, as she sucked on her straw.

"Meanness, I'm sure," the waitress said airily. "Just plain meanness."

She went off. Gage patted Cat's hand. "*Macbeth*'ll be a breeze after listening to town gossip, huh?"

Chelsea rolled her eyes. "I'm sure the story has been heavily embroidered."

"It's certainly juicy." Gage winked at her. "Remember, Ellen Smithers didn't like the old man who lived at the ranch, either. Jonas said she wouldn't sell him peacocks just because she didn't like the old man."

Chelsea met Gage's eyes. "Jonas could buy peacocks from someone else, I'm sure."

"Yeah. But he says hers are award-winning. And you know the Callahans. They have to do everything the hard way."

"You may have a point." Chelsea smiled at Cat. "See how much fun writing in a journal is going to be? You could dream up all kinds of stories just from Blanche's tales."

"My writing is going to be factual," Cat declared.

"A budding journalist," Gage said, smiling at Chelsea. He liked her, more than he'd let on to Cat. But as he'd told his daughter, there wasn't anything to worry about between the two of them.

"Tomorrow we go to the rodeo," he told Cat, who groaned.

"You'll come, too, won't you?" she asked Chelsea. "You'll need boots," she added, wise with her three-day-old purchase.

Gage watched Chelsea consider the invitation. Slowly, her eyes moved to Gage. "I'll go," she agreed.

"Good," Cat said.

Good, Gage thought.

Chapter Eleven

The Santa Fe rodeo was fun, and the weekend flew by. Cat had a blast, although she wouldn't admit it. She'd even taken a ride on a horse, clinging to her father as they cantered along. Traveling to Santa Fe had been relaxing. Chelsea had enjoyed seeing Moira have a good time, too. It felt as if Cat and she were becoming closer, almost like grandmother and granddaughter.

It did Chelsea's heart good to see that, because she knew her mother would never have a grandchild of her own. Chelsea didn't see herself ever marrying. She pretty much knew she would stay single, and hopefully be busy as a writer.

Maybe she was more like Jo March than she realized—although even Jo eventually had found the right man for her.

But that was fiction. Happy endings were written to fit. Chelsea couldn't see one of those prince-on-a-white-charger moments happening to her. Making love to Gage had been a stolen time. She would never have allowed herself to experience it if they hadn't been alone together in a place where she could let herself be different from who she was.

She understood Tempest so well. In a way, she was more Tempest than she was Jo March, more peacock or swan than sparrow.

I'd feel more settled if I knew where we'd be in two months.

It seemed as if the paperwork for her green card was taking forever. Chelsea buried herself in her writing, the slate clean now that she'd thrown out her first ten chapters, which was cathartic, and kept herself from fretting over the *what ifs*.

Then she found herself riding in Gage's truck with her mom, Gage and Cat, heading out to Rancho Diablo for the big Fourth of July picnic. Wearing earphones, she wrote madly on her laptop in the backseat.

The book, unlike her life, was proceeding as smoothly as ribbon now.

She pulled out one earphone when she thought she heard her mother talking to Gage about their future in Tempest.

"I can stay in the States longer than Chelsea can," Moira said. "I haven't been here as long. She came a few months before I did, so her visa is closer to expiring. But I wouldn't stay here without her."

Beside her, Cat piped up. "You don't want to go back to Ireland in the fall, Nana Moira. It's colder there."

Chelsea smiled. Cat had taken to calling her mum Nana, since she said Moira was the closest thing to a real grandmother she'd probably ever have. Chelsea hadn't asked, but she knew Gage's mother was still alive. Obviously, he didn't feel a desire to allow his mother and daughter to meet—yet.

"It's not so very cold," Moira said. "It's the dampness that bothers me more than anything, I think. That's my guess from being here, anyway. It's the only thing I can think of that's different."

"You can always stay with me, Moira," Gage said, and Chelsea's heart spilled over, shocking her with the sense of deep gratitude she felt at his offer.

"You don't need an old lady around to watch over," Moira said.

"Nana, do you know you say *yew* when you say *you?*" Cat asked. "Anyway, Dad needs you. Your cooking is the best. You always fix something he likes."

Moira laughed. Chelsea started to put her earphone in, then hesitated.

"It's true," Gage said, drumming his thumbs on the steering wheel as he drove. Chelsea thought that tic meant he was really thinking over her mother's situation. It touched her. "You've already applied for your green card, so yours may come before your visa expires. There's no reason to go back, even if Chelsea has to. Jonas would never, ever expect you to leave Dark Diablo, or if you were more comfortable there, Rancho Diablo."

"I don't want to ask. He's already done too much for us," Moira said steadfastly. "No, if Chelsea goes back to Ireland, I will, too. It won't be forever."

Chelsea sneaked her earphone back in, catching Cat looking at her with wide eyes, silently saying *Do something. Tell her it's okay.* Urging Chelsea to change her mother's mind.

It wasn't so simple. But Chelsea understood that the girl had become very attached to Moira, and vice versa. Still, Cat would go back home to Laredo when school started, probably in the middle of August. Moira wouldn't want to be here alone.

"Wow!" Cat exclaimed as Gage pulled into Rancho Diablo. "Look at all the babies!"

All the Callahan children were outside on the wide front lawn, inspecting a ring of walking ponies and a bounce house. Rancho Diablo was decorated for the Fourth of July, as Fiona Callahan always decorated for every holiday—with magical attention to fairyland detail.

The number of babies and toddlers was astonishing when one first encountered the Callahan clan. Chelsea thought she'd remembered that there were eighteen children now, since Fiona's plan to get her six nephews married with children had worked with phenomenal success.

"That pony has my name on it!" Cat said, her tone surprised and delighted. "Dad? Is that pony for me to ride?"

"You're the only Cat," Gage said, pulling the truck to a stop under an eave. "Let me introduce you to Fiona and Burke, who run this shindig."

"Look at all the kids," Cat repeated, sounding very wistful to Chelsea's ears, now completely unplugged. She wouldn't have missed Cat's joy for anything.

Gage opened her door and Chelsea slid out.

"Happy Fourth of July," he said.

She smiled, feeling his warmth touch her. "You, too. Your first one with your daughter."

"It's pretty cool."

Cat came around the truck with Moira. "Let's go, Dad!"

Moira smiled. "I'm going to find Fiona. We have a lot of catching up to do." Her mother hurried off, eager to visit with her friend.

"C'mon, Chelsea," Cat said, grabbing her hand. "You can't write every minute!"

"She has a point," Gage said. "But don't feel obligated."

Chelsea hesitated, not certain what to do.

She and Gage had been spending a lot of time together. There'd been Colorado, then the rodeo in Santa Fe, now this family picnic. The more time she spent with him, the more she was aware that this couldn't last, wouldn't last. This summer was simply a snapshot in time for them all.

He touched her hand, and she managed a brief smile. She did want to be with Cat. But she also wanted to be with Gage, even if she didn't want to admit it to herself.

She decided to do what she wanted to most.

"Let's go check out that pony, Cat," she said.

Gage's dark eyes glowed, and she sensed his pleasure. "Thank you," he said softly as they followed his excited daughter.

"No thanks necessary," Chelsea said, with an airy dismissal she didn't feel.

"I THINK I HAVE THEM straight," Cat told her father. "The munchkins are little Joe, Sarah Colleen, Devon Bridget, Sharon Marie, Sam Bear, Judith, Julianne, Janet, Molly Mavis, Jennifer Belle, Lincoln Rose, Suzanne, Ashley, Grace Marie, Joy Patrice, Elizabeth, Molly, and Fiona. That's in order of birthday. Alphabetically, they're Ashley, Devon Bridget, Elizabeth, Fiona, Grace Marie, Janet, Jennifer Belle, Joe, Joy Patrice, Judith, Julianne, Lincoln Rose, Molly, Molly Mavis, Sam Bear, Sarah Colleen, Sharon Marie and Suzanne. Alphabetically, I'd come after Ashley, but by age, I'd be last 'cause I'm oldest." She thought about it for a moment. "Did I leave anybody out?"

Gage smiled, and Jonas shook his head.

"You got them all. For now." Jonas handed Cat a sparkler and lit it, grinning as widely as she did as she waved it around.

"Fiona says all the kids are bedding down in the main house for story time. I'm invited, too. Bye, Dad!"

Cat tore off after the group slowly making their way inside. Chelsea had gone to chat with the other ladies, the Callahan wives and good friends, as they enjoyed the holiday together.

"So," Jonas said, "now what?"

"Now that I finally have your attention," Gage said, "we need to make an appointment to get together and discuss the plans I've come up with for Dark Diablo."

"You're going to tear everything down and start over," Jonas said.

"Exactly." He nodded. "How'd you guess?"

"Because it's all fifty years old, and in bad shape,

anyway. I don't think the old man had done anything to the place in the last ten years." Jonas shrugged. "I knew when I took it over that the project would be big. That's why I hired you."

"Well, you've been plenty hard to tie down to a discussion of getting started." Gage looked at his boss. "Sending me off on the peacock chase, for example."

He grinned. "You don't look like you suffered too greatly."

"All right." Gage hadn't, but wasn't going to give Jonas any reason to crow. "We need to go over some designs so I can get started."

Jonas rubbed his chin, then stretched out his legs as they seated themselves at one of the picnic tables. The fireworks were about to start, basic pyrotechnics run by the Callahan brothers, so the kids could watch from the windows inside. Then they'd have story time and bedtime.

His boss seemed in no hurry to discuss anything about the job, and Gage told himself that it was a holiday, after all. Only he seemed to feel a certain urgency to get everything set in motion.

"Gage."

"Still here."

"The family of the old man who lived there called me."

Gage looked at Jonas. "Yeah?"

He nodded. "They want to contest their father selling me the property. They feel he might have been coerced because he was elderly."

Gage blinked. "Can they do that after the sale and

after the old man's death? The estate was long settled, wasn't it?"

Jonas shrugged. "It's the issue of them feeling he might have been swindled. They say he had some mental issues."

"And that you took advantage of him?" Gage laughed. "Jonas, I've seen you in action. You can be a formidable opponent, but I've never seen you bully anybody. Certainly not elderly people in poor health."

"Still. I'm wondering how much improving I should do to the property, since clearly the heirs are looking for money."

Gage's heart sank. "I see."

"My brother Sam's checking into all the hooks and land mines in this matter."

"Sam's the one to do it," Gage agreed. "He saved this joint when it looked like that might be impossible."

Jonas nodded, glancing around Rancho Diablo. "Confidentially, I've had an architect draw up plans for a hospital out at Dark Diablo. But that's on ice, too, until I get this other problem nailed down."

"So I'm out of a job," Gage said.

"For the moment," Jonas said, sounding cheerful. "You can work here, of course. We always need hands. And you could start building the horse program from here. In fact, it might be easier for you to begin here because we've got plenty of barn space."

Gage turned to his friend. "What about Chelsea?"

Jonas looked toward the east as the first fireworks went up. From inside the house, they could hear the kids exclaiming with delight.

"Chelsea and Moira can stay at Dark Diablo as long as they want. I need someone to watch the place. Houses tend to get problems and fall into disrepair when no one's living in them, keeping them alive."

Gage nodded.

"And Cat's welcome either place, always."

Gage looked at him. "Thanks."

"No problem. I'll let you know when the coast is clear. Now, let's go inside and watch the women take pictures of the babies. Some of them have never seen fireworks before."

Gage grinned. "It's my first Fourth of July with Cat."

"Lucky dog. You get to experience all those firsts, just like a new dad. Heck, you *are* a new dad."

Gage followed Jonas inside, to where the kids watched through the windows, their noses pressed to the glass. Chelsea, he noticed, was taking pictures of Cat with her cell phone. He smiled to himself, warmed by her consideration of his daughter.

He liked Chelsea, more than he would ever admit. Liked her more every day.

But there was no way it could work out. He *was* an itinerant cowboy. Now he was out of a job, pretty much.

In fact, all things considered, Gage realized, as he watched his daughter applaud with the other, much younger children, it was time to go home, just as Kendall had said.

He had to do it for many reasons, but most of all, because he knew beyond a shadow of a doubt that he was falling in love with a certain redheaded firecracker of a woman.

As he'd told Chelsea when he'd met her, there were two red things a man should always stay well clear of: a redhead and dynamite.

And she was pretty much both, all wrapped up in one amazing, heart-stealing package.

I'm toast.

Chapter Twelve

"Oh, they're crazy as bedbugs," Blanche told Chelsea and Gage when they ran into her at the library. "Old man Taylor did exactly what he wanted to do with his money. His heirs—or non-heirs—will just have to deal with it. He was right in his mind and mean as a snake right up till the day he died, God rest his soul. Neither Jonas Callahan nor anybody else could have cheated Bud Taylor even if they'd thought about it." She laughed and shook her head. "Sorry you're out of work over it, though, Gage. We were kind of getting used to the sight of you in Tempest. Guess you won't be staying?"

Chelsea knew what Gage's answer had to be. Though she hadn't wanted him at Dark Diablo in the first place, now she feared she would miss him terribly when he left—and surely he had to.

And that meant Cat would leave, too. Chelsea's heart ached thinking about it. Yet the summer was only a break in Cat's life, a time for her to get to know her father.

I've gotten way too involved. Just when I let myself become fond of them, the story changes.

"Cat and I will probably move on," Gage said. "We have some other things we should attend to while Jonas works out his estate issues."

Cat glanced up from the books she was perusing. "Do we have to leave? I like Dark Diablo. I like Rancho Diablo. There are lots of kids around. Even though they're younger than me, it's fun, Dad."

Gage nodded. "I know, Cat. Things changed, though."

Blanche sighed, her dark eyes sympathetic. "It's a shame. Those Taylor heirs were troublemakers when the old man was alive, and nothing's changed. He didn't hold much affection for his heirs—called them hangers-on. And on days when he'd been drinking, he called them his own personal vultures."

Chelsea glanced at Gage. He seemed worried about his daughter, and regretful. Cat was happy in Tempest. But she'd be happy anywhere her father went.

"Our book group picked your last goose-pimpler to read, Chelsea," Blanche said. "We like having an author in Tempest. Never had one of those before. Got lots of scribblers, but no real deal. You won't go off with Gage, will you?"

Chelsea felt herself blush. "No. Jonas pays me to house sit. I'll be staying in Tempest for a while."

Blanche glanced at Cat, then Gage. "Well, guess I'll see you around then. Bye, Cat, honey."

She hugged the girl, then sailed off toward the checkout. Chelsea waited, feeling awkward.

"It's not fair," Cat said. "We should be able to stay.

If Mr. Taylor didn't like his family, and didn't leave them his money, why can't we stay?"

"Honey, you'll like visiting Aunt Kendall, too," Gage soothed.

"Come with us," Cat said to Chelsea. "You can write on the road—you do it all the time. And you said new scenery is good for your creativity."

Chelsea started. "Oh, Cat, I couldn't. But thank you."

"Dad would like it."

Chelsea glanced at Gage. "Your father has a lot to take care of, Cat. You can come back and visit us. Mum and I would love that. And who knows? Maybe the Taylor heirs will change their minds about suing Jonas."

Cat nodded, resigning herself to her fate. Chelsea didn't dare look at Gage. She knew how disappointed Cat was, and she knew Gage was unhappy that his job had changed.

"You know," he said, "I wasn't going to mention it, but Kendall did say I should bring you along."

Chelsea blinked. "Me?"

He nodded. "Yeah. Her specific words were 'When you come, bring Chelsea. If she's going to see the U.S., she wouldn't want to miss the dusty, one-horse town of Hell's Colony."

"I can't," Chelsea said. "It's your family time."

"I wouldn't necessarily call it that. I'm just going to sign some papers."

"Then what will you do?" she asked.

"I'm not sure yet." He shrugged. "I have only another month and a half with Cat. I'm wondering if Hell's Colony is the best place for her to be." He glanced toward his daughter, who was reading a thick book she'd pulled from a low shelf. She sat cross-legged on the floor, engrossed. "It will be a home-away-from-home for her, but I want to be cautious about all this."

Chelsea nodded. "She's such a good girl. But she's in a pretty fragile place. Mum says she thinks Cat's got a really high IQ. That that's why she gets easily bored, and why she does best with lots of intellectual stimulation. It's important for her to be around positive influences."

Gage shook his head. "I don't know about positive influences in my family. We're a pretty remote group. It's our survival skill." He shrugged, and she could tell he dreaded the whole idea of going home, especially with Cat.

His daughter was making so many good changes in her life. It was like watching a small white dove carefully sneak out of her nest, hoping there were no hard winds to blow her away.

"I'll come for a day," Chelsea decided.

"You will?" Cat rose to her feet, her book selections in her arms.

"Sure." Chelsea smiled. "I like to travel."

"That's cool. Now you don't have to be so stressed out, Dad." She looked at Chelsea. "He thinks I'm not going to be happy with his family. He'll feel more comfortable with you there."

Chelsea hesitated. "I don't know what good I can do."

"Dad hates his house," Cat said. "He wouldn't take me there except Aunt Kendall says he has to. And now he's lost his job, so he says he might as well do this." She smiled at him, taking his hand. "It's going to be fine, Dad."

"Sure," Gage said. "I know that. Let's not scare Chelsea away, all right? There's nothing sinister there. It's just a house that doesn't have much soul, because any soul that ever walked into it died from lack of…"

"Affection," Cat supplied. "It's okay, Dad. We've got each other."

Chelsea followed father and daughter into the sunshine. "Maybe it won't be that bad."

Gage nodded. "I haven't been there in years. My misgivings are ancient history. I'm sure everything has changed."

"He hasn't been home since his father died," Cat explained, sounding like the adult. "Dad says he's happier on the road."

"I know," Chelsea said, thinking, *But sometimes, home is good, too.*

THE PHILLIPS PLACE WAS like nothing Chelsea had ever seen. More office building than house, it was a hard-edged, sophisticated structure that spoke little of "home." To Chelsea, used to the green and misty landscapes of Ireland, the contemporary white, travertine exterior was blinding in the hot July sun.

"Wow," Cat said from the backseat. "It's huge."

The property *was* huge. Chelsea could easily understand Gage's discomfort here. She suspected he'd never felt right in this place, and had probably suffered under his father's expectations—and then disappointment—in his choices. Gage was a workingman, more blue collar than wheeler-dealer. He called the shots in his life, even if it meant living from job to job.

Kendall met them in the wide circle drive. "Gage! Welcome home!"

Gage shook his head at the uniformed driver who came to park his truck, and the uniformed attendant who reached to lift out their bags after he'd opened the doors for Cat and Chelsea. "We don't need help. Thanks. Cat, grab your backpack and bag."

She speedily complied, as did Chelsea. Gage looked at his sister. "Where do you want me to park my truck?"

"In the garage, as always, which you'd know if you ever came home to find out," Kendall said, amused. "Gage, let him park your truck so you can walk Cat and Chelsea inside."

Gage sighed and surrendered his keys. "Kendall, I don't know how you live like this."

"I don't know how you don't," she shot back with a smile. "Come on, Cat, Chelsea. We have tea waiting for us in the main room. Gage, relax."

He couldn't. Chelsea could feel the tension radiating from him. "Smile," she said softly. "You're scaring Cat half to death."

Surprised, he glanced at his daughter, noting that his apprehension was rubbing off on her. "Sorry," he said. "Cat, it's all right. Don't let my grouchiness upset you."

"I'm okay," she said in a small voice.

Chelsea went inside, following their hostess.

"I'm so happy you could come, too, Chelsea," Kendall said. "We're friendlier here than Gage lets on."

Her voice echoed in the travertine-and-marble foyer. Chelsea smiled. "Thank you, Kendall."

"Your mother couldn't come?" she asked.

"She stayed at Rancho Diablo with Fiona. They've known each other for many years, and wanted to spend more time catching up. I think they had shopping in mind."

"Plenty of shopping in Texas," Kendall said. "Neiman Marcus isn't too far from Hell's Colony."

Chelsea smiled politely, thinking that there was likely nothing at an upscale retailer her mother would want. "This is my first trip to Texas."

"Really?"

Kendall seated herself in what she called the main room, which felt like an auditorium to Chelsea. There was even a black piano that didn't have a fingerprint or speck of dust on it. The room was done in graphic black-and-white, with sculptures in every corner, and no plants to soften it. The bright note came from Kendall's heels, her signature color-explosion pumps accentuating her expensive, ebony suit. Today's pair were parrot-yellow. Chelsea felt a bit dowdy in her flat walking shoes and denim capris, though she knew it didn't matter what she wore; she wasn't here for an interview.

She glanced at Gage, feeling his growing anxiety more with every passing second. She sat on a white sofa and patted the cushion beside her. Cat bounced onto it with the enthusiasm of a teen who didn't worry about getting things dirty.

Gage hovered on the edge, his cowboy hat and worn boots an odd contrast to the museum-like room.

"Gage, sit," Kendall said. "You're making me nervous."

"Yeah, Dad," Cat said. "Sit by me and Chelsea."

He did his daughter's bidding, almost as if he was relieved to have her invite him. Chelsea was touched by the growing dependence the two had on each other. She smiled at Kendall and accepted the tea a butler handed her.

"So. How was the drive?" Kendall asked.

"Fine." Gage looked at his sister. "We can't stay long."

She stared at him. "How long is not long?"

"Probably just this afternoon. Do you have the papers here?" Gage asked.

"I do have. I'd have to get the lawyer out, but he's on call, of course—"

"You might put that call in." Gage's face had gone as cold as the marble floors.

"All right." Kendall looked at her brother, then stood. "The business documents, and the ones for your heir, as well?"

He nodded brusquely, and Kendall left the room.

"I'm sorry, girls," he said. "This is not my kind of place."

"It's okay, Daddy," Cat said.

"I'm good with whatever." Chelsea nodded.

Gage swallowed and gazed at her. "Listen. This is

going to sound crazy. Wild, even. Like I'm half out of my mind. Chelsea, marry me."

"What?" She stared at him. Cat's eyes went round as quarters.

"Marry me."

Chelsea stared at his resolute face. At his eyes, which had gone flat and emotionless. "Why?"

He glanced around the huge room, shook his head. "You need citizenship. You'll get that with me. Cat will get a stepmom she likes."

Cat stared at her father. "Dad, everybody knows you have to have a ring for a proposal."

He blinked. "I'm offering a green card, not romance."

Chelsea's breath left her. "You're serious."

"Yes, I am."

"But—" She shook her head. "Why?" she asked again, completely flummoxed.

"Because I need you." Gage shrugged. "That's why."

"Gage." Chelsea glanced at Cat, who was gazing at her with huge eyes, waiting for her answer. She had such a protective, concerned expression on her face, that Chelsea suspected the girl was worried she might turn her father down.

Chelsea took a deep breath, her heart accelerating. "I've already had a faux engagement. It's how I got to the States, how I got my mom here. But I don't want to do it again, not that way. Can you understand that?"

"No," Gage said. "I live my life practically. And the practical side of this is that your mother and you need to stay here, not return to Ireland. And I need you like I've never needed anyone in my life."

"I have to go back to Laredo in August," Cat said. "Dad needs you, or he'll be lonely. All alone."

Gage grasped his daughter's hand in his. "Take us on, Chelsea."

"I—"

"I never really wanted a stepmother," Cat said. "They always sounded horrible, like witches, you know? I always thought if I ever had a stepmother, I'd make her life miserable so she couldn't make *mine* miserable. Like Cinderella's stepmother was mean to her." Cat's eyes were huge in her pale face, and Chelsea realized she'd thought long and hard about this. "I never thought I had to worry about it, though, because I didn't know I had a father. Then I found out I did, and discovered I could end up with a stepmother, the worst thing I thought could ever happen."

"Oh, Cat," Chelsea said. "Lots of stepmothers and stepfathers are very nice."

"I don't like Larry," the girl said. "But I do like you."

"Thank you," Chelsea said softly.

"So at least I'd have this," she added. "I'd have you and Dad in the summers."

Chelsea's gaze met Gage's over the top of Cat's head. Her heart twisted as she thought of all the worries the teen carried inside her.

"And I love your mother," Cat said. "She's like my fairy godmother."

Gage smiled. "Cat, you don't have to make my case

for me. *I* have to convince Chelsea that she wants to marry me."

Cat didn't say anything more, but sat quietly gazing at Chelsea, clearly worried. Chelsea looked down at her hands, then nodded. "All right. I'll consider it."

"You'll consider marrying me?" Gage asked.

"And being my stepmom?"

"Yes," Chelsea said. "If your father and I get married, I would absolutely adore having you for a daughter."

Beaming, Cat threw her thin arms around Chelsea. Gage didn't say anything, but his face seemed less stony.

"Here are the documents," Kendall said, coming back into the room. "And the lawyer is on the way, so that the legal documents for Cat can be executed. It takes him about thirty minutes to get here by helicopter." Kendall looked at the three of them sitting on the white sofa. "Did I miss something?"

Gage shrugged. "The lawyer may need to draw up extra documents, so tell him to bring his legal-beagle briefcase and necessary flunkeys."

"Why?"

"Daddy asked Chelsea to marry him, Aunt Kendall," Cat said happily. "And she said she might!"

Kendall's gaze settled on Chelsea. "Found a way to get that green card, did you?"

"Maybe I did," she replied.

"Kendall..." Gage said, his tone warning.

Chelsea glanced at him, catching him looking at her. He wasn't smiling, but he didn't seem as tense anymore—even if Kendall did. Yet the funny thing was, Chelsea felt as if her whole world had suddenly changed.

Chapter Thirteen

"Yes," Gage said an hour later, when he and the lawyer and his sister were cloistered in the library to execute a mountain of documents. He wished he was out with Chelsea and Cat, who were getting a grand tour of the property by four-wheeler. But this had to be done, and the sooner he solved it, the faster he could leave the family compound. "Yes, I assign executorship of my estate to Chelsea Myers, who I hope will be Chelsea Phillips in the next seventy-two hours. She will direct the estate on behalf of my daughter, Cat, until Cat reaches her majority, at which time she may receive one-tenth of my estate so she can go to college, if she wishes."

Kendall stared at him. "Gage, I realize you're going to marry Chelsea, but we don't know her. I feel that as your sister and Cat's aunt, I'm in a better position to guide her finances—"

"Thanks, Kendall. I appreciate your offer to help Cat." He shrugged. "Truthfully, my estate isn't worth your time. I've got a truck and a few saddles, a lot of tools. I'm a builder and a dreamer and a helluva hard worker. That's it. Chelsea can handle it."

Kendall glanced at the bald-headed, elderly lawyer, who stared over his glasses at Gage. "Mr. Phillips, your portion of Gil Phillips, Inc., is worth several million dollars."

"And after you sign the papers that direct our purchase of a company in France and one in Dubai—" Kendall began.

"Dubai?" Gage interrupted.

"Happened over the weekend," Kendall said. "Didn't have a chance to mention it."

He shook his head, not entirely surprised by his sister's ability to do business. She was more like the old man than any of them. "My sister is kindly and graciously leaving out a few facts she isn't sharing with you," he told the lawyer. "First, I know nothing about Gil Phillips, Inc. Have no idea how the heavy equipment the family sells is transported to Dubai or France."

"Cargo planes," Kendall said helpfully.

"The fact is, my father disowned me a couple years before he died. And I'm happy with my circumstances," Gage said, not examining the painful memory of him and his father parting on bad terms and with harsh words. The old man hadn't liked him being a trade worker. Gage hadn't been able to stomach working with his father, didn't want to be anything like him.

He was happier not being tied to hearth and home.

Although that was changing on him pretty darn quick.

"Baloney." The female voice that spoke loudly in the room turned everyone's head as a fragile-looking but beautiful female was wheeled into the library in her wheelchair.

"Hello, Mother." Gage rose to give her a kiss and a hug. "It's good to see you looking so well."

"It's good to see you at all," Millicent Phillips shot back. "I just met your daughter. Beyond the scary hair and the face jewelry, she's a darling girl, Gage."

"Thanks." He doubted Cat would appreciate the terse compliment.

Millicent moved her wheelchair close to the large oval mahogany table they were seated around. "The point is, whatever your father claimed about your relationship to this family, Kendall, Xav and Shaman reversed a long time ago, with my blessings. Don't be a horse's ass, Gage. You have a daughter to think of now. Best be glad of it, too, because if Leslie had had her way, you'd never have known about Cat."

"My daughter and I don't need handouts," Gage said. "I'm happy living by my father's words."

Millicent pierced him with a glance, and for the thousandth time Gage thought it was she who'd been the power behind the throne. His father had believed he was the old, infallible lion, but it was his mother who'd been the steel in his spine. Kendall had very much inherited their mom's courage and determination. "Bring Cat and the new fiancée in, please," Millicent said.

"No," Gage declared.

"Yes," Millicent said. "If they are your family, then they become part of Gil Phillips, Inc., now."

"I don't want Cat ruined," Gage said, angry and annoyed. "Jonathan," he said to the butler, who'd gone to the door to do Millicent's bidding, "if you touch that doorknob, you won't have a hand left to open so much as a wine bottle with."

"Gage!" Kendall protested.

"I'm done here." He grabbed his hat. "Kendall, whatever papers you need signed for Dubai and France better appear in front of me in the next five seconds, because I'm taking my family out of here in the next sixty."

"Cool down," Millicent commanded.

"No," Gage said, "you're not going to steal my daughter's soul like you tried to steal mine. Kendall is you, carbon copy. Xav is pretty much the same. Shaman cut loose and may never come back. I don't belong here, either."

The lawyer quickly pushed a stack of documents his way. Gage signed them speedily, pushing the pen with knifelike strokes across every line the lawyer indicated. For a moment, the only sound was the rapid turning of papers.

"Gage," his mother said, her tone less strident, "Leslie called me for money."

Gage's pen stopped as he slowly looked up. "What are you saying?"

"I'm saying that the only reason you ever found out about Cat is that Leslie's gotten herself hooked up with a man who plans to blackmail us into paying them a large sum of money. Once he found out who Cat's father is, Larry called me to extract money to keep it from you and the rest of the world. These deals with Dubai and France were on the table, widely publicized in the *Wall Street Journal*. He threatened to release a story of a family that hid its dirty laundry when it was convenient."

"Cat is not dirty laundry," Gage said, fury flaming through him.

"Precisely." Millicent nodded. "I told Leslie that any child we had anywhere was part of this family, and if she didn't call you and tell you about Cat, I'd make her life miserable, starting with blackmail and extortion charges."

"Thanks," Gage said, still not happy with anything he was hearing. "You do have a soul, after all."

"Maybe," Millicent said. "At any rate, you'd never have known about Cat if Leslie hadn't gotten herself hooked up with this unfortunate individual."

"I will kill him," Gage stated.

"No," his mother replied. "What you will do is sit at this table and make decisions that reflect her best interests."

Gage leaned back in his chair, his eyes narrowing on his mother and sister. "What do you want?"

"I want Cat included in this family. I want all parts of this family's interests protected from unsavory types. No one is going to threaten Gil Phillips, Inc."

"This isn't so much about Cat as it is about the company and your reputation," Gage surmised.

"Gage, be reasonable," Kendall said. "Mom is trying to tell you that you need to sue Leslie for custody of Cat. You can't leave her in a home with a man who intends to use who she is for financial gain, and a mother who is too weak-willed to stop him."

As Gage considered the two women, Xav walked into the room, having heard the last of the conversation. He walked over to Gage, slapped him on the back. "The renegade returns. Welcome, bro."

"Whatever," Gage said. He looked at the lawyer. "I have the strangest feeling that you have the appropriate papers for this custody fight in your handy little black briefcase, don't you?"

The attorney swallowed, clearly not liking the dangerous glint in Gage's eyes. "It would have been a waste of your family's resources to make a second trip for paperwork that—"

"Never mind," Gage said. "I have to talk to Cat first. And Chelsea. Whatever Cat's circumstances, I'm not doing anything without discussing it with her."

"I suggest you plan on spending the night," Millicent said. "Give Cat a chance to get to know us."

Gage stared at his mother, his sister and her fraternal twin, all pretty much cut from the same cloth.

He didn't fit in.

But if his mother was telling the truth—and he had the feeling she was—he was going to have to do something about fitting in. His life had changed…but if he was lucky, maybe Chelsea would still agree to be his wife.

Even with this crowd she'd now be calling family.

"CHELSEA," GAGE SAID, when he got her alone on the stamped concrete patio that overlooked the huge, free-form pool. "I dig you a lot. Mostly I dig how you handle my family like they're not cold."

Chelsea smiled at him. He thought she was beautiful with her even gaze and long russet hair. He wanted to kiss her desperately, kiss her until she couldn't breathe, till their breath became one.

"Gage, everything is fine. I'm enjoying it here."

He shook his head. "No one does. It's too much like a museum."

She shrugged. "I like it. It's beautiful. Different, in a contemporary sense."

He wished he saw it that way. All he had to do was step onto the property and every cell of his body screamed *flight*. "There's a new situation we need to discuss."

"You've changed your mind, gotten over the craziness that drove you to propose—"

He kissed her, silencing her words, not wanting to hear anything about them not getting married.

"Wow," Chelsea said, when they finally pulled apart. "Must be big, whatever you want me to do."

"You could say that," Gage said. "How would you feel about living here?"

Chelsea froze, pulled away slightly. "You hate it here."

"Yeah. I do. But my family is trying to make me see the light."

"Must be a pretty bright light."

"Blinding," he agreed. "I'm not happy about this, Chelsea. I'll understand if you decide not to accept my proposal. I'm hoping you do say yes. But the fact is, I need to talk to Cat's mom about Cat living with me, and this is the closest thing to a home I've got at the moment."

"I can't say I'm totally surprised."

"I didn't think you would be."

Chelsea shook her head. "I've had the feeling that she's happy with you, and perhaps happier with you than she is normally."

Anger boiled inside him all over again as he remembered what he'd learned. "It's complicated. Turns out Cat's living situation may not be wholly desirable. I have to talk to her, but I believe it may be time for a change for her. A big one."

Chelsea nodded. "I understand."

He reached for her hand. "You'd be taking on more than you bargained for. There have to be easier ways to get a green card."

"Probably." She smiled. "I'll let you know when I find one."

He didn't know how he'd gotten to this place. Everything had changed in his life in the past month: Leslie, Cat, being part of The Family, Inc....

And yet he didn't feel the old urge to get the hell away as fast as he could. There was only one reason for the change, and that was the redhead standing beside him. She made him believe everything could work out, for Cat, for him.

For all of them.

"WE HAVE TO TALK," Gage told Cat the next day, sprawling next to her in the piano room. Chelsea had suggested that perhaps this first conversation about her future should be between him and his daughter, alone. Just the two of them.

He thought that was good idea, but he was nervous. Cat and he didn't know each other all that well. He thought she liked him. Certainly, he was happy with her. In fact, he was more than happy. Cat was the daughter he would have wanted if he'd planned for a child. So as a surprise, she was a pretty cool one.

He was going to protect her.

Cat looked at him with her wise, seen-too-much eyes. "We do need to talk, Dad. I know you like to be counterculture, but I want to encourage you to rethink something."

"*I* like to be counterculture?" He stared at his daughter with her half-shaved head and many piercings. "I'm a pretty basic guy."

"Dad, you've basically been a runaway for years." She gave him a stern look. "Aunt Kendall is not happy you won't come home."

"Yeah, well." He couldn't explain to Cat how hard it had been to deal with the old man. Gil Phillips had not been an easy character. There was no reason to burden her with the family skeletons. "I wasn't a runaway, Cat. I just wasn't a participator, I guess."

"Anyway, back to you and being different," Cat said. "You have to get Chelsea a ring. It's embarrassing, Dad."

He laughed and ruffled his daughter's hair. She stared at him solemnly. "You really didn't think my proposal was satisfactory, did you?"

"I wouldn't have liked it," Cat said, honest as always. "When a guy asks me to marry him, I hope he brings flowers and a ring."

"I'll bring my baseball bat when that day comes," Gage said under his breath, and Cat said, "What?"

"Never mind." He sighed, not wanting to think about that part of their future. He'd just found her; he didn't want to think about some boy stealing her away from him. "Listen, Cat. This is the thing. What would you think about living with me?"

Cat's dark brows rose. "For good?"

"Well, yeah." He weighed his words carefully. "For good. You, me, Chelsea."

"What about Mom?"

"I don't know," Gage said, not wanting to upset Cat. "We'd have to talk to her."

Cat looked around her at the huge family home, the distinctly manicured trees, the vast property. Beyond the pool was the helipad and several buildings. Offices for Gil Phillips, Inc., built by the most ornery man Hell's Colony had ever seen.

"I'd like being with you a lot," Cat said, her voice sounding kind of quivery. "Mom will never say yes."

He frowned. "Don't mention this conversation to her, please. Let me talk to her."

Cat stood. "Larry won't like it, either. He calls me the golden goose."

"What does that mean?" Gage asked, knowing full well exactly what it meant.

"I don't know, but when he says it, Mom gets upset."

I'm going to kill him. And maybe Leslie, too, for being so spineless and keeping my kid from me.

"Here's the deal," Gage said. "You let me talk to your mom, and don't worry about it, okay? If you really want to live with Chelsea and me, I'm pretty sure it can work out."

"Where will I go to school?" Cat asked. "Ms. Moira says I need to be taking accelerated classes."

"Seeing as how I've never had a house before, and seeing as I don't exactly know where all of us are going to live, that's a discussion for another day," Gage said. "Let's go tell the family the good news."

"Let's go buy a ring," Cat countered. "Dad, if you don't do this right, Chelsea may change her mind."

"All right." He grinned at his opinionated daughter. "Good thing I have you around to keep me straight."

"Yeah. It is," she agreed, following him to his truck. "You're pretty lucky, Dad."

"I am." He couldn't help smiling at her forthright opinions.

His cell phone rang, and Gage answered it, noting Leslie's number. "This is Gage."

"Gage?" she said. "Um, got a minute?"

"Just a minute," he replied. "I've got an errand to run."

"Okay. Listen," Leslie said, "I was wondering if you could bring Cat back home."

He frowned, watching his daughter get into his truck. "When?"

"Like…tomorrow," Leslie said.

"Why?"

"Because," she said, "I think it would be best."

"Why?" he asked again, annoyed.

"I talked to her last night," Leslie said, "and she said she's homesick."

He looked at his daughter, waving at him to hurry up. "I think she's fine, Leslie. Don't worry."

"But—"

"No, Leslie. I'll let you know if Cat's having a problem. Right now, she's not having a problem."

"She says she's not in Tempest anymore. That you've taken her to Hell's Colony." Leslie's tone was deliberately disinterested, yet inquiring, as if she really wanted to know something.

He smelled trouble.

"You wouldn't expect her not to meet the family, would you?" he asked, keeping his voice reasonable.

"No, but as a mother, I think you could have given me the courtesy of telling me your whereabouts."

He could hear whispering in the background. She was being instructed. Gage felt his temper starting to edge up. "We thought we were only staying the afternoon. Our plans have now changed. We don't know when we're leaving. When our plans are more definitive, we'll let you know."

"Cat says you're unemployed." *Again,* her voice implied.

"Don't worry about it, Leslie. I promise you that Cat is well cared for."

"I think she should come home."

He sighed. “Leslie, you wanted her with me because you said you needed a break. What’s changed?”

“C’mon, Dad!” Cat hollered through the open window of his truck. “The store’ll probably close in an hour!”

“Nothing,” Leslie said. “I’m just worried about our daughter.”

“Tell you what,” Gage said. “Don’t you worry about us. Enjoy your break. Everything’s fine.”

He clicked off his phone, felt like hurling it toward the pool. Instead, he took a deep breath and got in the truck. “That was your mom, calling to check on you.”

“Why? I just talked to her last night,” Cat said.

“She thinks you’re homesick.” Gage switched on the engine.

“I’m not,” Cat said. “I told her I missed her, but I always say that. It’s a daughter thing.”

“You don’t want to go back to Laredo?”

Cat looked at him. “Not if you can keep me, Dad.”

Her voice was so simple, so hopeful. Wistful. Gage nodded. “We’ll work on it.”

She didn’t say anything. Cat wasn’t the kind of kid who lived on empty hopes and dreams. He wondered if he was doing the right thing, and decided he had no choice.

“Glad you’re going to steer me on picking out a ring,” he said. “One guaranteed to make Chelsea keep me.”

“Us,” Cat said solemnly.

"Us," Gage agreed. "You, I know she'd keep. Me, maybe not so much."

"We'll work on it, Dad."

He smiled. It felt great having a daughter who had his back.

Chapter Fourteen

"So," Kendall said, nodding at the tray placed beside them by a silent butler, "you're going to marry my brother. A very interesting turn of events."

Chelsea was starving. She took a glass of sparkling water and a couple of tiny sandwiches that looked delicious. "Please tell me you're going to eat and not just watch me pig out."

Kendall took some food from the tray, delicately placing it on her plate. "There's a lot for us to do if you're going to be part of the family."

"Do?" Chelsea blinked. "Kendall, Gage and I haven't decided about getting married. But if so, all I'll be doing is getting married. Gage hasn't given me a to-do list."

Kendall looked at her. "I get the sense my brother is set on marrying you, despite the fact you've known each other only, what, a month?"

Chelsea nodded, letting that be her response to Kendall's pointed query.

"I'd like to help you, welcome you to the family."

Chelsea wasn't sure how much goodwill she would

actually receive from Kendall. "I don't need a whole lot of welcoming, to be honest. As I recall, you think I'm marrying your brother simply for legal status." She shrugged. "I think that sums up your attitude about me."

"I didn't mean to hurt your feelings."

"You didn't. My feelings aren't hurt that easily." Chelsea looked at the cucumber sandwiches and selected two more. "I *am* marrying your brother for legal status. That's what he offered." She gave Kendall an even look. "And I happen to be pretty fond of Cat."

Gage's sister returned her gaze. "Would you be willing to sign a prenuptial agreement?"

She shrugged. "If Gage wanted me to."

"Because I'm sure this marriage wouldn't be about money for you," Kendall said.

"Gage says he lives by his trade. He didn't offer me money." Chelsea frowned. "To be honest, I make a good living that's sufficient to take care of myself and my mother. Money has never come up in any conversation Gage and I have had."

"You can look around you and see that Gage is well-off," Kendall pointed out.

"He doesn't seem interested in claiming his fortune, and it's not something I care about," Chelsea said. "Is money why you invited me to tea? Not to welcome me to the family?" She put down her cucumber sandwich. "Not that I expected much more. Gage warned me that the family wasn't the welcoming sort. But I do take exception to your idea that I'm marrying him for money."

Kendall briefly lowered her lashes. "Please don't take it to heart. I'm looking out for my brother."

"I don't think so," Chelsea said cheerfully. "Gage doesn't seem to want anybody looking out for him, and if he did, I'm pretty certain it wouldn't be anyone in this house."

"You're pretty sure of yourself, aren't you?"

Chelsea smiled. "As Gage has said, he's not a complicated man. He's very forthright about what he wants."

Kendall took a bite of her first cucumber sandwich and chewed thoughtfully. "What about Cat?"

"Cat is wonderful." The thought of Gage's daughter made her smile again. "The more time I spend around her, the more I appreciate her bright mind and caring personality."

Kendall nodded. "I hope you can convince my brother to live here, he and Cat and you."

"Oh. No." She shook her head. "I'm afraid I won't be doing any convincing, Kendall. My laptop and I can move anywhere, and wherever he decides to go is where we'll go." She stood and held out her hand. "And now I have to get back to my work-in-progress. Things are flowing nicely, and as a fellow working girl, I'm sure you appreciate the value of hard work."

"Yes, I do," Kendall said. She took her hand. "I really do welcome you to the family, Chelsea. I can see what Gage likes about you. I hope we can be friends."

"Thanks, Kendall." Chelsea returned the smile and made her way up the stairs to the room where she'd slept last night. Her laptop was open, her heroine no longer in jeopardy. Now the villain was in danger and on the run, though he had no idea where the danger lay. She could feel his anxiety and his desperation. He needed to hide from his crime, hide from Bronwyn Sang. Sang was determined and focused, unlike other detectives who'd tried unsuccessfully to catch him. It was as if she never slept.

Bronwyn was a tough woman, and it felt as if she was gaining strength all the time.

Chelsea leaned back in her chair, staring out the window as she thought about her plot. Her mind wandered to Gage, and how much she liked him. He was a kind man, a good man, the antithesis of her villain. Though he'd mentioned he didn't get along with his family, she sensed a willingness among all the Phillipses to make amends. She hadn't been offended by Kendall's probing of her reasons for marrying Gage, because underneath the questions, she'd felt Kendall's sincere concern for her brother.

I'd be concerned about my brothers and sisters, if I had any. It was just me and Mum, though, most of my life. Maybe that's why I like the Phillipses; they're a family. Family is important. They will love Cat, they want to love Gage, and they would accept me.

But Chelsea hadn't been completely honest with Kendall. The marriage was not about a green card or legal status. Gage was offering her a temporary fix, and she'd probably say yes—gladly. That's what Chelsea had told Kendall, because she was comfortable with business transactions.

But the truth is, it's all about the man for me.

GAGE KNOCKED ON HER DOOR thirty minutes later, poking his head inside her room when she said, "Come in!"

"Working?" he asked. "I can come back later."

"I am working. My villain is trying to decide if he should keep running or trap my heroine with her own bravery." Chelsea looked at Gage, thinking he was a very handsome, very sexy man. Hopefully, he wasn't here to tell her that he'd changed his mind. Maybe Kendall had gotten to him. The very thought of that pained her. When he'd made love to her, Chelsea had felt something new, something different, a bond she'd never before experienced.

She tried to ignore her suddenly racing heart. "It's a good time to take a five-minute break. I want to talk to you, anyway."

He sat on the end of her bed near her. "About?"

Chelsea saw no reason to hesitate. "Your sister has suggested that I sign a prenup."

"Why?" Gage sounded surprised. "I don't want any of your income."

She blinked. "I think Kendall is worried about the reverse situation. That I might try to take advantage of you."

He sighed. "My sister is very protective of the family. Don't let it bother you. I don't need a prenup. If you want one, I'll sign it."

"I don't need one."

Then there was no reason to discuss his sister's concerns further. "How is Cat?"

"Thinking pretty seriously that she'd like to stay with me. With us."

Chelsea nodded. "I'm glad."

"I'll talk to her mother again later." He reached into his pocket and pulled out a jeweler's box. "Chelsea, my proposal the other night was more off-the-cuff than I wanted it to be. So Cat and I went shopping. I hope you'll accept this." He opened the box and handed it to her, his dark eyes searching her face.

"Gage, it's beautiful. Absolutely gorgeous."

But she didn't reach out to take the ring. Not yet. She had to know exactly what was on his mind. What were they actually going to be to each other?

"Cat picked it out, I'm not too proud to say." He grinned, clearly delighted with his daughter. "I'm really happy you're willing to marry me, Chelsea."

Slowly, she picked up the ring. "What are we doing, Gage?"

He looked into her eyes. "Being expedient, I guess."

"You need me, I need you."

He nodded. "I hope you need me. I sure as hell need you."

"Because of Cat."

Not replying, he leaned to slip the ring on her finger, where it sparkled and shone, catching the hot Texas sunlight spilling in the window. Three round oval stones glittered at her, more beautiful than anything she'd ever owned.

"Cat says there are three diamonds, one for each of us, all on the same band forever," Gage said.

"She's so sweet," Chelsea whispered, touched.

"Are you marrying me because of my child?" he asked.

"Yes," Chelsea said, and he laughed.

"Good. For a while there, I thought you might be marrying me for me," he teased.

"Cowboy, you think too much of yourself."

He kissed her on the lips, lingering for a moment, sending her blood into a crazy dance. "We won't worry about prenups. Our marriage will end when and if you decide it should, Chelsea. No forward-looking agreement necessary." He stood, his hands in his jeans pockets. "I'm going to let you get back to work. Dinner is at six. If you don't want to come down, a tray can easily be sent up."

"A tray?" She couldn't believe he thought she might not join his family for dinner.

He nodded, as if he hadn't said anything unusual. "Yes. One of the butlers will bring up whatever you want. Just push the button on the phone and order anything."

She watched Gage leave, stunned. When her door closed, she looked down at her ring, watching it throw dancing prisms of light around the room. She let her breath out slowly, somewhat painfully. She'd been holding it in too tight.

She wasn't going to ever plan on ending their marriage—because they weren't going to get married in the first place.

"I CAN'T MARRY GAGE," Chelsea told her mother when she called that night. "It's not fair. It's not honest. I know I'm in love with him, Mum. I'm crazy about Cat. But I know he's not in love with me. That was clear when he gave me this beautiful ring." She took a deep breath. "It's how fast he became a Phillips when he got here. The man I know is the man who lived day to day, job to job. He thrived on his independence. The truth is, Gage is vastly wealthy, and I'm not comfortable with that.

"I'm not like Kendall, or like his mother, Millicent. They're nice people, Mum. But they live differently. Not the way I saw us living together, needing each other. Gage doesn't really need me. He thinks he does, because of Cat. But he doesn't. He's got more staff around here than I've ever seen. Even the Callahans don't live like this. At Rancho Diablo they have help, foremen, trainers. But here they have actual buttons and bells. Push this button and your dinner arrives. Ring this bell and a uniformed attendant comes to do your bidding. And it's crazy how fast Gage got comfortable with it. He even told me they'd send up a dinner tray if I wanted one."

She was still surprised by his automatic acceptance of the Phillipses' routine, after he'd said many times that it didn't suit him, and never would. "I like the Gage I met in the beginning, who had to fight for every single thing."

"He may not decide to live in Hell's Colony," Moira soothed.

"Still, I didn't know him. The man I fell for is not this man. He has so much here, and Cat will have so much." Chelsea looked around her at the sumptuous surroundings, so different from anything she'd known in Ireland. Their backgrounds were vastly dissimilar—

and she would never fit in. "I'm going back to the farmhouse."

"Come to Rancho Diablo," Moira said. "I'm in the middle of major baking with Fiona. We're teaching each other a few things. In fact, I think I've talked her into letting me teach her lacto-fermentation of vegetables."

"My job is at the farmhouse," Chelsea said slowly. "I look after it for Jonas. And I can write there, where it's quiet. Gage needs to stay here and figure things out with his daughter. Get her ready for the new school year."

"It will all work out," Moira said.

"It's not bad," Chelsea said. "It's just not what I thought it would be."

"That's okay," her mother said. "Often things aren't. It's good to know now. Remember Tempest. She folded under her own expectations."

"Did she?" Chelsea frowned. "I thought she just went off to get away from her childhood."

"Sure," Moira said. "She wanted a lot out of life, to make up for what she had never had. But then she got it, and she went away. You don't want to trade yourself for something you don't want, love."

Chelsea hung up after telling her mother she loved her. Moira's words stayed in her mind.

It was true. She wasn't like Tempest, who'd scaled dizzying heights and then melted away. She wasn't like Bronwyn Sang, who was tough and tenacious and fought crime to keep from thinking about her painful childhood and the parents she'd lost to a bungled crime.

She was just Chelsea, an Irish girl who'd grown up without a father, a man who'd died in a fight with the law. The Trouble, it was called. The shadows of it had formed her childhood, misted over her later years with independence and an urge to create alternative realities.

Kendall had been right. Chelsea liked Gage the fighter. She couldn't marry Gage of Gil Phillips, Inc., the millionaire and man of privilege.

I'm pretty sure he thinks he needs to save me. It's the chivalry in him, and his good heart.

I just don't need to be rescued.

"WELL, DAD, WE'RE on our own," Cat said to Gage when they were about to go in for dinner. "It's just me and you now."

Gage looked at his daughter. "What do you mean, honey?"

"Chelsea told me she was going back to Dark Diablo. She left your ring upstairs." Cat gazed at him, and he could see she was worried about him. "Dad, it's going to be all right."

"I know it is.... But she told you she was going? How did she get back to Dark Diablo?"

Cat put her arm around his waist, giving him a squeeze intended to comfort him. He hugged her back, shaking his head. "Why didn't she talk to me?"

"She said you'd try to talk her out of it." Cat shrugged. "She's right. You would have, Dad. Chelsea says you come from stubborn stock."

"I think my little Irish friend has some stubborn in her, too."

"Yeah. She mentioned that. She said it never worked when two rocks ground against each other. Eventually, the rocks became dust." Cat sighed. "Chelsea said she needed to go back home. She talked Kendall into taking her into the bus depot in town."

Gage blinked. "The bus depot?"

"Well, Aunt Kendall says it's really a shuttle someone runs to Santa Fe."

"I'm going to have a word with her," Gage said, trying not to look as upset as he was. He didn't want Cat thinking she'd done something wrong.

"Won't do any good, Dad. Aunt Kendall did everything she could to talk Chelsea into staying. Then when she couldn't, she offered the helicopter, a taxi, even a butler to chauffeur her in one of the family cars. Then she pleaded with her to let her drive her herself. Aunt Kendall said she was just there last week, she knew full well how to get there, and it'd be a great time for them to get to know each other better." Cat looked at her dad with her wise eyes. "I heard the whole thing. You can't be mad at Aunt Kendall, Dad."

"All right. Thanks." He didn't feel any better, though.

"Chelsea told me that her decision had nothing to do with me," Cat said, her tone accepting. "She said she loved the ring I picked out, said it was the perfect one she'd want if she thought she was the woman who would make you happy." His daughter looked up at him, her expression worried. "Chelsea told me that she loved me. But that she wasn't the right woman for you."

He shoved his hands in his pockets. “I know she does love you, Cat.”

“Well, I’m lovable.” She put her head against his midsection, hugging him. “I think she’s just scared, Dad. I know how that feels.”

“Yeah. I guess I do, too.” He ran a hand over his daughter’s long hair, and sighed.

He remembered being scared. He was remembering it right now. “It will all work out.”

“I know. Let’s go eat, Dad. Grandma Millicent doesn’t like it when anyone is late.”

“This is true.” He followed his daughter toward the dining room, thinking the family mansion was going to be a lot lonelier without a certain Irish firecracker to make him smile.

Chapter Fifteen

Chelsea thought she'd write like crazy with no one else in the farmhouse. It was just her and her laptop.

But somehow the words had come to a stop again. A slow, torturous drip, drip, drip of jangled action and structure that never seemed coherent. Splices of dialogue, splinters of scenes—that was all.

The place was just too quiet.

She'd been here a week, alone with her thoughts and Bronwyn Sang.

"The thing is," she told her laptop, "I've always created best under pressure. Dysfunction. It's what I knew growing up, and I learned to compensate."

Too quiet. Too lonely.

She missed Gage. She missed Cat. And she missed her mum.

"I'm not leaving this chair until you tell me your next move," she told Bronwyn. "You're hiding your conflict, and your real desires. So I can wait as long as you can." She leaned back, read back over ten pages of story for inspiration.

The doorbell rang, surprising her. "I didn't even

know there was a doorbell in this house. Talk about ignoring one's surroundings." She smoothed her hair and went downstairs, expecting a delivery, maybe, or Jonas. He didn't usually call, just showed up. It was his house, after all, and it would be like her mother to make certain he checked on her.

She opened the door, astonished to see a tall, gorgeous, voluptuous blonde staring in the window to see if anyone was home.

"Tempest!" Chelsea exclaimed. "Tempest Thornbury!"

The larger-than-life portraits in Cactus Max's seemed to have materialized on the farmhouse porch.

"Yes," she said, nodding. "You must be Chelsea Myers."

Chelsea blinked. She couldn't believe she was actually speaking to Tempest Thornbury, the Zola Cupertino of Tempest, New Mexico. Tempest had a smooth, honey voice, and was even more stunning in person. "How do you know my name?"

"I've read all your books," Tempest said.

"You have?" It seemed unbelievable that this beautiful woman could have heard of her work.

"Yes. I like reading. It's my favorite thing to do." Tempest smiled, and the effect was blinding. "Besides cooking. I love to cook, too."

"Wait a minute." Chelsea held up a hand. "Why are you here?"

She shrugged delicately, her face relaxing into a smile. "A little girl asked me to come introduce myself to you."

"Cat," Chelsea said, light dawning. Cat had been very fond of reading her work and her notes. Chelsea had written a lot about Tempest, wondering about her life.

Her visitor nodded. "Seems you have quite a fan."

Rattled, Chelsea said, "Would you like to come in?"

"I would. Thanks. My flight was a long one. Delayed all over the place. And the security lines. You just can't believe how slow they can be."

Chelsea could believe that security lines and everything else moved with a turtle's pace when Tempest was around. People had to gawk at the beautiful woman. "Please sit down. Let me grab us some tea. Or water? Lemonade?"

Tempest smiled. "Water, please."

"I can't believe you're here, in my living room."

"I can't believe it, either." She laughed. "I couldn't turn Cat down. She's irresistible. And determined."

Chelsea poured water over ice in two glasses, grabbed some cookies and hurried back out to the front room. "Tell me exactly what happened. Please."

"Apparently, she's been reading your work," Tempest said, amused.

"I know." Chelsea offered her guest the cookies and a small plate to put them on. Tempest chose two and leaned back. "We talked about boundaries, but I don't know if Cat's had those before."

"She likes what you write." Tempest smiled. "As do a lot of other readers."

"Thanks. I always hope so. But go on, please." Tempest was drawing the story out as if she was in a Broadway play, and Chelsea's curiosity was killing her.

"Cat said you wanted to meet me. And that she thought I might help your story along. She told me you were having a little—"

"Argh," Chelsea said. "Everyone's a creativity muse."

Tempest laughed. "She loves you a lot. That was clear in her emails."

"Her emails." Chelsea shook her head, astonished. "She used my laptop to email you?"

"I think she used her father's." Tempest moved a languid hand through her long blond hair. "She said she wanted to help you because if your story went well, and if you finished your book, maybe you would have more time to spend with her dad. She said she didn't like you in the beginning, but now that she sees how happy you make him, she's hoping the three of you might one day become a family."

"Oh, no," Chelsea said. "That's not exactly the way it works. I'm so sorry you had to come all this way to...help me. Us."

Tempest shrugged. "I didn't come to help. I came back because it was time. Haven't been home in years. Cat merely provided the excuse. She reminds me a lot of myself." The statuesque blonde stood, putting a hand out for Chelsea to shake. "Thanks for seeing me. I called yesterday before I caught my flight, but there was no answer. So I took a chance that you'd be in."

"Where are you staying?" Chelsea asked, thinking about the broken-down Cupertino family home.

Shadows darkened her eyes for a split second. "I'm staying in Blanche and Shinny's bed-and-breakfast."

"Blanche and Shinny Tuck who run the ice cream shop?"

Tempest nodded, walking to the door. "I've known them since I was small. Shinny used to give me free ice cream, and Blanche was like a second mother to me."

"I know," Chelsea said. "Your portraits are on the walls of Cactus Max's."

Tempest walked onto the porch. "It's good to be back. I've forgotten how much I love being home."

Chelsea blinked. "You do?"

"Sure. Doesn't everyone?"

She wasn't sure. She didn't want to go back to Dublin, even thought she might have to soon. Gage hadn't wanted to go back to Hell's Colony—yet once he was there, he'd seemed to change into a man she didn't recognize.

"Home might not be so bad," Chelsea murmured.

"It's just hard to make yourself go back," Tempest said. "Goodbye, Chelsea. I hope your story goes well. Don't tell me what happens, but I have to admit, I'm hoping Bronwyn figures out how Detective Stone feels about her one day." She smiled. "Tell Cat I'm sorry I missed her. She sounds like a wonderful young lady. Very caring."

Chelsea nodded. "She is. Cat is the best."

Tempest walked out to her rental car, a Range Rover like Kendall had been driving.

"Thanks for taking the time to come by, Tempest," Chelsea called.

She smiled. "Call me Zola. Please. I'm Zola to my friends."

"Goodbye, Zola." Chelsea watched her drive away, completely stunned by the unexpected visit. It had been like a dream, a crazy, unimaginable dream come to life.

"Cat," Chelsea murmured. "You are amazing."

It had been sweet of Gage's daughter to try to make her happy. She sighed, locking the door behind her, then went up the stairs.

It was true what Tempest said. Going home was hard only if you kept putting it off.

THE DOORBELL RANG AGAIN a few hours later, and Chelsea put down a pencil with which she'd been writing notes on Bronwyn's inner thoughts, and went down the stairs. "Jonas," she said when she opened the door. "Why are you in Tempest?"

He followed her inside, and when she went into the kitchen, propped himself against the counter. "Your mother sent me to check on you."

She shook her head. "No, she didn't. Mum knows I retreat into a cave when I'm writing." Except when Cat and Gage had been with her, and then she'd written like mad.

It should have been just the opposite, if everything in her world was lining in the expected way, the normal way—before she'd let herself fall for a certain Texas cowboy.

Cowboy millionaire.

"Yeah, well, your mom did want me to check on

you. Actually, she wants me to bring you back to Rancho Diablo with me."

"Why?"

"She misses you." Jonas shrugged. "As your onetime fiancé, I think you coming back with me is a good idea."

She looked at him, knowing him too well to fall for his line. Jonas and she were friends, nothing more—but she could tell he was still trying to look out for her. "I'm supposed to be watching this house."

"Yes, but you can have a day off."

Chelsea sighed. "So what's the deal?"

"I don't know. Your mom's feeding the lovebirds until Cat gets back, and she said Cat was like a granddaughter to her, and she was worried you were going to have to go back to Ireland soon, and I said I was—"

"Jonas. What do you really want?" Chelsea demanded.

He looked undecided, then gave in. "Since your mail comes to Rancho Diablo, your mom said you probably needed to see this."

He handed her a stack of mail, on top of which was an envelope from Immigration. "My papers!"

"Yeah. Congratulations. Moira said she wanted me to bring you back so she could see your face when you got them. But you're never that easy to surprise."

"I'm surprised now." She hugged the envelope to her chest.

Jonas grinned. "Feel better?"

"You have no idea." She reached up and gave him

a quick kiss on the cheek. Then she grinned. "I owe this all to you."

"Nah. But if you're feeling grateful…" Jonas said.

She looked at him. "What?"

"Our favorite peacock dealer called. She says she might be willing to part with a pair of her prized babies."

Chelsea laid the envelope on the counter, feeling so happy she almost didn't care that Jonas was trying to dump another errand on her. "Did you tell her you'd be there pronto?"

He cleared his throat. "Actually, she asked if you could come get them."

"Me? Why me?"

He shrugged. "She says she feels more comfortable with a woman handling her treasured birds. It's a female thing, she says." He smiled, laughing a bit at the vagaries of womankind. "I told her I'd offer you the chance to visit Colorado. And now that you're perfectly legal, it's more like a celebration vacation than an errand, right?"

Chelsea gave him a why-am-I-not-surprised stare. "I'll go."

He glanced around. "I guess by yourself?"

"I can handle it, Jonas. Maybe Mum will want to ride with me."

"Are you sure?"

She nodded. "I'm sure."

"Long drive."

Chelsea gave him a light tap with her envelope. "You can always take Sabrina, and I'll babysit the kids.

Or you can wait until next year when you're free of lawsuits and can go get your peacocks yourself."

"I thought about it. But I'm afraid she'll get cold feet. I think the only reason Ms. Smithers changed her mind is because she felt like she could trust you."

"That's because I'm a nice girl."

"I know." Jonas shrugged and walked to the front door. "You're doing a great job keeping this place up. I appreciate it."

"Yeah. You better. You're about to get a bill for wooden blinds throughout the house." She gave him an impish smile. "Plantation-style. Expensive."

His mouth quirked. "Good to know. So, when do you expect Gage back?"

She blinked. "Why would I know? He's your employee."

"A little birdie told me he might be your fiancé." Jonas seemed happy about that, subtly trying to nose around for information without being overt.

It wasn't working.

"Jonas, I'm not engaged."

He nodded. "I guess now that you have your new status, marriage won't be on your mind anymore."

"It wasn't about my status, Jonas."

"Come on," he said, "you can tell ol' Jonas your love troubles."

She shook her head. "Nice try. But I don't have any love troubles."

"Okay. I'm always available to listen."

"I know. Thanks." She walked him to the door. "So when am I supposed to leave to see Ms. Smithers?"

"Oh," Jonas said. "Tomorrow would be good. How's your deadline coming?"

"It's actually a good time for a trip," Chelsea admitted, not happily. "Jonas, just one thing."

"Anything, Irish, you know that."

She nodded. "No coincidental sending of a certain cowboy on this trip with me."

"Ow," Jonas said. "Would I do that?"

"I won't dignify that with a response."

He laughed. "All right. It'll just be you and Ms. Smithers. Get me a pretty pair of birds, all right? I leave it in your capable hands. Take the ranch truck. You'll need it for the cages."

"That's great," Chelsea said, "but you'd better figure out who's going to build pens for those precious birds now that you have no skilled builder to do it. Ms. Smithers is very particular about knowing that proper protection is available for her babies. And I won't fib to her about it, so I suggest you get the specs from Gage, and then start Callahans hammering."

Jonas nodded. "You have a point."

She closed the door and went to pack. It was going to be a short night if she had to leave in the morning.

A long couple days on the road should jog my creativity. Peace, quiet...silence.

There was no time to celebrate her new immigration status. She had to meet her deadline—and Bronwyn wasn't exactly cooperating.

Silence would help.

IF SILENCE WAS GOLDEN, it wasn't really helping at the moment. Chelsea crossed the state line into Colorado the next morning, barely listening to any tunes on the radio. She was deep in thought about Gage and her feelings for him, and how long it took to get over a broken heart, when something moved in the backseat of the van.

"Where are we?" a voice asked, with a sleepy yawn.

Chapter Sixteen

Chelsea shrieked. Startled by her scream, Cat let out a yelp. "Why are you screaming?" she asked. "You scared me!"

"Why are you here?" Chelsea demanded. "Oh, my God, I can't believe you stowed away in my truck. And I've taken you over the state line. Oh, this is not good." She pulled off the highway, her pulse racing. "Honey, what were you thinking?"

"It's a long story," Cat said.

"Lovely." Chelsea drove up to a roadside café so they could talk. Maybe she could put in a surreptitious call to Gage, alert him that Cat was safe and sound. "When did you sneak into the van?"

"Last night."

Cat yawned again, seemingly unconcerned. Chelsea briefly considered wringing her neck, then told herself to stay calm. "You slept in here?"

"Yes. It's comfy."

Chelsea parked the truck and got out. Cat exited as well, staring up at her with huge eyes. "You're not going to yell at me, are you?"

"Maybe. A little. No." Chelsea sighed. "Let's go inside, order something to eat and think about what we're going to do."

They went in, seating themselves in a powder-blue vinyl booth. A waitress with two long black braids came over to take their order.

"Coffee," Chelsea said, "and a grilled cheese sandwich, please."

"Yum," Cat said. "I'll have the same."

Chelsea looked at her. "Do you drink coffee?"

"Never have before. But if you do, I will, too."

Chelsea looked at the waitress. "Maybe an iced tea for her, please."

The waitress went off, and Chelsea fixed her gaze on Cat. "I'm surprised your father doesn't have this place surrounded by the Army, Navy and Marines. Does he have any idea where you are?"

"No." Cat shook her head. "Though I did tell Aunt Kendall I was going to find you. She drove me to the bus station and gave me money to get to Dark Diablo."

The waitress delivered their drinks, and Chelsea sipped her coffee thoughtfully. Something wasn't adding up. Kendall had tried every way she knew how to talk her into taking one of the Phillipses' limos, or even the helicopter, back to Tempest. There was no way Gage's sister would have put Cat on a bus and said *good luck* to her niece. Chelsea pursed her lips. "So why did you leave?"

Cat took a sip of Chelsea's coffee, made a face and turned to her tea. She poured what seemed to be half a cup of sugar into it, nodding when she finally got it to her liking. "I'm not going back to Laredo."

"No one says you have to, do they?" Last she'd known, Gage was determined to keep his daughter with him.

"Mom says I have to go home. I'm not going to. I love Mom. She's my mother, you know? But I don't love Larry. I don't like Larry. And I want to be with Dad. If Dad can't make Mom let me stay with him, then I'd rather live somewhere else."

"Well, you can't live in the truck," Chelsea said.

"Yeah, well. I'll figure it out. Don't worry about me." Cat shrugged.

Chelsea felt so sorry for the teen. She had not had it easy. "Honey, your father has to be worried sick. Don't you want to use my cell phone to at least let him know you're safe?"

"I will in a minute. Right now, I want to eat this grilled cheese sandwich. I have to have a full stomach when Dad yells at me, and he is going to yell."

Chelsea thought that was a strong possibility.

"I just want to be like Tempest," Cat said around a mouthful of grilled cheese.

"You're thirteen," Chelsea gently pointed out. "A bit too young to transform yourself. And speaking of Tempest, I have a complaint to lodge with you about that."

Cat's eyes slanted toward her as she polished off her sandwich. "May I have another one of these, please, before you lodge your complaint?"

"When's the last time you ate?"

"Before Aunt Kendall took me to the bus station."

Chelsea shook her head. "You may order whatever you wish, but you must call your father. Please. I know that, somewhere, your poor dad is having heart failure, Cat, wondering where you are."

"All right. Can I have another sandwich, some tomato soup and a piece of chocolate cake?" she asked hopefully.

"Sure," Chelsea said, handing over her cell phone.

Chelsea placed the order while Cat called her father. "I'm okay, Dad. I'm sorry I left, but I don't want to go live with Larry and Mom. I just don't want to. And if you're too busy, and Mom doesn't want you to have me, then I'm going to…live with Chelsea," Cat said, making Chelsea jump.

"Don't get your father mad at me," she said. "I don't want him to think I had anything to do with your leaving!"

The last thing she expected was to see Gage walking into the café—and yet, knowing how he loved his daughter, she wasn't surprised at all. Cat was still on the phone, talking away, as Chelsea watched Gage walk toward the powder-blue booth. He looked hot and sexy in his dark aviator sunglasses, cowboy hat, black T-shirt and exactly-right worn jeans, and she felt her heart flip over.

He slid into the booth next to his daughter, giving Chelsea a wink that melted her. "Hey," he said, taking the phone and handing it back to Chelsea.

"Dad!" Cat threw her arms around his neck. "How did you know where I was?"

"Because," Gage said, "I followed the bus, I followed you to Dark Diablo, I watched you when you sneaked into the truck, and kept an eye on you while you slept." Gage ruffled her hair. "Not to tattle on Aunt Kendall, but she was willing to let you be a runaway only to a certain extent."

Cat hugged him again, and Chelsea breathed a sigh of relief. She should have known that the girl had never been out from under her father's watchful gaze. "Were you going to follow us all the way to Colorado?"

"Sure." Gage shrugged, shoving his phone into his jeans. "Couldn't let my two favorite girls go off on an adventure without me."

"I'm sorry, Dad." Cat looked at him with big eyes. "You just don't understand that I don't want to go home to Mom."

"It's all right." He kissed his daughter on the head. "Care to split that grilled cheese with your old dad?"

"Sure." Beaming, Cat handed her father half her sandwich.

Chelsea realized that if Cat hadn't eaten, Gage must not have, either. When the waitress came over, she ordered coffee for him and tomato soup for all of them. "And another slice of chocolate cake, please," she said, watching Gage look at his daughter. He pushed her hair, the strands on the long side, behind her ear tenderly, and Chelsea thought she'd never seen anything so sweet in her life.

Then she realized his gaze was on her.

"You gonna split that cake with me, Irish?"

"Sure, cowboy," she murmured.

After all, there was nothing she'd rather be doing

than sitting in this booth right here, right now, with Gage and Cat, Chelsea knew. She could run like Cat, but the truth was, she didn't want to.

She really didn't want to be anywhere but with them, even if she was fighting her own heart.

"THIS IS MY BEST PAIR," Ms. Smithers proudly told them. "They have your name on them."

Gage considered the birds, thinking that they were, indeed, stunning. Though his mind was barely on Jonas's unholy mission for lawn ornaments for Rancho Diablo. All he could think about was his child, and what he was going to do about her. It was obvious she absolutely wasn't going back to her mother; a line had been drawn in the sand over boyfriend Larry, something that Cat must have been trying to explain for a long time with her facial jewelry and crazy hair. It had not escaped Gage that since she'd come to him, the piercings had begun to disappear one by one, going the way of the wind. And her hair was growing out on the shaved side.

She seemed less resentful now, and happier.

He wasn't mad at Cat for trying to run away. If anything, he was worried. She hadn't once been out of his sight—this time. He suspected that if he told her she had to go back to Laredo, she'd disappear again—and he might not be so fortunate as to have Aunt Kendall running recon for him.

He sighed. *I remember those troubled teen years.*

Which got him to thinking about the redheaded rebel standing next to him. Chelsea leaving his ring and him and the Phillips mausoleum was no big shocker. He'd really hoped she could look past The Family, Inc., and see just him.

It was a lot to take in all at once. He'd never wanted to be around it, either. His father had wanted a son to take over the family business. He'd pushed relentlessly for Gage to do so. *It just wasn't in me to wheel and deal around the world. I liked building things. I liked being in the open air, not stuffy boardrooms filled with stuffy suits.*

I was a rebel, too.

"Just so you know, Ms. Smithers," Chelsea said, "these birds will be well cared for. They and their offspring will live either at Rancho Diablo or Dark Diablo, which is owned in part by Jonas Callahan of the New Mexico Callahan Ranches. We know you've been reluctant to sell to the previous owner of our ranch, but we are not the same as he was. We're trying to make Dark Diablo a better place, a happier place that gives back to the community. And we think your beautiful peacocks will enhance our family ranch and community."

Gage stared at Chelsea, admiring her tact with the reluctant Ms. Smithers. The die was cast now. He had no idea how the breeder would react.

"I knew that," she said, with a pointed look at him. "That's why I insisted *you* come get these birds," she told Chelsea. "I want you to understand that nothing comes easy, and these peacocks deserve the best. That old man didn't deserve them, but you…" She gazed at Chelsea. "I think you understand that a person's treasure isn't always measured in money. These are my babies," she said, with a sweep of her hand, "and I don't have to part with them. They only go to the very best homes." She nodded at Chelsea. "Thanks for being honest."

She sent a frown to Gage. "You *are* from Hell's Colony, but it wasn't too hard to figure out who Gage Phillips is, you know. The internet doesn't keep many secrets. You're not listed with the officials of the company, like your sister and brother are." Her brows lowered to indicate her displeasure with his dishonesty. "So I put in a call to ask where you were working these days. Very helpful woman—your mother, I believe—said that you were on a job in New Mexico at the Dark Diablo ranch. You honestly think I don't check where my babies are going? No one can even get a dog from a rescue society anymore without a thorough check."

She was right. "I apologize, Ms. Smithers. I should have been forthright about where your peacocks would live."

"Yeah, well. I gave you a small pass because you seemed knowledgeable and interested in proper penning. But if it wasn't for her," she said, poking a bent finger at Chelsea, "I wouldn't have considered your application at all."

He nodded. "I understand. We knew you had some bad feelings toward the previous owner."

"Mr. Taylor was a dishonest, horrible person and he sent men up here to steal my babies," she said indignantly. "Ask around Tempest sometime. Ask if some of his men didn't go back with a couple fannies full of buckshot."

Chelsea smiled. "You're a good woman, Ms. Smithers. No wonder your peacocks are the best anywhere. You love them so much."

She sniffed. "Some people say I'm crazy, that I act like they're my children. But if I never had any children, shouldn't I have something?"

Chelsea hugged her. "I'll tell Jonas Callahan that if he doesn't treat your peacocks with the reverence he gives his black Diablo mustangs, he will be in very hot water with you."

"I know. You, I trust." She looked at Cat, then smiled at the teen, who'd been listening to the exchange with well-mannered respect. "Come on, little one. Let's get you a snack while your daddy packs up my peafowl."

"Thank you," Cat said, docilely following her to the house.

Gage reached to touch Chelsea's hand. "Good job."

She nodded, giving him a relieved smile. "I'm going to tell Jonas I want a raise."

"You deserve one. And you deserve a lot of gratitude for what you did for Cat."

"Oh," Chelsea said, "I didn't do anything for Cat. She did more for me than I did for her."

"She trusts you." He understood completely why Ms. Smithers had instinctively trusted Chelsea. There was just something bright and honest about her that people recognized. "Thanks for having Cat call me."

"So how long were you going to follow us?"

He sighed, and she saw the worry and strain in his face. "I was going to step in when it became necessary. Trust me, it's not easy as a parent to let your child spread the proverbial wings, especially when I don't know Cat all that well. What I do understand clearly is that she's not happy with Leslie, and her mom's not happy with her. I told Leslie that Cat had left, and that I was following her, but that she and I were going to have a serious conversation about this Larry individual. Leslie got real quiet after that." He touched a strand of Chelsea's hair, drawing it through his fingers. Chelsea could feel the connection between them, and his understanding of why she, too, had left.

"I'm sorry, Gage," she said. "I really am."

He shook his head. "Don't be. I'm not."

They were talking about them now, and Chelsea felt tears prickle her eyes.

"So," Gage said, after a long moment, "now that you're on Ms. Smithers's good side, you think we should ask her to keep an eye on Cat for a while and give that rotating bed in the Peacock Cabin a test run? I'd probably get some cool ideas for a really upscale, technological pen for these birds that would blow Jonas's mind." Gage grinned as he tossed off his suggestion, and Chelsea couldn't help returning his smile.

"I think we'd better pack up these birds before Ms. Smithers changes her mind," she said, knowing that if things had turned out differently between them, she would have jumped into any bed where Gage was.

He was teasing her with a subtle mention that he'd enjoyed their lovemaking.

He wasn't the only one.

Chapter Seventeen

Chelsea drove Gage's truck, and Gage and Cat followed with the peacocks, carefully crated for traveling in the trailer hitched to the ranch truck. Fortunately, Chelsea liked to drive slowly, still acclimating to driving in the States.

Jonas had told Gage that she was leaving in the morning to go after the peacocks. Then he had told him that he could not under any circumstances follow her. But when Gage realized his daughter was about to be a surprise stowaway on a trip to Colorado, he'd said to hell with Jonas, and had taken off.

Now he had plenty of time to talk things over with his daughter—and concentrate on a certain redhead he was following through the mountains.

"Are you mad, Dad?" Cat asked.

"I'm not mad, honey. I'm worried."

"You weren't listening to me," she told him. "Mom never listens to me, either."

"I was listening," Gage said, "but I'm listening better now. If you want to live with me, I'm real willing to make that happen. I just don't know that I see us living in Hell's Colony with The Family, Inc."

"You always call them that. It annoys Aunt Kendall."

He smiled. "That's because it's more a consortium than a family. Kendall knows that. It's just that she loves the business, and I don't. We see it differently, and that's okay."

"We need a job, though," Cat said practically.

"I can work for Jonas at Rancho Diablo until he decides to start building again at Dark Diablo."

Cat sat up straighter. "Really? Could we?"

Gage glanced at his daughter. "Is that what you'd want?"

"It would be awesome!"

"There are, like, eighteen toddlers running around, getting into everything."

"I'd make a great big sister," Cat said. "Cousin, I guess, but it feels like they're my brothers and sisters!" She gave her father a wry glance. "I'll be in college before I get any little brothers and sisters of my own."

He laughed. "Give me a chance, would you?"

"I guess." She shook her head. "I don't know. You'll have to find a girlfriend, and that takes time, and then—"

"Whoa," Gage said, "I haven't given up on Chelsea yet."

"But she didn't take the ring."

He smiled at his daughter's directness. "Just because things don't work out immediately doesn't mean one should give up. The best things in life are worth time and effort, babe."

"I don't know, Dad. Chelsea seems pretty happy. And I don't know if you noticed or not, but there's a big envelope from Immigration sitting in her truck. I peeked at it when she went to the restroom in Colorado."

He knew he shouldn't encourage his daughter, but… "And?"

"I don't know what it was, exactly. She's asked me not to read her stuff anymore, and I'm trying real hard to respect boundaries."

It seemed as if boundaries were still a struggle for Cat.

"It is best to respect boundaries," he agreed. "Thanks for listening to Chelsea. She's right."

"So I didn't peek inside," Cat clarified. "I just peeked at the outside. It's still peeking, but…I get bored when I sit too long by myself."

He remembered Chelsea had said that her mother suggested Cat wasn't sufficiently challenged in school—and that tended to lead to boredom, and small mischiefs. "Cat," he said, "are you really thinking about going to college one day?"

"I think so. I'd like to be a doctor. I mean, I'd like to be like Tempest, but maybe that's a bit crazy." She considered that for a moment. "Anyway, I've always liked taking care of things. I've been taking care of Mom for years. So I think I'll be a doctor."

He winced. "You're going to be a little girl for a while yet. I want you to read the books Miss Moira suggests, and we'll go to Rancho Diablo. We'll find you a great school, and maybe a sports team or something."

"That'd be great, Dad."

She sounded distinctly happier than she had a few moments before, not troubled or weighed down. Gage thought about the envelope Chelsea had received from Immigration, realizing the long-awaited papers must have arrived.

She didn't need him anymore.

Thing was, he wanted her. He was in love with her. He wanted to be with her, all the time.

But as Cat had pointed out with her typical unsparing forthrightness, Chelsea seemed fine on her own.

"WE'RE GOING TO HEAD ON to Rancho Diablo." Gage stopped behind Chelsea's truck as she pulled into Dark Diablo. "Probably best to get these birds to their new home."

She nodded. "It's been a long drive. Does Jonas know you're bringing the birds out?"

"He can't wait." Gage grinned. "It's dumb, but it's a job, right?"

"We all keep Jonas happy." She closed the van door and stretched. "What are your plans?"

Gage looked at her, his eyes giving little away. She had the feeling he wanted their goodbye to be as easy as possible. "Cat wants to live with me," he said softly.

"I know. Seems best."

"Yeah. So I'm going to talk to Jonas about taking that job he offered me at Rancho Diablo. Cat wants to be around the kids and family atmosphere." He smiled. "She says she'd be just as happy in Hell's Colony, but she knows I don't want to work there. So she's thrilled to be going to Rancho Diablo."

"She's a good girl." Chelsea looked at Cat, who had climbed out of the truck and was running to check on the peacocks. "Mum's kept her lovebirds safe and happy, so Cat will enjoy that reunion."

He nodded. "So what are *your* plans?"

"Well," Chelsea said, brushing some stray red strands from her face as the breeze picked up, "writing like mad, for one thing. I'm almost finished. And I like the way everything is turning out. I'm going to close myself up in the farmhouse and hope for greatness."

He smiled. "I'm sure you'll get it."

She looked pensive. "Gage, I got my legal documentation."

He faced her, not saying anything, waiting for her to continue. "You don't have to worry about me anymore," she gently said.

Something flickered in his eyes, but she wasn't certain what. "Congratulations on your papers. I know you'll feel more settled now."

"I feel," Chelsea said, "like I can keep Mum safe and healthier now." The thought brought a smile to her face. "Keep an eye on her for me, will you?"

He looked at her. "I'll do it."

"Thanks." She turned her gaze to Cat. "If you can spare thirty minutes, I'd like to run your daughter into town."

"Any reason in particular?"

She smiled. "Girl talk. Nothing you'd be interested in."

He nodded. "I'll check on the birds and the crates while you girls go off and do your thing."

"Thanks. Cat!"

The teen came to stand beside them. "Yes, Chelsea?"

"I need to run to town real fast. Want to ride with me?"

She looked at her father. "Is it all right, Dad?"

He smiled. "Sure."

Cat followed after Chelsea, proudly wearing her new boots and a big smile. "Where are we going?"

"You'll see," Chelsea said. "You'll see."

CHELSEA FOLLOWED HER HUNCH and found what—who—she was looking for at Shinny's Ice Cream Shoppe. The stunning, larger-than-life blonde smiled at her when she walked in.

"Hello, Chelsea," Tempest said.

"Hi, Tempest. I brought a fan to meet you."

A sweet smile brought light to Tempest's eyes. "This must be my encouraging pen pal. Hi, Cat."

The teen appeared dumbstruck—but only for a moment. Then she reverted to her typical loquaciousness.

"You came back," Cat said.

"Sure," Tempest replied. "I was hoping to meet you."

"Wow," Cat said. "If my friends knew I was meeting a famous star, they'd be jealous!"

Tempest laughed. "Let's go sit in a booth, if you

have time?" She looked at Chelsea. "I'd love to enjoy Cat for a few minutes, if that's possible."

"We're delivering peacocks to the ranch near Diablo," Chelsea said. "Cat's father has given us about thirty minutes before they have to hit the road."

"Good. Shinny, can you bring us some ice cream, please?" Tempest asked the elderly gentleman as they seated themselves in the lipstick-colored booths.

"Like old times," Shinny said, coming over to shake Chelsea's hand and beam at Cat. "Is this the special writer who brought you back, Zola?"

The two women smiled at Cat. "Yes, Shinny, this is the sweet girl who made me realize what I was missing."

Shinny looked at Cat, his kindly face creased in a grin. "Would you like some ice cream, Cat?"

"Oh, yes, please," she said, delighted. "I'll have whatever Miss Tempest is having."

"Three of your specials, Shinny, please." Tempest turned to Cat, her face now free of the anxiety she'd worn the night she'd knocked on Chelsea's door. "You and I have so much to talk about."

Chapter Eighteen

Over the next three weeks, Chelsea finished her book, then sent it off to her editor, feeling good about volume three of her series. It turned out that Bronwyn Sang had known all along that she was stronger than she realized, and stronger even than the villain who had so bedeviled her. She solved her case, and in the hustle-bustle world she lived in, knew that it was only a matter of time before the next heinous villain darkened the world in which good always triumphed over evil, light over darkness, certainty over uncertainty.

And she fell a little bit more in love with Detective Stone.

Chelsea felt triumphant—and somehow empty now that she'd sent her manuscript off. She missed everything: Moira, Gage, Cat…noise, passion, light.

She hadn't taken time to celebrate her new immigration status, either. With a sigh of relief, she packed her bag and followed her longing for civilization and the people who meant the most to her.

But first, she had to say goodbye to someone she had come to admire.

She went first to Shinny's. From the time she'd been a young, unhappy, hungry little girl, Zola had known that Shinny and Blanche were safe harbors for her.

Shinny shook his nearly bald head with a smile. "Zola went back to Tuscany yesterday," he said. "Said she felt like Puff the Magic Dragon, waiting for her childhood to return. Tempest or Zola, it doesn't matter, she'll always be looking for that one thing she's missing."

"What is that?" Chelsea asked.

He grinned as he wiped the white counter. "Family. All her life Zola wanted a real family. She found it on Broadway, she found it in her fans, but deep down, she wants her very own family. She'd like a dozen little girls just like Cat, I imagine."

"I can understand that." Chelsea sank into a booth, and Blanche seated herself across from her. The long, old-style fluorescent lights dimly lit the ice cream shop in the late afternoon, and as Chelsea looked around, she realized probably nothing about this place had changed very much from the time that Zola was a child. "Do you think she'll ever come back to Tempest for good?" she asked, thinking that Shinny and Blanche had been pretty cool as stand-in parents.

"We always hope so," Blanche said, "and yet we realize that sometimes people keep looking when they have a hole in their heart that hasn't yet been filled. Sometimes we know where our family is, yet we still need a little more time to make that journey of self-discovery, yes?"

"I don't know," Chelsea murmured. Was that what

life was all about then? The journey every person had to undertake for themselves? Zola had gone away to become the legendary Tempest. Chelsea had left Ireland to find health for her mother—and maybe something more for herself. Gage had left Hell's Colony, even though he had wealth and family there. He would rather, as Cat succinctly put it, be a cowboy with just two nickels, as long as they were honest nickels.

"It's about being true to yourself," Chelsea murmured. "The dream only works if you are."

Blanche nodded. "I think so. We all know what we want. It's finding it and appreciating it that matters."

"So what happens now?" Chelsea asked.

Shinny set a tall, frosty glass of chocolate froth in front of her—one of his own legendary specials—and scooted in next to Blanche, who gave him a fond squeeze on the arm. "You tell us. What happens now?"

Chelsea spooned up some of the wonderful chocolate, closing her eyes briefly with pleasure. "This is better than any ice cream I've ever had."

He smiled. "You know, Blanche has been reading your last book to me, book two of the series. I like a good spine-tingler, I don't mind admitting. And I like to hear Blanche's voice, so she's gracious enough to read to me at night. It's comforting."

Blanche smiled, her eyes full of adoration for Shinny. Chelsea was misty watching how happy they were together.

"What I noticed about Bronwyn is that she's powerful because she's true to herself. She knows she is fighting the battle for good, and home is where she always returns to recharge after she's solved a case. But it's the way she fights for others that makes her compelling. Her strength is her home, and her desire to serve the people." Shinny sighed with satisfaction. "There's no place like home. And until we know where that is, we keep searching. It's our human frailty that blinds us. Oh, we all have our villains, don't we? But they're usually ones we've created ourselves."

Chelsea hesitated. Home. Where was hers? She *had* no permanent home. Didn't have plans for one. Her mother traveled with her, but she suspected Moira preferred Rancho Diablo to any place they'd been. Ireland was a distant world away. It would always be in her heart—she'd thought one day she'd move back—but now…

"Home is the journey," Chelsea said. "It's not the place, it's the people."

"That's what we think," Blanche said. "And that's what we think Zola will one day discover."

Chelsea had to go. "Thank you for the ice cream," she said, jumping to her feet. She hugged both of them warmly. "I'm so glad I got to know you, and Zola. Thank you for everything you've done for Cat, and for me." She gave them one last fond hug. "Don't think I don't know that you're trying to help me, just like you helped Cat. And Zola, too."

"We don't help anyone," Shinny said modestly. "We're just here to serve ice cream and talk. Mostly we like to talk to wonderful people who are kind enough to remember a couple of old folks from time to time."

"Goodbye," Blanche said. "Let us hear from you again."

Chelsea nodded, and as she left Tempest and Dark Diablo, she hoped there was still an open door waiting for her at the end of her journey.

Chapter Nineteen

Chelsea pulled into Rancho Diablo, somewhat surprised to see the Fourth of July lights and decorations still strung over the ranch, giving it a special twinkle and sparkle. Fiona Callahan was famous for her love of decorations, and this night was no exception. "No wonder Mum loves it here so much," Chelsea murmured, parking the van. "It feels like home should."

"Howdy," Jonas said as she got out. "You must have sent the long-awaited installment of Bronwyn Sang's adventures on to the eager editor. Did you find brilliance at Dark Diablo?"

"I feel good about it, and I feel great that I made my deadline." Chelsea smiled at him. "Why are you skulking around out here in the dark?"

"I saw your van pulling up. Thought I'd come out to greet the long-lost scribe." Jonas looked well satisfied with himself. "You can join us for pie and tea. Fiona, Moira and Cat have been baking up a storm."

"Yum." Chelsea followed him to the porch.

"I didn't figure we'd seen you this soon," Jonas said. "You've been quiet for the last week. If we didn't hear from you by tomorrow, I think your mother was planning on giving up her sojourn and going back to Dark Diablo."

Chelsea could use the excuse that she'd been so quiet because of her deadline—and that was partially true. But she'd mostly been thinking—about Gage, about herself, and about if they'd ever fit together as a family. Not The Family, Inc., but a homespun, traditional one. "I didn't mean to worry anyone."

"We weren't worried. But I did start to wonder if I'd made a mistake by bringing you to America, Irish."

She stared at Jonas. "Why?"

He waved her to the porch swing, and she sat, mystified.

"Listen, Chelsea." Jonas settled his gaze on her. "Remember when you agreed to be my fiancée, so I wouldn't have to come home alone and face Sabrina being pregnant and married to someone else?"

She laughed. "It was fun, Jonas. I enjoyed watching you turn yourself into an emotional pretzel once you realized she was pregnant with *your* child."

He smiled back at her. "But I always felt bad that once our charade was over, you had no one. I felt like I brought you here and then left you to fend for yourself."

"Jonas, I prefer fending for myself. Thanks. You gave me what I wanted, which was to travel with Mum, and then when I realized she seemed in better health, you gave me a job. Don't feel bad for me. I'm in a good place these days, I really am."

"Where does that leave you and Gage?"

"I don't know if we're anywhere."

"You're in love with him."

She smiled. "Not too hard to figure out, even for you, Callahan."

"Yeah, but I have backup to help me figure things out. Sabrina clued me in, and then Cat mentioned her father had proposed. And that you'd left the ring." He chuckled. "Cat heard Fiona and Moira discussing the magic wedding dress that all the Callahan women wore to their weddings, and she wanted to know whether, if you just tried it on, that might help you want to be a bride. She has a pretty agile mind."

"Magic wedding dress?" Chelsea shook her head. "I remember you didn't think you'd ever get Sabrina in the fabled dress."

"But I did," he said cheerfully, "and I tell myself with justifiable pride that Sabrina's never looked back."

"I don't believe much in fairy tales and fables," Chelsea stated.

"You can't live at Rancho Diablo and not believe in magic. That would be like saying the Diablo mustangs aren't real. Some things just can't be explained, you know. Anyway, you should always have room in your life for magic. Otherwise, what would we be? Just unfortunate humans slogging along on our unenlightened paths."

"I'll let you know when the spirit has moved me, Jonas."

He laughed. "You do believe in miraculous phenomena. Isn't Ireland the home of saints who send snakes running?" Jonas looked at her, his gaze bright with mischief. "Anyway, you have time to decompress from the storm of Shakespearean effort you've been weathering. Gage isn't here."

Her heart sank a little. But if Cat was here, then Gage wouldn't be far away for long. "You send him off on another wild-goose chase?"

"I resent you referring to my beautiful peacocks as geese." Jonas's face was scrunched in pretend disgust. "When the sun comes out and I let my babies out for the day, you'll be very surprised how much those peacocks seem like the beautiful greeters of Rancho Diablo."

"I'm glad you're pleased with them," Chelsea said wryly.

"Gage has gone to see Leslie," Jonas said.

"Cat's mom?" Chelsea blinked. "Did something happen?"

"He decided it was time to let her know that Cat would be staying here, with him." Jonas smiled. "I really admire a man who takes on fathering duties with such enthusiasm."

"Yes," Chelsea murmured. "It's a very appealing thing about Gage."

"Among others. Like what a hard worker he is."

Chelsea nodded, hardly realizing she was.

"And the ladies think he's quite a looker," Jonas continued.

"That's enough, Jonas," Chelsea said. "You don't have to sell him to me. I'm already sold."

"Good. When he and Sam get back—"

"Sam?"

Jonas shrugged. "Sam doesn't specialize in family law, but it never hurts to have a legal beagle along. At least that's what we told Gage. We really wanted to keep him from doing Larry mischief if the money issue were to arise again. We felt certain it might, and Sam is ever up for a troubleshoot, being that he's a meathead. Helluva smart meathead, but you get my drift. Sam's never said no to a little hand-to-hand discussion and arm-twisting."

"Oh," Chelsea said. "I keep forgetting about the Larry-money angle."

"Forgetting about money? Never do that." Jonas grinned. "You wouldn't want to marry a poor man."

"I would," Chelsea said with some heat. "I liked Gage just the way he was when I met him, when I thought he was broke and honest and the sexiest man I'd ever met." She could tell she'd surprised Jonas with her admission, but every word she'd spoken was true. "I liked him just the way I thought he was."

"So that's why you turned down his marriage proposal?"

She nodded. "The whole Family, Inc., thing was hard for me to be comfortable with. They operate differently there, and it felt like when we were in Hell's Colony, Gage began to change into something else. His family aren't bad people, you know. They just have different priorities than what I've experienced." She looked at Jonas. "I like Gage when he's a working man, a father, a friend. Not a corporate suit."

Jonas laughed. "Come on. Let's go inside. I hear the ladies calling that it's time for dessert."

"When do you expect Gage back?" Chelsea asked.

"Don't ask me," Jonas said, "I'm just the ever-ready listening ear around here."

"Poor thing," Chelsea said. "And yet I remember when you wheezed like an old car engine because you couldn't have the woman you loved."

He laughed, and held the door open for her. "Welcome home, Irish. Welcome home."

THE THING ABOUT BEING at Rancho Diablo was that it felt like home. Chelsea sat by her mother and Cat and watched all the little children enjoy spinning sparklers outside. Stars twinkled overhead in the New Mexico sky, a warm breeze barely blew—just enough to cool them—and Chelsea breathed it all in, feeling as if she'd finally come home.

Almost.

"I'm nervous," Chelsea told her mother, when Cat ran off to help oversee the older toddlers with the sparklers. "What if Gage can't convince Leslie that Cat is better off with him?"

Moira patted her on the arm. "Everything will work out for the best."

"I hope so." She knew how much Cat loved it here. The "face jewelry" was gone, and so were the dark clothes. Moira and Fiona had taken Cat shopping for some late summer clothes that could be used for school. Cat's hair was starting to take on the uneven look of growing-out-and-needs-to-be-shaped. She'd even mentioned maybe having it trimmed so it wouldn't be lopsided when she started school. It seemed to Chelsea that Cat had relaxed, felt less of a need to make a statement. "I can't imagine Gage without her."

Moira smiled. "I wish you could have seen them together the past few weeks. They were inseparable. Gage has got Cat riding a horse, says he's going to teach her to rope. Remember when we took her to that rodeo, and she didn't want to go?" Moira laughed. "Well, she's all about rodeo now, and horses, especially now that she's seen all the pictures of the Callahan brothers riding, and the buckles they won. Not to mention that since her father loves it, she does, too. Anything to be with her dad."

"That is truly a happy ending, isn't it?" Chelsea said. It felt so right, the way everything was turning out, like it had always been meant to be, the past softly segueing to the future in the best of ways.

She hoped there was a happy ending for her, too. Had she given up her best chance for that happiness by turning Gage down? It had been her fears speaking, just as Blanche and Shinny had pointed out so gently.

Of course, this was why she'd come to Rancho Diablo, to find her own happy ending. She'd do everything she could to show Gage how much she loved him, what a wonderful man she'd be so lucky to have—if he still wanted her.

If only.

The children squealed when sudden fireworks lit the dark velvet sky. Beautiful colors and bright white made magical patterns, and a diamond-white moon hung flat against the darkness. It was breathtakingly lovely, and Chelsea watched the fireworks with the same joy as the transfixed children. A small plane went overhead, not too far from the fireworks.

"How unusual," Moira said. "I only saw planes with banners attached to them when we went to Florida last summer, Chelsea."

It *was* a strange thing to see out here. Chelsea looked up, trying to read what the sign said. The Callahan women all watched the plane, but suddenly, settled their gazes on her with knowing smiles.

Marry me, Chelsea. I love you were the red-printed words on the banner.

"Oh," Chelsea said, and her mother hugged her, and all the Callahan women laughed. And suddenly, she realized that everyone had been in on the "big moment."

"Dad was afraid he didn't do the proposal right the first time," Cat said, bounding over to sit next to her. "He thought he better do something a bit more spectacular to seal the deal."

Chelsea laughed, hugging Cat joyously. "This is certainly spectacular!"

"Look," Cat said, "Rafe's flying over again, just in case you missed the sign the first time, I guess."

Chelsea smiled, tears in her eyes as she looked up. "I didn't miss the sign. I wouldn't miss it for anything."

"Good," Gage said, sitting down next to them on the porch, "because I'd hate to send Rafe back up there."

Chelsea turned to face him, with Cat in between. She smiled, feeling as if the whole world melted away except for them. "I thought you were gone."

"I was. Sam and I were already on the road when Jonas called to let me know you were here." Gage shrugged, his eyes twinkling. "We'd had this planned a while ago, but I wasn't certain when the best time to do it was. Wasn't sure how you felt about me. Then Jonas called and said I'd best strike while the iron was hot, because you'd about taken his head off when he mentioned that you wouldn't want to marry a man with no money. Jonas figured that was a positive indicator, and that it was time to send up the proposal."

Gage pulled out her ring, the ring she'd wished she hadn't had to leave behind, when she hadn't known that she loved him too much to give him up, no matter what. Chelsea put her hand in his and he slipped the ring on her finger, where the three stunning oval diamonds seemed to sparkle with happiness.

Chelsea couldn't stop smiling. "Jonas is right. It's a wonderful time to get a proposal. And the answer is definitely yes, Gage. I'll marry you." She hugged Cat and Gage to her, the three of them together as one, their own family.

"This is awesome!" Cat exclaimed, jumping up. "You're going to be my stepmother. I can't wait to tell Nana Moira she's going to be my grandma! Yay, Dad!" She ran off to share the good news, and Chelsea realized that the Callahan clan had melted away toward the corrals to give them some privacy.

"I was worried you wouldn't come," Gage whispered against her hair. "I knew I had to wait for you to make up your mind, and it was the hardest thing I ever did."

She kissed him, her lips lingering against his. "You weren't really worried."

"I was. Cat was after me every day," he said, kissing her lightly. "She kept telling me I needed a better proposal. That every woman wants her proposal to be something out of a fairy tale."

"This is almost perfect." Chelsea leaned against him, feeling his strength and his hard shoulders and chest, longing for him.

"Tell me what would make it perfect," Gage murmured against her temple.

"That you worked things out, and Cat will be with us," Chelsea said, squeezing her eyes closed.

She felt him smile, and he turned her face to his. "The three of us are a family," Gage said. "Wherever we are, we're together."

It *was* perfect, just as Chelsea had known it would be. Her heart soaring, she kissed him, wanting him to know that she was the happiest woman in the world. "Thank you," she said, and he held her tight. And as they looked into the star-studded sky, Chelsea was almost certain she could hear the Callahans' mystical Diablos running in the canyons.

And maybe they were.

Epilogue

The magic wedding dress fit—as everyone said it would—and Chelsea did see the man of her dreams when she put it on. Of course, she'd already seen him, on a hot day in June when he'd come into her life.

"You look lovely, daughter," Moira said, helping Chelsea place the veil on her red hair, which had been pinned up for this special day in a lovely updo.

"You are pretty, Chelsea," Cat agreed. She'd allowed her aunt to take her to the hair salon and get "the works." For her father's wedding day, Cat looked so pretty, Chelsea thought. Her new daughter's locks were evened up nicely. She looked so happy now, all the time, and that happiness radiated from her, lighting the room when she walked in. No, not walked—Cat never walked. She scampered, she scrambled. She chased babies with abandon, and she wasn't a bad storyteller, either. *Just like my mum. A born storyteller.* And she read to the kids constantly, when she wasn't riding with Gage.

Chelsea loved the simple magic of their new family. "I'm so happy. I thought I was happy before, Mum, when it was just me and you. But now…"

"Now you're going to be a wife and a mother, *and* a daughter." Moira smiled. "I'm so happy for you. All mothers have dreams for their children, and I can honestly say that mine have all come true for you."

Chelsea hugged her, and then held Cat close to her for a long moment. "Thank you, Mum, for everything you've done for me."

"'Twasn't that way," Moira said. "We took care of each other."

"Is there room for Jess and me?" Fiona asked, coming to join them in the room off the main library at Rancho Diablo. "Or is this a special mom-daughter-daughter time only?"

"Come in, girls," Moira said to Gage's cousin, who lived at Rancho Diablo, and the redoubtable Callahan aunt. "Look at my daughter, old friend, and tell me what you see."

"I see a woman in love," Fiona said gleefully. "And I just spied a man who's more in love and chomping at the bit to have you at the altar. Is there anything better than a July wedding?"

Jonas's wife, Sabrina, came into the room, smiling when she saw Chelsea. "Gage is going to have heart failure when he sees you," she told her. "He may not be able to wait for the *I dos*."

Chelsea laughed. "He won't have to wait long. I'm a legal resident, and now I'm ready to be a legal, eager wife."

Sabrina smiled. "You know my husband is taking full credit for you and Gage getting together? You'd think he was a matchmaking service, the way he's bragging."

Chelsea shook her head. "He's just happy because he's already got his bride. Thank you so much for agreeing to be my maid of honor."

Sabrina hugged her. "Wouldn't have missed it for the world. And your new sister-in-law, Kendall, wants to come in to see you."

"Good." Chelsea smiled at Cat. "Will you go get your aunt, sweetie?"

The girl raced off with a grin.

"She looks darling," Sabrina said. "That dress you helped her choose is perfect."

"It was wonderful shopping with her." Chelsea loved Cat, was thrilled she was going to be staying with her and Gage most of the time. Some holidays and summers Cat would be with Leslie—for as long as she wanted to be. Gage had made certain that his daughter didn't have to spend any more time than necessary in a place where she wasn't comfortable. "She's so easy to shop for." Picking out the full-length mint gown and the diamante barrettes had been so much fun. Cat looked like a teenager who was happy with her life, and it was good to see.

"Hi, everyone," Kendall said, walking into the room in a stunning white suit and silver high heels. She looked like a model, and Chelsea marveled that she and Gage were siblings. “Chelsea, you’re going to drop my brother to his knees in that dress. I hope I look that beautiful if I ever get married.”

“You will, Aunt Kendall,” Cat said quickly.

“We’ll see,” Kendall said, carefully hugging Chelsea so she wouldn’t crush the beautiful magic wedding dress. “I’m so glad you’re part of our family. And thank you for making my brother so happy. I haven’t seen him this happy in a long time.”

Chelsea hugged her back, glad they were going to be sisters. “Gage is a special guy.”

“He’s lucky to have you.”

“It might be your turn next, Aunt Kendall,” Cat interjected.

She smiled. “I wouldn’t bet the farm on it, sweetheart. But thanks for the vote of confidence.”

Chelsea thought that, lovely as she was, Kendall might find a man sooner than she thought. *After all, I never dreamed I’d find my prince here in New Mexico. But I’m so glad I did. No matter where we make our home, we’ll always be a family together. Always.*

“I hear the bride music, Chelsea,” Cat said. “We’d better go. We don’t want Dad to worry. He worries a lot, you know.”

The four women in the room smiled at her protectiveness of her father.

“The next time I hug you, you’ll be a wife,” Moira said, clasping Chelsea to her. “I might be losing you, in a way, but somehow I feel that I’m getting so much more. Thank you for being such a good daughter. You were my greatest blessing."

"I love you, Mum," Chelsea said. "If it wasn't for you, I wouldn't be the luckiest woman in the world. Thank you so much for all you've done for me."

They embraced one last time, and then Chelsea kissed her mum. Moira settled Chelsea's veil, and Sabrina picked up the train of the splendid magic wedding dress. Chelsea drew a deep breath. The moment was real, and it was more than she'd ever dreamed of. Smiling with joy, she reached for her bouquet. "Lead the way, Cat. Let's go get our cowboy."

THE WEDDING DAY WAS fairy-tale perfect, with not a cloud in the sky. Guests sat in white chairs draped with mint and pink ribbons; beside a punch bowl stood a three-tier wedding cake, the groom and bride on top holding tiny American flags to celebrate Chelsea's immigration status. Nearby, the peacocks fanned their spectacular tails, having decided in the past few weeks that Rancho Diablo suited them very well.

Cat tossed white rose petals on the ground as she walked, proud to have a role in the big day. Gage grinned, thinking his daughter was just about the best kid he could ever have had. Sabrina followed in a mint gown almost identical to Cat's, and beside him, best man Jonas puffed up like a proud rooster.

Gage could see Shinny and Blanche sitting together, smiling like proud parents, and Fiona sat near Moira, both women wearing pink, and huge grins of delight.

Moira wore a corsage of white roses he'd given her earlier, to match the bouquet Chelsea carried and the rose petals Cat had strewn in the aisle.

He held his breath, waiting for a first glimpse of his bride. Suddenly, his heart jumped as he saw Chelsea walking down the aisle on Shaman's arm—a surprise she and Kendall had obviously kept from him until this moment—and his heart nearly burst with love.

Chelsea was beautiful. He'd always known she was a special woman, with a kind heart, but today she was stunning in the magic wedding dress. He was surprised that he could fall more in love with her than he already was, but he could feel himself falling deeper, and was willing to let himself go without reserve.

"Hello, brother," he said to Shaman. "Good to see you. Real good." Shaman looked tall and strong—and pleased to be sharing this moment with him. He handed Chelsea over to Gage with a grin.

"Lucky guy," he said.

"Don't I know it," Gage replied.

His brother stepped back beside Jonas, leaving Chelsea all to Gage, a moment he'd hoped for almost since he'd met her.

"You're beautiful," he told her. "I don't know how I got you."

"I'll tell you how later," she said, her eyes sparkling up at him. "I love you."

"I love you, too. And I plan to tell you that about every hour on our honeymoon."

She looked at him, surprised. "Honeymoon?"

"No marriage is complete without a rotating bed in a Peacock Cabin, is it?"

Chelsea smiled. "Sounds good to me."

He took her hand in his. "Australia, love. We're going to Australia for the honeymoon. I don't know if they have rotating beds, but I figure we'll be just as happy on the Gold Coast. How's that for adventure?"

"Perfectly fabulous," Chelsea said, her eyes shining. "Thank you, Gage. It's a wonderful gift." She leaned up to kiss him, her heart in her eyes. "I wonder how you'd feel about working on a little sister or brother for Cat while we're on the Gold Coast?"

Gage laughed. "I'd feel great about that. Really great."

He could see his adventurous bride was thrilled, which was how he hoped she'd always feel about being with him. He brushed her hand against his lips, about to tell her that he had never known love the way she made him feel it. But then she kissed him again, and he knew she already knew all the feelings in his heart.

The guests applauded, delighted by the love they were witnessing, and Gage held his daughter and his Irish lady, letting the moment wash over them on the beautiful New Mexico day. Then they stepped up to the altar, and as the minister began the wedding ceremony, Gage saw many blessings to come with his new family.

This was the dream of a renegade, though maybe he'd never known it before. And the past had been but the prologue to the best part of his life. Gage knew it now beyond a shadow of a doubt.

Being a family was the most amazing magic of all. And he was a renegade no more.

* * * * *

There's one more bonus Callahan Cowboys story!
Shaman Phillips is about to meet his match
with none other than Tempest Thornbury!
Watch for THE COWBOY SOLDIER'S SONS,
coming September 2012 only from
Harlequin American Romance.

Texas Lullaby

Chapter One

"What doesn't kill a man makes him stronger"
—Josiah Morgan's parting advice to his teen-age sons when they walked out of his life.

The four Morgan brothers shared an unspoken belief, if nothing else: stubbornness equaled strength. A man who didn't have *stubborn* etched into his bones hadn't yet grown into big boots.

Some people used the word *jackasses* to describe the family of four brothers, but the Morgans preferred to think of themselves as independent loners. It was common for them to be approached by women who wanted to relieve their "loneliness." The Morgans had no problem breaking with their routine for beautiful women bent on their relief.

Fortunately, most people in Union Junction, Texas, understood that a solitary way of life was a good thing, if it was lived by choice. The Morgan brothers were moving to the area not by choice, but for two different reasons. The first was continued solitude, which had been confirmed by some family acquaintances, the

Jeffersons. Men after their own heart, the Jeffersons weren't loners, but they hadn't exactly been hanging out in bars every night sobbing about their sad lives before they'd all found the religion of love. They appreciated the need to be left the hell alone.

Yet the need for peace and quiet was just a cover for the real reason Gabriel Morgan had come home. This was about money. He stared at the two-story sprawling farmhouse set amongst native pecan trees and shouldered by farmland. For this house, this land, the Morgans were called to relocate to the Morgan Ranch near Union Junction. The first thing the brothers had all agreed on in years was that none of them was too happy about finding themselves the keeper of a large ranch. Five thousand acres as well as livestock—what the hell were they supposed to do with it? This was Pop's place. Light-footed Pop and his far-flung dreams, buying houses and land like he was buying up parts of earth to keep him alive and vital.

Pop was the true jackass.

Selling the ranch had been the first thing on Gabriel's mind, and he was pretty certain his brothers had the same idea. But no, Pop was too wily for that. Knowing full well his four sons weren't close, he'd come up with a brilliant plan to stick them all under one roof on acres and acres of loneliness where no one could witness the fireworks.

Pop was in Europe right now, in a new stone castle he'd bought in Pzenas, no doubt laughing his ass off at what he'd wrought. Oh, he couldn't buy just any old French countryside farmhouse—he'd bought an eighteen-hundreds Templar's commandery for a cool four million. It wasn't in the best of shape but just his style, he'd told his sons in the letters they'd each received outlining his wishes. Three floors, ten bedrooms, eight baths, plenty of room should they all ever decide to visit. It even had its own chapel, and he'd be in that chapel praying for them every day.

Gabriel doubted the prayers would help. Pop would be praying for family harmony, and truthfully, some growth in the family tree, some tiny feet to run on the floors of the stone castle, sweet angelic voices to learn how to say Grandpop in French. *Grand-père.*

Like hell. Family expansion wasn't on Gabriel's mind. He was looking for peace and quiet in this rural town, and he was going to get it. He'd live in the house just as his father had decreed, for the year he'd specified, take his part of the bribe money—money was always involved with Pop—and leave no different than he was today. Except he'd be a million dollars richer.

Easy pickings.

Gabriel would take the money. As for the unspoken part of the deal… The pleasure of putting one over on his father, spitting in his eye, so to speak, would be a roundabout kick from one jackass to another. Pop hadn't said his sons had to be close-bonded Templar knights; he'd just stated they had to live in the house for a year. Like a family.

He could do that—if for no other reason than to show the old man he hadn't fazed Gabriel in the least.

"Hi!"

He turned to see a woman waving to him from a car

window. She parked, got out and handed him a freshly baked cherry pie.

"Welcome to Union Junction, stranger." Her blue eyes gleamed at him; her blond hair swung in a braid. "My name's Mimi Jefferson. I'm from the Double M ranch, once known as Malfunction Junction. I'm Mason's wife. And also the sheriff."

"Hello, Mimi." He'd met Mason months ago through Pop's business dealings, and Mason's wonderful wife had often been mentioned. "Thanks for the pie."

"No problem." She glanced at the farmhouse. "So what do you think of it? Hasn't changed much since you were last here."

Pop had made some additions to the house, rendering it more sprawling than Gabriel thought necessary. He'd added more acreage, too, but that was his dad's agenda. Always the grand visionary. "I haven't been inside."

She smiled. "It needs work."

That he could see from the outside. "I noticed."

"Should keep you real busy."

He nodded. "Seems that was my dad's plan."

She laughed. "Your father fit in real well here in Union Junction. I'm sure you will, too."

He didn't need to, wouldn't be here long enough to put down deep roots.

"By the way, I believe the ladies will be stopping by with some other goodies. We figured your dad left the fridge pretty empty when he went to France."

"The ladies?"

"You'll see." With a cryptic smile, she got into the

truck. "I'll tell Mason you'll be by to see him when you've settled in."

That meant it was time to head into the old hacienda of dread and bar the door. He had no desire to be the target of gray-haired, well-meaning church ladies toting fried chicken. "Thanks again for the pie."

She waved at him and drove off. Gabriel dug into his pocket for the key marked Number Four—he supposed that was because he was the fourth son or maybe because his father had four keys made—and headed toward the wraparound porch. It groaned under his weight, protesting his presence.

Then he heard a sound, like the growing din of a schoolyard at recess. As a code breaker for the Marines, he was tuned to hear the slightest bit of noise, and could even decipher murmured language. But what assaulted his ears wasn't trying to be secretive in any way. He watched as ten vehicles pulled into the graveled drive. His jaw tensed as approximately twenty women and children hopped out of the cars and trucks, each bearing a sack. Not just a covered dish or salad bowl, but a bag, clearly destined for him.

He was going to go crazy—and get fat in the process.

"We're the welcoming committee." A pretty blonde smiled at him as she approached the porch. "Don't be scared."

She'd nailed his emotion.

"I'm Laura Adams," she said. "These ladies—most of us—are from the hair salon, bakery, et cetera, in town. We formed the Union Junction Welcoming Committee some time ago after we received such a warm greeting when we arrived in this town. Many of us weren't raised in Union Junction. Our turn to do a good deed, you might say."

Except he didn't want the deed done to *him.* She smelled nice, though. Her voice was soft and pleasant and he liked the delicate frosting of freckles across her nose and cheeks. Big blue eyes gazed at him with a warmth he couldn't return at the moment.

The porch shook under his feet with the sound of more approaching women. He hadn't taken his eyes off Laura, for reasons he couldn't quite explain to himself. She opened her pretty pink lips to say more, introduce all her gift-bearing friends, when suddenly something wrapped itself around his thigh.

Glancing down, he saw a tiny towhead comfortably smiling up at him. "Daddy," she said, hugging his leg for all she was worth. "Daddy."

For the first time in his life, including the time he'd temporarily lost part of his hearing from an underwater mine explosion near a sub he'd been monitoring, he felt panic. But the women laughed, and Laura didn't seem embarrassed as she disengaged her daughter from his leg.

"Oh, sweetie, he might be a daddy, or he will be one day. Can you say Mr. Morgan?"

The child smiled at him beatifically, completely convinced that the world was a wonderful, happy place. "Morgan," she said softly.

So he'd be Morgan, just like Pop. He could remember people yelling his father's name, cursing his father's name, cheering his father's name. It was always something along the lines of either "Morgan, you jackass!" or "Morgan, you old dog!"

It didn't feel as bad as he thought it might. Gabriel wondered where the child's father was, and then decided it was none of his business. "I should invite you in," he said reluctantly to the gathering at large, his gaze on Laura. He could tell by their instant smiles that being invited in was exactly what they wanted. "Too hot in June to keep ladies on the porch. We can all see the new place at the same time and make some introductions."

"You haven't been inside your home yet?" Laura asked. "Mimi said she thought you might have arrived later than you planned."

"Tell me something," he said as he worked at the lock on the front door. The lock obviously hadn't been used in a long time and didn't want to move. "I'd heard Union Junction was great for peace and quiet. Is this one of those places where everybody knows everybody's business?"

That made everyone laugh. Not him—for Gabriel it was a serious question.

"Yes," Laura said. "That's one of the best parts of our town. Everyone cares about everybody."

Great. The lock finally gave in to his impatient twisting of Key Number Four and he swung the door open. The first thing he realized was how hot the house was—like an oven.

The smell was the next thing to register. Musty, unused, closed-up. The ladies peered around his shoulders to the dark interior.

"Girls, we've got our work cut out for us," an older lady pronounced.

"That won't be necessary," Gabriel said as they brushed past him. Laura smiled at him, swinging her grocery sack to the opposite hip and taking her daughter's hand in hers.

"It's necessary," she said. "They can clean this place so fast it'll make your head spin. Besides, we've seen worse. Not much worse, of course. But your father's been gone a long time. Almost six months." She smiled kindly. "Frankly, we expected you a lot sooner."

"I wasn't in a hurry to get here." Neither were any of his brothers. During their curt email transmissions, exchanged since their father's letter had been delivered to them, Dane had said he might swing by in January if he'd finished with his Texas Ranger duties by then, Pete said he might make it by February—depending upon the secret agent assignments he couldn't discuss—and Jack hadn't answered at all. Jack was the least likely of them all to give a damn about Pop, the ranch, or a million dollars.

His chicken brothers were making excuses, putting off the inevitable—except for Jack, who really was the wild card.

"Well, we're glad you're here now." She didn't seem to notice his grimness as she set her grocery sack on the counter. "Hope you like chicken, baby peas and rice."

"You don't have to do that." He heard the sound of

a vacuum start up somewhere in the house, and windows opening. The fragrance of lemon oil began to waft from one of the rooms. The little girl clung to her mom, her eyes watching Gabriel's every move. "Really, I'm not hungry, and your little girl probably needs to be at home in bed." It was six o'clock—what time did children go to bed, anyway? He and his brothers had a strict bedtime of nine o'clock when they were kids, which they'd always ignored. Pop never came up the stairs to check on them, and they used a tree branch outside the house to cheat their curfew. Then one year, Pop sawed off the limb, claiming the old live oak was too close to the roof. They devised a rope ladder which they flung out on grappling hooks whenever they had a yen to meet up with girls or camp in the woods.

Or watch Jack practice at the forbidden rodeo in the fields lit only by the moon.

"Oh, Penny's fine. Don't worry about her. You're always happy, aren't you, Penny?"

Penny beamed at Gabriel. "Morgan," she murmured in a small child's breathy recitation. He felt his heart flip over in his chest as he returned the child's gaze. *Heartburn. I'm getting heartburn at the age of twenty-six.*

"I have a smaller version of Penny who is being watched for me right now." Laura smiled proudly as she unloaded the grocery sacks the ladies had loaded onto the kitchen counter. "Perrin is nine months old, and looks just like his father. You love your baby brother, don't you, Penny?" She looked down at her child, who nodded, though she didn't break her stare from Gabriel.

Gabriel felt his heart sink strangely in his chest. This woman was married, apparently happily so.

He was an idiot, and probably horny. The house was swarming with women and he had to get the preliminary hots for a married mom.

Good thing his yen was in the early stages—one pretty face could replace another easily enough. "Listen, I don't want to be rude, but I just got in. I appreciate you and your friends trying to help, but—"

"But you would rather be alone."

He nodded.

"I understand." She flicked the oven on Warm and slid the casserole inside. "I would, too, if I was you."

She knew nothing about him. He decided a reply wasn't needed.

"You know, I really liked your father," she said, hesitating. She stared at him with eyes he felt tugging at his desire. "I hated to see Mr. Morgan go."

"Josiah," he murmured.

"I didn't call him by his first name."

He shrugged. "You didn't know him too well, then."

"Because I didn't call him by his name or because I liked him?"

He looked at her, thinking, *Both, lady.*

"Mr. Morgan was fond of my children."

His radar went on alert. Here came the your-father-wants-you-to-settle-down chorus. He steeled himself.

She ran a gentle hand through Penny's long fine

hair. "Of course, he dreamed of having his own grandchildren."

Gabriel frowned. That topic was none of her business. His family was too raw a subject for him to discuss with a stranger.

"You're going to hear this sooner or later." She gazed at him suddenly with clear, determined focus. "I'd rather you hear it from me."

He shrugged. "I'm listening." He reminded himself that whatever she had to say didn't matter to him. What Pop had meant to the town of Union Junction was not his concern.

"Your father put a hundred thousand dollars into a trust for my children."

She'd caught his attention. Not because of the amount, but because Pop had to have lost his mind to have gone that soft. Pop was as miserly as he was stubborn, even complaining over church donations. All he was interested in was himself.

Or at least that had been the Pop of Gabriel's youth.

Truthfully, it astonished him that this tiny woman had the nerve to tell him she'd managed to wheedle money out of his father. Maybe Pop had finally begun to crack, all the years of selfishness taking their toll. More importantly, Laura was obviously the kind of woman with whom Gabriel should exercise great distance and caution. "Congratulations," he finally said, trying not to smirk. "A hundred grand is a nice chunk of change."

"Each."

He stared at her. "Each?"

"Each child got their own trust. Penny and Perrin both received a hundred thousand dollars. Your father said it wasn't a lot, but he wanted them to have something later in their lives. He doesn't want them to know about his gift, though, not until they're grown up." She smiled, and it seemed to Gabriel that her expression was sad. "They won't even remember him, then."

He had no idea what the hell to say to this woman. He was suspicious. He was dumbstruck. Perhaps he was even a little envious that she'd gained some type of affection in his father's heart, when he and his brothers had struggled for years and had received none.

She picked up Penny. "I just thought you should know."

He watched as she turned, heading for the front door. Over her mother's shoulder, Penny watched him with wistful eyes. What had been the relationship between Pop and Laura that such an astonishing gift would be given to her kids?

He could remember a cold, wet night in Poland, hunched behind a snowbank, listening to a radio he'd held with frozen fingers to pick up conversation in a bedroom in Gdan′sk. He'd retrieved the information he'd needed, turned it in and got cleared to return home. Chilled, he'd called his father, thinking maybe his soul could use a good thawing and their relationship a delayed shot of warmth. He was young, idealistic, mostly broke, lonely. Damned cold in every area of his life.

He needed a bus ticket from the base, he'd told his

father. The military would get him stateside, but he only had a few zloty in his pocket.

Pop had told him not to come crying to him for money. He said the greatest gift he could ever give him was the knowledge of how to stand on his own two feet.

That was ten years ago, and he could still hear the sound of the receiver slamming in his ear. He followed behind Laura, catching up to open the front door for her. "You must have meant a lot to my father."

She turned, slowly, her gaze meeting his, questioning. In a split second, she got the gist of his unspoken assumption. "Your reputation preceded you," she said softly. "You really are a jackass."

The door slammed behind her. Gabriel nodded to himself, silently agreeing with her assessment. Then he went to shoo his well-meaning friends out of the house he didn't want.

Chapter Two

Laura returned to her house, steaming. She put Penny down on the sofa and went to find Mimi, whom she could hear quietly singing to Perrin in the back of the house. "Thank you for watching my little man, Mimi." She looked down into the crib at her baby, and all the tension flowed from her.

Together they walked from the nursery. "So what did you think of Gabriel Morgan?" Mimi asked.

"Not much. He thinks I sucked up to his father to weasel money out of him." Laura shrugged her shoulders. "He's everything Mr. Morgan said he was. Cocky, brash, annoying."

Mimi laughed. "Not a man's best qualities. Wasn't he nice at all? He just seemed sort of shy to me."

Laura went to fix them both an iced tea. "I suppose I compare every man to my husband." Her gaze was reluctantly drawn to the framed, fingerprint-covered photo of Dave. Penny liked to look at the picture of her father, enjoyed hearing stories about him.

Dave had been such a kind man. Warm. Funny. Easy to talk to. Nothing like the man she'd met today.

Laura wrinkled her nose and tried not to think so tears wouldn't spring into her eyes. Heaven only knew Dave had his moments; he was no angel. They'd had their spats. But he'd been her first love and that counted for so much. It had been such a shock to lose him.

At least she had his children.

"I suppose it would be hard for me not to compare every man to Mason." Mimi smiled. "No one would measure up."

Laura nodded, appreciating her friend's understanding.

"Some would say there never was a tougher nut to crack than Mason Jefferson."

"Really?" Laura found that hard to believe. Mason loved his wife, loved his kids. Was always looking at Mimi, or holding her hand.

"Suffice it to say he was really difficult to get to the altar. Sometimes I even wondered why I wanted him there." Mimi laughed. "Talk about stubborn and hard to get along with."

"Dave was easy," Laura murmured. "Don't get me wrong, I'm not looking to replace Dave in my life at all. But I was hoping for a connection with Gabriel, something like the one I'd had with his father. I miss the old gentleman." She smiled sadly at Mimi. "I can't understand why his boys don't want to be close with him."

"Mr. Morgan was a different person with us than he was with his sons. They say people show themselves differently to everyone, and we probably saw his best side. He was a good man."

"Obviously his sons believe they understand him

better, and they probably do." She and Mimi moved to the kitchen table. Penny came into the kitchen and crawled into her mother's lap. Laura handed her a vanilla wafer from a box left out on the table since yesterday. "I swear I do keep house. We don't always have food left out from the day before." She glanced at the sink where the pots were piled up from making the welcome meal for Gabriel.

"Try living in a house where grown men come and go all the time. They make a bigger mess than the kids." Mimi sipped her tea. "I'll help you clean it up in a bit."

Laura shook her head, appreciating the offer but not wanting the help. She didn't mind washing dishes. It was soothing to have her hands in warm dishwater, and somehow comforting to submerge dirty dishes in suds and then pull them gleaming from the water. "I didn't want him to misunderstand my relationship with his father."

Mimi nodded. "Men don't always temper their thoughts before they speak. Anyway, nobody tells Josiah Morgan what to do. Gabriel knows that."

Gabriel, too, struck Laura as the kind of man willing to fight any battle life threw at him.

"Besides, it's really none of Gabriel's business."

That was also true. She'd only told him about his father's gift to her children because she wanted him to know up front. "Okay, I give up on being mad. It's a waste of time."

Mimi got up from the table. "Let's wash these dishes."

"No, you go on home to your family. You've done enough for me, Mimi. I really appreciate you watching Perrin so he could nap."

"Did the doctor say how long it would take for the medicine to do some good?"

Perrin had colic, long bouts at night that worried Laura. Someone had suggested that the colic was stress-induced, and that Perrin was sensing his mother's sadness. It had been a shock when Dave had died, and she certainly had grieved—was still grieving—but it was an additional guilt that she was causing her son's pain. "The doctor said babies sometimes go through colic. The medicine might help, and putting him on a different formula. Or he could grow out of it."

Mimi patted her hand. "I'll come by to see you later at the school."

Laura nodded. "I'd like that."

She closed the door behind Mimi. Penny handed her a vanilla wafer, and for the first time that day, Laura felt content.

ON FRIDAY NIGHT, THREE days later, Gabriel finally drove into the small town of Union Junction. He could see what had drawn his father to this place. For one thing, it looked like a melding of the old West and a Norman Rockwell card. There was a main street where families were enjoying a warm June stroll, ice-cream cones or sodas in hand. A kissing booth sat in front of a bakery. Other booths lined the street in front of various shops.

He glanced at the kissing booth again, caught by a glimpse of blond hair and the long line outside the booth. All the booths had lines, but none as long as the kissing booth, which Gabriel figured was probably appropriate. If he was offered the choice of getting a kiss or throwing rings over a bottle, he'd definitely take the kiss.

"What's going on?" he asked a young cowboy at the back of the line.

"Town fair." The young man grinned at him. "You're Morgan, aren't you?"

He looked at him. "Aren't you too young to be buying kisses?"

He got a laugh for that. "Get in line and spend a buck, Mr. Morgan."

"Why?" He wasn't inclined to participate in the fun of a town fair. He'd just been looking around, trying to figure out why Pop had settled near here, trying to stave off some boredom.

"We're raising money for the elementary school. Need more desks. The town is certainly growing."

"Shouldn't the town be paying for that from taxes or something?"

"We like to do some recreational fundraising, too."

Gabriel reluctantly fell into line. "So who are we kissing?"

"Laura Adams."

"We can't kiss her!" He had to admit the idea was inviting, but he also wanted to jerk the young man out of line—and every other man, too.

The line kept growing behind him.

"Why not?" His companion appeared puzzled.

Gabriel frowned. "She's married. And she's a mom."

The young man laughed. "Mimi Jefferson was working the booth an hour ago. It's the only time any of us can get near Mimi without getting our tails kicked by Mason, so most of us went through twice."

Gabriel's frown deepened.

"It's for a good cause," his new friend said. "Besides which, Laura's not married anymore."

Gabriel's mood lifted slightly. He felt his boots shuffling closer to the booth behind his talkative friend. "She's not?"

"Nah. Her husband died shortly after she gave birth to Perrin." His friend looked at him with surprise. "You should know all this. Your dad loved Laura's kids. Said they were probably the only—"

"I know. I know. Jeez." Gabriel rubbed at his chin, trying to decide if he liked how quickly the line was moving. And the young man was right. The gentlemen were leaving the line to catcalls and whistles and hurrying to the back of the line for another kiss. It was a never-ending kiss line of rascals. "I'm pretty sure I don't belong here."

"No better way to get to know people," his friend said cheerfully. "My name's Buck, by the way."

"Hi, Buck." He absently shook his hand. "I guess kissing's as good a way as any to get to know someone." He supposed he should get to know Laura better since they sort of had a connection.

Buck stared at him. "Hanging out at the town fair being sociable is the way to get to know people."

"That's what I meant." Gabriel noticed there were only five people in front of him now. His heart rate sped up. Should he kiss a woman his father had such a close relationship with? Clearly Pop had depended upon Laura for the sense of family he was lacking. It almost felt like Laura could be a sister.

He heard cheers as Buck laid a smooch on Laura. To Gabriel's relief, it was mercifully short and definitely respectful. *Just good clean fun.*

He found himself standing in front of her booth, staring down at her like a nervous schoolboy. Her blue eyes lit on him with curiosity and nothing else, no lingering resentment over their initial meeting. He noted a distressing jump in his jeans, a problem he hadn't anticipated. But he'd always been a sucker for full lips and fine cheekbones. He could smell a sweet perfume, something like flowers in summer.

Laura was nothing like a sister to him.

He laid a twenty-dollar bill on the booth ledge and walked away.

GABRIEL FOUND A BETTER way to support the local elementary school: drinking keg beer some thoughtful and enterprising young man had set up far away from the kissing booth. Here he was safe. No one bothered him while he sat on a hay bale and people-watched, which was good because he really needed to think. He hadn't expected his father to have a family connection in Union Junction.

He sat up. Surely his father hadn't been trying to

build his own family here? With a ready-made mom and grandchildren? All it would take was one out of the four brothers to meet the lady and her children, to whom some of the Morgan money had been put in trust, and maybe, just maybe, Pop might get that family he'd been itching for?

He wouldn't put it past Pop. Throw in a scheme that required all four brothers to be on the premises for a year, and Pop had a one in four chance of seeing that dream come true.

Gabriel resolved not to fall for it. In fact, he congratulated himself for staying one step ahead of the wily old man. He didn't know for sure that was what Pop had been up to, but with Pop there was always an angle.

He'd be very cautious.

"Hi." Someone soft and warm slid onto the hay bale beside him. Laura didn't smile at him, but her lips were full and plump from being kissed. "Guess you changed your mind about kissing me."

He hung between fear and self-loathing for being a coward. "Seems we should keep our relationship professional."

"Awkward."

"That, too."

"Fine by me."

He slid her a glance. She had nice breasts under her blue-flowered dress—very feminine. A breast man by nature, he was shocked he hadn't taken note of her physical charms before. He'd been completely preoccupied by the swarm of women descending upon him. Although he had to admit that after just thirty minutes of being in his house, it looked and smelled more welcoming than it was ever going to be under his watch. But now he was checking out Laura's attributes, a subconscious flick of his gaze that dismayed him. God, they really were gorgeous. And he hadn't noticed her small, graceful hands before, either.

He felt his temperature rise uncomfortably. "Where are the kids?" Not that he was really interested, but it was best to remind himself that this woman was a mother, not someone to be ogled as if she were single and available for some casual fun.

Which was all he was interested in, for now and for always. *Damn Pop for throwing temptation my way.*

"Penny and Perrin are being held by some ladies from the church. They're spoiled rotten by them." She pointed to an outdoor play area that had been set up. Lots of older ladies were inside, holding infants and playing games with toddlers.

He could see Penny's light hair, just like her mother's, as she sat in a woman's lap and colored in a book. It wasn't difficult to see what had drawn Pop to this gentle fatherless trio.

Who would have thought Pop would have had a protective bone in his body?

"You know, we're not swindlers. Nor did we lure your father into feeling like we were his family."

He turned to Laura. "I shouldn't have implied that there was anything unusual about my father leaving someone outside the family money. I apologize for that."

"Thank you." She raised her chin. "I knew you

could be a difficult person. I choose to ignore that for your father's sake."

He frowned. "I don't want anything for my father's sake."

She shrugged. "He was a nice old man."

"You didn't know him."

"Maybe not as well as you. But maybe better in some ways."

He couldn't argue that. Didn't even want to. "Why?"

"When my husband got sick with cancer, and then died, your father said the least he could do was make certain my kids had college educations. There was a fundraiser here in town to help us...because Dave had no insurance. He was a self-employed carpenter, a dreamer, really." Her voice got soft remembering. "He loved to build homes. The bigger, the better, the more intricate, the better. He did lots of work on your father's place."

This was all beginning to make sense. "Listen, none of this is my business. What my father wants to do with his time and his life is his concern."

She nodded. "I've got to go back to the booth. I've got one more half-hour shift."

He could see the line queuing from here; could count at least twenty men waiting their turn. It looked as if Union Junction had no lack of horny males. "Do you have to kiss all of them?"

"Most of them just kiss my cheek." She smiled. "Only the younger ones try for something more, and a few of the bachelors."

That's what he was afraid of. He thought about his

father, and what a jackass he was. He looked at the line, and the men grinning back toward Laura, obviously impatient for her break to be over.

Out of the corner of his eye, he could see Penny, who'd spotted her mother. Mom and daughter waved at each other, and he could see the longing in Laura's eyes to be with her daughter.

What the hell. He lived to be a jackass. He was just keeping the family name alive.

"All right," he announced loudly, ambling to the front of the line, "I'm buying out Ms. Adams's thirty minutes of time." He placed five one-hundred-dollar bills—all he had on him at the moment besides some stray ones and a couple of twenties—on the booth ledge where everyone could see his money. Grumbling erupted, but also some applause for the donation. He grunted. "Move along, fellows. The booth is closed for this lady."

Chapter Three

Gabriel's buyout of Laura's time in the kissing booth won him lots of winks from the guys and smiles from the ladies as he walked toward his truck. He hadn't said anything to a shocked Laura—just figured he'd introduced himself to the town in the most obvious way he could have for a man who preferred being a loner.

He didn't even know why he'd done it.

Maybe it was Pop, egging him on to be a gentleman, which was a real stinker of a reason. Mason met him at his truck.

"Have a good time?"

Gabriel checked Mason's eyes for laughter but the question seemed sincere. "Seems like everyone is enjoying themselves."

"Good to see you around. We've been wondering what you're going to do with yourself out there if you stay holed up at the ranch."

"I imagine I'll figure out something."

Mason handed him an envelope. "Mimi said to give you this."

"Mimi?" Gabriel scanned the envelope. It had his name written in his father's handwriting, and no postmark.

"Mimi's the law around here." Mason winked at him.

"What does that have to do with me?"

"Your father left that with her. She asked me to deliver it to you. I've been meaning to get out to your place, but here you are, getting to know the good folks of Union Junction."

Again Gabriel studied him for sarcasm. There appeared to be nothing more to the man's intentions than good old friendliness.

"Why didn't Pop just mail this to me? Or courier it like he did before?"

Mason shrugged. "He said something to Mimi along the lines of when and if any of his sons ever got here, they were to have that. Josiah figured you'd be the first, though. In fact, we wagered on it. I owe your father a twenty." He handed Gabriel a twenty-dollar bill.

Gabriel shook his head. "Put it toward the school fund." He looked at the envelope, wondering why his father would have wagered he'd be the first brother to the ranch. "Who'd you bet on?"

Mason laughed. "Jack. He's the unpredictable one. I always go with the dark horse."

"Cost you this time, buddy."

Mason slapped him on the back. "Sure did. Come on out to the Double M when you have time. We'll introduce you to the kids."

"Maybe I will," Gabriel said, knowing he probably wouldn't.

"Congratulations, by the way," Mason said as he walked away.

"For what?"

"For spending that much money for a kiss and then not getting it. Nerves of steel." Mason waved goodbye. Gabriel glanced back down at the envelope, aware that Mason was now giving him a gentle ribbing. "Jackass," he muttered under his breath and got into his truck.

But it was kind of funny coming from Mason, and even Gabriel had to wonder why he'd passed up the chance to kiss Laura after he'd so obviously put his mark on her.

Not that he was going to think about it too hard.

"NOTHING," LAURA TOLD the girls at the Union Junction Beauty Salon. "I'm telling you, there's nothing between us. He didn't kiss me. Gabriel's barely civil to me."

The girls oohed and then giggled. Laura had received a fair bit of teasing and she expected the kissing booth incident had been thoroughly dissected. Privately, Laura wondered what it would have been like to have Gabriel's lips on hers. It had been so long since she'd kissed a man—well, kissed a man as she had Dave. She didn't count those chaste, predictable pecks in the kissing booth. Even the old ladies and the elderly librarian got their turn in the kissing booth, and the men lined up for them just as quickly. The older ladies—particularly teachers—received grandmotherly busses on the cheek from favorite students.

Everyone was anxious to see the elementary school succeed. There was so much goodwill in this town.

Laura was never going to regret moving here with Dave those five years ago. He'd said Union Junction was a growing town, he'd have lots of work, they'd make a family and be happy out away from the big city....

It had worked out just that way for just over five years. Five perfect years.

So she shouldn't really be thinking about what it would have felt like to kiss Gabriel. She was twenty-six, too old for dreamy longings; she was a mom and a widow.

"I bet he kisses great," one of the stylists said to another, and Laura blushed.

"Aren't you curious?" someone asked her.

Laura ran her hand through Penny's hair as she often did. The feel of the corn-silk softness comforted her, as did the powdery smell of Perrin. "No," she murmured, easy with the lie. "Gabriel is not my kind of man."

They all fell quiet, silenced by the uncomfortable position they had put her in.

"She doesn't need to tiptoe around Dave forever," someone finally spoke up bravely. "Honey, we know you loved him, but you're alive and he wouldn't want you being sad forever."

Tears jumped into Laura's eyes. Several ladies came over to hug her. She felt Penny press closer to her leg. "I know."

"All right, then." They all patted her, then went back to their places. "So next time you get a chance to kiss a hunk like Gabriel Morgan, you just grin and bear it if you want to, okay?"

"Maybe," Laura said, smiling as she wiped away the unwanted tears.

"Wish he'd buy out *my* booth," someone said, and everyone laughed, even Laura, although she really didn't think it was funny. What they didn't realize is that Gabriel hadn't wanted to kiss her, hadn't even looked tempted. He'd sort of picked up his father's responsibility—and then he'd headed off.

A woman knew when a man was interested in her. All fairy tales included a kiss—a man knew how to get what he wanted, even in books. Dave had been a gentle pursuer, slow and careful as if she were a fine porcelain doll.

Gabriel owned no such gentle genes. If he wanted a woman, she figured the indication of his desire would be swift, like a roiling wave breaking over a boat at sea, claiming it with powerful intent.

Gabriel pretty much turned to stone every time he laid eyes on her.

Dear Gabriel,

By now you are at the house and are beginning a year of time you no doubt resent like hell. But money talks and though it might not talk very loud to you, I know you'll stick out the year just to prove yourself. This need of yours to be a tough guy living on the edge is exactly what I now need to lean on.

Remember when I bought that extra acreage

and added on to my own hacienda out here? I bought it from a man who was down on his luck, and partly down on his luck thanks to me, which he has discovered. Now don't go getting all high and mighty like I cheated this man out of his birthright, because the man is a scoundrel. And anyway, he needed the money.

The problem is, I bought the land suspecting there was an underground oil source. I had it surveyed without his knowledge. He has since found out I paid for a geological survey of his property and feels cheated.

Fact is, maybe he was and maybe he wasn't. He could have paid for his own damn survey.

The trouble in this is that the man is Laura Adams's father, with whom she has no contact due to the fact that he didn't approve of her marrying a carpenter. Didn't like her husband, felt he wasn't good enough for his only child, which didn't sit well with Laura. He needed her to marry big to save his sorry ass.

You see my predicament. I could sell the man back his land but the price would include a terrific profit which he cannot afford. I gave Laura's children a tiny portion of what is rightfully theirs, since it would have been anyhow, I suppose, though I believe her father would have drunk up the estate. You might say I just hijacked

Penny's and Perrin's inheritance, robbing from the poor to give to the poorer.

Unfortunately, the jackanapes took to threatening me. He really feels cheated by life, and I suppose he has been, but the big dog runs off the little dog and that's life, isn't it? But for the grace of God go I.

Anyway, you'll be seeing him, as he lives to create trouble. But I have faith that you'll smooth everything over in due time, as you were always the responsible one in the family, even though it really chaps your ass that I say that. It just happens to be true.

Pop

"IT DOES CHAP MY ASS." Gabriel forced himself not to shred his father's letter. "It does indeed chap me like you can't even imagine, Pop."

He did not appreciate being appointed the protector of the family fortunes, but even less so the knight of Laura Adams's little brood. He couldn't even make himself kiss her; how the hell was he going to start thinking of her as part and parcel of the Morgan family?

And yet, according to Pop, they owed her something.

What exactly that was, Gabriel wasn't certain.

THE STORM THAT SWEPT Union Junction and the outlying countryside that night kept Gabriel inside and feeling caged. He paced the house, watching lightning crack through the windows of the two-story house. The TV had gone out; the phone lines were dead. He could hear water dripping frenzied and fast into the overgrown gardens.

There wasn't a lot to do in a house one didn't call home. So far he'd mainly confined himself to his room on the second floor, and the den. He passed through the kitchen occasionally to forage from the goodies the ladies had left for him. The house, he estimated, was around six thousand square feet. Eventually, he'd have to investigate the rest of Pop's place.

Actually, there was no better time than the present, he decided. The sound of something not quite right caught his ear; instantly he listened intently, all the old survival skills surging into action. Someone was at the front door; someone with a key that wouldn't fit easily. Gabriel considered flinging the door open and confronting whoever was out there, some idiot so dumb they didn't know it was storming like hell outside, then relented. Let the water drown them. If they made it inside, then he'd deal with them.

He thought about Laura's father's threats against Pop and figured he couldn't kill the man in cold blood. So he selected one of his father's many travel guides he had in the den—the heaviest one, something about the South Seas—and waited behind the door.

It suddenly blew open with a gust of wind and rain and vituperative cursing. Gabriel raised the eight-hundred-page tourist guide high over his head, preparing to crack it over his visitor's skull.

"Damn it, I *hate* Texas with a passion!" he heard, and lowered his arms.

"Dane?"

His brother swung to look at him. "What the hell are you hiding back there for? And with a book on the South Seas?"

"Preparing to coldcock you." Gabriel closed the door.

"I'm *supposed* to be here." Dane glared at him, his coat dripping water all over the floor.

"Your email said you were coming in January."

"And I've since changed my mind. You got a problem with that?" Dane asked as he threw his bags in a corner.

Gabriel sighed. "Calm down, Sam Houston. Food's in the fridge."

"Don't call me that. I detest Texas."

In the kitchen, Gabriel settled into a chair. "Are you starting your year of duty early?"

"Figured I might as well get it over with." Dane stuck his head inside the refrigerator door, ending the conversation for the moment. "Fried chicken! Watermelon!"

Gabriel shook his head and began to read the travel guide to the South Seas, which was starting to sound appealing.

"You get your letter from Pop?" Dane asked while he emptied the contents of the fridge on to the kitchen counter.

"What letter?"

"The one with the sob story about watching over

this woman and her twins who have no man in the house."

"Twins?" Gabriel sat up. Laura only had a toddler and a baby—didn't she?

"I despise kids almost as much as I hate Texas," Dane said.

Gabriel couldn't think for the shock of adding more kids to Laura's equation. "You're a Texas Ranger. Get over it."

"I'm done. I retired from active duty."

"Congratulations. So back to the family of four—"

"Yeah. I'm supposed to look out for this little mom because of some mess Pop made."

Gabriel frowned. *He* was supposed to be the reluctant knight in shining armor. Possessive emotions and a sense of *I saw her first* crowded his skull.

Dane shuddered. "Her name is Suzy something."

"Suzy? Not Laura?"

Dane sat down across from him with a beer and a plate of fried chicken. "How do you get Laura from Suzy?"

Gabriel shook his head. "This doesn't sound good."

"Tell me about it. I nearly took off for New York, never to be seen or heard from again. But in the end, I knew I had to do this, or I'd really never be free of Pop. He'll try to rule us from the grave if we don't prove to him that nothing he does can screw up our lives anymore."

"And then there's the million bucks."

"A small price for putting up with Pop," Dane said

glumly. "You know it's going to get ugly. *Suzy.*" He shuddered.

At least it wasn't Laura Pop had sent Dane to rescue. It didn't really matter, Gabriel reminded himself. One year and he was gone. *Outta here.*

But now apparently there was a family of four in the mix, and an additional *problem* to be solved. Gabriel stared out the window at the pelting rain.

It was indeed beginning to get ugly.

Chapter Four

"So who's Laura, anyway? Girlfriend?"

Gabriel stared at his elder brother, elder being twenty-eight to his own twenty-six. "Hell, no. I just met her. Pop left her children a trust. It's complicated."

"Isn't everything Pop touches complicated?"

Gabriel nodded. "This as much as anything. So what's the deal with Suzy?"

"Don't really know. The letter just said that he owed her something and he'd like me to see to it."

"Pop's matchmaking by making disasters for us to fix."

Dane quit chewing. "You think?"

"Sure. He wants grandkids. He's been busy finding himself some ready-made families."

"Man," Dane said, "that's not fair. I'm glad you figured that out because I might've stepped right into the snare."

Gabriel nodded. "Pop never does anything without a reason."

"But still...family-making?" Dane shook his head. "That's so underhanded."

Gabriel returned to staring out the window.

"So is Laura at least somewhat easy on the eyes?"

Gabriel shrugged. "She is. But she's not my type."

"That would be pretty hard to identify."

He frowned. "What's that supposed to mean?"

Dane looked at him. "Pop's not a sphinx. He can choose all he wants for us, but he can't figure out who'd be that special girl, which personally, I believe is a fairy tale spun to young boys by parents who want grandkids. So we're safe."

"Oh." Gabriel relaxed a little now that he understood his brother wasn't saying he was tough to please. Then he tensed all over again. Pop *had* selected someone Gabriel was attracted to, in a breath-stealing, jaw-tightening way he hadn't anticipated. "I'd still be careful," he warned. "Suzy might be just your thing."

"Nah." Dane shuddered. "I could never hear myself saying 'Suzy, make me breakfast, baby.'"

Gabriel stared at his brother. "You wouldn't say that to a woman without getting a frying pan upside the head."

Dane sipped his beer. "I like girls who can cook."

Gabriel considered that. If the chicken and rice and peas were any forewarning, Laura could definitely cook.

"Great cooking, great sex. Very important qualities in a woman, if I was looking for one. I'd say Pop's run into a brick wall with me. Now, you might not be as safe."

Gabriel stood. "I'm going to bed. Make yourself at home, such as it is." He wasn't going to think about sex and Laura; he wasn't going to even kiss her. Or imagine what she tasted like.

"You realize if Pop cooked up a mess for me and one for you, the other two probably have assigned families as well," Dane pointed out.

"Yeah, well, good luck with Jack. We haven't seen him in ten years. And Pete, almost as long." He shrugged. "What's a secret agent going to do with a family?"

"I see Jack's scores every once in a while. He posts a few wins, breaks a few bones. Got stomped in Amarillo."

Gabriel looked at his brother. "Stomped?"

"Not bad. Slight concussion."

He sat again in spite of himself. "You've seen Jack."

"I was a Ranger. I have connections. People tell me things, let me know what's happening on the rodeo circuit." Dane finished the chicken and started on some watermelon. "Sure. When he got stomped, I checked in on him at the hospital. Don't think he knew I was there. He was out of it for a while, but I did see him pat the nurse's ass. And he didn't get his hand slapped."

"I didn't know about Jack being in the hospital."

"You weren't stateside much."

That was true. But even if he had been home, he wouldn't have known much anyway. "So since you hear things, fill me in on Pete."

"He slipped into my house in Watauga about a year ago. I thought I was going to have cardiac arrest when he sat down at my breakfast table with me. I hate that spy crap secret agent voodoo thing he's got going on."

Gabriel grunted. "Thought Rangers had sonar hearing and X-ray vision."

Dane laughed. "We're not quite superhuman, jarhead."

He wasn't a jarhead anymore. Since he'd gotten his discharge, his dark hair had grown out some. He'd expected a bit of gray, and saw a few strands mixed in. No bald spot or thinning hair, though, which made him think he might just keep growing the stuff. It felt strange long. Old habits died hard. "So what did Pete have on his mind?"

"Just checking in. He was on his way somewhere. Didn't say. Said he was getting tired."

They were all getting older. Even Gabriel felt the gradual march of time slowing his body down, his need for action yet speeding up. Not military action. Something else he hadn't quite put his finger on.

"I don't know if I can live out here for a year," Dane said. "Watauga seemed like hell to me, but this would be worse."

Gabriel took Dane's plate to the sink. "Do any of us really have a choice?" He walked back to the fridge and tossed Dane a beer. "Look. We have to do this. For the sake of our own futures. Pop's crazy, no doubt, but crazy like a fox. Remember? He was always working a deal."

Dane cracked his beer and focused on the label. "I know you're right but it still stinks. I resent Pop for controlling our lives with a snap of his thin fingers."

"Look," Gabriel said, "what if the old man died?" He looked at Dane with a serious expression. "He'd get the last laugh, man. We'd be holding the whole damn bag of emotional dirt."

Dane shook his head. "That's too 'tortured soul' for me."

"Well, think it over, because it's true." He sighed and leaned back in his chair, not wanting the conversation, not really wanting the beer, not wanting anything but a flight to Tokyo, maybe. Away from here. "So we're going to do this. And what about Suzy?"

"Now, that isn't anything I have to deal with. Whatever mess Pop made, I just have to make certain some money changes hands, some responsibilities are seen to and that's it. I live here for a year, a paltry three hundred and sixty-five days, and then my time is done."

He thought about Laura. "So cut-and-dried."

"So cut-and-dried." Dane nodded. "You got that right."

"Good game plan. I'm turning in."

Gabriel rose, poured the beer into the sink and headed upstairs, mulling over Dane's game plan. It was fairly detached, and Gabriel liked detached and unemotional.

It just might work for him.

LAURA FROWNED AT THE NOTE that had been stuck to the front door of her small house. *Hey, baby, be by to see you later.*

Chills ran through her. Nobody *baby'd* her—no one except her father. She didn't want to see him. Didn't want him near her children. The fact that he'd found out where she lived made her want to move far away, as fast as she could.

He was her father by blood, but Mr. Morgan had acted more fatherly toward her. There was something wrong with the man whose genes she bore—Ben had problems with thinking the world owed him something. A chip on his shoulder kept him from being the responsible human he might have been.

Laura wanted no part of him.

She took her children inside and locked the door. Penny went straight to her stuffed animals, so Laura put Perrin in his playpen before she sank into a chair at the kitchen table to think.

There was a reason Ben had chosen this moment to filter back into her life. Months ago, Ben had claimed Mr. Morgan had done him a disservice, which the old man had denied. Ben had told her that Mr. Morgan had cheated him out of money. She didn't think Mr. Morgan was the cheating type but after Dave died, he had put that money into trust for her kids. Was it guilt money? At the time, tired and grief-stricken, she'd assumed it was exactly what he'd said it was, a gift of college education for kids whose company he'd enjoyed. As a teacher, she'd certainly appreciated the gesture. A lot of people had been very generous after the funeral. In fact, the Jeffersons had helped pay down the mortgage on this house so that Laura wouldn't have to struggle so much. It was just the type of caring thing Laura had seen done many times over in this town.

She hadn't thought about guilt money. And Ben had always been the kind of man who whined. It was part of the reason she was determined to shoulder her burdens without complaining, without relying on other people. She wanted independence and that didn't come by whining and blaming.

She thought about Gabriel. He seemed very independent, too. He wouldn't blame other people for any misery he incurred. She'd heard from Mr. Morgan that none of their family was close, a fact that disheartened him. In his twilight years—he'd started to say he was feeling his age—he had hoped to knit his family back together.

He'd never said exactly what the problem had been.

Laura wanted a family for her children, though. If she ever remarried, she would want a man who was close to his kin. Penny and Perrin deserved a father who didn't have skeletons rattling in his closet; they had enough bones with Ben. Although they'd never met him, it was only a matter of time before that family skeleton made a nuisance of itself with some whiny rattling.

She tore up the note and threw it into the trash, pushing it down deep before closing the shutters and checking the locks on the doors.

TWO HOURS LATER, LAURA had the kids in bed. She'd been spending some time making plans for the upcoming school year; it would be her second year teaching seventh-grade science. Laura had plans for setting up some conservation composts and doing a rocket launch. If the students were ready, she planned to jump right into some in-class science projects so that they could record data over the course of the whole year.

She'd completely put Ben out of her mind.

Someone knocked at the door, and the dreaded prickles ran up her back. She closed her eyes, reminding herself that Ben was her father, that he had never been violent. He just hadn't liked Dave and had been disagreeable and opinionated about him.

It was Mr. Morgan he'd really been at odds with. Maybe she'd been influenced by those stories.

Yet there was the money. Funny that Ben would be showing up in her life when he knew that her children had been the recipients of various gifts of goodwill from the town. Ben wasn't a coincidental kind of man; he planned everything almost down to an obsession. Then again, she'd heard through the grapevine that Ben had picked up heavy drinking in the town that bordered Union Junction.

The knock sounded again. Now was as good a time as any to face her father. Then again, it could be Mimi.

Mimi would call first.

"Who is it?"

"Gabriel Morgan."

She put a hand to her chest to still her thundering heart, then realized he made her just as nervous—in an unexpected, different way.

She turned on the porch light and opened the door. "Hello."

There he was, wearing a Western hat and jeans. He wasn't smiling, but he hadn't smiled the other times she'd met him, either. He had bought out her kissing booth—and then disappeared. She'd expected to hear something from him…she hadn't been sure what.

"I would have called, but I didn't have your number. Guess it's unlisted."

She nodded. "It is."

"Would have called Mason for it, but…hope you don't mind me stopping by."

He seemed uncomfortable and Laura didn't blame him. Apparently he was only in the area because of his duty to his father. She held the door open so Gabriel could come inside. "If you'd called Mason, he would have asked why you needed to see me. I can ask you myself." Laura pointed to a sofa so he could sit down. He did, gingerly hovering on the flowered sofa.

"Just seems we got off on the wrong foot."

She nodded. "Maybe. What other foot is there, though?"

He hesitated. "I think I was surprised my father left me instructions about you."

"He did?" That wasn't welcome news. She didn't want Gabriel to feel obligated to her in any way.

"Yeah. Apparently you have some issues with your father, who may or may not have your best interests at heart."

She thought about the note on the door. "It's not something I really want to talk about."

"I fully understand. I don't want to talk about my dad, either."

"So don't." She felt more awkward by the second. "Look, Gabriel, despite whatever your father told you, I can take care of myself. I have lots of friends. I have a great job. I love my kids. I don't need a protector or anything like that."

He glanced down at his hands for a moment before looking back at her. "You're sure you're all right?"

"Of course I am! Your father was ultraprotective of me because of my children. But you don't have to take on a parenting role, Gabriel. I wouldn't want you to. They had a father." She took a deep breath. "He was a wonderful man, and…I'm not looking to fill his role in our lives."

He appeared to consider her words. "You'd let me know if you need something?"

"Honestly, no." She shook her head. "I wouldn't. I'd call Mimi or some of my girlfriends. But I can tell you I would if that's the closure you need. It just won't be true. You're completely off the hook."

A knock at the door startled both of them. A shaky premonition snapped into Laura.

"I'm sorry. I didn't realize you were expecting company." Gabriel got to his feet.

"Laura! Baby! Let me in!"

Gabriel frowned. Laura glanced at the door, making certain it was securely locked after she'd let Gabriel in. To her relief, it was.

"Laura! It's your father. Don't keep me out here!"

"I didn't realize you were still on speaking terms with Ben." Gabriel's eyes searched hers. "Thought I'd heard the opposite."

It was her family's private business. "I don't want to discuss this with you." If she did, he would feel responsible for her.

The glass pane smashed, and Laura screamed in spite of herself. She flung open the door. "Ben, what the hell? You could have hurt one of the children!"

"Hi, baby." Her father tipped unsteadily to one side, listing, before righting himself. "I know I taught you better manners than to leave your old dad standing outside."

She felt Gabriel move behind her. She pushed him back with one hand. This was her problem. "Ben, take your drunk and sorry self off my property and don't come back. We said all we had to say years ago. If you ever come around here again, or if I catch you near my children, I'm going to have you put in jail."

He squinted at her. "Who's that in there with you?"

"Ben, pay attention to what I'm saying to you—" Laura began, but her father shoved the door back so fast she couldn't stop him.

"Morgan," her father said, his tone a curse. "I should have known Morgan's pups wouldn't be far away from the prize."

Gabriel literally moved her from the door, filling the opening with his large frame. "Ben, whatever happened between you and my dad is old news. It has no part with me, and it has no part with Laura. You need to let it go."

"The money your father gets from the oil rights on that property should be mine."

"So take it to court," Gabriel said calmly. "You can't get any money that Laura has because it's all tied up in trust for her children."

"That's why you're hanging around. The children." Ben's face grew surly. "Like little pieces of gold."

"I'd be a fairly useless human if I had to wait around for fifteen years to get some little kid's trust. Move along, Ben. It's all over. Laura said she didn't want you here, and you need to respect that."

"Because you say so?"

Laura tried to edge in front of Gabriel but he held her back.

"Because I say so," Gabriel confirmed. "I'd be going if I was you, or you're not going to be in one piece to do it on your own."

Ben's face wrinkled with hate. "You haven't heard the last of me, Morgan."

"I'm certain of that." Gabriel shut the door, waiting until he heard Ben's boots leave the porch before he turned to Laura. "I'll fix this pane before I go. I can tape it tonight, and then get some glass tomorrow at the hardware shop."

She straightened her five-foot-two frame. "Don't ever fight my battles for me again. Don't assume I can't take care of myself."

"It wasn't about you," Gabriel said, "it was about my father and his schemes." He glanced around the room. "I'll be sleeping here tonight."

Chapter Five

Gabriel's pronouncement clearly didn't suit Laura, but he hadn't expected it would. She gave him a determined stare. "You will not be sleeping here tonight, or any other time."

"Mommy?"

Gabriel turned to face a tiny blue-eyed, blond version of her mother. Penny stood in the hallway, rubbing sleepy eyes.

"Yes, honey?" Laura said, going to her.

"I heard a loud noise."

Laura shot Gabriel a warning glance. "A pane on the door accidentally broke. Don't worry about a thing."

In the background, Perrin began to cry. Gabriel focused on the sound. If he had to guess—and he had zero experience with infants—it was a *comfort me* cry.

Laura went down the hall to Perrin. Penny looked solemnly at Gabriel. "Who's going to fix the window?"

"I am," he told her. "Tomorrow morning."

"No, you're not," Laura said, entering the family room with Perrin, who was happy now that he was being held. "And you're definitely not—" she glanced at Penny "—you're definitely not staying here," she said in a low voice.

"Either I stay here or your family comes to my ranch. You can't stay here with your father in a hot-headed state." Protective emotions inside him rushed to the surface. Laura looked vulnerable with her two children in her arms. She was trying to be tough but her eyes held confusion. He knew she had to be scared. No woman wanted to sleep in a house with a broken window. If Ben came back—and he probably was watching to see when Gabriel's truck left—he'd simply reach through that pane and unlock the door.

To Gabriel's mind, any battle Ben wanted to put up should be with Gabriel, not Laura. He was after money, pure and simple. The easiest way to get it was to panhandle his own daughter.

"I'm going to put my children back to bed."

Laura turned and went down the hall. Penny followed with a backward glance at Morgan, her face somber. His heart lurched, twisted. Despite his vow to never want children of his own, Penny's big eyes and soft voice saying his name stole his heart. Perrin's plump cheeks and soft hair made him want to see the little boy have his chance at growing up safe and strong. Actually, he would have loved to hold the baby if Laura would let him—but he knew she would not. She had definitely warned him off her deceased husband's territory. He couldn't blame her for that. But she did need some help, whether she wanted to admit it or not.

Maybe Pop hadn't been so crazy after all.

Laura walked into the kitchen with Penny, getting the little girl a drink of water. She held her daughter in her lap, singing softly to her, ignoring Gabriel. That was fine with him. Frankly, he'd never seen anything so beautiful as Laura comforting her daughter.

Then he heard Perrin crying again, an inconsolable sobbing. Gabriel started to mention to Laura that the baby was upset again, then thought better of it. Penny was enjoying her mother's attention. Gabriel quietly went down the hall in the direction of the crying—three bedrooms, bathroom on the hall to the left—and found the nursery.

Perrin had wedged himself under his tiny pillow and flailed a blanket over himself, and was not happy about his predicament.

"Hey, little guy." Gabriel removed the blanket. The baby stared up at him. "Don't be so upset, dude. Your mom's trying to calm your sister down, and they just need a moment together. You've got this soft bed, and everything's going good for you, right? So calm down." He reached into the crib, stroking the baby's cheek. Perrin watched him with big eyes. Gabriel couldn't stand it any longer. Laura would not appreciate this, but the lure was too strong.

He scooped the baby up and cradled him to his chest.

There was nothing, he decided, quite like the smell of a baby. The feel of a baby. And this one…this one was so rotund and squeezable… Gabriel closed his eyes as the baby laid his head against his chest. He felt like he was holding one of those fat cherubim he'd seen in paintings in the Louvre.

The baby had gotten himself agitated with all his wailing. Gabriel swept back Perrin's tiny curls from his forehead. "Little man, you've got to learn to chill. There's nothing quite as annoying as getting yourself wrapped up in your blanket, but you've got to learn to think your way out of your predicament." He leaned his cheek against the baby's head. "When you're older, of course. Right now, you have the luxury of having a good wail on the world. When you're my age, you learn to suck it up." Gently, he placed Perrin back in his crib, and quietly hummed a Texas cowboy lullaby he'd learned long ago. Soothed, the baby curled into his sheet, opened his eyes once more, then shut them peacefully.

Gabriel backed away from the crib, yet kept his eye on the baby, kept humming. That hadn't been so bad.

"What are you doing?"

Gabriel turned. "He was crying."

"I can take care of my own family, Gabriel."

He looked at Laura. "I noticed. Relax. Where's Penny?"

"In bed."

He nodded. "Guess I'll head to the sofa and do the same." Brushing past her, knowing the storm of protest was brewing at his back, he almost smiled. Laura was independent, she was in a bad spot and there was nothing like the combination to make a woman like her mad.

"It's inappropriate for a man to stay in a house

with a newly widowed woman and her children. What would my neighbors say?"

"Folks'll understand when they hear about your visitor."

"*I* won't understand!" She had her hands on her hips and was building anger. He gave her credit for stubbornness.

"Suit yourself." He nodded. "I'll be back tomorrow to fix the window."

"I'll call a handyman."

She sure didn't seem to like him. It hurt his feelings a bit since she'd been so fond of his father. Or had she? Had her affection been a ruse for his money?

It didn't matter—all those answers would come in time. "Good night." He headed outside, got in his truck and made himself comfortable.

Ten minutes later, she was at his truck window.

"What are you doing?" she demanded.

He turned down the radio, which was playing soft country tunes. "Watching out for the boogeyman."

"I don't need you to protect me." Laura shook her head. "What's it going to take to get that through your thick skull?"

"Something more than you've got, lady, because I'm not convinced you don't need a little help. And as long as I'm out here, and you're in there, I'd say your virtue is safe."

She gave him a glare that would have curdled milk.

"What's the problem?" he asked reasonably. "I'm not bothering you."

"You're the problem. Go away."

He got out of the truck, considering her. "I'm slowly starting to figure you out."

"You are not."

"Yeah. I am. Here's my offer. I'll stay out here until I'm satisfied you're safe. In the morning, you call the handyman, or Mason, and I'll go." He put his hands on either side of her, capturing her against the truck. "And in the meantime, I'll be a gentleman. I promise."

Then he kissed her.

Gently, but he kissed her all the same.

At the moment, it felt awesome. For days afterward, he'd wish he hadn't.

SHOCKED BY GABRIEL'S KISS, Laura pushed his arms away. She stared at him, trying to figure out why he'd done it—hadn't he just said he'd be a gentleman?—then stalked inside her house, locking the door.

She let out her breath and waited for her thundering heart to still. He was everything Josiah Morgan had said his son was: arrogant, opinionated, stubborn.

Nothing like Dave, who'd been gentle, kind, nurturing.

And she'd been lying when she'd told Gabriel she didn't need him standing guard. She was indeed afraid, mostly for Penny and Perrin. Her father wouldn't hurt her children, but it was nerve-racking and wearying when Ben was drunk like that.

Yet no woman wanted to be a responsibility. She knew Mr. Morgan's bequest made Gabriel feel he had to have a part in looking after her and her children.

She touched a finger to her lips, still surprised that she remembered the way his kiss had felt.

She was afraid of feeling anything.

It hadn't been long enough since her husband's passing to feel anything. Hadn't she promised to love and honor Dave until the day she died? Her heart would never forget him.

No other man should have a part in her children's lives. Perhaps that's why she'd felt so comfortable with Mr. Morgan's affection for Penny and Perrin; it was grandfatherly and safe. Their own grandfather was rough around the edges; Dave's family lived up north and sent presents at Christmas. Mr. Morgan had provided the love the children needed through Laura's most devastating hours. She would not feel the same about Gabriel sharing their lives.

Yet he was out in her driveway, standing guard over them. She'd frozen when she'd heard him singing to Perrin; very few men would sing to another man's children. She'd found that quiet act of his astonishingly sexy. Tingles sizzled over her skin, jolting her with a memory she'd shared only with her husband.

Yet those emotions were impossible. Ignoring the tug of desire she would never acknowledge, she went to put on her nightgown and go to bed.

"THEN WHAT HAPPENED?" Dane stared at his brother. Hot Texas sun rose to nearly overhead, indicating the noon hour. The steaming humidity was suffocating. "Did you kick Ben's ass?"

"No." Gabriel peered at the cracked rocky earth

where the old dividing line had been, before Pop had bought Ben's property. "I sent him on his way and then stayed to make certain he didn't return."

Dane knelt, watching Gabriel dig around in the soil. "So now what? What are we looking for?"

"I don't know. Pop and his wild tale of oil under the land he bought from Ben. I don't believe it should be causing this much trouble, because if there was enough oil to fight over, Pop would have had drillers out here by now." He looked at Dane. "So what if it was one of Pop's wild tales? What if he was trying to stir Ben up on purpose?"

"Why would he?"

"I just don't trust Pop." He couldn't tell anything about the earth. The soil didn't look any different to him, from the miles he and Dane had walked together. He didn't really need Dane tagging along, but he couldn't say it had been a bother. Pop had claimed he'd noticed a difference in the soil that led him to speculate that the land was holding a secret, but Gabriel was more inclined to believe a fairy tale had been dreamed up for all of them.

"Well, I will be damned," Dane said, and Gabriel glanced up.

"What?"

"Look what the wind just blew into town."

There wasn't so much as a breeze to stir the humidity. Gabriel turned. "Pete," he murmured, shocked. "I'll be damned right along with you."

Their brother rode up on a horse, a chestnut Gabriel recognized as one of their own. "It isn't February."

"Nope." Pete got down. "But thanks for the trail you left for me."

"Trail?" Gabriel stared at his brother, realizing that the years had left them all a little older, a little leaner, maybe a little meaner. Pete's eyes were a hard dark granite; his cheeks sculpted by whatever demons secret agents battled. He was surprised that he was glad to see his brother. "We didn't leave you a trail."

"Tire marks to the side of the field, hay bent after that. Looked like a bear had crossed the field instead of two men."

"We weren't trying to hide where we were," Dane said. "Good to see you, Pete. Didn't know you were in the country."

"You might have thought about hiding if you knew Ben Smith was at the house, hollering about wanting Gabriel to come out and take his punishment."

"Oh, hell." Gabriel winced. "He's becoming a pain."

"I sent him on his way, but he's convinced we owe him money," Pete said. "He shared that at the top of his lungs, over and over again. Do we?"

Gabriel shrugged. "I doubt it." He glanced at the ground. "Think Pop's got everybody all stirred up for nothing."

"You mean this isn't going to be the next King Ranch?" Pete asked, his hard gaze turning lighter for a moment. "Ben seems to think we're sitting on a Spindletop-sized gusher."

"Don't think so." Gabriel turned toward the truck. "Thanks for the warning, though."

Dane followed, and Pete remounted, riding alongside. "We probably want to keep an eye on him."

Something—maybe a fly—whizzed past Gabriel's ear. He flicked at it, then realized the fly had been accompanied by a sound in the distance.

"What the hell was that?" Dane suddenly flattened Gabriel to the ground.

Gabriel heard hoofbeats rhythmically charging away from them. "Did that sorry sack of crap just take a shot at me?"

"Pete's going after him. Lie low until we know Pete's ridden him down."

Hay crackled in Gabriel's face and itched at his hot skin. He wasn't too keen that his brother felt he had to protect him. "Get the hell off of me. I'm not china, and that goofball couldn't hit the broadside of a barn." Gabriel preferred to take his own hit—he didn't need to rely on his brothers. Dane didn't move, and Gabriel couldn't hold back a snarl. "Get *off,* damn it!"

Dane rolled away. Gabriel jumped to his feet, making a primo target of himself in his red T-shirt and jeans.

"I'd get down if I were you until Pete signals. Who's going to look after Mrs. Adams and the children if you're gone?"

Gabriel glared hotly enough at his brother to scorch the hay around him. "Be very careful, brother."

"Oh, hell. You always were the sensitive one." Dane laughed, untroubled by his brother's foul mood.

Gabriel ignored the desire to jump on Dane and

whale him a good one. "I suppose you don't think Pete makes a bigger target on the back of a horse."

"Ben's aiming for you, not Pete."

Gabriel grunted. "I'm walking to the truck. If Ben could have hit me, he would have by now."

"It just takes one lucky shot."

He wasn't going to cower on the ground while his brother fought his battle. If he got his hands on Ben, he was going to wring his skinny neck.

Then again, Ben was Laura's father. Theoretically, he shouldn't strangle the ornery little coward. Laura would probably say he'd bullied Ben, and she sure wouldn't want any help solving her own family issues. Something round in the dry grass caught his eye. Gabriel bent to pick it up. "Not that I'm any happier about a BB, but at least I'm not going to have to kill him."

They got in the truck and he and Dane drove back to the house in silence. Dane got out and glanced over his shoulder. "Coming in?"

He shook his head. "Got to get some glass for Laura's window in town."

Dane studied him for a long moment, then nodded. "I'll see what Pete found."

Gabriel didn't really care. All he was thinking about was Laura and the kids.

LAURA KNEW GABRIEL WAS out there. She knew when he drove into the driveway. She didn't answer the door when he rang the bell. Holding her breath, she waited for him to leave, knowing she was being unkind, maybe even rude, by not thanking him for his care of her.

She didn't want big, strong Gabriel Morgan pushing his way into her life, storming her heart. It could happen so easily. But she was going to fight the onslaught of his charisma with all her might, for the sake of her own sanity.

Would she even breathe until she heard his truck drive away? She didn't think so; her chest physically pained her. He rang the bell again, calling, "Laura! Your door needs to be repaired!"

He wasn't leaving until he did what he'd come to do. She opened the door silently, unsmiling. He tipped his cowboy hat to her, then puttied in the window efficiently and quietly, never meeting her gaze.

When he finished, he closed the door and went whistling down the porch. Now that he was gone, she could relax. Her house was safe again.

Except it wasn't. There might not be a broken window anymore, but there was a very strong chance of a broken heart that had too few pieces left to risk shattering.

She locked the door.

LAURA THOUGHT SHE WAS free until she heard Gabriel's truck pull back into her drive at eight o'clock that night. She tensed, waiting for a knock on the door, but none came. Burning curiosity tweaked at her. She peeked out the window. He'd simply shut off the engine and pulled out a newspaper.

An hour later she couldn't ignore him any longer.

She went outside to confront him. “This is not necessary.”

“Caution is a good thing. Besides, your old man took a shot at me this morning.”

She gasped, not wanting to believe him. The honest depth of his eyes made her realize he was being completely truthful. She felt sick over her father’s spiral into violence. “Did you call the sheriff?”

He shook his head. “Nah. It was only a BB. Pete ran your father down and Ben said he’d just been shooting at a duck. I didn’t see any ducks, but whatever.” He looked at her with some sympathy. “Maybe there’s a way you know of that we can calm him down, get him to stop acting like he’s out of his tree.”

“I appreciate you trying to be understanding, but I don’t know what Ben’s problem is. We haven’t been close since the day I got married.” Instinctively, she lifted her chin. It was still a memory that hurt. “I’m not sure why he’d want to hurt you, though.”

“He was just trying to get attention.” Gabriel shrugged. “Pete paid him some.”

“Pete? How many of you are at the ranch now?”

“Three.”

She smiled. “That leaves just one more. Guess your father knew what he was doing.”

That rankled. “Go on in before the kids start looking for you. I’m going to read the newspaper.”

She sighed, wearing a slightly annoyed expression. “I have a phone. I’ll call you if Ben comes back. How’s that? You go on home and visit with your brothers, the way your father intended.”

He squinted at her. "How do you know what my dad intended?"

She shrugged. "Josiah wasn't exactly quiet about how much he missed his sons being around."

That seemed strange. He'd pretty much run them off when they were old enough to be gone.

"Do you think your father really stole from my father the way Ben claims?"

Gabriel considered that. "I don't know what to believe. And I'm not sure it really matters."

"It matters to Ben."

"Are you taking sides?"

She shook her head. "Merely stating a fact."

"Even if my father did steal from him, that doesn't mean he has the right to knock out your window and take a shot at me."

"I didn't say it did. I simply said that he certainly feels wronged."

"Yeah, well." He wished she'd get on another topic that was friendlier to both of them, and a little easier. Getting a laugh or a smile out of Laura was rare. The shame of it was, he liked looking at her so much. He wished she'd stop cornering him all the time so he could just sit and stare at her full lips and blue eyes. Right now she was wearing a white blouse and a blue skirt that looked cool and feminine. He liked the whole modest thing she had going on. "Well, I'd best turn in," he said, before he started hungering for something he couldn't have.

"Turn in?"

"Get some shut-eye." He settled the newspaper over

his face. "I've got some chores to take care of early in the morning."

"Nothing is going to happen. You really don't have to stay."

He slid the newspaper off and met her gaze, not to be polite but because he wanted an excuse to look at her. "I know it won't, not as long as I'm sitting in your driveway."

"You're the most stubborn man I ever met."

"Yes, ma'am."

"Have it your way." She turned away, and without any guilt he watched her fanny sashay to the house and up the steps.

He knew he shouldn't look. A gentleman wouldn't.

Damn.

Chapter Six

One hour after he'd read the sports section, the business section and the larger community section of Union Junction's newspaper—a one-page epistle—Gabriel was surprised when the passenger-side door of his truck opened and Laura slid into the seat.

"Hello," he said cautiously.

She gave him a determined look. "Why did you kiss me?"

He didn't have an easy answer for that question; he'd pondered it and come up empty. The only reason he could think of was that the old rascal inside him had risen up and acted impulsively. "Paid for it, I guess. Just cashed in a bit late."

She nodded at his reply. "Gabriel, I can't have you sitting in my drive every night. It's only six o'clock now, and here you are already. It's not good for me."

"The neighbors will talk?"

"You and I both know that was just an excuse."

"So what's the real reason you don't want me around?"

"So when do you find out about the mysterious Suzy?" Gabriel put off going out to talk to Laura and Ben. They seemed calm together, maybe even enjoying each other's company for the first time in God only knew how many years.

"Never." Dane grinned, then high-fived his brother. "Dad only said we had to live in the house for a year. The letter asked if I'd take care of Suzy's situation. I did, through a mediator."

Gabriel had to admit it was a smooth move he hadn't considered. "That was smart."

"Watching you moon around after Laura hasn't been pretty. If you got snagged so easily, it could happen to anyone. I had to measure my risk appetite, and I decided it was pretty low."

"I have not been snagged." Gabriel felt his ill humor returning.

"Then back away from the window," Pete said. "I'm sure she can see you from behind those blinds."

Laura probably could. She'd probably be unsurprised that he was keeping watch over her. He sighed, realized she also wouldn't appreciate it and slid away from the window, feeling silly.

"Again, you could just go say hi." Pete stood, stretching. "Anybody for banana fritters?"

Gabriel frowned. "Fritters? Who's going to make those?"

"Laura said she would since she was coming over. It's either that or we grill burgers. I offered burgers because I'm not exactly a banana man. She said the choice was yours since you'd been through a lot lately. We all agreed that was the case."

His life was out of control, hijacked by people he didn't really know that well. He was thinking about the past, and everybody else seemed happy to go along with the cards Pop had dealt them, singularly unsuspicious about the old man's true motives.

"Burgers," he said, "and I guess I'll ring the damn dinner bell." Feeling almost relieved, he jerked open the door. Ben jumped to his feet, startled, and Laura stared at him with shock.

"Morgan," Penny said, a sweet smile on her face.

"Are we bothering you?" Laura asked. "Pete and Dane said we could come inside, but we prefer to sit outside. It's a lovely evening."

"Ben," Gabriel said, "what the hell are you doing on my porch, anyway?"

"Got no place to go at the moment." Ben didn't seem too concerned by that. "Your dad bought my place. This is as close to home as I can get."

"But where were you before that?" Gabriel demanded. "You were somewhere, weren't you?" He looked at Laura, who didn't seem that disturbed by his bad manners. Stepping around him, Dane and Pete went to brush leaves and blown dirt off the picnic table and set up the grill for burgers.

Ben scratched his head. "Well, I've sort of been in this town and that town looking for work. Then you boys came back, and I pretty much figured it wouldn't hurt if I hung around here a bit."

"You tried to shoot me." Gabriel wasn't sure how he

was supposed to forget about that. Turning the other cheek in this case would be a trifle hard.

"Didn't try too hard, son. I really didn't give it my best shot. And I was under the influence of some booze and self-pity, I don't mind admitting." The old man scratched his head and rubbed his chin ruefully. "Sorry I scared you, though. Won't happen again. I gave your brothers my word."

"I wasn't scared. It's against the law to take potshots at people." Gabriel felt annoyance rising inside him. This was not a Hallmark card moment, never would be for him. Anger and mistrust were wrung up together inside him. Why did he get the feeling that this new family was being thrust upon him? "I don't trust you, Ben, to be perfectly honest."

"I respect that," Ben said calmly, "but on the bright side, it's not like I'm in the running to be your father-in-law or anything."

Pete and Dane swung around to stare at them. Laura's eyes went huge. The words hung silent and awkward in the twilight air.

Ben glanced around at everyone. "Well, I'm not," Ben reiterated, "so there's the bright side, right?"

It would be hell having Ben for a father-in-law. Whatever foolish daydreams he'd had concerning Laura were blown to dust. He should never have kissed her, should never have toyed with her affections.

Now that she and her father were coming to some type of reunion, he could excuse himself from the picture-perfect moment he didn't want to be painted into. "Think I'll go check on the horses. Good night."

He headed off, leaving everyone else to enjoy what had become a family picnic.

Almost.

LAURA STARED AFTER GABRIEL, disappointed by his reaction. She could feel his withdrawal from the gathering, from her. Even from the children, and that hurt the most. He was big and strong and caring, and she had kept him at arm's length. There were reasons for that, but she didn't want him resenting her, or her father.

Although it was easy to resent Ben. He had lost his temper. No one would forgive someone who shot at them.

"I've made a mess of this," Ben said sadly. "I'm never touching another drop of drink."

Dane and Pete went back to scrubbing off the grill. It looked like it hadn't been scrubbed properly or even used in years. "Listen, Ben," she said, sitting down on the porch beside him, "it's great that you're not going to drink anymore. It's great for you, it's great for the kids. You might even consider some counseling or A.A. In the meantime, don't worry about Gabriel. There was nothing to mess up."

"I was just so mad thinking Josiah had cheated me. I always hated getting cheated." Ben sniffed, rubbing his nose on his shirt. "Josiah is a tricky one, too. He's a smart man. He didn't get so wealthy by being a sucker." He sighed deeply. "Unlike me."

"This is the time to stop feeling sorry for yourself, don't you think, Ben?" She shifted Perrin in her arms;

Penny sat quietly between them. "If you see yourself as a victim, then you'll be one."

He slowly nodded. "I guess I fell into that trap when your mother went away. I thought she was happy with me. Never dreamed she'd go off."

Laura had read the letter from her mother many times over the years. She'd long since made peace with the fact that her mother hadn't been able to handle life with a drifter who moved from town to town. She'd gone back north where she had friends. It wasn't that she didn't love her baby, she'd said in the letter. She just felt Ben would be the better parent.

It had been like being given up for adoption. Painful in the growing years, hard as a teenager and probably contributing to Laura's desire to marry a kind, gentle man who seemed solid as a rock, someone who'd be there for her forever. "Ben, it's all right about Mom. We did fine on our own."

"I've been an ass." He looked down at Penny, who stared up at his whiskered face without judgment. "I'm sorry I was hard on your husband, Laura. When he died, I relapsed. I blamed myself for letting my stubbornness get between us."

The familiar knife of pain went through Laura at all the time wasted between them, when Dave had been alive, when her father could have been part of their family. It was time that could never be replaced.

"And now I've shot at your new boyfriend and ruined things for you," he said. "He's never going to want me around."

"Gabriel's not my boyfriend," Laura said firmly,

"and if you're sincere about quitting drinking, I want you around and that's all that matters."

He nodded, glancing at Penny and Perrin wistfully. "I am."

"And no more feeling sorry for yourself."

"No." He shook his head. "I've got a lot to live for now."

"And you forget about that oil business you think Josiah pulled over on you," she said sternly.

A grimace wrinkled his face. "That's a little more difficult. A man hates to have something taken from him."

"I don't think there's anything here. There'd be drillers out here if there was. And do you know what the start-up costs on an operation like that would be?" She looked at her father sincerely. "Unless it was an oil find the size of, I don't know, something in the Gulf, it probably wouldn't be worth the drilling costs."

He blinked. "You're right."

She nodded.

He thought about that for a minute. "But why'd he give you all that money for the kids if it wasn't guilt money?"

"Because Mr. Morgan was a nice old man."

Ben shook his head. "No, Josiah Morgan is not."

"It doesn't matter, does it? He felt like he could help our family when Dave died. That's a good thing, isn't it?"

Ben glanced over at Dane and Pete. "He couldn't get along with his own family, though. Never did understand how that came to pass."

"It's none of our business. People probably say the same thing about us." She kissed Perrin and Penny on their heads.

"Hamburgers? Or hot dogs?" Pete asked. "What does everyone want?"

Laura stood, feeling awkward. "I'm not sure we should stay for dinner. Gabriel made his feelings about our presence pretty plain."

Pete grinned at her. "Gabriel was always the slow child among us. He'll cool off in a bit."

Dane laughed, overhearing his brother's comment. "Besides Jack, he's definitely the most temperamental."

She sat Penny at the picnic table. Somewhat sheepishly, Ben sat down beside Penny.

"It's awfully nice of you boys to forgive me," Ben said.

"You don't have to sing for your supper, Ben," Dane said kindly. "Let's just enjoy the wonderful summer evening."

"Every one of us here is a sinner," Pete added, plopping a big juicy burger in front of Ben. A hot dog followed for Penny, and then a burger for Laura. Perrin sat in her lap, watching everything with big eyes and his fist in his mouth.

"It's a bit charred because we overfired the grill. We'll get better in time," Dane said.

Dane and Pete served themselves, then sat across from Ben and Laura. "I'll say a blessing," Pete offered, and they all bowed their heads until they heard the back door slam.

They glanced up to see Gabriel standing in the doorway.

"The prodigal brother returns," Pete said. "Grab a burger."

Gabriel looked at the picnic table, divided with Laura's family on one side, the Morgans on the other. He had no appetite, except maybe for Laura, something he'd discovered that was growing in spite of his objection to those emotions. "I don't think I'm going to be able to stay here."

They all stared at him.

"Tonight?" Pete asked.

He couldn't meet Laura's steadfast gaze. "At all."

Chapter Seven

Laura's heart sank at Gabriel's words. He obviously had a problem with her family. He definitely did not want them there. She couldn't blame him, either. She held Perrin tighter to her. Maybe she'd made a bad judgment call, believing that because Mr. Morgan had welcomed them, his sons would, too.

"Ben," Gabriel said, "how are you at doing odd jobs on a ranch?"

Ben looked at him. "Could do a good-sized bit of work in my day."

Gabriel folded his arms across his chest. "Are you wanting a job?"

"Depends." Ben jutted out his chin, letting everyone know his pride was at stake.

Gabriel's gaze briefly flicked to Laura. "We've got one open here. This place needs a lot of work."

Ben's jaw sagged. "Do you mean it?" He glanced around at Pete and Dane, whom Laura noticed were staring at Gabriel with approval.

Gabriel nodded. "My brothers feel you could be helpful. You have good knowledge of a working ranch."

It seemed Ben's eyes shone brighter. "I'll take you up on that offer, then."

Gabriel nodded. "You'll have to ask my brothers the particulars of where you should start." He glanced around at the gathering. "Laura, Ben, thank you for coming by." He fondly tousled Penny's and Perrin's hair, surprising Laura. "I'll be heading out."

They all watched in silence as Gabriel left.

"Uh, anybody want pickles with their burgers?" Dane asked to cover the awkward silence. Penny ate her hot dog, and Perrin strained to get down and crawl on the ground. Laura had the strangest sensation that she was missing something in Gabriel's words. He sure hadn't seemed happy. "Can you watch my kids, Ben?" she asked her dad.

"Sure," Ben said, happy to be asked.

Laura handed Perrin to her father, then hurried around to the front of the house so she could catch Gabriel before he departed. He'd said he wasn't going to stick out the year on the ranch—something was bothering him. Badly.

She had to know it wasn't her—or her family.

"Gabriel, wait." She hurried across to where he was backing his truck down the drive. "What is your problem?"

He gazed at her, his eyes pensive. "If I have one, I'm keeping it to myself."

Wasn't that just stubborn as a mule? She shrugged. "I think something's on your mind."

He resumed backing down the drive. She let him

go this time, hating his withdrawal. Hiding your emotions was too easy.

She watched him stop his truck, then pull slowly back up the drive, like a magnet moving toward her.

"Maybe we should talk," he said.

"As long as it's your idea," she said sweetly, and got into his truck.

"It wasn't my idea to offer your father a job," he said, heading away from the ranch.

"I thought not. Why did you?"

"My brothers thought we should. And I'm not exactly objective about the situation, considering I don't completely trust him."

"Nor should you," Laura said, not hurt in the least. "He hasn't always been trustworthy." She took a deep breath. "If it makes your decision any easier, I'm taking some leaps of faith where Ben is concerned these days, as well."

"I don't think I'd be able to be friends as easily with my father if he suddenly came back."

She figured that hadn't been an easy admission to make. "I have children, Gabriel. Ben deserves a chance to be a good grandfather, even if he didn't agree with my choice of life partner. That's always going to hurt, but he regrets it now. And I can't wish those years we spent apart never happened, because they did."

"That's one of the things I like about you. You're steadfast." Gabriel glanced toward her briefly. "I just don't think I'll ever be close to my father, especially now that he's got us all tied here for whatever purpose."

"Parenthood isn't easy at any age."

He stopped the truck outside a roadside ice-cream stand. "Would it bother you if you were part of a setup?"

"No, because I don't see myself that way."

Gabriel looked at her. "Even though Josiah gave your kids money, even though he asked me to look after you, you don't see this as part of a grand scheme?" He sighed. "I do. I resent the hell out of it."

She felt prickles run over her skin. "You're safe from me."

"Oh, I know that. You've got an honest-to-God electric fence up around you." Gabriel stared at her so intently she felt her bones turn to water. "It would almost be easier if you didn't."

"Meaning you could sleep with me and then move on? As easily as you're going to move on from your father's request?" She lifted her chin. "I didn't see you as the type of man who looks for the easy way out. Even Ben's got more spirit than that."

Well, that little minx, Gabriel thought. How dare she decide he was spineless? If she knew how badly he wanted to kiss her, shut those pretty lips up so they'd stop taunting him, she'd jump right out of his truck and run back to her safe little family.

He hated indecision, despised fear and inaction. Strength for a man lay in his stubborn attachment to his ideals, and she was shaking every one he had. He hadn't wanted to hire Ben, but part of him knew he'd win approval from her for it. Now he realized how desperately he craved that approval.

But he didn't want to feel this way, not so deeply.

About *any* woman, and no million dollars was worth it. A man worth his salt earned his own damn money, he didn't get paid to go to the altar.

That's what he felt like. That's what he'd really meant when he'd said he might not stick out the year. As ticked as he was at his brothers for making him hire Ben—a problem lodged in his own brain because Pete and Dane seemed to think it was a brilliant plan—he really didn't want to admit his father was controlling his life.

His choice of bride. His will to marry.

Dane, he'd noticed, had to feel the same because he didn't give two flips about who this mysterious Suzy was. "Do you know a Suzy in this town? I believe she may have a few children."

Laura turned big eyes on him. "Suzy? Don't you know, since you're asking about her?"

Gabriel shrugged. "Pop left Dane a letter about someone named Suzy."

"Oh." Laura seemed surprised by that. "She's not exactly his type."

"Really? What type is Dane's?" He watched her, obviously interested in her reply. What made her think she knew his brother at all?

"She has twin baby girls. I'm not certain any of you Morgans would want to take on parenting duties," Laura said slowly, then shook her head. "I see what's bothering you. Your father seemed to have planned to get you brothers women with ready-made families."

"Would be awful devious of him."

She nodded. "What I think you're underestimating is that he wanted grandchildren and doesn't mind adopting them into his family. I don't think he's actually crazy enough to assume he can induce four hardened bachelors to get to the altar."

"Yeah, Pop is that ornery." He nodded. "As least your father only took a shot at me. Mine's trying to shoot holes in our lives."

"You probably learned a lot about being bulletproof in the military," she said smoothly. "But your father wants the same thing mine does—to be close to his family. And if he uses money or connections to make that happen, can you blame him? He's not getting any younger."

"I prefer the direct approach."

She shook her head. "No, you don't. You've been running from me ever since you kissed me."

That was certainly direct coming from a young widow with children. "I've been trying not to do it again. You didn't seem too happy about it, and a gentleman respects a lady's wishes."

"I do appreciate you hiring my father, Gabriel. I saw something come into his eyes I haven't seen in years. I think it was hope. He seems to be changing."

"Wasn't easy. He's made an ass of himself."

She tapped his hand, which was resting on the steering wheel. "All of us probably have. I doubt he'll let you down, though."

"Hope not," he grumbled.

"So you've done what your father asked of you. You've watched out for me, employed my dad. You can go on with your life now and not worry about me."

"It's not that easy," Gabriel said with reluctance. "Your kids have gotten under my skin."

Laura looked at him. "What do you mean?"

"See, this is the part I wasn't expecting," he said, realizing all of a sudden what he hadn't been able to put into words before. "I didn't expect to find myself caring about your children."

She seemed to withdraw from him. He knew he had headed into deep water, and there was no going back to shore. "Guess I see why Pop liked them so much. Penny's adorable and Perrin… I hate it when he cries. He makes me want to comfort him."

Her face was a blank he couldn't read.

"It's okay," he said, steeling his heart. "I just find myself thinking about them…and even if I wanted to leave, I don't think I could leave *them*."

Laura didn't know what to say. Perhaps Gabriel was only offering himself in a brotherly capacity. He didn't act like a man who was interested in her—beyond that initial quick kiss, he hadn't made a move toward her.

He wouldn't. Behind that wolf's coat hid a chivalrous heart. Just like his father, just like his brothers. These men all walked dangerous paths, but they wanted the heart and soul of life: family, friends, community.

They just didn't want to admit it.

"If you're offering to take a man's role in my children's lives, I wouldn't turn that down," Laura said. "Mason spends a lot of time with them, and—"

He took her hand in his. Laura stopped speaking, held herself stiffly. Nothing in her body would relax.

Gently, he pressed her palm to his lips. His eyes were dark and fathomless.

Oh, boy. She was pretty sure he wasn't thinking *uncle* now. Her heart beat too hard; her breath went shallow. She couldn't take her hand away from his warm lips. She couldn't think. She felt herself falling under Gabriel's spell, falling faster than she'd ever fallen in her life. There was nothing safe here; this was not a gentle friendship he was offering.

She knew he was waiting for her to speak. A man like him would probably only offer his protection once…and yet, she could not reach into the flames to feel the desire he was offering to ignite.

She lowered her gaze, her pulse racing. After a moment, he put her hand in her lap and rolled down his window. "Ice cream?" he asked, his tone respectful.

"No, thank you."

"Think I'll get a limeade." He pressed the button, placed an order for two and stared out the front window pensively.

"Gabriel, I—"

"You know," he said, "I'll always be here for you, no matter what."

"For a year."

He nodded.

"Because your father asked you to watch out for me."

He turned to look at her. "It won't hurt me to spend time around your children. I know how to observe the boundaries you've set."

It was over, whatever he'd been offering her a mo-

"Hell, no. Didn't talk to him in America, sure as hell aren't going to cross the world to do it." Why would he, anyway? They hadn't had anything to say to each other in years.

"So what was it exactly that happened? Do you mind me asking?"

He did mind, but since it was Laura, he could tolerate the question. "There's no easy answer, other than we all got tired of being on the rough side of Pop's tongue." It had been hard facing constant criticism. None of them had ever lived up to Pop's ideals. "Pop was a hard taskmaster."

"I know. It's how he made his money."

"I guess. But his way wasn't my way, nor Dane's, nor Pete's and sure as hell not Jack's." If there was ever a man who'd had all his ambition for steady living driven out of him, it was Jack. Jack was perfectly suited to rodeo because it was a gamble, a walk on the wild side. Just man pitted against beast and a score that determined the outcome.

In other words, it was pretty much a day-to-day test of survival skills. "Beyond the fact we couldn't please Pop and we knew he'd never be proud of us, we did something he just couldn't tolerate. We knew he'd never forgive us, so we left. Unfortunately, when we left, none of us felt good about it, so we sort of drifted apart. Ten years moves a lot faster than you think it might. People say they get busy and they do, but it's just all noise for the relationships they're avoiding."

"Oh, I know how fast time can slip away."

Damn, he'd sounded like he was preaching. "We

were pretty much of a handful for Pop to raise. Chafing against authority and all that."

She smiled. "As a teacher, I have to ask if you did well in school."

"None of us did particularly well in regular school. All of us enlisted except Jack, and from there we found our own niches. I'm proud to say that the military put me through four years of college, and then I made top grades."

"Good for you."

"Yeah." He hadn't had Pop chewing on him to do well, so he'd done it for himself. "So then I served out the rest of my time and now I'm answering the call to family duty."

"Very honorable."

"Not really, I guess. Just trying to beat Pop at his own game."

She laughed. "I don't think you realize how much he's mellowed in his old age."

He grunted.

"And I don't really believe the reason you're doing all this is because you're trying to best your father," she said, "because that would mean you still care very much about his opinion, and you don't. Do you?"

Ah, she was being sneaky. He liked that. "Not sure."

"I know families can be messy. I also believe it's best to let the past go, if possible. Even if you felt your father was never proud of you, you're proud of your choices. You're your own man."

"You're a regular mind reader, aren't you?" He wasn't sure he liked her picking at his emotions.

"Teachers do some of that," she said coolly, "but having known your father, I know that he isn't a man who is truly comfortable with his emotions. Most people aren't."

He stopped at the ranch. "I'd better feed you a hamburger before you blow a circuit."

She smiled and got out of the truck. "Do you feel better now that you've cooled off some?"

"Maybe." He stared down at her, thinking he wasn't cool at all. He was on a slow boil around Laura.

"Just don't say you're not going to stick out the year again, at least not because of me." She looked up at him with those endless eyes, and he felt his resistance melting. "You're as easy to get attached to as your father, you know," she told him.

He didn't know what to make of that. Or her. He shook his head and followed her around to the back patio.

Ben was enjoying his grandkids. Pete and Dane were throwing a Frisbee around, and not too well, either. Gabriel scowled at the makeshift family gathering.

Then he looked at Perrin and Penny and broke out in a grin. They were cute, unafraid of Ben. He wasn't sure he could ever forgive Ben—the man could have killed him in a drunken stupor—but Laura was right. It would be better for Penny and Perrin if their grandfather was active in their lives.

If Ben was serious about turning his life around.

"I really do appreciate the job," Ben told him, his eyes shining over the heads of his grandchildren. "Feel like I have a purpose now. Your brothers told me I can start tomorrow."

"Great," Gabriel said, his voice stern. "You have to lock your guns in a gun cabinet or get rid of them altogether now that you've got grandkids. Even BB guns, air rifles, pellet guns. Hell, even water guns." He jutted out his chin.

The Frisbee landed on the grass. Pete and Dane stared at him. Laura nodded.

"He's right, Dad. It's a good idea."

Her gaze met Gabriel's. He knew she understood that he might not ever trust Ben, but she also thought he was trying to be cool about what happened. A man had a right to be ticked about being shot at, didn't he?

"It was a BB gun and he was far away," Pete told him. "Not that it couldn't have harmed you but we're not talking the need for a bulletproof vest, either, bro."

"Yeah, well." He'd been in the military too long to appreciate someone aiming a gun at him. Any kind of accident could happen with toddlers around. "For that matter, we're locking ours away in the attic. I don't think that's too cautious, do you?" He couldn't stand the thought of Penny and Perrin accidentally getting near a hunting rifle or… His chest constricted, his mouth went dry. Clearly his brothers thought he had gone mental, then they shrugged and went on with their game. Laura watched him, her expression concerned, but with a soft smile on her face. His mind raced, still on Penny and Perrin. There was a pond on the property, knives in the kitchen. The fireplace had sharp corners on it where Perrin could fall and hurt himself. There were two staircases that the children could tumble down. Acres of farmland surrounded them. He scanned the perimeter of the property, thinking that if one of the children wandered away, he wasn't sure they could find them easily.

He realized he was panicked. He could count on one hand the times he'd been scared in the military, and that was when he'd been in a war zone.

He couldn't imagine actually being a parent.

"Are you all right, Gabriel?" Laura asked.

He was beginning to wonder.

DANE WAS WONDERING, TOO, mostly what was eating at Gabriel. He jerked his head at Pete and they slipped inside the house. From the kitchen, they watched Laura and Ben play with the grandkids, and Gabriel hover nearby like an uncertain bear.

"Think he likes her?" Dane asked.

"Pop probably hoped he would."

They sprawled in the wooden, rounded-back chairs set at six places around the table. "There were four of us, and Pop. Guess we never needed the sixth chair unless we had company." Dane remembered they all used to toss their coats in the sixth chair, and Pop had gotten so mad.

"If he gets married before his year is up, does that mean he forfeits if he moves away?" Dane was thinking that if Gabriel wasn't open to getting serious, he was probably crazy. Laura was a beautiful woman. She was sweet. Her kids were great. He didn't give Pop much credit for anything, but he'd certainly picked a nice family to associate himself with.

"I don't know." Pete shook his head. "No one knows but Pop. I wouldn't say that to Gabriel, though."

"Oh, hell, no. Although he did consider leaving, briefly."

Pete laughed. "He hates being boxed in. Even when he was a kid, he hated being told what to do."

"So do I." They were all stubborn chips off the block like their dad. "Wonder why Pop never remarried if he was so set on family."

They sat quietly, listening to Gabriel and Laura calling to Penny as they tried to teach her to throw the Frisbee.

"Dunno. Didn't he always say marriage was for suckers?" Pete kicked his boots up onto a chair.

"He did." He'd been pretty bitter when their mom left. Refused to speak of her for years. "So if it's for suckers, he'll understand none of us choosing to settle down."

They heard Perrin's happy squeal, saw Ben go by the window holding his grandchild.

"Maybe one house can only hold so much bitterness," Pete said. "I don't understand why Pop didn't match me to a bride."

"Hey!" Dane sat up. "This Suzy girl is not my match!"

Laura came inside the kitchen, smiling when she saw them relaxing at the table. "Too much activity out there for you boys? You're not used to being around children. They can be overwhelming."

"I can handle it," Dane said.

"That's good." She got out glasses and a tumbler. "Gabriel says you're supposed to meet with Suzy Winterstone at some point? She has darling twins." She filled the pitcher with water and ice.

Dane sat up. "How old?"

"About twelve months old. Why?" She glanced at him curiously.

"Where's the father?" His mouth felt completely dry. Damn Pop! He could almost feel a trap ensnaring him.

"There isn't one. Well, not in residence anyway. Suzy had a boyfriend. She thought they were serious, but apparently, he wasn't. She's not heard from him since he went back to Australia or wherever he was from. Mr. Morgan hired a couple of nannies to help her and now they're doing just fine."

"Nannies?" Dane didn't really know what a nanny did. Didn't they just push around big fluffy strollers with oversized wheels?

"Well, she has the money to have help. Definitely having two children at once is challenging. And being alone would be hard. Plus, she had a C-section that had some complications."

"But if she has money, then she doesn't need...like, a man or anything." Dane knew he sounded like he was desperate to run away from the situation, and he was, but he didn't want to sound completely unchivalrous.

"She has money because of your father's generosity."

She took the tray of drinks outside, leaving Dane to stare at Pete.

"Pretty weird hobby Pop had."

"So was collecting huge acreages. Made him a lot of money, though." Pete sounded untroubled by that.

"You're just not worried because you didn't get a letter of doom." Dane felt annoyed by that. "Maybe Pop only felt that Gabriel and I were suitable choices for—"

"His schemes. I'd buy that. You guys are the youngest. And the most impressionable."

Dane shook his head. "I don't need a woman with two babies. That sounds high maintenance."

Pete laughed. "So is Pop."

LAURA STAYED LATER THAN she'd planned, watching Ben play with her children, feeling like her life was a completed circle now. Wholeness eased her heart. Penny and Perrin would have a father figure to look up to; Ben appeared to have a new lease on life.

She could forget the past. Not Dave, of course. Her heart still burned with sadness when she thought about him. But healing old pain made her feel brighter about everything. It was the start of summer, a great time for new beginnings.

Gabriel made her feel a snap of excitement, too, as much as she didn't want him to be part of her emotional healing process. With Ben in their lives, the father-figure gap she'd worried about would be alleviated.

She stood. "I have to take the children home and put them to bed. Thank you for a lovely evening."

Penny tiredly rubbed her eyes; Perrin's were drifting shut as he lay against Gabriel's chest. Gabriel and

Ben followed her as she picked Penny up and walked her to the car.

"I'll be by tomorrow," Ben said eagerly. "We could take the kids for a ride into town. I'd like to show them off to my buddies."

Laura smiled. "They'd love that."

Ben glanced at Gabriel self-consciously, then said, "Thanks for everything, Morgan."

Gabriel watched as Ben ambled away. "I can't get used to people calling me that in my father's house."

She strapped Penny into her car seat, then took Perrin from Gabriel to do the same. "What did they call you in the service?"

"Morgan. But I hear it here, and I look around for Pop."

"It took me a few weeks to get used to being Mrs. Adams."

It was then that the idea hit Gabriel, blooming big in his brain, like facing the worst fear he'd ever had.

Chapter Nine

"Try getting used to Mrs. Morgan," Gabriel said.

Laura turned around. "What do you mean?"

"It could be your name. For a year, anyway."

Her heart skipped strangely inside her. She wanted to run and hide in the worst way. "I don't want a husband."

"I don't want a wife in the traditional sense. But it wouldn't kill me to have some help making this year more bearable, I'll admit."

She sank into the seat and closed the car door. "I have to get my kids home."

He nodded, his eyes dark, his gaze unfathomable, before his attention switched to the kids in the backseat. "They look like they've had a full day. I'm glad I got to see them."

She hesitated, Gabriel's words just sinking in. "I'm sorry, but did you just propose to me?"

"I am proposing, yes. You can call it a business proposal, a merger or an idea to make my life easier. Whatever you want to call it."

She shook her head. "You are your father's son."

"Laura, I understand that you're still grieving. Whatever limits you'd want on a partnership between us would be fine by me."

She felt her fingers tremble. He didn't understand that she wasn't that much of a daredevil. Besides the obvious thrill of being married to a man like Gabriel, she wouldn't be able to count on the snuggling, the gentle companionship that Dave had offered.

"Just think about it for now. The option's open. Good night, kids." He reached through the window and touched each child's hand. "See you tomorrow."

She backed up the car and drove away, her mind whirling over Gabriel's proposal. She didn't want to get married. He didn't want to get married.

The only reason he'd asked her was because of his father. It had something to do with the wager his father had set upon his sons.

On the other hand, Gabriel really seemed to enjoy her children. He had even offered Ben a job, which she knew was against his better judgment, and maybe even hers. But the fact that he'd been willing to give her father a chance caught her attention. Sometimes a chance was all someone needed to start over, jump into better luck.

Her eyes widened as she realized he was giving her a chance, much like he had Ben. Gabriel was a giver, hiding behind a gruff exterior. She'd been fooled—or frightened—by his seeming harshness.

Marriage to him would be a business, just like everything else in the Morgan family. Because of their father, they couldn't help but think coolly, strategically.

She missed Dave's uncomplicated style. Day by day, come what may.

However, that lifestyle had led to being alone with two small children and financial hardship. Had it not been for Josiah Morgan—who'd seen fit to give her a chance—she'd still be knocked off her feet.

She was surprised to find herself mulling Gabriel's offer.

The temptation shocked her.

Her gaze found Penny and Perrin in the backseat through the rearview mirror, and she knew she was looking at the one reason she would consider Gabriel's offer. A chance for a wonderful father for her children didn't come along that often. Maybe she was being selfish, but secretly she longed for that chance for them.

It didn't hurt that Gabriel was sexier than any man had a right to be.

WHATEVER LABEL ANYONE wanted to put on marriage—partnership or love at first sight—Gabriel had never considered the option. He was too old to be fooled by sexual attraction, but he was insanely attracted to the little mother. Nor did he care that he was falling into his father's plan willingly.

Fact was, he didn't give a damn what his father or his brothers thought. He liked Penny and Perrin. He liked Laura. The piece of his life they'd begun to occupy felt like home to him, and he was smart enough to realize that all the houses and land Pop had acquired over the years were probably a filler for the feeling of home.

Bottom line, a man shouldn't be so dumb he let his pride rule him.

He knew Laura probably would never love him. Actually, his chances weren't great on that score, since she was still in love with her deceased husband. He understood, but he didn't mind waiting that out. The desire to own that piece of life they'd embedded in his heart, that intangible thing he'd craved all his life, was simply too strong. He was a risk taker; he wasn't afraid of it. In fact, he almost relished the challenge.

A great chunk of the challenge—and he wasn't afraid to admit it—was that he'd never planned to have children of his own. But he could be a father to two kids who needed one—at least he could try. This was the toughest part of proposing marriage: not knowing if he could be an adequate father. It required settling down for real commitment. Living in one town. This town.

And what if they stayed married beyond the year he needed to put in at the ranch? Little League, dance recitals, trying not to beat on teenage boys who would come to date his daughter, learning golf with his son. Golf was probably a good thing to learn, he mused. He'd have to attend church with them, something he had refused to do. God had been a very faraway component of his life in the world's hidden outposts.

He'd have to change a lot about himself. Being a parent required sacrifice. He wasn't afraid of sacrifice.

But the reality that he might let them down sent

sweat trickling down the back of his neck. He'd had a stern role model for fatherhood—he hoped Laura didn't factor that into her consideration of his proposal.

He really craved the piece of home she represented.

"HOME, SWEET HOME!"

The bellow from the foyer at 5:00 a.m. shot Gabriel upright in his bed. The voice was a nightmare; he remembered the lashing roughness of it.

It couldn't be. He'd simply had a nightmare.

He heard familiar heavy boots clomping on the hardwood floor downstairs. His pulse rate jacked up. He went to stare over the rail. Dane and Pete met him there.

Suddenly he was an awkward teenager again, wishing he didn't have to face the critical appraisal of his father. "What the hell, Pop?" he demanded.

The white-haired and strong Josiah Morgan looked up at his three sons. "I see money *can* buy a man everything." His weathered face folded into a frown. "Except Jack. Where the hell is Jack?"

"Not being bought," Gabriel replied. "Helluva price to pay for a family reunion, if that's what you wanted."

His father shrugged. "A good businessman checks up on his investments."

"I'm leaving," Dane said under his breath. "I don't need this crap."

Pete nodded. "Damn if he doesn't make me remember all over again how much I despise him. Old goat."

"Shh," Gabriel said. "Don't disrespect the chance to learn from life's mistakes."

"Are you crazy?" Pete asked. "The man isn't a father. He's a human computer."

"Maybe he can be reprogrammed."

"I don't care," Pete said. Their father ignored them, headed into the kitchen. They could hear his boots striding through to the den. "He doesn't own me."

"If Ben can turn over a new leaf, it's possible Pop can, too." Gabriel wasn't going to run from his father's dark bitterness. "He wouldn't be here if he wasn't up to something. Wasn't it you who said we should keep our enemy tucked close to our chest?"

"Yeah, but that was when it was your ass in hot water," Pete said, and Dane nodded.

"I personally don't believe in that enemy theory," Dane said. "It isn't the way I handled being a Ranger."

"I preferred distance between me and the enemy. The old saw about close enough for hand grenades worked for me," Pete said.

"God hates a coward." Gabriel turned to go downstairs to face his father.

"Nope, God gave me legs to depart." Dane shrugged. "I don't have a big enough shovel for all the crap Pop's gonna give us. And it ticks me off that he lured us here under false pretenses. He just wanted us home."

"I agree with Dane. I'm too old to be trapped into one of Pop's sorry-ass confrontations. His approval hasn't mattered to me in years. Gabriel, you're on your own if you're fool enough to stay." Pete went to his room.

Gabriel figured he was used to that. Hell, they all were. "Well, maybe Pop's carping won't bother me as much as it would you. Otherwise, my backup plan for getting along with Pop is to get married," he said, and grinned when his brothers stuck their heads back into the hall.

"Married?" Pete repeated.

Gabriel nodded. "I asked Laura to marry me."

"Whoa," Dane said, "you're setting a bad precedent here. Do not think that I intend to do the same. In fact, I tore up Pop's letter about that Suzy chick. I'll be telling him that before I leave, too."

"Why are you falling in line with Pop's scheming?" Pete demanded. "This isn't the military, you know. You don't have to jump when sarge commands. Once Pop knows he can buy you, you'll be screwed."

"I'm doing it because Laura needs me," Gabriel said, "although Laura would disagree." Actually that reason was too simplified, but he wasn't going to pour his heart out to his boneheaded brothers. They'd never understand.

"Well, probably no one can save you," Pete said. "Good luck."

"Yeah. Let me know where to send a gift," Dane said.

Gabriel replied, "Here, of course. I'm sticking out my year like I planned."

"With Pop in residence? Does Laura know?" Pete asked. His expression said Gabriel was nuts.

"Doesn't matter to me if Pop's here or not. Doesn't matter to me what Pop thinks about my marriage proposal." Gabriel's heart was singing at the freedom of not caring anymore. "To be honest, I couldn't care less. Everything is in the past and that's where it's going to stay."

"The optimism of a baby," Dane said. "I hope you know what you're doing."

Gabriel shrugged and went downstairs. "So. What ill wind blew you in?"

His father looked up. "How the hell was I to know my place was being looked after?"

"You knew I'd be here. I'd bet you expected all of us to be here." Gabriel slung himself into a leather chair opposite his father. For being apart ten years, he couldn't say there was an outpouring of emotion at the reunion. Nor had the old man changed much. He was craggier, whiter of hair, maybe, but still looked strong as a bull and was obviously marching to his own drummer. "You set this all up knowing we'd all do what you wanted."

"I wish it were that easy." Josiah looked at him. "Are you still in the military?"

"Did my time. Now I'm house-sitting for you."

"Mooching off me, you mean," Josiah said sourly.

"Okay," Gabriel said easily, rising to his feet. "I didn't realize you regretted your own scheme. Ben will be arriving every morning at 5:00 a.m. to water and feed the horses you left for the neighbors to look after."

"Ben? Ben Smith?"

Gabriel nodded. "You said you owed him something. So we gave him a job."

"No one consulted me." Josiah's brows pulled together. "The man is a leech."

"Well," Gabriel said, putting on a hat, "fire him if

you want, but you'll let Laura down. Those kids of hers are something, aren't they?" he said, not ashamed to be as sly as his father. "I'll be seeing you."

He went out, not listening to the expletives his father unleashed at him. Getting into his truck, he drove deserted country roads for hours. Then he headed to Laura's. He sat staring at her house, thinking, trying to pull a plan of action together.

He knew she wasn't likely to accept his proposal. But he could use the buffer between him and Pop. Pop liked Laura; she brought out his less antagonistic side.

She opened the door and seemed to hesitate. Then she waved at him to come inside.

He did before she changed her mind.

"I'm glad you came by," Laura said, "because we should probably talk."

That sounded good to him. He slid onto the bar stool she offered and watched as she made lemonade in the small, bright kitchen. "Where are the kids?"

"Napping. They've been tired lately, and I think it's the June heat." She pinched some mint sprigs, and he could smell the sweet green freshness. "The other night, you made me a proposal."

He nodded. He pretty much knew what her answer was going to be. She looked so calm and refreshing in a white top and blue jean shorts, cute sandals. "I probably didn't handle that as well as I should have."

She looked at him. "But you were sincere?"

"Oh, yeah. Definitely."

She took a deep breath. "I'm not going to fall in love with you."

"I know." Still, hearing the words stated so flatly threw a knife into his chest. He knew his odds were slimmer than a crack in a window. He thought about Pop, angry and pissed off at home, and wondered if he'd ever known real love. "I'm not the romantic type who expects notes signed with a heart."

Pain seemed to jump into her eyes. "I'm not looking for romance. In fact, it would bother me if that's what you're looking for. I just don't have that emotion available to me right now."

"I understand."

"I'd like to accept your proposal."

He sat up straight. "You would?"

She nodded, holding his gaze. "With a couple of modifications."

"Name them." Suddenly, his heart was skidding with joy. He didn't care what the qualifications were; he had never wanted anything so much in his life.

"My children," she said, "come first."

"I wouldn't expect anything else."

"You would in a marriage where you'd been my first love. You would have come first. But I understand that you're offering me a proposition that's pretty much cut-and-dried. As a single mother, I'll admit I see benefits to what you're offering."

She had no idea what benefits he'd be getting. A family. A real wife and kids. Okay, maybe not totally real, but close. Closer than he'd ever expected. "What else?"

For a long moment she looked at him, then took a

deep breath. "I know that you're supposed to live in your father's house for a year—"

"He's back," Gabriel interrupted. "As far as I can guess, he's nullified his own game. Pop never did like to give up control."

"I know Mr. Morgan's back." She motioned him to follow her into the garden and turned on a baby monitor. They sat an awkward distance away from each other, but at ten o'clock in the morning, there was no moonlight to confuse romance with negotiations. "Everyone knows he's back. He left a generous donation to the church, the library and the school. And then there's that." She pointed, and Gabriel saw a plastic sandbox shaped like a dinosaur and bags of sand. Shovels and buckets lay in a gaily decorated basket nearby.

"I can't figure him out. Pop came in the house snarling like his old self."

"The whole town is reeling this morning from the gifts." She shook her head. "Maybe you four were problem children?"

"Oh, he'd like you to think that. He'd like everyone to see his good, benevolent side. Thing is, it's so much easier to be nice to people on the surface. Family requires time and effort. It requires being close enough to give a damn."

"Which is why I really shouldn't ask this of you," she said, hesitating, "especially since you should be focusing on your father..."

He was afraid she'd get hung up on Pop and do

something generous like decide to crawfish out of his marriage proposal. "Let me worry about Josiah."

"You have to live here with us," she said calmly, her tone serious.

He stared at her, his heart instantly shifting into a slow thudding beat. "Here."

She nodded. "I can't take the children from the only home they've ever known, even if it's only for a year."

"I guess you can't." He wouldn't want them up-rooted from their security, especially so soon after losing their father.

"I realize doing so would break the agreement between you and your father—"

"He wasn't going to give any of us a million dollars, anyway," Gabriel said. "It was one of his ruses to trap us. Because he can't come right out and ask for what he wants."

Her eyes went wide at the bitterness in his tone. "I don't want to come between family—"

He got up, pulled her to her feet and kissed her on the mouth, long and hard, definitely not allowing her to retreat. She would never be able to say no to this man about anything, she realized, her heart falling.

Gabriel pulled slowly away from their kiss, brushed her cheek with his fingers, stroked her neck with his palms. "Don't mention him again. This is the family I want."

"I just think—"

"No, you don't." Gabriel shook his head. "Thinking

about the old man invites decay into my life. I choose you and Penny and Perrin."

"Your father has been giving away a lot of money," Laura said. "Maybe he is sincere. Maybe he's using his money to bring you closer to him."

"Then he has no idea what I really want in life." Gabriel kissed her hand. "Your children come first, and I live here with you. Have I got it?"

She nodded.

He felt happier than he had in a long, long time. "I'll move in after we're married."

"All right."

"We can probably get the marriage license and blood work done in a week—"

"Or we could go to Las Vegas," Laura said quickly.

He blinked. Was she hot for him? He didn't think so. If anything, she looked scared to death. "What about the children?"

"Mimi and Mason would be happy to keep them."

He didn't really want an Elvis wedding, or one away from her children. Penny would make a darling flower girl. Perrin would be a cute ring bearer of sorts. "Are you sure?"

"Definitely. As soon as possible. Just the two of us."

"I'll pick you up tomorrow." He walked to his truck, not feeling good about the arrangement.

It didn't matter. He could wait a couple of days to find out what Mrs. Adams had up her sleeve. She was taking advantage of his offer of marriage for a reason—but she was forgetting who'd raised him. He knew all about ulterior motives, and he wasn't afraid of hers.

He was finally getting a real family of his own.

GABRIEL FIGURED HE'D BUNKED in enough out-of-the-way places that he could sleep in the foreman's cottage overnight. Hell, he could sleep in a barn if it meant staying away from Pop. Why the hell had the old man really returned? He hadn't accomplished anything he'd supposedly wanted; Pete was gone, Dane had high-tailed it and he wasn't providing a sounding board for his father's bitching.

Yep, he'd take the foreman's deserted shack. Unlocking the door with the key hidden in a secret wall crevice, he went inside, glad to be finally alone.

It had been an exciting day. He'd made plane reservations, wedding reservations, had gotten Laura a ring. Of course, he couldn't get married without buying a couple of stuffed animals for his new kids: a soft, fluffy horse for Penny, a paunchy, huggable teddy bear for Perrin. He couldn't wait—he would be a hundred times better father than Pop.

The foreman's shack hadn't changed, and to his relief it wasn't in the terrible condition he'd expected. He and his brothers had spent some happy hours here hiding from their father. They'd used it as a home away from home. Pop had never been able to keep much help around, so the cottage went for long periods of time unoccupied.

He flipped on one of the bedroom lights, and a figure rose from the bed.

"What the hell?" the figure demanded.

Gabriel frowned. "Ben, what the devil are you doing here?"

Ben rubbed his eyes. "Trying to sleep! What are you doing here?"

"This house is on Morgan property," Gabriel reminded him.

"If you want me taking care of your livestock at five a.m., this is my house." Ben stuck out his jaw. "I can't sleep in fields forever."

Gabriel considered that. The man would be his father-in-law tomorrow. He supposed it was churlish of him to begrudge the man a home. "You think you could have asked?"

Ben shrugged. "The door hadn't been opened in probably five years. Didn't figure as it mattered."

It probably didn't. "I'm avoiding Pop."

"You think *you* are?" Ben swung his legs to the side of the bed. "He wouldn't exactly be jumping for joy to find me on his property." He squinted at him. "Did you tell him you hired me?"

"Yeah." Gabriel sank into an old leather chair that had seen better days. "I'd say he wasn't happy, except he wasn't happy about anything. That's sort of the groove he stays stuck in."

"I don't mind sharing the place with you if you'll sleep," Ben said. "Five o'clock comes early, you know, and my bosses are real jackasses." He snickered and slid back in bed. "Nice of them to hire me, though."

Gabriel rubbed his chin. "Yeah, about that, Ben."

"You promised you'd be silent as a mouse," Ben told him. "So far all I hear is yak, yak, yak."

"I'm marrying your daughter tomorrow."

A long pause met his words. Then Ben sat up.

"Nope," he said, "that ain't gonna do."

Chapter Ten

Laura was nervous. Accepting Gabriel's marriage proposal filled her with a strange type of dread. She'd said yes for all the wrong reasons.

Gabriel was a handsome man. He was sexy, the kind of man most women wanted. But there was something she'd kept from him: she was the reason Josiah Morgan had returned.

Mr. Morgan had made her promise that if any of his sons came home to Union Junction, he was to be notified. She didn't know any of the Morgan boys, and innocently, she had thought it was awful the way they never came to visit their father. Maybe she'd even felt a sad yearning for the relationship she lacked with her own father. Because of the gifts Mr. Morgan had given her children, she'd readily agreed to his request.

She hadn't realized how much they despised him—and she hadn't dreamed he meant to return home to confront them. Mr. Morgan's return had driven Gabriel to a marriage proposal. He claimed he wanted the one thing he'd never had: a real family. Children he could love and hold and call his own. Secretly, she couldn't say that she didn't adore the idea that her children would have a father like Gabriel.

She wasn't going to deny to herself that Gabriel didn't make her blood run hot. A fantasy or two or ten had definitely played in her mind, hotter ones than she'd care to admit.

Yet if he knew that Mr. Morgan had planned to return, had basically lured them, and she had helped—she was pretty certain it was a betrayal that Gabriel would not be able to forgive.

She wasn't going to tell Gabriel. He had offered marriage for one year. She had been honest, told him that she wouldn't fall in love with him. She'd had love before, knew what it felt like, how deep it lodged in her heart. What she felt now was lust and a desire to have safety for her children, nothing more.

And when Gabriel left in a year, she would tell Penny and Perrin that Gabriel would always be part of their lives. He would, she knew, just as Mr. Morgan remained part of their world.

Gabriel just wouldn't stay in hers.

Knowing that kept the guilt she felt at bay. Even if she felt like a traitor, it had been an innocent mistake. She'd thought she was doing the right thing, and she couldn't change that now.

JOSIAH MORGAN HAD FEW friends. He had no family who cared for him. It was ironic how much he wanted what he couldn't have, when he could buy everything in sight.

An old journal lay open on his desk. Pictures of him

and his wife at their wedding stayed between the pages of the heavy journal; they were slightly grainy with age and wrinkled at the corners. He treasured those two pictures more than anything he owned.

He knew where his wife had gone. With the money he'd accumulated in his life, he'd been able to hire an investigator. Gisella was living in France, in the countryside, with people who remembered her from her childhood. Her own parents were long deceased, but Gisella still fit in to the surroundings of her youth. He would never contact her, but he needed to know where she'd gone.

He'd met Gisella in the military, in London, when he'd been stationed there as a cook. Back then he hadn't had two pounds in his pocket, but Gisella hadn't cared. They'd found plenty of activities to fill their time, and then Jack had been conceived. Head over heels in love, Josiah married Gisella. He smiled, remembering that day. Never had he seen a woman look more beautiful. Nowadays most women wore too much makeup, had their bodies artificially plumped or toned or browned—Gisella had been the salt of the earth.

As soon as he'd gotten out of the military, he'd begun his lifelong habit of acquisition. He was determined to deserve this wonderful woman, give her everything she didn't have. It was rough financially while they were married, but she believed in his dreams. She gave him four beautiful sons.

He was moody, struggling with start-up businesses. He was under the weight of trying to deserve the woman he loved. They fought a lot. Gisella hated being left alone on the ranch; she was afraid of the dark.

Their few cattle started disappearing, and Gisella became nervous with fear. Always edgy, afraid for the boys. Terrified for herself.

He was gone on a business trip to Dallas when he got the worried call from Jack. All of eight years old, Jack tried manfully to tell him his mother was gone—in the end, he dissolved into tears that Josiah would never forget hearing him cry. He hurried home, finding the boys were being kept by Ben Smith, whom Gisella had called for help.

He would never, ever forgive Ben Smith for driving his wife to the airport.

It had been years, and he was still mad as hell. Ben told him that Gisella had planned to call a taxi, but he'd driven her to Dallas to try to talk her out of leaving. Gisella had left a babysitter at the house, with instructions to stay with her sons until their father returned.

He could feel his blood boil all over again. Betrayal, by everyone he knew.

The boys would never understand that from that day forward, he had to teach them to be men. They needed to know that life was hard, and there were disappointments. Nothing was easy, nothing was free. Nobody gave a man a single thing, he earned every bit, and if he was smart, he made that lesson the bedrock of his soul.

Josiah shut the journal and stared at it for a long moment. In the journal, he wrote words daily that he wanted his sons to know about him, about their mother. He was aware they disliked him intensely. But they would know that he had loved them, and whether they considered his love too harsh was something they could decide after he was gone.

His kidneys were failing and he had maybe a year, possibly less. He would not take treatment, would not be chained to a machine. Would not show weakness, nor the fatigue that robbed his strength. Not even the depression that came upon him from time to time. A kidney transplant could save him, but that was not an option he chose. There were many more deserving people in the world who had something to live for. He'd been given his own chances to do something good with his life, and God would judge that.

He'd leave the healing to those who deserved it. He'd struck his deal with life, now he was determined to go out with fireworks. He would be no wimpy candle that blew out unresisting at the slightest puff of wind.

"NOPE," BEN SAID, "you ain't marrying my daughter. And if that's why you gave me a job, then you can sure as hell shove it, Morgan."

Gabriel threw himself on the sofa and closed his eyes. The sofa was scratchy and old, made of a plaid fabric that had seen better days. It felt lumpy and out of shape, but Gabriel was too tired to care. "Go to sleep, Ben. We'll argue in the morning."

"Morning or night, next week or next year, I ain't giving you my blessing. You damn Morgans ruin everything you touch, and you ain't gonna upset Laura."

"Listen, Ben, you're no angel. And Laura's old enough to make her own decisions."

"That's just like a Morgan, thinking they can bend everybody else to their will. I'm telling you, leave Laura and the kids out of your screwed-up life."

Ben had a point. He had several points, in fact, but nothing was going to stop Gabriel from marrying Laura, not even her own father. He wanted her so badly that he could practically taste her. Desire washed through him, tugging at him, binding him to her in a way he could never explain.

"She deserves a man who can love her," Ben said, standing over him, "and you come from stock that loves no one but themselves."

"It's not entirely true." Gabriel grimaced.

"Yes, it is. Your whole clan turns on each other at the snap of a finger. Where are your brothers?"

"Not here."

"And how many words have you spoken to your father?"

"Under fifty, maybe," Gabriel admitted.

"Which is why you're hiding out here, and why you're trying to rope my daughter into marrying you. Fact is, you're doing this to get your father's approval."

Gabriel blinked. "You could have a point."

"Yeah. I do. You know your father provided for my grandchildren. So what do you do? You go and ask their mother to marry you. You haven't even known Laura a week. It's not love at first sight or something romantic like that—it's trophy bagging. Like she's some kind of prized deer you can brag that you shot."

"Hey!" Gabriel jerked up on the sofa. "Ben, shut your mouth before I shut it for you. That's a terrible way to talk about your daughter!" There might have been some family psychology at work—he didn't mind admitting that Laura represented wholeness and a sense of family he craved—but he would never see her as a trophy.

Ben stuck out his chin belligerently. "I'm talking about you, not my daughter. You're the hunter here. She's just the innocent prey in your quest for game."

Gabriel shook his head. "I don't know what to say, except you sort of worry me. Didn't you act up about Laura's first husband?"

Ben raised a finger, wagging it at Gabriel. "He wasn't good enough for Laura."

"Is anybody?" Gabriel honestly wanted to know.

"Probably not," Ben barked. "She hasn't yet met the man who deserves her. But I don't expect you to understand that, because you're your father's son."

Gabriel sighed. "Ben, you gotta calm down. It's going to be hard to share Christmas dinners if you talk like that all the time."

"I'm being honest."

"And I appreciate that, but I'm not the devil. And Laura's a smart woman. She wouldn't have said yes if she didn't think marrying me had some merit."

Ben snorted. "Laura is a grieving widow. She thinks you'll be a good father. Maybe you can be, but maybe you won't be. But, son, I know more about you and your family than you'll ever know, and I'll be willing to bet you've never had a relationship with a woman that lasted a year."

Gabriel's brows furrowed.

"Have you?" Ben demanded.

"How do my past relationships affect my future ability to be a good husband?"

Ben put a boot on the side of the sofa and leaned close. "Rumor has it you and your brothers make sport of women."

"Not true," Gabriel said defensively. "While I can't speak for my brothers, I can't exactly say I personally ever met the woman I wanted to spend my life with."

"And did you tell my daughter you planned to stay with her for the long haul?" Ben asked. "I'm just curious, because marriage is a long-term thing. It's a commitment. Something I haven't ever known you Morgans to be good with."

"I was in the military. Can't think of a more demanding commitment than that."

"That's a paycheck. It was also an escape from your father." Ben left the room, heading back to his own exile. "Marriage should not be an escape route, Morgan."

He closed his eyes. "True," he muttered. "I'll take it under advisement."

"I'll be saying the same to Laura."

"Probably a good idea." He'd be worried about having himself for a son-in-law if he was in Ben's boots. Why had he even mentioned it to Ben?

He stared up into the darkness, examining his conscience. It was traditional to ask a father for his daughter's hand in marriage. Perhaps he'd hoped for his future father-in-law's blessing. He really cared about Laura and her family, and that included Ben to some degree. He didn't blame Ben for feeling the way he did. Yet Gabriel knew he was marrying Laura—unless she changed her mind about having him. He briefly considered tying Ben to his bunk, at least until the *I dos* were spoken, but the old man had a right to do his damnedest. It didn't matter what Ben did, anyway. Laura had said yes, and she wasn't the kind of woman to go back on her word.

Chapter Eleven

"I'm getting married," Gabriel told his father the next day before he left to pick up Laura on the way to the airport. "I know news travels fast here, so I wanted you to hear it from me." He figured Ben had probably already run a marathon to tell his old man, but Josiah looked surprised.

"You are?"

Gabriel nodded. "I'm marrying Laura in Las Vegas today. We'll be back by nightfall."

Josiah's brows beetled. "Not much of a honeymoon."

Gabriel shrugged. "She has two young children. She'd rather not leave them long." He wouldn't tell his father they didn't need any real *honeymooning.*

"Penny and Perrin would be fine with me. They like me," Josiah offered.

"Thanks. But Laura's got her heart set on coming home."

Josiah grunted. "Your brothers slunk out of here without saying much to me. Guess you'd be gone, too, if it wasn't for Laura and the kids."

He probably would. Pop's gaze was on him, inspecting him, waiting for an answer. What was the right answer? What did Pop want to hear? He didn't know. "Since you're back, you can take care of the place yourself, right? And you've got Ben."

Josiah scowled. "I don't need Ben."

"Well, get along with him." Gabriel tossed some stuff into his truck. "I probably won't be seeing you for a while."

"You probably won't. I'm planning on going back to France early next week."

Gabriel turned to look at his father. "Why did you really come home?"

Josiah shook his head. "It's my house, isn't it?"

"So what was the deal about the million dollars if we stayed here for a year?"

Josiah fixed dark eyes on him. "None of you seem to be planning to do it, so what does it matter?"

True enough. Gabriel knew his father had simply been moving them around like chess pieces.

"Gabriel, I have to admit I'm glad you and Laura are getting married."

"I guess so. It makes you a grandfather. Wasn't that what this was all about?" Gabriel felt a little bitter about satisfying one of his father's desires, the familiar resentment welling up inside him that Josiah Morgan was always behind every move in his life.

"Actually, I never dreamed she'd have you," Josiah said. "She was pretty torn up when Dave died. I just wanted you to look after her and the kids while I was gone."

"Did you cheat Ben on purpose?"

Josiah frowned. "I saw value in something that Mr. Smith did not. Including his own family, I might add."

He had a point. But that didn't make it right with Gabriel.

"Pop, have you ever thought that maybe you shouldn't capitalize on people's weaknesses?"

"Hell, no. It's a dog-eat-dog world. Don't kid yourself."

Gabriel shook his head. "Listen, I've got to head out."

He looked at the man who was his father, and yet who felt like he was something else: judge, jury, prosecutor. Time had stretched the bonds between them and deepened the scars. He didn't think either of them would really ever heal the wounds.

"Gabriel, thanks for telling me about the wedding." Josiah turned to go inside his house. For just a moment, Gabriel felt sorry for his father, then decided it was a wasted emotion. Josiah played by his own rules, and they were rules he was comfortable with. Gabriel wasn't going to make the mistake of judging his father.

He drove off to pick up his soon-to-be bride, and it belatedly occurred to him that he had received his father's approval. It felt good.

Marrying Laura would feel good. He'd counted the hours since yesterday.

He was going to be a husband and a father. He couldn't wait.

But when he got to Laura's house, she wasn't there. Instead, he found a note taped to the door.

Gabriel, Dad was having chest pains. I've taken him to the hospital. Laura

LAURA WAS NEARLY SICK WITH fear. Her father looked so pale. Nurses scurried to hook him up to various monitors and an IV. She didn't want him to have a heart attack, she wanted him to be well. Life was short, and she'd wasted time Ben could have had with his grandchildren. She regretted every moment of her stubborn pride.

She should have tried harder to make her father understand how much she loved Dave—although as much as she hated to admit it, Dave hadn't helped to ease Ben's worries. In retrospect, she realized how much Dave's laconic approach to life had worried Ben.

Ben had mumbled how sorry he was that she had to take him to the hospital when she was supposed to be leaving for a wedding in Las Vegas. Laura comforted her father, telling him that everything would work out eventually. She didn't want him upset.

Gabriel strode into the hospital, coming straight to her to close her in his embrace. She allowed herself to be enveloped in his strong warmth, appreciating his caring. "He got sick all of a sudden."

He stroked her hair. "He'll be fine."

She wasn't certain. "I hope so." Through the small window, she could see her father being wheeled down the hall. "It just came on so quickly."

"They'll get him fixed up."

She looked up at Gabriel. "Sorry about the wedding."

"Las Vegas has weddings every day. We can reschedule."

"Like a business meeting," she murmured.

He stroked her cheek. "Ben was sleeping in the old foreman's shack. He may be getting too old to live the life of a gypsy."

"How do you know where he was sleeping?"

"I found him there. I tried to ask him for your hand in marriage, but it wasn't the most encouraging conversation."

An old, painful memory slid forward. "Oh?"

"Yeah. I can't say he exactly gave me his blessing, but I made it clear how much I wanted to marry you. We left it at that."

Laura doubted anything had been *left.* Ben had refused his blessing when Dave had asked him, as well. And now Ben was in the hospital with sudden chest pains. Was a short-term marriage, a year of life with Gabriel, worth going through this again? She should have seen this coming. Ben was uneasy about the Morgans and he definitely wasn't going to give her away to them without a fight. "Was he upset?"

"No more or less than usual. At least he didn't take another shot at me." He turned her chin up so he could look into her eyes. "Ben's illness is not because we plan to get married."

She hated how worried she'd sounded. "I'd like to wait until he's better before we…before we do anything."

"I agree." Gabriel nodded, gently releasing her. "Where are the children?"

"Mimi's looking after them."

"I'll swing by and grab them, if you want. I can keep them while you're here with your father."

She looked at him, her blue eyes a bit guilty. "Are you sure you're ready for that? They can be a handful."

He grinned. "I think I can handle your crew."

He certainly seemed to look forward to the challenge. "I hope you know what you're signing on for."

He shook his head. "I've enlisted before. This will be a piece of cake. Call me if you need anything."

He went off, not the least bit bothered by her hesitation to marry him, not worried about Ben's non-blessing. Dave had been bothered by it, but she had the sudden impression that Gabriel was not the kind of man who would give a damn. He'd love the blessing, but if not, he sure wouldn't lose any sleep over it.

Maybe Ben had a simple case of heartburn, and then none of this would matter. Perhaps Gabriel had misunderstood her father's reticence about their marriage.

She knew Gabriel had misunderstood nothing.

"Mrs. Adams?"

She turned to face a doctor. "Yes?"

"I'm Dr. Carlson. I understand that you're your father's only relative who can see to his care?"

"I am." Chills suddenly ran through her.

"He's had a mild heart attack. Nothing severe, but we're going to keep him here overnight. We're evaluating his condition and need to run some tests. We'll look for a blockage, or other issue that may have caused this."

"Thank you." She felt ashamed for wondering

whether her father had staged a heart attack to keep her from marrying Gabriel. "Can I see him?"

"For a minute. Then I want you to go home and get some rest."

She nodded, following the doctor into her father's hospital room. "How are you doing?"

"I'm fine," Ben said. "These doctors need to let me out of here."

She patted his hand. "Stay calm, Dad. Don't get excited."

He sighed. "I am not a good patient."

She nodded. "Most people aren't. But the doctor says I can only stay a moment."

"Guess I messed up your wedding." He didn't look too unhappy about that. "I told Gabriel I didn't think he deserved you."

"I know. He told me."

Ben twisted his lips. "Guess I worried myself into a little chest pain."

Guilt jumped inside her. "You shouldn't have. I'm a big girl, Dad."

"Fathers worry. That's what we do."

She shook her head. "You need to let go."

He nodded. "I guess it was just a shock. I felt like you and I had just patched things together, and then suddenly I needed to keep you to myself. Felt like I had to fight for you. You know I don't trust those damn Morgans."

"This is my decision, Dad. Gabriel's a good man."

"You say that about Josiah, too, and he's a scoundrel."

She laughed and kissed her father lightly on his forehead. "He's not the only scoundrel in Union Junction."

Ben grunted.

"I'm leaving before your blood pressure skyrockets."

"I think it already did," he said, in a bid to get more attention.

She smiled. "I'll be back tomorrow."

He looked at her, his eyes big and sad. "I wish you could stay my little girl."

She blew him a kiss and backed away, feeling like the worst daughter in the world.

GABRIEL SMILED WHEN MIMI opened the door. "Hello, Mimi."

"Come in, Gabriel. How's the patient?"

He looked around the big, welcoming entry of the house at the Double M ranch. Gabriel could honestly say he wouldn't mind having a place like this one day, where little feet could run and play, and he and Laura could raise their family.

He seemed to think about Laura and the life he wanted with her all the time. "Nice place, by the way."

"Thank you."

"The patient isn't pleased to be a patient," Gabriel said.

"I wouldn't expect Mr. Smith would be happy to be in the hospital." Mimi ushered Gabriel into the kitchen. Through the window, he could see Penny and Perrin playing with Mimi's brood. Though Mimi's children were a bit older, they included Laura's children in their activities. There was a large swing set and fort, a sandbox and a couple of Hoppity Hops littering the lawn.

He remembered having a Hoppity Hop. Jack had been the best of all of them when it came to racing on them; maybe it had been good early training for the rodeo.

Mimi glanced over her shoulder at the children. "They make me smile, too. Laura's done a great job with her kids."

"Yeah." He couldn't wipe the smile from his face.

"So I hear congratulations are in order?"

He dragged his gaze away from the children. "I hope so. When Ben gets well, congratulations will be in order."

Mimi smiled. "Laura sounded happy about marrying you."

That shocked him. If anything, she'd seemed reluctant to him. "Glad to hear it."

"She asked me not to tell anyone what you were planning, but she felt like you two are very comfortable despite only knowing each other a short while. I take it you want a low-key wedding?"

He nodded, not certain what Laura would want if the circumstances were romantic rather than advantageous.

"I know you'd planned for an elopement," Mimi said carefully, "but I also know you were having to plan spur of the moment. So Mason and I were wondering if perhaps—when Ben gets well, of course—if you'd like to get married at the Double M."

He blinked, instantly able to see Laura in a pretty dress on the wide green lawns of the Double M. It was the kind of wedding she deserved. “That’s very generous of you and Mason.”

Mimi smiled. “It would be our wedding gift to you and Laura. Then Penny and Perrin could be at the wedding, and by then Ben will be well enough to give his daughter away.”

Gabriel wasn’t sure Ben would be up to the task. Laura would have to be pried out of his grasp.

“You know he didn’t get to give her away before.”

Gabriel shook his head. “I didn’t know that.”

“Ben was so dead set against Laura marrying Dave that Laura ended up eloping. Coincidentally, they married in Vegas. She said it wasn’t what she’d wanted, but she’d had no choice.” Mimi put some biscuits on the counter and covered them with a plaid napkin. She set some fresh fruit out in a bowl, and the washed fruit shone in the light. “Laura may feel differently, and my feelings won’t be hurt if you don’t take Mason and me up on our offer, but it does seem that a woman should have one hometown wedding in her life. Don’t you think?”

He certainly agreed. In fact, he wanted no reminders of Laura’s first wedding. “Thank you, Mimi. I’ll see if I can budge her on the matter.” He wasn’t sure what Laura would say. Pieces of the future were fitting together in his mind, and the more he thought about a traditional wedding, with vows spoken in front of family, and Penny and Perrin there, the more he knew he wanted this moment to feel like forever.

He could see wanting Laura for the rest of his life.

Now that his father had returned, and the deal was off, he didn't need a one-year marriage. He didn't need to get married at all. He could go back to being as unattached as he was before.

But that wasn't what he wanted, not his freedom nor a one-year marriage. Suddenly, he was grateful that Ben's heart condition had slowed everything down. Somehow he needed to convince Laura that he had changed—she could trust him for something deeper than a fast fix.

Chapter Twelve

Gabriel drove Penny and Perrin to his house, feeling pretty good about how excited they'd acted to see him. Of course, Perrin didn't show his enthusiasm quite like Penny, but the baby definitely seemed pleased. He'd debated whether to take them to Laura's house where they'd be among familiar things, then decided he'd head over to Josiah's. His father would enjoy seeing the kids—it might even soften the old man up a bit.

Penny and Perrin might be the only way to put a smile on Josiah's face. Penny saw Josiah on the front porch and ran to be enveloped in his arms.

"This is a surprise," Josiah told Gabriel. Josiah's eyes glimmered gratefully at Gabriel. In that moment, Gabriel knew he was going to spend extra energy trying to connect with his father. It could be his father lying in that hospital. As cranky as Josiah was, he didn't want to shortchange their relationship.

"Didn't figure you'd mind," Gabriel said.

"Nope. Come out here, kids. I have something to show you."

The four of them walked to a south paddock. A

small white pony stood grazing, glancing up at them before returning her attention to the grass.

"Horse!" Penny exclaimed. "Can I ride her?"

Josiah laughed. "As soon as she gets settled in, you may ride her. Perrin, too, when he's old enough. I bought that pony for you kids."

Gabriel raised a brow at his father. "You bought them a pony?"

"Every child should have a pony. At least every child who wants one, and who has a little land."

Gabriel watched as Penny held out a piece of grass to try to lure the pony to her. "You never bought us a pony."

Josiah grinned. "You boys were too busy rappelling out your bedroom window to need a pony. You got plenty of exercise."

"So you cut that limb off on purpose?"

Josiah nodded. "Just hadn't figured on the rope ladder."

It felt good to talk about the past. The moments of ease that peeked into their relationship felt healing.

"So, how's my thin-skinned farmhand doing?"

Gabriel snorted. "Ben's tough."

"I didn't need you hiring half a man to work this place."

Gabriel looked at his dad. "You weren't supposed to be here. So I made an appropriate hire. The man has plenty of experience. Not to mention that you ran off two able-bodied sons."

"I didn't run them off. They deserted."

"You didn't make them feel welcome." He didn't

feel welcome, either, but he had Penny and Perrin to think of.

"What was I supposed to do? Buy them a pony?" Josiah asked.

"You're supposed to just be nice," Gabriel said. "It gets you what you want. Especially after you've gone to the trouble to gather everybody around."

Josiah grunted.

"You might as well tell me," he said, helping Perrin to put his feet on the bottom of a wood rail, "why you went to the trouble of scheming to get us all home."

His father picked Penny up, kissed her on the cheek. "So did Ben ruin any chance of you and Laura getting married? You know he's pulling this sickly routine on purpose."

"I don't know that to be true."

"Ah, hell, yeah, Ben was probably one of those kids who threw fits."

"Shh, that's their grandfather," Gabriel cautioned.

Josiah shrugged. "It's true. Anyway, here comes Laura. We'll ask her how the hypochondriac is doing."

"I wouldn't phrase it that way," Gabriel said, making Josiah laugh.

"Hi," Gabriel said, when Laura walked to the fence. "How did you know we were here?"

"Where else would you go?" She looked up at him, her eyes dark with fatigue. "This is your home."

True. He didn't glance at his father. "How's Ben?"

"Fine, for the moment," Laura said. "Still, he needs a change in diet and an improved lifestyle. The doctor feels he's under too much stress."

Josiah turned away with Penny in his arms. Gabriel thought he'd seen a grin on Josiah's face. "Glad he's going to be all right."

"Gabriel, can I talk to you?"

"I'll take the kids in for a snack," Josiah offered. "Good news about your father, Laura."

"Thank you." She pushed her hair back, though the early-morning breeze pulled it forward again. "Gabriel, maybe we were moving too quickly."

He watched her intently. Damned if Ben didn't appear to be winning the battle. "Maybe. Maybe not."

Laura looked uncertain. "I don't want to cause my father any stress."

"Of course not." Gabriel shook his head in sympathy.

"Since you and your father appear to be getting along better, you probably don't need my help any longer."

"Your help?"

"By marrying you," Laura said quickly.

"Oh." Her face was so drawn that Gabriel realized it was Laura who was stressed, maybe more than Ben. She was afraid. Afraid that her relationship with her father might be forever on hold if he suddenly died. She was afraid that marrying against her father's wishes a second time might be too much for him to take. "I understand your position."

"Thank you," she said on a rush. "I've got to get back to the hospital."

"Leave the kids here," he said quietly. "Dad and I are enjoying them."

"Dad?" she said. "Not Pop?"

He shook his head. "It doesn't matter. You go on. I'll take good care of the children."

"Thank you so much for understanding."

"Yeah. I'm just that kind of a great guy," he said as she got into her small seen-better-days car. He waved as she drove away, though it was hard to pull off the lightheartedness. The pony neared the fence, eying him curiously. "There went my bride," he told the pony. "She has no idea I want to marry her for real. I've fallen in love with her, and I don't think she sees me quite the same way."

It hurt. And he was pretty sure that a gentleman would back off and be an understanding kind of guy. He could do that, in fact, would do that, since she'd asked it of him, but he recognized it was going to take a chunk of his soul to act like he was good with it.

At least he still had Penny and Perrin. He was pretty sure they liked him. He headed inside to find out.

Penny and Perrin were riding on Josiah like he was an energetic *horsey.* For his part, Josiah seemed to enjoy the game as much as the kids. He neighed, pawed the air and generally acted silly. "I can't remember you doing that for us," Gabriel commented.

Josiah let out a gleeful neigh, his white hair shaking as he pretended to be a horse. "Where do you think I got these skills?"

"I thought Penny and Perrin conned you into being a substitute for the pony you bought them. Does Laura know you did that?"

"We need not share that just yet." Josiah carefully

rode Perrin across the "creek," a swath of the den where the furniture had been pushed away. "She was in a bit of a hurry to get back to Ben, wasn't she? Think he's really all right?"

"I guess so." Gabriel went into the kitchen to make tea and grab some of the cookies the church ladies had recently left. The realization that Josiah was in town and bearing gifts had brought many containers of delicious treats to their house. It was too bad Pete and Dane had elected to leave—the eats were fantastic. Gabriel munched on a double chocolate chip cookie from a box labeled Thank You For Everything, Mrs. Gaines.

"What'd you do for Mrs. Gaines?" He set the cookie tray on the table and pulled Perrin into his lap. "No cookies for you, sir. You get something more delicious, like one of these meat stick thingies your mom left you. Ugh. Probably better for you, but still."

"She's the town librarian. They had a wish list last Christmas that asked for a new reference set. Times have changed, you know. Nobody hardly wants the big fat books as much. They want the CD versions, or the website subscriptions, and that takes updated technology. I left a little money to cover the technology." He swiped a cookie, set Penny beside him, stuck a napkin in her hand—the picture of a happy grandfather. "It's especially important for the high schoolers who want to study in the library. Not everybody has a computer in their home."

"Yeah, Dad, about that." Gabriel sipped at some iced tea, carefully moving Perrin's hand away from the cookie tray and giving him an animal cracker instead.

"I know kids don't always remember everything their parents did for them, but it does seem that you've entered a new, more benevolent stage of your life. One we aren't familiar with."

"You're asking why I didn't coddle you boys since I had so much money. Why I kicked your asses instead of giving out hugs. Why I tried to make men out of you instead of pansy-assed good-for-nothings who were always looking for a handout."

"In so many words," Gabriel said, "I suppose you just gave me the answer."

"Kids who have everything handed to them generally don't fare well. You boys were already a little wild. You had no mother to soften you. I was busy running things and couldn't mother hen you. I figured if you had it in you to be successful, you'd get there on your own. And if you didn't, you'd only have yourself to blame."

Gabriel nodded. "I see your point." He saw it, but that didn't address the affection part of the parenting equation, the pleasure of enjoying your child. "So the reason you're spoiling Penny and Perrin is—"

"I can enjoy being a doting grandfather if I want."

"I can't speak for my brothers, of course, but seeing the softer side of you—"

"I'll tell you something, Gabriel. Since you're being honest, and since you hung around, which frankly shows some of what I was trying to teach you boys sunk in—which is to face the hardest parts of life bravely—I liked watching you kids struggle. I liked seeing you get tough. Raising men is a hard thing.

Raising whiners is easy." He kissed Penny on the forehead and handed her another cookie. "But in case you feel left out—and I suspect you do or you wouldn't be trying to improve my parenting skills—I'll tell you a little secret."

"Shoot," Gabriel said dryly. "I'm all ears."

"Now, this is just between you and me—"

"Absolutely," Gabriel said. Who the hell would he tell?

"I put the million dollars that you would have received for staying here one year into a bank draft in your name this morning."

Gabriel looked at his father. "What's the hook?"

Josiah laughed. "There is no hook. You proved yourself. You came here, and you would have stayed. You alone cared enough to try to patch up our differences. I see in you a son I can be proud of."

That meant more to him than the money. "Thank you."

Josiah nodded. "Jack didn't even bother to show up. He doesn't give a damn. He'll still get his chance, but—" Josiah shrugged "—he and the rest of your brothers have to live under the same rules you played by."

"Okay," Gabriel said, "did you come home because you wanted to see us, or was it all just a test?"

Josiah grabbed a red ball, scooted near the fireplace and rolled it to Penny, who rolled it back. He then rolled it to Perrin, who couldn't roll so well, so Gabriel helped him.

"When Laura let me know you had come home,

I chose to come home," Josiah said. "It was a test, maybe, but I also wanted very much to see you."

"Laura?" Gabriel frowned.

"Did you think I was psychic?" Josiah grinned. "Laura had instructions to let me know if any of my sons returned."

Gabriel wondered what else she was keeping to herself. "Guess she did her job."

"I'm leaving in the morning." Josiah stood, his shaggy hair bushing out around his shoulders. "I have to get back to work. It keeps a man alive, you know."

"I hope so." It was all he had right now. "So what are your plans for this place?"

"You're here. You can take care of it. You have the money to do whatever else you like, but I wouldn't tell anyone, if you want to know if they care for you."

Gabriel wondered if that was a veiled reference to Laura, but he didn't think she was fixated on money or she would have said yes to him instead of backing out on him when her father had chest pains.

"There's an account and books for the ranch specifically. I know I can trust you with the running of it."

"Ever thought about selling?"

Josiah shook his head. "Nope. I love my place in France and I'm thinking on buying one in Florida, but this ranch represents what I believe is best about life. Feel free to make it your home as long as you want."

"And if Pete and Dane come back?"

Josiah shrugged and headed up the stairs.

"Jeez," he said to Penny and Perrin. "He's got me stuck right in the middle."

Penny smiled at him. "Morgan," she said, enjoying saying the name.

"That's me," he said, and wondered why he suddenly felt okay with that.

WHEN LAURA CAME TO PICK up the kids that night, Gabriel had a surprise for her. "Chicken on the grill, canned corn and a salad. Not as good as you made me when I first arrived in Union Junction, but as good as I can do. I know you're probably worn out."

"I'm all right." She glanced at the food. Penny and Perrin were seated at the table. Somewhere Gabriel had found a small chair he'd sort of roped Perrin into; sailor's knots held her son's roundness into the chair. Mashed peas decorated the table in front of Perrin. "It's hard babysitting when you're not used to it."

"It's good practice for me. And Dad's been helping."

She slid into the chair. "Thank you. It looks delicious."

"So. This is what we'll look like every night if you keep my proposal in mind." He lit two candles in the center of the table with a flourish. "I'm just saying."

"I can't." Laura shook her head. "Ben is just too upset about it. And I can't go through that again. I'm sorry, Gabriel."

"You have no idea what you're passing up." He'd thought a lot about it, and he wasn't about to let this woman go just because Ben was having a coronary. If anything was killing the man, it was his own bitterness.

Steps sounded on the stairs. Josiah came into the

room, his laugh booming when he saw the children at the table. "You two don't need to eat. You need to see a pony!"

"Yay!" Penny jumped up from the table.

"Young lady!" Laura shook her head. "Mr. Morgan, they must excuse themselves."

"All right. Excuse us all," Josiah said, rescuing Perrin from his sailor's knots. "We have to go walk a pony, and then I need to do some things in town. I'll only be gone a couple of hours, Laura, so don't get jittery. You and Gabriel enjoy the food. He's been cussing at the grill for an hour."

Gabriel nodded. "It's true. I am not the griller that my brothers are."

"Looks like you did a fine job," Josiah said, looking at the meal, "but the kids and I are having ice cream for dinner. Even Perrin can have ice cream instead of those peas, can't he?" he asked, nuzzling the baby as he carried him out. "And I saw my son feed you that nasty meat stick thingie from a jar earlier. If I was you, Perrin, I'd complain. Come on, Penny, honey, you and I will have a swirl with candies on top."

The door closed behind them. Gabriel shook his head. "I didn't even know he knew that there was a roadside ice-cream store that offered swirls with candies on top."

"He's always been this way with my children." Laura seemed resigned to it. "The gifts are getting bigger, however."

He'd just had a huge one tossed into his life. He wasn't sure how to take the fact that he now had a million dollars to his name, free and clear. He didn't even have to live here, didn't have to put up with Josiah, didn't have to take care of Laura.

He was free.

"So, Laura," he said, "I understand you're the little birdie who let Josiah know I was here."

She hesitated as she served them corn. "Yes, I did."

"You weren't going to tell me."

"No. Do you have a problem with that?"

He grinned. "I probably should, but I like that mysterious edge you've got going on." Reaching over, he captured her hand in his. She dropped the spoon into the corn as he pulled her into his lap. "Suddenly, this dinner doesn't seem as inviting as what I've got in my lap right now."

He kissed her, and Laura had no desire to pull away. She knew her father would be so angry—Ben really thought he was looking out for her best interests—but just like before, she was falling for the man and not the approval. Gabriel kissed differently than her husband had and she relished that. She wanted everything about this to be different.

It was important that she never look back. She didn't ever want to feel the same. She wanted this, and more and everything Gabriel wanted to give her—except marriage. She couldn't do that. She knew that now. Ben falling ill had convinced her that she had agreed to marriage for all the wrong reasons. She was agreeing to marry for stability, when all she really wanted was to feel alive again.

Gabriel moved his hand to her waist, and then along

her sides to her breasts. Her breath caught. She sensed him waiting, asking permission. Gabriel was a gentleman; he would never override her wishes. But she wanted him, wanted what he was offering her and so she kissed him back, letting her hands move down his chest—and then lower.

His breath hitched, and she knew he wanted her the way she wanted him.

"You're making me crazy," he told her.

"I want to."

"I'm going to drive you crazy, too," he said, "and then make you the happiest woman on earth."

He already was. Her blood steamed in her body, her skin craved his touch. But she feared Josiah and the children would walk in and see them.

Gabriel carried her upstairs, laid her in his bed. Kissed her inch by inch, her entire body, chasing away her fears. Made her know that everything about this moment would be different from anything she'd ever known—and when he finally claimed her, Laura knew she'd never be the same again.

Hunger had been born inside her, and only Gabriel could satisfy it.

"GET OUT OF BED, OLD MAN."

Josiah looked down at his nemesis, allowing his lips to curl. Ben's eyes flew open—then he grinned at Josiah.

"I'm quite comfortable, thank you. Appreciate the visit, though." Ben glanced around. "What brings you? An apology?"

"Hell, no. What would I apologize for?"

"For trying to kill me when you learned I took Gisella to the airport. I was trying to do a neighborly deed, caught between a rock and a hard place was I—"

"Let's not live in the past," Josiah snapped. "Forgiveness isn't one of my more saintly qualities."

"I'll say." Ben shuddered. "They'll not be putting your name forth for beatification no matter how much money you give away."

Josiah sighed. "The kids want to see their sad sack of a grandfather. Right now, they're eating fruit cups in the cafeteria with a nurse friend of mine. You and I have something to discuss."

Ben glared at him. "I'm on my deathbed."

"You're throwing a pity party, and I want it to cease. Or I'll consider myself invited."

Ben wrinkled his face. "You've never been much fun at a party."

Josiah laughed heartily. "Now, listen, old man, you think you're playing me and everyone else like a well-strung fiddle. But you leave Gabriel and Laura alone."

Ben's gaze narrowed. "Why should I? He's trying to marry my daughter, and that just ain't gonna happen."

"Thanks to you, it probably won't."

"I see no reason to mingle my blood with yours, Morgan. It would dilute the purity of my good name."

"Ben, you sorry ass—if you weren't connected to an IV, I'd kick your selfish butt."

Ben shrugged. "And everybody would say look at poor Ben being picked on by that awful Josiah Morgan."

"No, they wouldn't. They'd say poor Josiah Morgan, having to put up with that conniving Ben Smith."

"Damn you!" Ben looked like he wanted to hop out of bed and take a swing at Josiah. "I'm not a conniver! No more so than you, Josiah Morgan!"

"You are if you're lying in this bed making your daughter feel guilty about wanting to be with my son."

"How the hell do you expect me to feel? After you cheated me?"

Josiah grimaced. "I didn't cheat you. You think you put one over on me, and I'm letting you gloat on that, but if you don't give my son your blessing, I'm going to put an end to your game."

Ben looked at him suspiciously. "What are you talking about?"

Josiah tapped him on the arm. "Old friend, I'm talking about that false rumor you put about that there was oil on your property."

Ben blinked. "Don't know what you're talking about."

"Sure you do. You told everyone you thought there might be oil. Then you asked me to buy your land at an inflated price. Then you ran around screaming about how I'd taken advantage of you. I knew there was no oil, I knew there was little value to your land and that you were hard up for cash. What happened to that cash, by the way?" Josiah asked, a gleam in his eyes.

"It's...in a safe." Ben waved a hand. "Anyway, it's none of your business."

"Funny how you're shacking up in my foreman's house if you have the money somewhere. Over a half million dollars, and you don't even buy your grandchildren a trip to the county fair. Yet I hear you going all over town about how I cheated you."

"Probably you did, Josiah. You always get the best of a person."

Josiah's white brows raised. "Did you gamble away that money?"

"No!"

"Did you drink it up?"

"No!"

Josiah leaned close. "Then tell me what happened to it."

Ben sighed. "I put it in a vault in the bank so it couldn't be traced to me for taxes."

Josiah frowned. "You would have had to report the sale of your land."

"That's why I tell everyone you cheated me. So I won't have to pay capital gains."

Josiah wondered if the man truly didn't understand the law. "Do you understand that few people cheat Uncle Sam and get away with it?"

"Do you understand that that is the only time I'll see that much money? Do you know how hard it is to make it as a farmer?" Ben crossed his arms. "I'm not giving one cent of it to the government. I've paid taxes for years. When did the government ever help me?"

Josiah scratched his head. "At the very minimum, when you get caught, you'll have to pay interest on what you owe."

"I'll be dead by then."

Josiah shrugged. "And your estate will still have

to pay. I'm not sure what you've done helps Penny and Perrin."

Ben sighed. "It was just hard to give up any of that dough. I wanted money all my life, just a little something in the bank that gave me security. Something I could pass to my daughter without everybody thinking I'd been a failure all my life."

"Don't you think she'd have been just as happy with you being honorable?"

Ben shook his head. "I can take care of her, and my grandkids, without asking anybody for a dime if we ever fall on hard times."

"Laura seems independent to me. Besides, Ben, sleeping in my foreman's shack isn't exactly living the high life."

"It's free. Seems like a bargain to me, and I'm satisfied with that."

Josiah had to admire the man's desire to keep what was his. "But you've just about done in your ticker."

"That's because your son is trying to take my daughter away from me."

"You're just trying to keep her away from me." Josiah sat down near his nemesis. "Be honest and don't juggle facts for a change."

Ben snorted. "I don't completely cotton to Morgans, I'll admit. Some are better than others."

"But is that fair to your grandchildren?" He leaned close to stare Ben down. "Gabriel would do fine by them."

Ben's gaze slid away. "Not sure about that. But if

it'll make you quit harping on me, I promise to pay the taxes on the money you paid me for the land."

Josiah sighed. "Don't get me back on that. This entire matter is between you and me, and you need to butt out of Laura's life. You nearly got yourself sidelined for good, you know. Interfering is not healthy."

"Says the greatest interferer I ever met." Ben's eyes closed. "Anyway, you don't even like your own sons. Why should I?"

Josiah shook his head. Ben had it all wrong. He clearly didn't understand the Bible's instruction: *What son is there whom a father does not chasten?* The way he'd raised his sons was the only way to raise good men. But Ben was so stubborn it was hard to move him. Laura probably had some of those stubborn genes in her, which didn't bode well for Gabriel, who was pretty mulish himself.

Josiah wished he could make it all better, but he couldn't. The die had already been cast. He went to get Penny and Perrin to sneak them in to see their grandfather—no kids allowed in this area, especially past visiting hours—but he figured what the hell. He'd given enough money to the hospital to buy beds for a new wing. One day, it might be him lying in one of these beds, and he sure hoped Ben would care enough to sneak the kids in to see him.

Maybe he would, and maybe he wouldn't. Josiah couldn't divine whether forgiveness lay in store for him, from anyone. But life was all about family, and Josiah was doing his damnedest to try to build one.

Chapter Thirteen

The moment he made love to Laura, Gabriel was even more determined to romance her until she couldn't say no to his marriage proposal. But he was aware this wouldn't be easy. He moved her arms above her head, trapping them against the pillows, then languidly licked each nipple. He loved the gasp he pulled from her.

"Gabriel," she murmured, a slight protest, and since he knew she was going to use going to visit her father as an excuse, he slid inside her, keeping her with him for a few more minutes.

"Yes?" he asked.

She moved up against him, welcoming him. "Don't stop."

He laughed. "Are you sure?" He teased her with another slow thrust.

She clutched at him, pulled his head down so that he could kiss her. This closeness with one person was what he'd been missing all his life. He kissed her fast, hard, possessively, and let himself enjoy the feel of her unresisting in his arms.

AN HOUR LATER, LAURA GASPED and jumped from the bed, grabbing at her clothes. "I hear your father's truck!"

"It's all right. It'll take him a minute to get the kids out of their seat belts."

Laura gasped again, jumping into her clothes. "The children can't see me like this! Hurry, Gabriel!"

The joys of parenthood. Gabriel grinned. "That's what you said not an hour ago."

"Don't tease me now," she said. "No mother wants her children to find her naked in bed with a man she's not married to."

"Yes, we should fix that."

She tossed him his shirt. "Some things can't be fixed, you know."

He handed her the tiny black panties that had gotten hung on his belt buckle. "Female undergarments amaze me. Are they utilitarian or just for turning a man on? These certainly seem more sexy than functional. Can't say that's a bad thing."

"Gabriel!" She moved his boots over to him and slipped on her panties and then her sandals. Her fingers flew through her hair as she glanced out the window. "Oh, they're looking at the pony. Why did your father buy a pony when he won't be here long?"

"He bought it for your kids," Gabriel said absently, thinking through the logic of what Laura had just said. He followed her down the stairs. Josiah had said he was leaving in the morning. Why would he have bought a pony that couldn't be ridden yet?

"My kids! Penny and Perrin aren't really old enough to ride. Besides, we're never over here."

"I know." They sat down at the dinner table they'd abandoned two hours ago. The candles were burned down to the sticks and had put themselves out. The food was cold, but Gabriel would have eaten it anyway except for the look on Laura's face. "What?"

"He bought a pony for my children," she repeated. "Obviously he plans on them being around here. With you."

"You'd have to ask Pop about that. I don't really understand him myself. I'm just now learning the whole father-son thing in a new way. It's a whole new language I'm decoding."

"Gabriel!"

"Yes?" He looked at Laura. "Do you know you're beautiful when you're not wearing makeup and your hair is out of place?"

She opened her mouth to say something when Josiah walked in with the kids. He had Penny by the hand and Perrin soundly sleeping tucked up against his chest. "You two still eating?" Josiah asked. "Must be some hungry folk."

He glanced at the plates and saw that they hadn't been touched. "Ah, you know in France and Italy people tend to take longer meals. It's good for the digestion," he said to cover Laura's embarrassment. She could barely look at Josiah.

He handed her Perrin gently. "This one's a snoozer. He was awake for visiting your father, though."

"My father?" Laura looked at Josiah. "You went to see Ben in the hospital?"

"Sure." He put Penny in a chair at the table, glancing at Gabriel like he had something he wanted to say but wouldn't share it in front of Laura. "He's my employee."

Could Ben and Josiah spend five minutes in the same room without a battle breaking out? Gabriel wasn't sure. "So how did that go?"

"He was his usual irascible self, which I attribute to his general well-being." Josiah tucked in to cold corn and chicken. "This is delicious, Gabriel. For a man who lived off of military grub, you seasoned this chicken just right."

"Mr. Morgan," Laura said sternly, "you did not go to pay a social call to Ben."

"I took the grandkids by." Josiah shrugged, his face innocent. "I had some things to say to him. Never know when I might see him again."

Gabriel stared at his father, the pieces falling into place. "Dad," he said, "you gave us a referendum and a game plan, but then you came home in the middle of the playing rules. You gave me money I wasn't expecting. You're gifting the whole town. You bought these kids a pony they're not really old enough to ride and which you will not be here to put them on. You've gone to see your archenemy or rival or whatever you want to call the relationship you've had over the years with Mr. Smith."

Josiah looked at him, his brows furrowed. "So?"

Gabriel glanced at Laura, then at the kids and saw

the family setting his father wanted so badly. "A man would have to be knocking on heaven's door to change as much as you are," he said quietly.

Josiah blinked. He didn't reply, confirm, deny.

"Are you sick, Dad?" Gabriel asked.

Josiah shrugged. "Depends upon a man's perception of himself. I happen to think I'm just fine."

"But the doctors don't agree?" Laura asked.

"Now, missy, you just worry about your own father," Josiah said.

Laura shot back, "You're family, too!" which brought an amazing change to Josiah that Gabriel had never seen in all his life.

Tears in Josiah Morgan's eyes.

LAURA WAS SHOCKED BY THE look on Gabriel's face. He looked heartbroken by his father's slight admission of illness. Briefly she wondered how ill Mr. Morgan could truly be—certainly he looked fit. But he wouldn't lean on frailty to get his way, something Ben might do, she conceded unwillingly.

Here at this table sat many of the people she knew as family, and yet one of them had been holding up all the rest of them. "I'm worried about you," she told Mr. Morgan.

"Don't," he said shortly. "Damn doctors don't know what's in God's plan."

"True, but is there something I can do for you?" She glanced at Gabriel, saw that he appreciated her asking the question he apparently could not. Gabriel looked like he'd had his horse shot out from underneath him.

He'd made a lucky guess on his father's latest machinations, trying to second-guess him when the truth was much more simple. The man was trying to cobble his family back together.

"No, thank you," Mr. Morgan said, "it's not in my hands."

"Excuse me." Gabriel left the room.

"Now, see, I don't want anybody worrying," Gabriel's father said. "There's too much of life to live without everyone being down."

"He is your son," Laura said gently. "Wouldn't you expect him to be concerned?"

"I'd rather him focus on getting married and having a family. He's traveled around for years," Mr. Morgan said, warming to his subject. "The honest truth is that family is a great thing. I made a lot of mistakes, I know, but family gave me more pleasure in my life than anything else, including making money. Some people would find that shocking."

Laura felt it was best to skip the marriage comments. "I don't think Gabriel getting married will help your health issue."

"Sure it will. That old geezer you call Ben is lying up in a bed because he doesn't want you to marry my son."

Laura sighed. "Mr. Morgan, it's not that easy. And anyway, you can't really say that Ben doesn't know what's best for me when you're busy impressing your will upon your sons, claiming you know what's best for them."

"True," he answered, "but I have to consider my

own longevity. And, Laura, won't you please start calling me Josiah?"

Laura refused to allow him off the topic. "You and my father both think that parenting is managing. I'm going to try not to do that with my children." Penny got down from Josiah's lap and went to find her ball. Perrin snoozed comfortably on her shoulder. She loved her children; she could see how she might want to make decisions for them.

"Well, enough of that kind of talk," Josiah said. "I heard there were chocolate chip cookies in the kitchen, so if you'll excuse me, I think I'll brew up some coffee and have a few."

He got up from the table. She watched him walk into the kitchen, big and broad-shouldered. He appeared more robust than Ben, but he wouldn't fake an illness. He wanted to see his sons married more than anything.

She understood that—but it was not something she could help with. Making love with Gabriel had clearly been a mistake. There was no future for them; she knew in her heart she could not go into a second marriage—not now. When they'd planned a temporary marriage, when she'd thought she was helping Gabriel, that had been different. She'd been able to see the beginning and the end of their marriage. Open and shut, like a book. No emotions.

Now it was too complicated. She couldn't see the end, or where the heartache was. She'd barely pulled herself through the abyss this time; she didn't know if she could rescue herself again. The Morgans were unpredictable men. No matter how much she'd fallen for Gabriel, she had to keep herself from the edge, especially for her children's sakes.

Slowly, she stood. "Will you tell Gabriel I said goodbye, Josiah?"

He came out of the kitchen. "Must you leave so soon?"

She knew Gabriel was upset by his father's news. He needed time to think. "I need to get to the hospital early in the morning in case they release Ben."

He nodded. "Let me know if I can help."

She shook her head. "I appreciate everything you've done, Josiah. Everything except the pony."

He grinned. "Every child should ride."

"I'd tell you to quit scheming," she said, "but maybe it's medicinal for you. It's probably keeping you alive."

He roared with laughter, pleased by her outspokenness. But she had a feeling she was right.

GABRIEL WATCHED FROM HIS window as his father said goodbye to Laura and the kids. He saw Josiah kiss each child, saw him laugh at something Laura said before hugging her. Gabriel saw softness and kindness that he'd never experienced from his father, and realized Josiah had reprioritized his life. It wasn't so much Perrin and Penny that had changed his father, though that had something to do with it. Gabriel saw that Josiah had accepted the changes life was pressing upon him. His father was a different man.

He felt sad for all the time that had passed between them, when he had allowed silence to set solid and inflexible between them. After a moment, he pulled out his cell phone.

He hunted around for Dane's number, then made the call. "Dane," he said. "It's Gabriel. Got a minute? I need to talk."

"Great," Dane said, "I was just about to call you. Have you heard from Pete yet?"

"No." Gabriel watched Laura drive away, saw his father look after the car until it was long gone and then still he stood, eyeing the distance. "What's up?"

"You might want to think about a road trip and be quick about it," Dane said. "Jack took a real ass-stomping in Kearney and this time he's hurt pretty bad."

Chapter Fourteen

As he stared at Jack in intensive care, wired into every machine known to man, Gabriel knew he had to change his whole life. His brother lay very still, his head bandaged, his eyes closed. Pete and Dane had visited first, then Gabriel went in with Josiah. Josiah hadn't had to be dragged to see his son, which surprised Gabriel. In fact, his father had seemed eager to get to Kearney, his fingers drumming anxiously on his knees as Gabriel drove.

Josiah's drawn face hovered over the face of the son he hadn't seen in ten years. Gabriel wanted to push back time. Jack was battered, bruised—almost unrecognizable. "Jack," he whispered, but his brother didn't move. Josiah's shoulders slumped. Slowly, he reached to touch his eldest son's hand, his fingers trembling.

"Has he spoken?" Gabriel asked the nurse, who was changing a bag of IV fluids.

"No. But we know from the cowboys who rode in the ambulance with him that he had a helluva ride before the bull caught him against the rail and dragged him off. His foot caught in a stirrup and he couldn't free it. The clowns did what they could, probably saved his life, according to your brother's friends."

It was the risk that came with rodeo. Gabriel shook his head. They all worked dangerous jobs, and each of them loved their chosen professions. They had the fever to live on the edge. Many times he'd sat shivering in Gdan′sk, or baking in San Salvador, wondering why he did what he did.

The answer was easy: the Morgan brothers all did what they did to prove themselves to the old man. And the old man was keeping his own secret of fallibility. *So we're just bashing ourselves on the rocks, trying to get to someplace that doesn't exist.*

"Jack," he murmured again, hoping to see his brother's eyes move. Josiah looked truly distraught. Gabriel wanted to comfort him but he didn't know how. He did know, however, that their father had raised them as he'd thought best as a parent.

Gabriel sighed. The nurse glanced at him. "I'm sorry, we have to keep his visits very short."

"I understand." Gabriel stood, but Josiah lingered at the bedside of his firstborn.

"Come on," Josiah said. "Jack?"

But Jack didn't move. Josiah turned and silently left the room.

"We'll be back tomorrow," Gabriel told the nurse. "Will you call us if there's any change?"

But the only change the next day was that they were told Jack didn't want visitors. Nor the next day. At the end of the week, the family was told that he'd checked himself out. The hospital could give them no further information.

The three remaining brothers and Josiah stood awkwardly in the waiting room digesting the news. Josiah looked as if he'd aged fifteen years. Gabriel watched as Pete and Dane tried to absorb what they'd learned. Finally, they left after giving Josiah an awkward handshake.

Josiah looked at Gabriel. "Was I that bad a parent?"

Gabriel sighed, shaking his head. "We all make mistakes. I've made more than my share." He pulled his stunned father to the sliding doors leading outside. "Come on, Dad. Let's go home."

LAURA HAD JUST PUT THE kids to bed when she heard a knock on the door, an impatient rapping she recognized. She hurried to open the door. "How is your brother?" she asked Gabriel.

"Tough as cowhide." Gabriel reached to grab her, not allowing her to keep an inch between them.

"And your father?" Laura asked breathlessly.

"Equally tough."

His lips searched hers hungrily. "Wait." She pulled away, feeling a new intensity in him. "What happened?"

"Jack disappeared. Crawled off like a wounded animal, I guess. He just went away before any of us ever got to see him conscious."

She gave him a gentle push toward the sofa, which he sank into. "Where are the kids?"

"In bed. Do you want a drink? Food?"

He shook his head. "I'd like to see the kids. I was hoping to catch them before they went to sleep."

As if she'd been listening at the door—and probably she had—Penny came into the room. She crawled up in Gabriel's lap. A warning flashed in Laura's mind. Her daughter was becoming attached to Gabriel, as was she. There was no denying it. Panic spread through her as she recognized a blossoming hope in her chest. She got up to get Perrin out of his crib so they could all be together.

The three of them looked at her with winsome eyes. She knew Gabriel wanted to be with the children; she knew he had to be upset from visiting his brother. "It is a special occasion," she said.

They snuggled up to Gabriel, each child resting against one side of his body. Perrin put his thumb in his mouth, then thought better of it. Penny's eyelids slowly lowered.

"Life is short. Let's make this more than a special occasion," Gabriel said.

Laura looked at him, her senses on alert.

"I want this to be an every night thing," he told her. "You deserve a guy like me, Laura."

She couldn't say no. In spite of her misgivings—and she was scared to death—she couldn't look in those dark eyes and honestly say she didn't want to be his, didn't want him to be a father to her children. "All right," she said, knowing there was no turning back now and not really wanting to anyway.

MIMI WAS DELIGHTED TO help plan a wedding for Laura. She had a friend in a neighboring town who made bridal gowns, so she dragged Laura over to Tulips, Texas, to have her fit in something that "would make Gabriel's mouth water," Mimi said with a flourish. In town, Valentine Jefferson would make her a lovely wedding cake. Mimi assured her no one did them better.

They had Perrin outfitted in a little tuxedo and Penny in a darling flower girl gown. Mimi agreed to serve as the matron of honor. The ladies of the Union Junction salon agreed to do the hair for the wedding, and even trim Gabriel's just a bit. Not enough to take away from the rascal look he had going on, they assured her. They liked his hair growing out of its military cut.

Ben had recovered enough to give Laura away, though he was balking. "Don't know if I should willingly give you to a Morgan," he said, before asking Josiah if he planned on hanging around or hotfooting around the globe. This seemed to annoy Josiah for a minute, before he recovered his good humor at being invited to the wedding.

Pete and Dane sent congratulations. Jack, they never heard from at all. Gabriel was worried, but he knew that his brother was still recovering. He tried not to think about the fact that none of his brothers would be at his wedding, and asked his father to be his best man, an invitation which Josiah readily accepted. His return to France was postponed.

It would have been perfect except that before the rehearsal dinner, Gabriel discovered just how cold his bride's feet actually were. He went by to give Laura the ring he'd bought weeks before and knew by the pink of her nose that she'd been crying.

"You're not having second thoughts?" he asked, remembering how anxious she'd been to marry him before and then how quickly she'd backed away when her father became ill. It was all understandable—but he had to admit to a spur of worry.

She shook her head. "I'm just nervous, I think. You?"

"No way. I'm going to be a husband and a father. Life is good."

She took a deep breath. "Thank you."

"For what?"

"For not being afraid of…stepparenting."

He laid a finger over her lips. "Parenting. No *step*. When we slow down and you catch your breath, I'd like to adopt Penny and Perrin, if you'll let me."

"I—I have to think about that," she said, wondering why she held back. But the very act of allowing the children to be adopted seemed to push her deceased husband very far into the children's background. Was that the right thing to do?

"There's plenty of time. Right now I'm going to drink a beer with Josiah as my bachelor celebration. I'll see you at the rehearsal tonight." He kissed her goodbye. More than anything, Laura was afraid that she was going to awaken and find this had all been a fairy tale dream just beyond her grasp.

And then she realized why: Gabriel had never told her he loved her. That he was *in* love with her. He loved her children. He really wanted to be a father.

As for love—that word had never crossed Gabriel's lips.

THE REHEARSAL WOULD BE an easy step toward marrying Gabriel. Laura tried to keep calm, telling herself that just because the wedding had grown a little bigger and more elaborate than she'd expected, this was no cause for nerves. Nor was marrying one of the finest men she'd ever met. If she was a little disappointed Gabriel hadn't ever actually said he loved her, she was sure that was something that would come with time.

She reminded herself she was the one who'd insisted on boundaries when he'd first asked her. He was probably trying not to scare her. This time, there was no reason for them to be marrying, except good old-fashioned romance.

The dress she was wearing tonight was a straight column of light silk she'd worn to church many times. Gabriel would never know this gown was old. But her wedding gown was brand-new. Designed by Mimi's friend in Tulip, it was a shell-pink wrapping of silk and lace, falling straight to her ankles without any fuss. She loved the simplicity of it. Nothing about it reminded her of her first wedding, and she felt beautiful when she put it on.

Gabriel would be very handsome in a charcoal-gray tuxedo. She got the kids ready, and headed over to the Morgan ranch. Picnic tables and chairs had been set up on the lawn for the rehearsal dinner. White tents protected the guests from any shower which might fall, but the skies were clear.

She pushed down her rising panic, resenting it. Where were these feelings of worry coming from? Normal bridal nerves, she assured herself. Every bride probably got them.

She hadn't when she'd married Dave.

But she'd been young and idealistic then. Now there were many more people counting on her to make the right decision. The diamond Gabriel had given her sparkled on her finger. It was a bigger diamond than she expected; she'd never dreamed of owning anything so beautiful. Despite the sun, goose pimples ran over her arms.

The minister had asked them to be early, so that he could have a private discussion with Gabriel and Laura. She saw his car parked in the drive so she hurried to knock on the door. It swung open, and Josiah engulfed her in a hug. "You're family now! You don't have to knock on the door like a guest, Laura!"

"Thank you," she said, letting herself enjoy Josiah's bear hug. Across the room, Gabriel smiled at her. The minister smiled at her. It was a happy occasion—nothing to be afraid of.

"I want to go over the solemnity of the vows with

you and Gabriel," Pastor Riley said. "This is just some quiet time for us to reflect on the meaning of the ceremony before you say your vows in front of your guests."

"All right." She slid into the chair he held out for her, unable to meet Gabriel's gaze.

"Did either of you want to write any of your own vows?" Pastor Riley asked.

"I don't think so," Laura murmured. They hadn't talked about it—maybe traditional vows were best. Gabriel shook his head.

Nodding, Pastor Riley put on his glasses. "Marriage is a holy occasion, as you know. From the beginning of the vows, which ends with the final instruction 'till death do you part—'"

Laura stood. Gabriel followed suit, surprised. "I'm sorry. I can't do this. Gabriel, forgive me. I truly thought I was having simple bridal nerves. But it's more than that." She took a deep breath, struggled for the right words. "This feels like a test I know I'm not going to pass."

"Laura," Gabriel said, his tone sympathetic, "would a few moments alone with Pastor Riley help?"

She shook her head, alarmed by the panic spreading inside her. They couldn't possibly understand. She'd done the death-do-you-part thing once. Death did part her from her beloved, cruelly early, and she'd never be able to say those words again knowing how sinister they were. They weren't romantic at all.

"I'm sorry," she repeated. She handed Gabriel the

ring and backed away from the table. "I— Maybe it's just too soon," she said.

Gabriel followed her. "Laura. Are you all right?"

She gathered up Penny and Perrin, walking them to the car. She strapped the children into their seats. "I can't do it. I suppose in retrospect I wanted a Vegas drive-through type of wedding so it wouldn't seem so momentous. I realize that now. I'm just too scared to get married again, Gabriel. Which sounds silly, I know, but it's not like falling off a bicycle. As Pastor Riley said, the vows are solemn and meaningful—but they don't always last."

"All right. Don't worry. Somehow we'll get this to work out."

"I don't want you to think I'm crazy," she said, trying not to cry.

"No crazier than anybody else around here. Frankly, if we got to the altar without a couple of misfires, we probably wouldn't be doing ourselves any good. Practice makes perfect."

"Do you mean it?" Laura wasn't sure she deserved this much forgiveness.

"Oh, hell, yeah." He shrugged. "Go home. Change your clothes. Forget about this whole thing. Call me when…when you can."

She nodded. "Thank you."

He shrugged. "Bye, Penny. Bye, Perrin."

They looked at him through the window and Laura turned on the car and drove away, feeling like she'd just given up the best thing that could have ever happened to her.

"I am so, so sorry," she murmured to the children. "You have no idea what your mother just took from your life."

She had taken the coward's way out, and now she knew she was in love with Gabriel Morgan. And the thought of losing him, the way she had Dave, was a fear she could not face.

"WHAT THE HELL JUST HAPPENED?" Josiah demanded. Pastor Riley looked at Gabriel sympathetically.

Gabriel shrugged. He appreciated the concern, but he really wasn't surprised. "My bride got the jitters."

"Huh." Josiah shook his head. "Laura's always been a cool, practical kind of girl. Usually knows what she wants."

"Oh, she knows what she wants. She just can't figure out how to get there." Gabriel ushered the minister into the kitchen and poured them all some tea. "I bet wedding cake freezes just fine. Tuxes can be reordered. Pastor, you can use the flowers for this weekend's services, can't you?"

"Or I can have them delivered to some older folks' homes. They'd really appreciate that, Gabriel." Pastor Riley shook his head. "I've known Laura Adams a long time. She's a wonderful woman. She'll come around."

"I know. She's just not a marrying kind of girl. At least not right now," Gabriel replied.

"You know, I think you have a point," Josiah said. "The best things in life don't come easy."

"See? All those good lessons you gave us growing up are coming in handy now," Gabriel said wryly. "A lesser man might give up on a good thing if he hadn't learned that patience is a virtue."

Josiah grunted. "You didn't learn patience in my house."

"That was the military. You taught me life wasn't always easy. I can wait on Laura."

Pastor Riley nodded. "I'll notify Mimi, and she can help me let the guests know. I'm always available when Laura is ready."

"Thanks." He walked Pastor Riley to the door, then headed upstairs. Grabbing a duffel bag, he tossed in shirts, jeans, all his clothing. His father stood in the doorway, watching.

"What are you doing now?"

Gabriel wasn't sure how to explain his plan. "For now, leaving Ben with the upkeep of the ranch."

"I thought you said you were okay with Laura having second thoughts."

Gabriel looked at his father. "She says it's the ceremony she can't go through again. I think she was fine up until the 'I do forever' part." He shrugged. "Luckily for her, I learned life could be very short in the military. If she doesn't want to put the words on it right now, I understand. But I'm still going to be with her, as a husband, and as a father to her children."

Josiah handed him his boots. "And what if she says—"

"She won't," Gabriel said. He'd held that woman, made love to her. He knew how she felt about him. "It's up to me to give her space."

"By moving in with her?"

"By going slow." Gabriel picked up his duffel and shook his father's hand. "When are you leaving for France?"

Josiah grunted. "I was leaving after we threw the paper hearts at the happy couple."

Gabriel grinned. "Plan on making a return trip in the near future."

He walked away, confident that Laura and he could pass whatever test she was worried about—together. She just needed a teacher to help her study, and he had lots of lessons left to give her.

And a wedding ring.

Chapter Fifteen

"I'm so sorry, Mimi, about all your hard work." Knowing that guests needed to be notified, Laura had driven from Gabriel's ranch straight to the Double M. "I just couldn't make myself do it. It was like there was a giant sign that said Go The Other Way flashing at me."

"Well, you're not exactly a runaway bride," Mimi said, hugging her. "You told Gabriel what was happening, and he understood. Believe me, there are a lot of couples in this town who didn't make it to the altar smoothly, and I'm one of them."

Laura couldn't imagine Mason and Mimi not having an easy courtship, but she did remember rumors that Mason had jumped through a few complicated hoops to win Mimi. "Thank you."

"I bet Josiah just about cried." Mimi smiled. "He's been itching to get his boys to the altar."

Laura didn't feel good about that. Josiah had been so good to her and she felt she'd let him down. "I left so quickly I barely saw Josiah. But he'd been so nice, even telling me not to knock on the door anymore now that I was family."

Mimi patted her hand. "You're still family. Josiah made that clear a long time ago."

She felt better. Slowly but surely, her panic ebbed away.

"You did the right thing," Mimi said. "It's never good to feel pushed toward a decision."

"I really do like Gabriel."

Mimi smiled. "I know."

Laura hoped she hadn't lost any chance she'd had with him. He was gorgeous, sexy, kind. Loving. She was in love with him. "I think I was a little nervous that he hasn't told me he loved me."

Mimi paused in the wrapping up of some hors d'oeuvres that had been meant for the rehearsal dinner. "He hasn't?"

Laura shook her head.

"Men don't always talk about their emotions. Sometimes they expect us to divine their feelings."

"I'm not good with divining," Laura said, and Mimi laughed.

"I can't remember how long it took for Mason to tell me he loved me, but it does seem like forever. It was like pulling a mule out of a barn in winter." She put some food into the refrigerator. "Gabriel seems a lot like Mason. You can read a lot about their feelings from their actions."

Gabriel was a man of action. She could count on him to never be boring. "Can I help you with anything?"

Mimi shook her head. "Right now, I want you to go home and put your feet up. Play with your children. Do something relaxing. You've been through a lot lately. Take some time to smell the roses, as they say."

Laura gathered up her children and embraced her friend. Mimi held her for a good long hug, and Laura thought for the hundredth time how lucky she was to have such wonderful people around her.

She drove home, realizing she'd expected Gabriel to be parked in her driveway. He walked over to help her take the kids out of the car. "I hope you know how glad I am to see you," she told him.

He nodded, grinned at her. Desire melted through her, right down to her bones. "I know you want me."

She shook her head and helped Penny to the house; Gabriel carried Perrin. "I wonder why you still want *me*."

"Because I do. That's all I know," Gabriel said, putting Perrin on the floor with his toys. "I'm moving in, unless you object."

"I was hoping you would," Laura said, surprising herself.

"And what about gossip?" he asked.

"I'll try to save your reputation eventually," she said.

He slid her ring across the kitchen table. "Put that in your jewelry box until you're ready for it."

She picked up the beautiful sparkling ring, then handed it back to him with a shake of her head. "Thank you for trying to be a hero. It hasn't gone unnoticed."

He shrugged and got down on the floor with Perrin. Penny came to sit beside him. "I'm going to like this parenting stuff."

Gabriel told himself he was doing the right thing. Even if Laura looked nervous, she hadn't kicked him out.

He decided the best path was to start off as friends.

It was going to be hard, but he vowed to go slow. Let her make all the moves. The prize would be worth it in the end.

A persistent ringing of the doorbell sounded. He glanced around for Laura, but she'd gone to the back of the house. Shrugging, he decided that since this was now his home, he could open the door just as well.

Dane and Pete grinned at him. "Hey. You're not supposed to see the bride before the wedding," Pete said. He came inside the house, looking around with approval. "Small. Clean. Bright. I like it."

"The wedding is canceled. Sorry you made the trip." Gabriel looked his brothers over. "You look like just fell out of a laundry bag."

"We've been doing something I never thought I'd do," Dane said. "We volunteered as clowns at a rodeo. Then made a side trip. Can we sit down or not?"

"It's not really my house," Gabriel said, then remembered he was practicing fathering and marriage. "Sure, have a seat. Play with my kids."

Pete eyed him as he sat. "How are they yours if the wedding is canceled? Sorry about that, by the way."

"Don't be. Some things turn out for the best."

"Always the optimist. Did you get cold feet?" Dane shook his head. "Marriage and Morgans don't mix well."

"Laura had second thoughts. So I decided to move in and show her what she's missing out on."

"Brave. Egotistical, but brave." Dane grinned. "I decided that while I was in town for your nuptials, I'd best take a look at this Miss Suzy Winterstone."

"And?" Gabriel pulled Perrin in to his lap.

"I'm so glad I didn't allow Pop to guilt me into anything. She isn't my type."

"How do you know? Did you talk to her?"

"I watched her playing at the playground with her twins." He glanced at Penny and Perrin. "I'm not cut out for the playground lifestyle. I'm not even cut out for living in Texas."

"You live in Watauga, you're a Texas Ranger," Gabriel reminded him for the hundredth time. "I've never understood you being something you didn't want to be."

"What, like a housemate instead of a husband?" Dane asked, taking a small dig at Gabriel's circumstances. "Jeez, Gabriel, take it easy on a guy. Part of my issue is that I let Pop kick me into the military. I got out as fast as I could, but what else was I suited for besides protecting, keeping order and handling guns?"

"Sounds like an excellent résumé to me," Gabriel said dryly. "So back to the playful Miss Winterstone."

"Okay. She's cute, I have to admit, but a little fuller-figured than I like."

"Because she has year-old twins."

"Perhaps. But I sense she's just one of those big-boned girls."

"Not a bad thing, in my book." Laura was nice and

petite, but nobody would call her thin. She had lots of curves he'd love to discover all over again.

"I think she might be German or French or something." Dane shook his head. "If I'd had your skills, I could have probably understood what she was saying to her children."

"Yeah." Gabriel grinned. It sounded as if his brother had happened upon the babysitter at work, but he wasn't going to share that. Let Dane figure it all out on his own—it was more fun that way. "So where are you headed now?"

"Well, since there'll be no wedding, I guess I'm free for the weekend. What's Pop doing?"

"Last I heard, he was heading out."

"And you're staying here?"

"Nothing's moving me," Gabriel said. "This is my family now."

"Wow." Pete shook his head, walked to the door. "You actually already seem like an old married man. Congratulations."

"Thanks." He hated to ask but made himself do it. "Ever hear from Jack?"

"Nah. He went off to lick his wounds. We'll probably never know what happened, you know?" Pete said.

Pete and Dane seemed resigned to this, but it bothered Gabriel. Their family was so sporadic, unsettled. "Keep in touch, all right?"

"I will." Dane waved at him. "Give my regards to the family."

"Why? Aren't you stopping by to see Josiah?"

Dane shook his head. "I've been thinking about

that million dollars Pop promised us if we lived in the house for one year."

"Oh, yeah?" Gabriel kept his face blank. "What about it?"

"Do you think he ever meant to give us any money? Or was he just playing a game? Not that it matters, as far as the money goes. I just resent being jerked around by Pop. Don't think I can forgive that."

Gabriel thought about the money that was already in his bank account. His father had sworn him to secrecy, and he figured Josiah knew something about what he was doing. "Can't say, myself."

"You're not going to live there, though."

"Laura wants her children to stay here where they can keep some stability in their life."

"Doesn't bother you to live where her husband lived?" Pete asked.

Gabriel paused. "Can't say it's going to bother me." Pop was right; some things were better left unsaid.

"Sorry. Shouldn't have opened my big fat mouth."

"Don't worry about it. I'm not." He waved goodbye to his brothers and closed the door. Home was where the heart was; he knew that from spending too much time in dangerous places hungering for the promise of home. Penny and Perrin and Laura belonged here. Hopefully he did, too.

"Who was that?" Laura asked, coming into the room. She was freshly showered, her face glowing. He loved seeing her completely natural; he loved being with her in her home.

"Nobody but trouble," he said.

WHEN THE DOORBELL RANG an hour later, Gabriel half expected to see another wedding guest who hadn't yet received the news about the postponement—he refused to say *cancellation*. He and Laura were simply delaying the inevitable.

It was Ben standing on the porch, looking like he'd rather be anywhere but his own daughter's house. "Hi," he said, walking inside. "Can I talk to you, Gabriel?"

"Sure." Why the hell not? Apparently it was his day for surprise visitors, misery loves company for the jilted groom. He motioned Laura's father over to where he'd been sitting with the children.

"Hi, Dad," she said. She walked into the room with her kids. "We're going outside to play in the new sandbox now that it's all put together."

"You do that," Ben said. "I need to talk to Gabriel for a moment."

"Oh? About what?" Laura asked.

"Now don't you worry about that." He kissed his daughter on the forehead. "Sorry about the wedding, but I do understand. Perhaps it's a wee bit soon."

Her glance slid to Gabriel. "I think so."

"Have fun," he told her.

She managed a tentative smile for Gabriel and closed the door behind them.

Ben wasted no time getting to his topic. "Gabriel, I'm sorry as hell the wedding didn't go off like you wanted."

Gabriel looked at Ben, not completely certain he was being truthful.

"But I hear from your father that you're planning on

moving in here with my daughter. I have to be honest with you, I don't think that's a good idea."

"Because?"

"Son, you're rushing things. The girl is still grieving for her husband. Not that he was any great favorite of mine, as you know, but I know Laura, and she's a one-man woman."

That didn't make him feel better. "She didn't seem unhappy to have me here."

"See, that's the problem. Laura doesn't know what she wants. Ever since Laura was a baby, she's known exactly what she wanted and had no trouble speaking up about it. This is why I think you're making a terrible mistake."

Gabriel looked at the man he'd known could be both slippery and untrustworthy. "Why would you try to help me?"

"Because of Perrin and Penny," he said simply. "I knew Laura wasn't ready to get married. I believe I tried to steer you away from that."

That's not exactly what he would have called it, but whatever. "I think it's just marriage she was saying no to, not me."

"Well, it's all wrapped up together." Ben raised his hand and waved it airily. "It's all pressure."

Gabriel considered that. "I can see your point."

"I know you want to be here, understand that you want to make a family with my daughter. Truth is, you haven't even taken care of your own house, son. And now you're staking a claim on Laura, when maybe you should be giving her some breathing room."

"I'll take it under advisement." Gabriel didn't like anything he was hearing. He wasn't certain he could trust Ben.

What worried him was wondering if Laura would ever trust him, and want him despite her fears. A cramp hit his gut. He wanted to be here with Penny and Perrin; in fact, he wanted an even bigger family with Laura.

But her father knew her best, and he believed Laura wasn't ready for marriage.

He saw Ben out, then considered his options. Tonight he was going to spend time with the family he wanted. Later, he'd figure out whether his father-in-law-to-be dispensed helpful advice or not.

From the kitchen window he could see Laura and her kids building a small sand castle. It wasn't as grand as the knight's castle Josiah had purchased in France, but big or small, everyone wanted their own castle. He wanted sand castles and Little League and high school proms in his kids' lives. It did his heart good to see Laura enjoying her family. If he was very lucky, maybe one day they would have a child together.

A child seemed like a faraway dream right now. He went into the kitchen and grabbed some hamburger to make patties, veggies for a salad, a little fruit for a child-friendly dessert. He set the table for four and brewed up fresh tea.

Laura smiled when she came inside. She was tousled from playing with Penny and Perrin, and he liked seeing the happiness in her eyes. "You're making dinner?"

"I'm at your service. What time does the family normally eat?"

"This crowd likes to be at the table by six. We eat, then play, maybe watch a video for thirty minutes, have our bath and they go right to bed." Laura seemed uncertain about how much he could stand of kid play. "Feel free to skip the *Little Bear* video if you want."

He shrugged. "It all sounds great."

She smiled. "I'm going to wash the children up. We hosed off outside but we're still a wee bit sandy."

He wanted to help with that but Ben's words held him back. He hated that he felt he had to retrench his emotions; he felt more like a visitor than a part of the family.

Whether he liked it or not, that was exactly what he was, until Laura said *yes.* Said *I do* with enthusiasm and true joy.

When Laura came back to the table, she sensed a subtle change in Gabriel. He'd gone from being upbeat to quiet. This was supposed to be their rehearsal dinner night, and here he sat eating burgers and watching *Little Bear.*

She didn't want to lose him. He could have had his choice of women, but he'd picked her and her brood. "I'm sorry about tonight, Gabriel. And the wedding."

"Don't be. Everything works out for the best usually."

But she sensed a lack of conviction in his words, as if he was repeating them simply to reassure himself.

Chapter Sixteen

Gabriel had finally figured out his father. Money wasn't everything to Josiah, though he'd kept a penny-pincher's handle on every cent until lately. Josiah had given Gabriel his portion of the one-year money because he had made an honest effort to rebuild the relationship with his father. Family was more important to Josiah than money.

Gabriel wanted family, too. This family he was watching play on the floor after dinner. He wanted Laura to want him as much as he wanted her. Ben's words rang true to him now. Maybe he'd never be certain of Ben's motivation, but staying here wasn't the way to find out if Laura would ever want him the way he hoped she would.

He stood. Penny and Perrin looked up. Laura looked at him, too. This was going to break his heart, but in the end, it had to be Laura who felt sure of what she could handle in life. "I'm going to head to the ranch."

She hesitated. "I thought you were staying here."

He nodded. "I had planned on it, but I accomplished what I came here for. We shared our evening together.

I don't need a rehearsal to know how much I want to marry you, but I did want to be with you and the children tonight." Gently, he ran a palm over her cheek. "I'll show myself out."

She followed him to the door. "I don't know what to say right now. I think I understand how you feel, but part of me isn't sure."

He smiled. "It'll all get straightened out in time."

He leaned down and kissed her lightly on the lips. "Be seeing you," he said, and went to his truck.

Leaving didn't feel good, but it did feel like the only right thing to do. His heart heavy, knowing now the agony his father had felt wondering if his boys would ever come home, Gabriel drove toward the Morgan ranch.

"WELL," LAURA SAID TO her children, "let's pick up these toys. Maybe we should crawl in my bed together and watch a movie."

The children were silent, helping their mother tidy up. Perrin didn't really help but he picked up a block and handed it to his mother. Penny industriously put the toys in the toy box before turning to look at her mother. "Where is Morgan?"

"He's gone to his house, sweetie," Laura said, before realizing what her daughter called Gabriel. She had always called him Morgan—but Laura knew he wanted to be called *Dad.* He'd gone from calling his father *Pop* to *Dad,* a subtle but noticeable shift in their relationship. She liked that Gabriel was stubborn; he hung on to a situation, no matter how unpleasant or awkward, until he had the right answer. He had commitment bred into his soul.

She knew he would always be there for her and her children.

The only thing holding her back was the fear of the unknown.

"PERFECTLY NORMAL," VALENTINE Jefferson said the next day when Laura went to thank her for the lovely wedding cake, which had ended up in the freezer. "My path to the altar with Crockett was definitely not easy."

"It's a lovely cake." Laura smiled. "Thank you for everything."

Valentine smiled. "Believe it or not, you'll probably appreciate Gabriel more now that you've been through this."

Laura left the shop and went to visit the girls at the Union Junction salon to apologize for taking a day out of their appointments for a wedding that didn't happen.

"Love is a wonderful thing," Delilah said. The head hairstylist had married her truck-driver beau, Jerry, and all had been right in her world ever since. "It just takes time and understanding. You'll know."

Laura shook her head. "I hope so. I thought I was ready—I just didn't realize I wasn't."

"You have a lot to fit into your life." Delilah sat her down, pulled her hair into a ponytail, pressed it into some pretty curls. "Where's my little Penny and Perrin? Perrin should be just about ready for his first haircut."

Laura shook her head. "Gabriel came by and got

them this morning. He said he wanted to get to know them, and that it was a day without Mom. He wanted me to have some time to myself. I have a suspicion that he wanted to get them on the new pony Josiah bought and didn't want me around worrying."

Delilah smiled. "He sure does like those kids of yours."

"They like him, too." The knowledge gave her a sense of comfort.

"And your father?"

"Ben hasn't said much lately," Laura said. "It's odd for him, because he had plenty to say about Dave, and about Gabriel, too, at first. Once Dad turned over a new leaf, he seems to be determined to stay in everyone's good graces."

"I've seen people change for the better that I never thought would," Delilah said. "My sister and I battled for years, but once Marvella decided to make positive decisions in her life, she's been a completely different person. She's a joy to be around."

Laura thought about Delilah's words for a long time after she left the salon. Then she realized that everybody around her was making changes in their lives—everyone except her. It was as if she were stuck, rooted to one spot, wanting everything in her world to stay completely still and unmoving. She would always love Dave; he was the father of her children. But what she felt for Gabriel was more mature, more balanced. She didn't need to be ashamed of her feelings or feel obligated to Dave's memory. He'd always hold a special place in her heart.

As Gabriel did now. The place he had in her heart felt warmed, and loved.

She went home to her house. Hesitating only a moment, she went and pulled out the family photo album, wistfully opening it.

The first pages showed photos of her and Dave on various dates: at the movies, snuggling on the sofa, hanging out with friends. A few wedding pictures followed, both of them smiling with happiness. There were many photos from when the children were born; she'd forgotten how snap-happy Dave had been. He'd spent hours compiling photos in an orderly fashion that chronicled pregnancies, first steps, first teeth. Tears of happiness and sadness jumped bittersweet to her eyes. The last photo was of Dave, taken by Laura, of him holding both the children. When he learned he had a life-threatening disease, he said he wanted a photo of him and the children so they would always remember what he looked when he'd been strong and fit. He wanted them to know he'd loved them.

She closed the album and cried one last time for the innocence of her marriage and the good friend she'd lost.

But Dave would know she had loved him, grieved for him, and he'd also want her to move on with a good life for their children. He would not want her making a silent shrine to his memory. The husband, the father in the album he had put together, was the man he'd wanted remembered.

She drove to the Morgan ranch, smiling when she saw Penny on top of the white pony. Perrin was held securely in Gabriel's arm as he walked the pony by halter. Each child wore a cowboy hat. Nearby, Ben took pictures, grinning as he recorded his grandchildren's first ride for posterity.

Ben was a changed man, no doubt about that.

She got out of her car and walked to the fence. "Hey, cowboy," she called.

"Hey," Gabriel said, "you made it in time for the big event."

"What's the pony's name?"

"Sugar." Gabriel grinned proudly. "Penny says she's white as sugar. I figured snow was the obvious choice, but she surprised me."

Laura smiled. "Hi, Dad."

Ben held up the camera. "Step inside the paddock and let me snap a photo." He seemed to consider his words. "A family photo."

Laura ducked under the fence and went to stand beside Penny. Gabriel held Perrin and stood stiffly next to Laura.

"Closer," Ben said with a wave of his hand. "I can't fit everything into the picture."

Gabriel and Laura moved slightly together.

"Closer," Ben instructed. "It's hard to get everybody in the shot 'cause Penny's on the pony."

They moved together again. Laura was pretty sure they were close enough for the smallest camera in the world.

"Closer!" Ben examined the picture he'd just taken. "Gabriel, you have to—"

Laura tugged Gabriel's face toward hers and gave

him a meaningful kiss. "Close enough?" she asked her father.

"That one's a keeper," Ben replied.

Gabriel looked down at her, his gaze questioning. "Am I getting a message here?"

"I don't know. How are your code-breaking skills?"

"They were always pretty good." Gabriel grinned. "Try me again to make certain I got the right information."

She kissed him, and he held her tightly against him, despite Perrin's attempt to squiggle free and Penny's giggling behind them.

Gabriel's eyes warmed. "That code was easy to decipher."

She took a deep breath. "After everything I've put you through, do you still want to marry me, Gabriel?"

"You're worth the wait," Gabriel said huskily. "You're talking to a man who waited ten years to be a son. I would have waited forever for you. Fortunately, you come around more easily than I do."

"Dad, hand me that camera, please," Laura said. "And if you don't mind, go stand next to the kids and your future son-in-law."

Ben hopped over the fence and stood next to Gabriel, smiling proudly. Laura clicked the camera, then checked the photo. Everyone was smiling and happy. Tears of happiness jumped into her eyes. She would treasure this picture of her new family for always.

Gabriel helped Penny down from the pony. "There'll be steaks and potatoes tonight for dinner," Gabriel said as they walked toward the house. "Stay and eat with us, Ben."

"I'm going to put Sugar up and bed down for the night." Ben grinned at his daughter. "Think I'm going to try to talk my boss into a new bed and maybe some sheets and blankets for the foreman's house. That plaid stuff is old as the hills, and I'm developing a taste for the finer things in life."

Gabriel snorted. "Get what you need, Ben. The cottage needs an update and you might as well make it yours for as long as you want it."

Smiling, Laura took the children upstairs to wash up. Gabriel looked at Ben. "Are you good with me marrying your daughter now?"

Ben gave him a toothy grin. "She came here on her own, didn't she?"

Laura had, indeed, surprising him. She didn't seem so spooked anymore; instead, she radiated calm and happiness. "Yeah. She did."

"I told you you'd be happier if you waited. Good thing you listened to me. Does no good to rush a woman."

"So, Ben," Gabriel said, "there's one thing I have to know. Did you pull a fast one on my father about oil on your property?"

Ben gave him a coy look. "No one pulls a fast one on Josiah Morgan."

He left, and as he walked to his truck, Gabriel saw the old man jump up into the air and kick his heels. He was celebrating, and Gabriel felt like doing the same.

"Hey," Laura said, as she put her children on the floor, "what can I help with?"

He took her into his arms. "Teaching me how to be a good father and husband."

She smiled up into his eyes. "I think you're already on your way. In fact, I was thinking that maybe it's time for me to give you something you say you want. Weddings are a good time for new beginnings of all kinds, right?"

"Definitely. What am I getting?" he asked, playfully picking her up.

"I was thinking adopting Penny and Perry might make you the—"

"Luckiest man in the world?" He kissed her with gratitude and joy. "I've waited a long time for this moment, and it feels even better than I imagined it would."

Happiness shone in his eyes, and Laura was glad she could bring him joy.

"Home really is where the heart is," Gabriel said, his voice catching. He kissed her again, taking his time to show her how much he cared for her. "I'm in love with you, little mama. I liked you the minute you stood on my porch with chicken and peas."

Hearing Gabriel say he loved her was a pleasure Laura hadn't expected again in her life. "I fell in love with you when I realized you loved my kids like your very own." There was a time she might not have wanted that, but now she knew how blessed her family was to have Gabriel's love.

"I used to think I didn't want kids," he said. "Good thing I'm not stubborn or anything."

She smiled. “Penny and Perrin will try your patience. Be forewarned.”

He laughed. “I waited out their mom. I’m a very patient man.”

He kissed her, long and sweet, and Laura knew she would always be safe with Gabriel. But even more important, she knew they would always be a family.

Epilogue

This time Gabriel and Laura's wedding went off without a hitch. They married two weeks later on a beautiful cloudless day, and invited everyone in Union Junction who wanted to come celebrate with them. Laura said they'd just needed time to work the kinks out of things, and Gabriel said he was going to keep her busy working kinks out of him for the next fifty years so waiting two weeks hadn't killed him. But happily he'd slid her engagement ring back on her finger, a sweet reclaiming of the woman he loved.

Gabriel thought Laura was the most beautiful bride he'd ever seen. She made him hungry for her just walking around in her shell-pink wedding gown, holding Perrin and keeping a sweetly-dressed Penny at her side. His mind took rapid-fire pictures of his new family, putting them in a mental photo album he would always treasure. Perrin never had colic anymore, and Penny was becoming quite the little pony rider, all positive changes for which Gabriel felt some proud dad ownership.

Ben gave his daughter away willingly. Josiah grinned,

a proud best man, his face alight with joy. His approval meant everything to Gabriel, and just seeing his father's happiness healed the old emotional scars for good.

Pete and Dane made it to the wedding this time to serve as groomsmen, and though they never heard from Jack, Gabriel figured his brother's well wishes were with him. Peace was coming over the family, and it felt good to Gabriel. They had a long way to go in the Morgan clan before all the old wounds were healed. Dane and Pete were having a harder time with forgiveness than Gabriel, but the Morgans were getting closer to harmony than they'd been in a decade.

"You've made me a happy man," he told Laura, pulling her to him for a kiss. "Have I told you yet that I love you? Because if I haven't, I'm happy to tell you that I love you, Mrs. Morgan."

Laura laughed. "Not that I'll ever get tired of hearing it, but you have said it a few times in the last hour."

Gabriel grinned at his bride. "When Pastor Riley said I could kiss the bride, I wanted to grab you and never let you go."

Laura smiled at her handsome husband. "*Did* you let go of me willingly? I thought your father tapped you on the shoulder to remind you our wedding guests were waiting for some wedding cake and dancing."

"Remember the kissing booth?" He ran a hand down her back, giving her a gentle hug. "I wanted to beat all those guys away from you. I figured today they can just sit and suffer watching me romance my bride. They'll never get another kiss from you."

She gave him a teasing smile. "Mason lets Mimi volunteer at the kissing booth."

"That's Mason," he said. His eyes held a possessive gleam that made Laura shiver with delight. "I'm a Morgan, and we have never been ones to play well with others."

"We play well together," Laura said. "I love you just the way you are." Their children snuggled close, and Gabriel wrapped them all into his embrace. For Gabriel, this was heaven, his very own Texas lullaby come true.

* * * * *

COMING NEXT MONTH from Harlequin® American Romance®

AVAILABLE AUGUST 7, 2012

#1413 COLTON: RODEO COWBOY

Harts of the Rodeo

C.J. Carmichael

Years ago Colt Hart made a big mistake. Now he's fallen in love with single mom Leah Stockton. Can she accept what he did? More important, can he forgive himself?

#1414 A COWBOY'S DUTY

Rodeo Rebels

Marin Thomas

Gavin Tucker wants to do right by Dixie Cash after getting her pregnant. But Dixie's past has taught her that she and her baby are better off on their own!

#1415 A SEAL'S SECRET BABY

Operation: Family

Laura Marie Altom

When navy SEAL Deacon Murphy learns a long-ago affair produced a daughter, guilt nearly destroys him. At least until he opens himself to loving Ellie...

#1416 HONORABLE RANCHER

Barbara White Daille

Bound by a promise to watch over his best friend's widow, what can Ben Sawyer do when Dana fights him at every turn?

Angie Bartlett and Michael Robinson are friends. And following the death of his wife, Angie's best friend, their bond has grown even more. But that's all there is…right?

Read on for an exciting excerpt of WITHIN REACH by Sarah Mayberry, available August 2012 from Harlequin® Superromance®.

"HEY. RIGHT ON TIME," Michael said as he opened the door.

The first thing Angie registered was his fresh haircut and that he was clean shaven—a significant change from the last time she'd visited. Then her gaze dropped to his broad chest and the skintight black running pants molded to his muscular legs. The words died on her lips and she blinked, momentarily stunned by her acute awareness of him.

"You've cut your hair," she said stupidly.

"Yeah. Decided it was time to stop doing my caveman impersonation."

He gestured for her to enter. As she brushed past him she caught the scent of his spicy deodorant. He preceded her to the kitchen and her gaze traveled across his shoulders before dropping to his backside. Angie had always made a point of not noticing Michael's body. They were friends and she didn't want to know that kind of stuff. Now, however, she was forcibly reminded that he was a *very* attractive man.

Suddenly she didn't know where to look.

It was then that she noticed the other changes—the clean kitchen, the polished dining table and the living room free of clutter and abandoned clothes.

"Look at you go." Surely these efforts meant he was rejoining life.

He shrugged, but seemed pleased she'd noticed. "Getting there."

They maintained eye contact and the moment expanded. A connection that went beyond the boundaries of their friendship formed between them. Suddenly Angie wanted Michael in ways she'd never felt before. *Ever.*

"Okay. Let's get this show on the road," his six-year-old daughter, Eva, announced as she marched into the room.

Angie shook her head to break the spell and focused on Eva. "Great. Looking forward to a little light shopping?"

"Yes!" Eva gave a squeal of delight, then kissed her father goodbye.

Angie didn't feel 100 percent comfortable until she was sliding into the driver's seat.

Which was dumb. It was nothing. A stupid, odd bit of awareness that meant *nothing*. Michael was still Michael, even if he was gorgeous. Just because she'd tuned in to that fact for a few seconds didn't change anything.

Does Angie's new awareness mark a permanent shift in their relationship? Find out in WITHIN REACH by Sarah Mayberry, available August 2012 from Harlequin® Superromance®.

HSREXP0812